"WE DON'T HAVE TO BE ENEMIES, AIMEE."

Her animosity was so real, Nick could almost touch it. Yet there was more than hatred between them.

Aimee held her breath as Nick walked toward her—broad of shoulder, hard and lean, undeniably male. "I never wanted to hurt you," he said softly. "We shared something special that night." His eyes traveled down the length of her. "You're still exquisite."

Aimee closed her eyes, and when she opened them, Nick was standing so close that his warm breath fanned her cheek. "Let me take away your anger."

Before she could fling back a retort, his mouth closed hotly over hers....

SURRENDER to the FURY

CONNIE MASON

LOVE SPELL BOOKS   NEW YORK CITY

LOVE SPELL®

June 1998

Published by

Dorchester Publishing Co., Inc.
276 Fifth Avenue
New York, NY 10001

ISBN 0-505-52266-7

Printed in the United States of America.

Prologue

~~~ᗡᑕ~~~

Aboard the Dixie Belle 1859

He strolled into the smoke-filled room at the stroke of midnight. The width of his shoulders first caught her attention, then his eyes, which were an incredible, startling green, fringed with long, thick lashes as black as his hair. Beneath the superfine material of his exquisitely tailored suit, his body was strong, almost leonine. He strode through the crowded gambling salon with the supreme confidence of a man who knew what he wanted.

Their eyes met as he reached her side. Thick cigar smoke rose above the cardplayers seated around the poker table, curling around his head like a halo. Instinct warned her that this man was no angel—he looked more like a devil.

"I'm Nick Drummond. May I join the game?"

Her first thought was: He's a damn Yank! Rumors of impending war made her leery of all northerners. His clipped accent set her teeth on edge.

The four men engaged in the poker game with the lovely lady gambler slid their chairs closer together to make room for the newcomer. Nick grabbed a nearby chair, wedged it in place, and sat down. The four players grunted out their names. Nick nodded to each in turn, raising an inquiring brow when his eyes settled on the sultry beauty who had drawn him to the poker game like a moth to flame. He already knew her name was Aimee Fortune. He had heard all about her before he boarded the *Dixie Belle* in New Orleans. Aimee Fortune. Obviously that wasn't her real name, but she was so damn beautiful, who in the hell cared?

She wore vivid red, quite appropriate, Nick thought, given her rather flamboyant calling. Her honey brown eyes and golden hair were a perfect foil for the creamy expanse of skin revealed by the deep décolletage of her gown. Though the low neckline was daring, he'd seen more revealing displays at society functions on proper ladies. She looked cool and composed and confident, as if she knew exactly what she wanted and how to get it. He'd never seen a more cocksure professional gambler anywhere.

He has a dimple! Right in the middle of his strong, square jaw. Aimee frowned. Where had that thought come from?

"They call me—"

"Aimee Fortune." Nick grinned. "I've heard of you, Miss Fortune." Her voice was cool and cultured, with just the barest hint of an accent. French? Nick was intrigued. The mysterious lady gambler created a heat in his blood he hadn't felt in a long time.

He wanted her.

Aimee stared boldly at Nick Drummond. For the first time since she had taken up gambling as a means to reverse her rather dismal fortune, she felt a thrill of apprehension shoot down her spine.

Nick returned the stare, thoroughly enjoying the sensual journey over Aimee Fortune's lovely features and enticing curves. Lady gamblers weren't all that common, though there were a few, but this lady was unique in the fact that she was young— surely no more than twenty—fresh and enchantingly lovely in an innocent way that belied her unladylike profession. Nick was enthralled by thick strands of long blond hair artfully arranged around a flawless face—wide eyes a warm light brown fringed with long lashes, lush red lips which begged to be kissed. Slim, bewitching, alluringly fashioned, her body alone was exquisite.

Nick watched Aimee closely as she picked up the deck and shuffled. Satisfied that she wasn't cheating, he relaxed, keeping his eyes on the cards. Though not new to the game of poker, Nick wasn't the professional gambler Aimee assumed him to be. In New Orleans to visit friends, he had heard of Aimee Fortune, and curiosity compelled him to book passage aboard the *Dixie Belle* to Natchez on his way back to Chicago. Nick had always liked poker and enjoyed incredible luck whenever he played, but had little time to indulge in the game. But he knew enough about it to spot a cheater, and he was convinced that Aimee Fortune wasn't dealing from the bottom or palming cards.

Aimee concentrated on the play of the cards, carefully avoiding Nick Drummond's eyes. They were devil's eyes, clear and green and compelling. As long as she was able to resist the lure of those eyes, she was confident of winning. She had learned poker at her father's knee and had honed and perfected the game in the months following his tragic death. Though she loved her father dearly, the man had been a gambler and rake and had left her deeply in debt.

After the funeral she had gathered her wits and realized she lacked the necessary skills to support herself and her faithful nanny, Savannah, who was the only mother she'd known since she was twelve. She had maternal relatives in England who had disowned her mother when she had married her ne'er-do-well father, and an uncle somewhere in Texas. But for all intents and purposes, she was alone in the world, dependent on her indomitable spirit, her wits, and her extraordinary skill at poker. She didn't include her beauty, for she didn't consider herself classically beautiful.

During the past six months she had won enough money to comfortably support herself and Savannah. A few months more and she could retire and start a new life away from the gossipmongers of New Orleans, who never let her forget that her father had been killed in a duel over a woman.

Nick smiled as he raked in another pot. He had been lucky tonight, which pumped up his confidence. Everything seemed to be going his way; he could do no wrong. As the pile of chips in front of him grew, Aimee's hoard of chips dwindled. When he caught her looking at him, he winked. She rewarded him with a scowl. Nick couldn't help but notice that she carefully avoided looking him in the eye and he chuckled, pleased that he discomfited her enough to make her lose her composure.

Aimee's scowl deepened. Things weren't going

according to plan. She knew the only way the damn Yankee could win nearly every pot was by cheating, but for the life of her, she couldn't detect how. But she wasn't going to let him get away with it. She'd encountered cheaters before and bested the scoundrels.

Nick Drummond continued to win at an alarming rate, sweeping in every last cent Aimee had amassed thus far as well as the reserve she kept in her reticule resting on her lap. One by one the other gamblers dropped out to seek their beds.

"Are you ready to call it a night, Miss Fortune?" Nick asked with a mocking smile when he noted that he and Aimee were now the only two people left in the gambling salon.

Aimee's slim fingers delved inside her reticule, searching for money she knew wasn't there. Nick Drummond had beggered her with startling efficiency. Abruptly her hand touched cold steel. She had nearly forgotten the pistol she unfailingly carried for protection. Its weight felt comforting.

Her temper flared when she thought of how easily he had won her money. "You cheated!" Her mind utterly rejected the notion that Nick Drummond could have won honestly, though she had no concrete evidence suggesting otherwise.

"I don't cheat at cards." His voice was quietly menacing. Had Aimee been a man, Nick would have challenged her.

"No one could be so lucky. You had to cheat."

Nick grinned and gave a careless shrug.

To Aimee that shrug served only to reinforce her belief that Nick Drummond was a hard-bitten Yankee cheater who cared little for his hapless victims or the havoc his cheating wrought. Before she had time to consider her reckless behavior, she whipped the pistol from her reticule and waved it in Nick's face. Nick blanched, leaping to his feet.

"Dammit, Aimee, what in the hell are you doing? I didn't cheat. I won fair and square." Aimee stared at him with accusing eyes.

Nick had to blink to break the spell. Never had such overwhelming hostility been directed at him by another human being. For a moment he considered himself a dead man. But the feeling quickly dissipated when he looked into Aimee's warm honey eyes and knew she wasn't capable of pulling the trigger. Still, it was damn annoying looking down the barrel of a gun.

Aimee's hand trembled, but instinct told Nick she wouldn't shoot him. She wasn't the type. She might be a gambler and a whore, but she was no killer.

"Put the gun down, Miss Fortune."

Aimee faltered. Nick Drummond had ruined her. He'd won every cent she'd accumulated except for a small amount she'd left with Savannah for safekeeping. Her mind told her that no one would condemn her for killing a cheater, but her heart whispered that she hadn't the instinct for killing another human being. Her finger caressed the trigger. Nick smiled, the cleft in his chin deepening. Dismayed, Aimee gaped at the arrogant rogue. What kind of a man laughed in the face of death?

"You're a gambler," Nick taunted, "not a killer. Let's compromise. I'll give you a fair chance to recoup your losses. I dare you to draw against me. Winner take all."

Aimee gasped. "You want to draw against me?"

"I didn't mean a duel with guns. We'll cut the deck for high card. If you win, everything I've accumulated tonight is yours."

"What's in it for you? You've already cleaned me out; I've nothing of value left." Why was he taunting her? She knew better than to trust a cheater, but his challenge had goaded her into recklessness.

A look of pure deviltry turned Nick's eyes into gleaming emeralds as they raked her voluptuous figure. "I'll think of something," he drawled. The underlying sensuality of his voice sent a ripple of awareness through her.

His highly charged words left little doubt in Aimee's mind what he wanted from her if he won. If she lost, he'd strip her of her last valuable asset. Aimee chewed her bottom lip. Surely her luck was bound to change. If there was a God, he wouldn't let her lose to a Yankee devil like Nick Drummond. Too much depended on her winning. She needed the money to survive, but it was merely a game with him. The gambler in her accepted the challenge before her practical mind could reject it.

"Well, Aimee Fortune, which will it be? I seriously doubt you'll shoot an unarmed man. You can walk away a loser or accept my challenge and take a chance on winning a fortune. It's your choice."

The choice he so gallantly offered was really no choice at all. No damn Yankee was smart enough to beat her at cards. She knew she was good at the game, and until tonight, no one had even come close to beating her.

"Very well, I accept, but only if I'm allowed to

shuffle. One draw only. High card wins." She felt her heart beating rapidly.

"Agreed," Nick conceded, sketching a mocking bow. "Be my guest."

Aimee's hands shook as she slowly and carefully shuffled the deck. She was all too aware of Nick's amused scrutiny and she did her best to avoid looking into his eyes. When she finished, she placed the deck on the table between them.

Nick gestured toward the deck. "Ladies first."

Aimee held her breath as she reached out and quickly cut the deck. She turned over the ten of spades. Not bad, she thought. She gave a loud, shaky sigh.

Nick rewarded her with a devastating smile. "Very good, sweetheart, but is it good enough?"

His mocking endearment infuriated her, but her eyes remained on his large brown hand as it paused briefly atop the deck before dipping down and flipping over the top card. The queen of hearts!

Aimee groaned.

Nick laughed.

The gun clattered to the floor.

"My win, sweetheart."

Utter disbelief seemed to turn Aimee to stone. How could she have lost?

"Are you prepared to honor your debt?" His voice held a note of contempt that made Aimee bristle indignantly. She considered a gambling debt a debt of honor.

Unable to speak, she merely nodded her head in affirmation. Grinning with slow relish, Nick bowed and offered his arm. "I'll collect my debt in private. Actually, I've thought of nothing else since

I set eyes on you. We've many hours left before the *Dixie Belle* docks."

Aimee moved on wooden legs as Nick led her from the gambling salon to his cabin. She entered Nick's cabin just as the first blush of dawn made an unheralded appearance in the eastern sky.

Nine months later.

"Push, Aimee, push dat baby out. C'mon, chile, dat's it, I can see his head."

"The devil take you and this baby!" Aimee sobbed, nearly senseless with pain. "He's the spawn of the devil, just like his father."

Savannah shook her gray head. Her black face was bathed in sweat, her clothes soaked with it. Her beloved Aimee was bearing a child she didn't want, and Savannah could do or say nothing to ease her pain. "Don't talk like dat, chile; de babe is innocent in all dis. You got only yourself to blame, Aimee LaMotte. I done tole you you were in over your head when you started gambling on dat boat and called yourself Aimee Fortune instead of the name your parents gave you. I knew no good would come of it. We woulda survived somehow."

"Oh God!" Aimee let out a loud shriek. The dreadful knowledge of giving birth to a child she knew she would hate made her pain even more difficult to bear.

"I can see his head!" Savannah cried, jubilant. "He's got dark hair, honey. Push; it's all gonna be over in a few minutes."

"Over," Aimee panted bitterly as she bore

down. "You're wrong, Savannah, it's only the beginning."

The words were ripped from her throat as her body contorted in agony. She uttered a single scream and the baby slid into Savannah's waiting hands.

"It's a boy, honey, a perfect baby boy with dark hair." As if to confirm her words, the room suddenly reverberated with the child's lusty cries. Savannah chuckled in delight as she gently cleansed mucus from the baby's mouth and nose, and wiped his body clean with a soft cloth she had prepared beforehand. Still smiling, she held him aloft for Aimee's inspection.

Aimee stiffened and turned away, refusing to look at the tiny mite she had given birth to. "Take him away; I don't want to look at him."

"Honey lamb!" gasped Savannah. "Don't talk like dat."

"I mean it. I'll have to live the rest of my life knowing how this child was conceived. His father walked out on me without a backward glance."

Savannah looked troubled. "He's your own flesh and blood, honey. Who's gonna look after him if you don't? He needs his mama."

"Don't you understand, Savannah? I don't want him. Every time I look at him I'll be reminded of his father."

Shaking her head and clucking her tongue in obvious disapproval, Savannah lay the babe in a small cradle beside the bed while she tended her mistress. Then, her lips compressed in a thin line, she gathered up the soiled linen and carried it from the room. Aimee was nearly asleep when the child's whimpers jerked her awake. For a long time she tried to ignore him while his soft mewlings continued. Then Savannah's words came back to haunt her. *He's your own flesh and blood. He needs his mama.* Rising on her elbow, she cast a resentful glance at the tiny mite lying in the cradle, expecting to see the face of a devil. Instead she saw an angel.

The tiny, wizened face was screwed up into the most endearing expression she had ever seen. He was sucking vigorously on one fist while waving the other in the air. A tuft of dark fuzz covered the perfect, round head, and his eyes were wide open, staring back at Aimee in a bold, demanding way that reminded her of his father.

Nick Drummond.

The handsome, arrogant rogue who had demanded her body in payment for a debt of honor and took her virginity without ever realizing she had been a virgin, piercing her innocence in one swift thrust that changed her life forever. He had assumed she was a whore and took her in a fury of passion. She had gained no honor by submitting to Nick Drummond. In a few short hours he had cheated her out of her winnings, robbed her of her virginity, and planted his Satan's seed in her. What made it all the more unbearable was the damning fact that she had surrendered to the fury.

He had introduced her to a splendor she had never imagined existed. He had taken something only a husband had a right to take, and made her feel as if it belonged to him. His sizzling passion had made him senseless to her virginity, not that it would have made any difference to the rogue.

She hated Nick Drummond.

Hated him for transporting her to paradise, despised him for being a Yankee and for planting his babe in her. Detested him for walking out on her the next morning without a word of good-bye. Loved every damn minute she had spent in his arms.

She had relived those perfect moments so often, they were etched forever in her brain. The thought of looking at a part of him every day for the rest of her life filled her with dread.

A soft whimper interrupted her reverie, and a force stronger than her own sense of survival compelled Aimee to reach out a finger and touch the child's cheek. His skin felt like the softest velvet. He gurgled contentedly. One tiny fist closed around her finger, trying to drag it into his mouth. Despite her solemn vow to hate the product of Nick Drummond's loins, Aimee lifted the baby from his cradle and snuggled him in her arms.

Savannah watched from the open doorway, holding her breath as Aimee cuddled her child. When Aimee placed him at her breast to suckle, the faithful old nanny offered up a prayer of thanks. For one terrible moment she feared Aimee would reject her child utterly.

For Aimee, this special bonding with the child she was prepared to hate was for life. In a flash, she realized the tiny, helpless being she had given birth to was innocent of his father's sins and had a personality all his own.

"What are you gonna call him, honey?"

Aimee smiled up at Savannah, gratefully aware that she couldn't have managed without the loving care the aging woman had lavished on her. "You name him, Savannah."

Savannah looked startled, then inordinately

pleased. It took only a moment to make the choice. "Brand. His name is Brand."

Aimee couldn't help but ask, "Why Brand? It's an unusual name. I don't think I've ever heard of it before."

Savannah grinned. "The instant you held him in your arms, he placed a brand of love on your heart."

"Brand. Brand LaMotte. I like it; it's a good name."

Chapter 1

Tall Oaks Plantation, Atlanta, Georgia 1864

Captain Nicholas Drummond halted his company of Union cavalrymen at the entrance of a winding dusty road lined with stately oaks that appeared to stretch up to the sky. It was a surprisingly peaceful setting amidst a land ravaged by war, curiously untouched by time and man's injustice to his fellow man. Yet the bloody, senseless war between the North and South, pitting brother against brother, had been raging for three years.

Though the issue forcing the war was slavery, Nick knew the reasons went far deeper than that, and for the sake of humanity, he prayed it would end soon. But until then he had a duty to perform. He had joined the Union army because the cause was just and his honor demanded that he fight for justice and equality for all men.

Nick twisted in the saddle, waiting for Lieutenant Dill to ride up beside him. "Is this the place, Lieutenant?" His voice was gritty with exhaustion, and his gaunt face gave mute testimony to the many battles he had fought and survived through sheer grit and determination.

14

"Yes, sir," Dill acknowledged. "Tall Oaks. It belongs to the Widow Trevor and her young son. Because of its size and proximity to Atlanta, it was purposely left standing to serve as an observation post in the area."

"I suspect Widow Trevor won't take kindly to having her home occupied by Union soldiers," Nick mused, stroking his stubbly chin. He felt grubby and dirty and couldn't wait to feel a real bed beneath his aching bones. "How long has her husband been dead?"

"Intelligence reports he was killed at Richmond back in sixty-two."

"Very well, Lieutenant," Nick said dismissively, "Mrs. Trevor will just have to live with our presence whether she likes it or not. Warn the men that she's likely to be bitter over the death of her husband, but that neither the widow, her son, nor any of her people are to be harmed. Is that clear?"

"Yes, sir, I'll see to it." Dill wheeled his mount and rode back to convey Nick's orders to the men.

Younger than Nick, Lieutenant Clifton Dill was a handsome man with a wry sense of humor and boyish charm most women found irresistible. In contrast, Nick was a seasoned soldier who learned the hard way to protect his back, be wary of the obvious, and trust no one but himself. His philosophy had brought him through the war unscathed thus far, and he expected to outlast most of the young, inexperienced men under his command.

The tough veneer Nick had assumed made him no less appealing to women. He was the kind of man women found challenging. The hard planes of his face were saved from austerity by the deep cleft in his square chin and by his devastating smile, when he chose to show it.

The plantation house sat majestically at the end of the driveway nearly one half mile long. As Nick drew near he could see signs of ravage wrought by years of neglect. In his mind's eye he could picture how the house must have looked at one time with slaves bustling about performing all the chores necessary to maintain such an imposing mansion. The entrance rose three stories high, supported by tall, stately columns. The paint was peeling now, the acres surrounding the house lay fallow, and the slave cabins out back sat rotting beneath the hot Georgia sun. Nick saw no signs of life as he rode into the yard at the head of his company.

Had Widow Trevor and her son vacated the premises? he wondered curiously. As a precaution against an unwelcome reception lying in wait for them, his hand hovered inches from his gun. Nick dismounted. His men followed suit. "Spread out," he snapped. "Sergeant Jones, take some men and search the slave quarters. Lieutenant Dill, follow me into the house. The rest of you set up camp beneath those trees yonder."

"The place looks deserted, Captain," Dill observed. "It must have been difficult for a widow to survive out here on her own."

"More like hell," Nick muttered. Food was so scarce, his men had to scrounge for enough to keep them alive between quartermaster deliveries. He could well imagine what it was like for a woman with a child and no means of support.

They approached the door, and Nick used the butt of his gun to knock. The sound reverberated hollowly inside the house. When no one answered, he tried the knob. It turned easily beneath his fingertips. The door was thick but somewhat battered, as if someone had tried at one time or another to hammer it down. Nick shoved it open with his foot.

She stood facing him, an old, rusty pistol aimed at his midsection. Her face was set in grim lines, and Nick was assailed by a vague memory of having lived this same scenario one other time in his life. It was eerie, yet so vibrant that he had to squint his eyes in the dim recesses of the vast foyer in order to bring the woman's features into sharp focus.

Neither the purple shadows marring the delicate flesh surrounding her honey brown eyes nor the gaunt hollows beneath her cheekbones detracted from her beauty. The much patched and faded blue dress hung loosely on her spare frame. But Nick noted that she still had sufficient curves to identify her as a lovely young woman. Her blond hair was pulled back from her face in a taut bun, emphasizing fine bone structure beneath pale ivory skin.

Nick's heart beat a rapid tattoo as he gazed into those hate-filled eyes. He felt himself being swept five years into the past to a night of unforgettable passion aboard the *Delta Belle*. His gaze rested on her, steady, unflinching, unfathomable.

Aimee Fortune.

He had taken her in a moment of splendid madness in payment for a gambling debt.

And he had never been able to forget her. The first time he had seen her, he'd felt lust, pure and simple, and he had satisfied it, handily, unforgettably. He regretted the haste with which he had left her the next morning, but she was sleeping so soundly, he didn't have the heart to awaken her. He had slipped ashore at Natchez and immediately boarded a train for Chicago. But he had thought of Aimee Fortune often since then, and made an effort to travel aboard riverboats several times in the ensuing years, hoping to encounter once again the enchanting lady gambler who portrayed innocence so effectively. She was either a very talented actress or so experienced, she knew all the right moves.

There were so many questions he wanted to ask her. Yet no one in New Orleans or Natchez seemed to know a lady gambler named Aimee Fortune or what had happened to her. She had virtually disappeared from the face of the earth, and Nick was forced to relegate the memory to a part of his past that somehow refused to die.

The gun pointing at his middle wavered slightly. "What do you want here? Haven't you and your kind taken enough from me? I've nothing more to give." Her voice was ripe with bitterness, raw with hatred, and Nick couldn't find it in his heart to blame her.

"We mean you no harm, Mrs. Trevor," Nick said softly. He stepped into a patch of sunlight streaming through a dingy window in the dim foyer and removed his hat.

Aimee drew in a ragged breath. Thick, black hair emphasized the coppery tone of his complexion, his bronzed skin dark against the stark blue of his uniform. He was much more deeply tanned and his face more rugged than when she had last

seen him. Her heart hammered against her breast
when his startling green eyes gazed upon her face.
They had a hypnotic power that left her paralyzed
and unaware of the peculiar way she was staring
at his sensual mouth, at the cleft in his square
chin, at the frown that drew his brows together
and shadowed those incredible eyes. Eyes satu-
rated with a secret knowledge that brought a rush
of color to Aimee's pale face. Devil's eyes.

Nick Drummond.

He looked older, hardened by the war, his jaw
more firmly set than she remembered. His expression was determined, the lines somewhat tempered by the cleft in his chin.

Numb terror held Aimee speechless. She knew
by his words that he had recognized her, though
she had changed greatly during the past five
years. Does he know about Brand? she wondered,
desperately searching his face for a hint of his
thoughts. His eyes remained carefully hooded. It
took very little effort for her to hate Nick
Drummond—even less for her to recall the way
his loving had made her feel so long ago and the
precious gift he had given her in the form of her
son. Brand was the only person left in the world
besides Savannah whom she truly loved and who
loved her in return. She was seized by an obsessive fear that Nick Drummond had come to take
her son from her. She had lived with that fear for
five years and wanted desperately for Nick to
leave before he saw Brand.

"You're trespassing on my land. State your business," she said.

"The widow Trevor," Nick mused, still stunned
at having finally found the woman who had

haunted his dreams for the past five years. He had never recovered from the guilt of leaving her so abruptly aboard the *Delta Belle*. It was unlike his usual behavior with women, but he had had a train to catch. "Perhaps you don't remember me, Mrs. Trevor, but I recall every moment of our last meeting. Five years ago, aboard the *Delta Belle*. I knew you as Aimee Fortune. Does that jog your memory?"

Jog her memory? Dear sweet Lord, how could she forget when she had living proof of their brief encounter? On the heels of that thought came the memory of a tantalizing smile and erotic mouth that kissed and caressed her until she was senseless with rapturous pleasure.

A look of bemusement settled on Lieutenant Dill's face as he listened to the interchange between Widow Trevor and his captain. Her thinness took nothing from her natural beauty, and Dill looked forward with delight to becoming better acquainted with her. It puzzled him that even though Captain Drummond appeared to know her, she gave no indication of having met him before. A very interesting situation, to say the least, thought Dill.

"Perhaps I did meet you," Aimee admitted sourly. "But it was a very long time ago, and if I did, I hardly recall the encounter."

That observation did not sit well with Nick. How could Aimee Fortune forget him when he remembered every passionate detail of their one and only time together? "I looked for you, you know, for a long time. No one seemed to know a damn thing about a woman called Aimee Fortune."

Aimee shrugged. She wasn't going to admit a

damn thing. Brand belonged to her, and no one was going to take him from her, especially not a damn Yank captain who spread death and destruction across the South. Who besides Savannah would testify in court in her defense if Nick took it into his head to petition for custody of Brand? She knew she was being obsessive about the whole thing, but she couldn't help it. She'd lived with that fear for too long. "You still haven't told me what you Yankees are doing here." Her voice was cool and uncompromising as she kept the gun trained on Nick's midsection.

"Put the gun down, Mrs. Trevor; we mean you no harm."

Nick smiled in an attempt to defuse the situation, bringing the dimple in his chin into sharp focus. Even though it was covered with dark stubble, Aimee had noticed it immediately. A bitter taste of apprehension spurted into her mouth.

"I realize you're not going to like this, Mrs. Trevor, but your home is to be used as headquarters for myself and my men." He directed an appraising glance toward the stairs, silently speculating on how many men could be accommodated in the bedrooms above. "You need only billet Lieutenant Dill"—he nodded toward the silent Dill—"and myself in the house. The men can set up tents on the lawn. Starting with supper tonight, the Lieutenant and myself will share meals with you and your family."

Aimee gave a bitter laugh and lowered the gun. "You're welcome to all the food you find in the house. We're not exactly prepared for company. You'd do well to seek accommodations elsewhere."

Nick appeared undaunted. "In case you haven't noticed, few plantations in the area are fit for occupation."

"Whose fault is that?" Aimee snorted sarcastically. "You've taken our men, left our children orphans, destroyed our homes, and expect to be welcomed with opened arms. Get off my land, Captain."

"The name is Drummond, in case you've forgotten. Nick Drummond. I'm afraid you'll have to put up with us until such a time as we're ordered to move on. The decision to occupy Tall Oaks was decided by those in higher authority than myself."

"You havin' trouble with dese no-good Yankee devils, honey?" Savannah materialized from a nearby hallway, brandishing a shotgun. She had used the weapon more than once in staunch defense of her mistress since the war had started, and she was prepared to use it again.

Nick glanced at the once substantial black woman whose flesh now hung in loose folds. "No one will be harmed," Nick assured her, "as long as everyone cooperates. We're occupying the plantation until further notice. See that two rooms are prepared for Lieutenant Dill and myself."

"How dare you come in here and take over my household!" Aimee bristled indignantly, furious at Nick for issuing orders as if he owned her. "Your president freed the slaves long ago. Savannah is my companion. She was freed even before that."

"My error," Nick said with a hint of sarcasm. "Then *you* may see to our rooms. And our supper."

"Like hell! I don't grovel before damn Yankees."

"Supper!" Savannah snorted in obvious disgust.

"Ain't no food in dis house. Not for no Yankees. Brand gets whatever we's able to scrounge."

Aimee blanched. "Savannah!" What if Nick demanded to see Brand? What if . . . No, she decided, men had no idea about children and their ages. He'd never suspect Brand belonged to anyone but her dead husband, Beauregard Trevor. Everyone thought the lovely young bride Beauregard Trevor had brought home with him from a visit to Memphis early in 1860 was a widow with a young child. Beau had wanted it that way, and that's the way it had been. Beau couldn't have loved Brand any more if he had been Beau's own son.

Beauregard Trevor had fallen deeply in love with Aimee at first sight. They'd met by chance while he was visiting relatives in Memphis, where Aimee had fled when she learned she was expecting Nick's child. With Savannah's help she had sold all her possessions, which were few indeed, and left the city of her birth in shame. When she and Beau had met, Aimee had already given birth and was at her wits' end. She had little money and no prospects for a job. Savannah did what she could to earn their keep, but it wasn't enough to support three people. When Beau proposed, Aimee briefly considered letting him continue to believe, as her few acquaintances in Memphis did, that she was a widow. But Aimee was too honest for that kind of subterfuge. Instead she confessed everything, every sordid detail of her short-lived career as a gambler and the astonishing outcome. Beau was more understanding than she had a right to deserve after her reckless behavior.

Beau still wanted Aimee for his wife and gladly

accepted Brand as his own son. They lived together as husband and wife briefly and barely got
to know each other before Beau went off to war in
'61, but during those short months Aimee couldn't
have asked for a better husband or father for her
son. If she never found the passion she had hoped
for, the blame was entirely hers. She deeply regretted not having been a more loving wife to Beau,
though he had never complained, and when he
was killed at Richmond in 1862, she was troubled
by the thought that he never knew how very
much she had appreciated him. Her consuming
hatred for one man and preoccupation with a war
kept her marriage from reaching its full potential.
They had barely known each other before he left,
never to return. There were many, many things for
which she held Nick Drummond accountable.

Nick realized Brand must be Aimee's son, and a
jolt of jealousy shot through him. The thought of
another man fathering a child with Aimee made
him feel strangely uncomfortable. He had never
forgotten the sweet innocence of her response,
even though he knew it was all pretense. But another thought intruded upon his reverie. Both
women implied there was no food in the house.
He knew things were bad, but surely a plantation
this size had food hoarded away somewhere. The
thought that Aimee and her child were starving
was shocking.

"You said there was nothing in the house to
eat," Nick probed gruffly. "Are you telling the
truth or have you hidden away a cache of food
someplace where it can't be found?"

"I don't lie," Aimee said tiredly. "What we had
was stolen long ago by Union soldiers, brigands,

and deserters who took great pleasure in leaving us nothing on which to survive. If not for Savannah . . ." Her sentence trailed off, leaving Nick furious enough to want to seek out those men who had made Aimee suffer.

"As long as I'm here, I'll personally see that there is enough to eat in the house. Unless, of course, I learn that you're lying to me." He turned to Lieutenant Dill. "Lieutenant, send a detail of men immediately on a food-seeking expedition. I don't care how they get it, just see that there's food for the house and troops. Dispatch a messenger to the quartermaster. The army can't very well let us starve."

"Yes, sir." Dill saluted smartly as he spun on his heel and left the foyer.

"I'll return after I check on the men," Nick told the two women. "I'd like a bath before supper." He sketched a hasty bow and followed Dill out the door.

Savannah, with the shotgun hanging loosely in the crook of her arm, stared at him in astonishment. "Well, if dat don't beat all! I ain't gonna like all dem Yankees underfoot. Mr. Beau must be turnin' in his grave. And dat captain, talkin' jest like he owns de place. What we gonna do, honey?"

"What can we do?" Aimee said bitterly. "I suppose we'll just have to exist the best we can until they leave. I for one intend to keep out of the captain's way. And I don't want him to see Brand if I can help it. No telling what kind of ideas he'll put in the child's head."

Strange as it may seem, Aimee had never revealed to Savannah the name of Brand's father.

And Savannah, thinking it was too painful for Aimee to discuss, never questioned her. It was enough for Savannah to know that the man had callously taken Aimee's virginity without a thought for the consequences. Not that either of them ever regretted the joy Brand brought into their lives.

"I'll do my best to keep Brand away from dem Yankees, honey, but you know what a curious little rascal he is. The only thing good about dis is dat maybe we'll get enough to eat for a change. If de captain can be believed."

"I wouldn't put too much faith in the word of a Yankee." Aimee's voice was ripe with contempt as she turned away from Savannah. It wouldn't do for her faithful friend to see just how deeply she had been affected by the reappearance of Captain Nick Drummond. "And don't you dare do anything to those rooms upstairs. The Yanks will just have to put up with a little dust. Where is Brand?"

"I put de little scamp down for a nap. He didn't give me too much trouble. He ain't gettin' enough food lately to keep up his energy level. I sure hope . . ." Savannah turned away, her shoulders drooping. She had done her best for Aimee and Brand, but it wasn't enough. They were all teetering on the edge of starvation, with little hope for reprieve. In a way, having the Yankees occupy Tall Oaks was the best thing that could have happened. She wisely kept that observation to herself as she trailed Aimee up the long, curved staircase that had once been the pride of Tall Oaks, but like the rest of the house, had long since fallen into disrepair.

* * *

Nick surveyed with a jaundiced eye the elegant room he was to occupy during his stay at Tall Oaks. The room had definitely seen better days, but its faded elegance was undeniable. The feather-bed looked comfortable enough despite the layer of dust covering it and the sparse furnishings. Nick couldn't recall when he'd last slept in a real bed. The room boasted a fireplace but little furniture. Had marauders carried it off or had it been used as firewood during difficult times? He located a brass tub behind a screen and dragged it to the center of the room. Then he perched on the edge of the bed to removed his boots. When a knock sounded on the door, he called out permission to enter. The door swung open and Aimee appeared, her lips turned down into a scowl. "Your bathwater is heated."

"Is there no one available to do the heavy chores?" Nick asked, frowning. Aimee looked so fragile, he didn't want her performing the arduous task of carrying buckets of water up the stairs. He hadn't meant to be unreasonable when he had requested a bath earlier, he just thought . . .

"Just Savannah, and she isn't as young as I am."

"I'll assign a man to help with the chores."

"There's no need," Aimee said tightly. "We'll manage." She didn't want to be beholden to Nick Drummond for anything.

Nick leaped to his feet, grasping her wrist when she picked up the buckets. "I'm trying to make things easier for you, you little fool."

"I don't need your help."

"Dammit, Aimee Fortune, or Mrs. Trevor, or whatever you call yourself, what happened between us happened a long time ago." Aimee flushed and looked away. "It's too late to deny we've met," he continued, "or to forget the outcome of that poker game those long years ago. You owed me a debt and I collected. If my memory serves, you enjoyed the encounter as much as I did." His knowing grin sent her temper soaring.

"Let me go!"

Ignoring her plea, Nick dragged her tightly against the rock hardness of his superbly fit body. "Do you know that I looked for you afterward? Many nights I lay awake wondering who you really were, if you were all right, and why I could find no trace of you when I returned to the area. That night was like an erotic dream, one I've relived many times over. I can perceive no good reason why you should hate me. I was merely collecting a debt of honor."

His gaze met hers. It was an unrelenting look, sparing her nothing as he cocked a questioning eyebrow, demanding an answer.

"I don't owe you an explanation, Nick Drummond." Her body was molded to his, and she could feel every brass button on his dusty jacket. "Just being a damn Yankee is enough to earn my hatred."

"Perhaps, Aimee Trevor, but I have a feeling that fate has a plan for us. A plan set into motion on the night we met." The timbre of his voice was deep and oddly compelling. Aimee knew he was going to kiss her before he lowered his lips to hers; the devil hiding in his green eyes leaped out to warn her.

His kiss was a sensual exploration of taste and texture. Five years melted away as if they had never existed as she vividly recalled the touch of his mouth, the unique taste and smell of him. Five years of the same dream caused her memories to mingle with reality. This was the man she had reason to hate above all others. This was the man to whom she had surrendered her virginity, the man who had calmly walked out of her life the next morning. This was the man who never realized she had been untouched! This man was the father of the child she adored!

Nick Drummond was a devil.

Aimee felt herself being dragged backward toward the bed, felt rough hands slide around to fondle her breasts, felt the hard, unrelenting thrust of his sex against the softness between her legs. She recognized a profound terror.

"No, let me go! I don't want this; you have no right!"

Nick was so aroused, Aimee's words barely registered in his befuddled brain. He wanted her. He'd wanted her the first time he saw her and he still wanted her. But as her words registered, he realized he indeed had no right to assume she'd fall into his arms. He never deluded himself about the hatred she bore him for winning the wager, and the years had done little to change her feelings.

"Why are you hurting my mama?"

The tiny voice had the same effect on Nick as a dash of cold water. Abruptly he released Aimee and she stumbled out of his arms. Her breath was ragged, her eyes fraught with terror. Her hands flew to tidy the bun at her nape where long tendrils of blond hair had become loose and spilled down her back.

Nick stared at the child who had burst into his room like a tiny whirlwind. He was suddenly at a

loss for words, but knew he must somehow placate the boy or play the villain during his stay at
Tall Oaks.

"I'm not hurting your mama, son. I mean no
harm to her or anyone in this house."

Wide hazel eyes stared back at Nick with an intensity far beyond his meager years. Tousled black
hair the color of a raven's wing framed a thin, serious face that seemed to pierce directly into
Nick's heart. The boy's features were hauntingly
familiar, almost as if Nick recognized him. Nick
hadn't been around children much, but this small
imp could easily occupy a place in his heart.

"What are you doing in my papa's bedroom?"

Nick shot a quizzical glance at Aimee. He had
no idea he had been given the master bedroom.
"This is one of the few bedrooms fit for use,"
Aimee explained as she started to shoo Brand
from the room. She didn't want her son and Nick
together longer than necessary.

"Wait," Nick ordered. "I haven't met your son
yet. I'm Captain Drummond." Smiling broadly, he
held out his hand to the boy.

Brand peered resentfully at Nick's blue uniform,
not too young to recognize an enemy when he saw
one. Many Union soldiers had stopped at Tall
Oaks during the past few years, and he had been
taught to be wary of anyone wearing a blue uniform. "I don't like you."

"Brand!" Aimee cautioned, looking fearfully at
Nick. She knew so little about him, she had no
inkling what his reaction would be to Brand's mu-
tinous outburst.

"It's all right, Mrs. Trevor." He carefully ad-
dressed Aimee in a formal manner for her son's

benefit. "So your name is Brand," he said, kneeling before the boy. "My uniform is blue because I'm a Union soldier, but that doesn't mean I'm here to harm you or your mother. On the contrary, I intend to see that you get enough to eat during my stay here. Can we be friends?"

Aimee couldn't believe Nick was taking so much time and effort with her son. She had hated him for so long, it was difficult to imagine him possessing redeeming qualities.

Brand's small face grew solemn as he studied Nick. He was very young when his papa went away, and he hardly remembered him. Since then, he'd known no other adult male well. Naturally distrustful, he wanted desperately to accept Nick's friendly overtures but feared offending his mother, who seemed to have an aversion to anyone in a blue uniform. Rather than hurt her, Brand remained mute.

"He's shy," Aimee offered, sensing the reason for Brand's reticence. The sensitive child was too young to remember Beau, yet old enough to know a Union bullet had deprived him of a father. "So many of the raiders who stopped here wore blue uniforms. They threatened our existence and left us nothing to eat. Often we had to flee for our lives when we saw them approaching."

"I'm sorry," Nick said, rising to his feet. "I promise you have nothing to fear from us."

Nothing to fear? Aimee shuddered at the thought of what Nick's reaction would be if he found out Brand was his son. She would live in a state of constant anxiety until he and his men left Tall Oaks. "May we go now?"

"Of course. Tell Lieutenant Dill I said to assign one of the men to carry water up for my bath."

Aimee turned to leave, but Brand hung back, as if there were something he wanted to say but didn't dare. Nick noticed the boy's troubled expression and asked, "Is there something you wanted to ask me, Brand?"

Aimee frowned, trying to guide Brand from the room. But the child dug in his heels and refused to budge—until he had asked the question that had burned on the tip of his tongue since the moment he saw Nick's blue uniform.

"Yes, sir," Brand said with the guileless innocence of a five-year-old. "Did you shoot my papa?"

Nick blanched. He barely heard Aimee's sharp intake of breath as he grappled with Brand's question. What could he say to this small child who had been deprived of a father's love by a Union bullet? Yet the question demanded an answer—one a small child could understand. He dropped down to one knee, seizing Brand by the shoulders.

"No, Brand, I didn't shoot your papa. In war times, terrible things happen, things that most men wouldn't think of doing during normal times. I don't like killing, but I'm doing what I think is right for our country. So was your father. He died a hero, son, never forget that. Only God knows which of us is right. One day history will judge the issue. I want you to know I don't consider either you or your mother my enemy. Do you believe me?"

Much of what Nick said was lost on Brand. But knowing that the tall captain hadn't killed his papa made accepting him in the house much easier. He looked to his mother for guidance, but she was staring at Nick, and Brand couldn't tell what she was thinking. He decided to reserve judgment until the blue-coated captain proved himself worthy of friendship.

"I believe you didn't shoot my papa, but I'm still not sure I like you."

"I can live with that." Nick grinned, giving the child a quick squeeze before sending him on his way.

As he watched Aimee and Brand leave, he made a solemn vow. He promised he'd find some way to earn the child's trust and to teach him that not everyone in a blue uniform was bad. And Aimee? The mother was another story. He wanted Aimee. Her sizzling hatred was a challenge to his virility, one he couldn't resist.

Chapter 2

There was more food on the table than Aimee and Brand had seen in months. Brand's hazel eyes widened when Savannah carried a platter of roasted pork surrounded by browned potatoes and carrots from the kitchen and placed it in the center of the table. The fine china and silver had long since been sold or stolen, but the odd assortment of chipped earthenware made little difference to those assembled for the meal.

Nick noted with compassion Brand's eagerness to dig in to his food when a small portion was ladled onto his plate, as if it might be whisked away before he had his fill. Aimee's appetite was more subdued, but Nick could tell by the way she concentrated on her food that it had been a long time since her hunger had been satisfied.

His men had scoured the countryside and flushed out a wild boar. The fresh meat provided a welcome supplement to the dreary rations provided by quartermaster. Lieutenant Dill had informed Nick that a wagonload of rations as well as fresh beef and pork would arrive from quartermaster in a few days. Nudging Dill, Nick indicated that they were to eat sparingly of the food, leaving the bulk of it for the young widow, her son, and her servant. Dill understood Nick's meaning immediately, setting his fork down and complaining that he had little appetite after a large noontime meal with the troops. Truth to tell, Nick felt as if he could have eaten the whole boar himself, but his pleasure at seeing Brand wolf down the food was reward enough for leaving the table hungry.

The meal ended quickly, too quickly to suit Nick. He was as intrigued with Aimee today as he had been five years ago. Though Aimee was plainly dressed in a patched and faded gown, her hands rough from physical labor, her face honed fine and her body as slim and fragile as a wraith, Nick vividly recalled the torrid passion he unleashed in her during one perfect night of bliss. And he wanted to do it again; he craved it more than he'd ever craved anything in his life.

Aimee sat back and sighed, full for the first time in a very long time. She smiled at Brand, who was just shoveling the last morsel of pork into his mouth. She hadn't wanted to be beholden to Nick Drummond for anything, but seeing Brand's smiling face now was worth more than her pride. From beneath lowered lids she gave Nick a covert glance and was flustered when she found his hooded gaze resting on her.

Nick searched Aimee's face, a frown tugging at the corners of his mouth. Her skin was pale pink; her lips full and rounded over even white teeth. When she smiled at Brand, he found himself wishing she would smile at him like that. But she despised him with an intensity that went beyond the color of his uniform and the place of his birth. She hated him for reasons that puzzled him—he damn well couldn't figure them out.

Fidgeting beneath Nick's avid scrutiny, Aimee rose stiffly to her feet. Nick and Lieutenant Dill both stood politely.

"It's Brand's bedtime. If you gentlemen will excuse me, I'll see to my son."

"Will you return later?" Nick asked.

"I think not," Aimee replied. "It's been a long day."

"I insist," Nick said. "There are a few rules I must lay down while my men are in residence here. We have yet to discuss them."

"Can't it wait until tomorrow?"

"No."

Aimee twisted her hands nervously. What did he want? She was terrified that Nick had recognized something of himself in Brand. Could she afford to make him angry by refusing his request?

"It is rather late, Captain," Lieutenant Dill objected, sensing Aimee's reluctance and feeling pity for the young widow. He couldn't figure out why Nick was deliberately baiting the woman, unless— unless there was more between them than they were letting on.

"I agree, Lieutenant, and I suggest you seek your bed immediately. You're to lead a patrol into enemy territory at first light tomorrow. As for you, Mrs. Trevor, I'll meet you in the study in an hour. That should give you sufficient time to see to your son."

Finding himself abruptly dismissed, Dill left the room in a huff. If his captain had designs on the young widow, he wouldn't bet money on his success. Aimee Trevor didn't look the sort to meekly submit to a man she obviously despised.

"Good night, Mrs. Trevor," he said. "Pleasant dreams."

Aimee quickly took her son by the hand and led him from the room, refusing to look at Nick as she swept past.

"Good night, Brand," Nick called as the child was hustled from the room. "One hour, Mrs. Trevor," he repeated for Aimee's benefit.

"Is Captain Drummond a bad man, Mama?" Brand asked once they had reached the privacy of his room. The child was deeply aware of his mother's hostility toward the Yankee, which confused him since the captain had told them he hadn't shot his papa.

Aimee was hard-pressed not to blurt out that Captain Drummond was the worst kind of devil imaginable. He had taken so much from her—so much. He had cheated her out of her money and stolen her virginity without being aware of his theft. But something deep inside her wouldn't allow her to revile the obnoxious Yankee to his son. Even though Brand would never know Nick Drummond as his father, she couldn't quite utter the words that would condemn him in the eyes of his small son. The animosity she felt for Nick Drummond was so personal that Aimee could share it with no one, least of all her child—Nick's child.

"Captain Drummond is a Yankee, Brand. I imagine there are good Yankees, though I've yet to meet one."

"Is Captain Drummond one of the good ones? He seems so nice."

"That's something you'll have to judge for yourself. Personally, I don't like the man."

"Then I'll try not to like him," Brand said loyally. "But you won't be mad if I talk to him sometimes, will you?"

"No, darling, I won't be mad, but I'd prefer you stayed away from him. He's far too busy with the war to concern himself with you."

"But how can I learn if he's a bad man or a good one if I don't talk to him?"

Aimee ground her teeth in frustration. "He's a Yankee, isn't he? Enough, Brand; you make my head spin with all your questions. Hop into bed, son. I'll look in on you again before I retire."

"Yes, Mama." Though he acquiesced dutifully, Brand was far from appeased. His mother just wasn't making sense. Her answers, usually so forthright and honest, had been brief and confusing. He knew she was troubled, that she didn't want the Yankee soldiers on their land, but there was no denying that the captain had provided a meal for them tonight the likes of which they hadn't seen in months. For the first time since he could remember, he was going to bed with a full stomach.

Aimee took her time returning downstairs for her confrontation with Nick. The allotted hour had long since passed and a tiny smile tugged at her lips when she thought of Nick pacing the small study waiting for her to appear. He might be the enemy, but she was far from being conquered by him. He probably felt a certain smugness about the wanton way she had responded to him those long years ago, but in her heart she knew she had merely been paying a debt of honor. Her passionate response was something she hadn't counted on or expected. She placed no special importance on the event or the act, except as a means of repaying a debt. Nick Drummond was an experienced man proficient in the art of love, and she had been too inexperienced to resist.

Squaring her narrow shoulders, Aimee sucked in a fortifying breath and rapped lightly on the study door. The room hadn't been used since Beau had left in '61, and it rankled her to think that a Yankee was now making it his. Without waiting for a reply, she opened the door and stepped inside. A single lamp burned in the small room, creating dancing shadows on Nick's broad back. He was staring out the window into the darkness, hands clasped behind his back, feet planted wide apart. She shifted impatiently from foot to foot and cleared her throat twice before he turned to acknowledge her.

"You took your time." His hooded eyes glowed emerald green in the flickering lamplight. His brooding features revealed nothing of his thoughts.

Dear God, why did he have to be so handsome? "My son needed me. What is so important that it couldn't wait until tomorrow?"

"I've duties to perform tomorrow and a company of men to deploy on their various missions."

She looks so young, Nick thought, and so fragile. Had her marriage been a happy one? he wondered. Had her husband found the secret that unleashed the passion in her exquisite body? He wanted to think he had been the only one to taste the full flavor of the magnificent fire that dwelled inside her, but he realized how unlikely that was.

She probably had many lovers before and after he met her.

"This won't take long, Mrs. Trevor—Aimee," Nick said. He was more tired than he cared to admit, and his weariness showed in the deep lines trailing outward from the corners of his eyes and mouth. War was hell; he wished it were over and all the senseless killing ended for all time. "Would you care to sit?"

"I'll stand." Aimee felt safer standing—somehow he seemed less intimidating.

Nick nodded. "Very well. First I have a few simple questions to ask. From the looks of your son, I'd say you married almost immediately after our meeting. How old is Brand?" Nick knew the question was irrelevant, but some devil inside him prodded him. A preposterous notion had formed in his brain the moment he saw Brand, and he needed more information before he discarded it. He knew how unlikely it was that their one night together had produced a child, but something in the boy struck a responsive chord in him.

Aimee froze. Did Nick suspect? "What's Brand got to do with anything? Leave him out of this."

"Humor me, Aimee; I'm merely being inquisitive. After all, we are old friends."

"Acquaintances but hardly friends. But if you must know, I met Beau shortly after—after our meeting. He swept me off my feet and we married a few weeks later. Brand was born nine months after our wedding. He's just four years old. He's big for his age, but Beau was a big man. Are you satisfied?"

"Was your husband dark?"

Dear God, would he never be satisfied? "Yes, he was dark."

Nick's shoulders slumped in disappointment. He had no idea what he wanted to hear and wondered vaguely if Aimee was being truthful with him.

"I'll take your word for it," he said. "While my men and I are here, I'll expect you to remain within the boundaries of the house and yard. No one from the household will be allowed to go into town. Vital information will arrive by messenger from time to time, and I must ensure that utmost secrecy is maintained."

"Vital information to whom?" Aimee inquired haughtily. "Are you accusing me of being a spy?"

"I'm accusing no one. I'm merely issuing a warning. I won't tolerate disobedience."

"And I won't be dictated to. You've taken over my home, turned my companion into your slave, asked me personal questions that are none of your business, and now you accuse me of being a spy. I want nothing to do with you or your men. The sooner you leave me in peace, the better."

The hard lines in Nick's face softened and a slow, thoughtful smile spread across his handsome features. "We don't have to be enemies, Aimee." Her animosity was so real, Nick could almost touch it, yet there was more than hatred between them. There was something live and palpable that danced around them like spikes of white lightning.

Aimee held her breath as Nick walked toward her—broad of shoulder, hard and lean, undeniably male. An unwanted memory of that hard body naked and pulsing with raw, lusty energy pounded the breath from her lungs.

His eyes traveled down the length of her. "You're still exquisite. I remember—"

"No, don't! Don't remind me of that night! I can't bear it." Turbulent emotions twisted Aimee's gut. Those hours spent in Nick's arms had cast her from heaven into the violent paradise of damnation. She was thrust from girlhood to womanhood in a matter of hours.

"I never wanted to hurt you in any way," Nick said softly. "We shared something special that night."

Aimee closed her eyes, and when she opened them, Nick was standing so close that his warm breath fanned her cheek. "Let me take away your anger." His arms swept her against him, his gentle hands stroking her back as he would a hurt child. "Finding you again is like a miracle. I want you as much today as I did five years ago."

"What we shared was lust," Aimee spat in disgust. "That's all it ever was."

"Perhaps. Shall we test the theory?" The intensity of his voice sent a jolt of awareness surging through her veins.

Before she could fling back a retort, his mouth closed hotly over hers. Aimee's struggle was short-lived as she surrendered to his kiss, for a brief moment reveling in sensations she'd never felt with Beau. Nick's arms tightened. The fever of lust raged through him. Licking her lips, he nudged them apart with his tongue. He curved his tongue around hers, drawing it deep inside his mouth. Then he dipped his head and lightly licked the slender column of her neck, down into the cleavage between her breasts.

When his hands grasped the taut mounds of her buttocks, pressing her into the incredible hardness of his body, Aimee suppressed a shudder of pure joy. This couldn't be happening! She hated Nick Drummond too much to respond to his passion. Her feet left the floor as Nick lifted her high into his arms, burying his face into the sweet fullness of her breasts. She smelled and tasted delicious; he wanted to devour her.

"I want to love you, Aimee," he rasped into her ear. "I want to recapture that moment five years ago. I've not forgotten, you know."

His words brought her plummeting back to earth. He had forgotten her the moment he walked out on her. The fire that had heated her blood in a moment of weakness was replaced by cold fury. Men like Nick Drummond took and took, and gave nothing in return. She wanted him out of her life before he discovered Brand was his son. He wasn't the type of man who was easily fooled.

"I wouldn't let you love me if you were the last man on earth," she said ruefully as she fought to free herself from his embrace.

He gave her a derisive laugh. "You could have fooled me. Judging from your response just now, I'd say you haven't forgotten how wonderful it was between us once. I certainly haven't."

"I forgot you the moment you left me aboard the *Dixie Belle*," Aimee lied. Color rushed to her cheeks, brushing the fragile, almost translucent skin like rose dust. Her lips were red and swollen from his kisses, and Nick thought her the most beautiful woman he'd ever seen. And the most charming liar.

"I don't believe you. No one could maintain a hatred for five years unless they thought about the object of their hatred during that time."

"Damn you, Nick Drummond, let me go! I'd rather bed every man in your company than submit to you."

Nick froze. Abruptly he released her, his green eyes dark with fury. "Do you hate me so much?"

"Yes." She felt his gaze on her and stepped back. "You're not wanted here. Take your men and leave my family in peace." Her eyes were dark and stormy as they raked him with contempt.

"Is that why you responded to me just now? Because you can't stand the sight of me? Or is it because you've been without a man for a long time?"

His mocking words were deceptively calm as he reached out and dragged her against the hard wall of his chest. He seized the hair at the nape of her neck and pulled, lifting her face to his while he lowered his face to hers. His kiss was not gentle, but a bold, insolent assault on her mouth that left her shaken and frightened. His hands found her breasts, and Aimee gasped in outrage as he rolled the nipples between forefinger and thumb before pressing slowly downward. Her skirt rose inch by inch as his hands slid underneath and skimmed the satiny flesh of her inner thighs. Her moist warmth enticed him as he drew closer to that private part of her that he longed to explore. Then his fingers reached inside her pantaloons, touching her intimately, bringing a sigh to her lips.

Never had Aimee experienced such overwhelming helplessness. Her body was no longer hers to command; a cheating Yankee rogue had stolen her mind and her will. Yet she knew that if she submitted to Nick Drummond now, she'd lose the most important battle of her life. She had more pride than to let Nick seduce her again. For Brand's sake she had to preserve her hatred for the man who could shatter her life.

"Please, don't do this to me." Her quiet dignity must have made an impression on Nick, for he immediately turned her loose.

"Forgive me, Mrs. Trevor; I had no reason to assume you'd return my interest." His eyes chilled her: two chips of clear emerald green. "I've let my imagination run away with me. I deluded myself into thinking you wanted me as much as I wanted you. From now on my behavior will be nothing but circumspect. You may leave."

Her eyes full of distrust, Aimee scooted around Nick, fleeing the room as fast as her legs could carry her. Another two minutes with Nick Drummond and he'd have reduced her to a blathering idiot, begging him to make love to her. How could she hate someone so thoroughly yet at the same time be aroused by him? She thought she was rid of the man five years ago. For all she knew, Nick Drummond was married and had a house full of children. That notion brought her thoughts to a skidding halt. Married? For some odd reason that assumption brought an uncomfortable jolt to her senses.

She tossed restlessly in her sleep, but the howling wind outside did not awaken her from the vivid reality of her dream.

He shut the door behind them, enclosing her in a private hell of her own making. The room was illuminated by lamplight. He turned the key in the lock and smiled at her. Soft light played against his handsome features, and she noticed the strong curve of his broad shoulders and his muscular frame. He pulled her into his arms and kissed her. When his lips met hers, she had an inkling of just what these next hours would be like. He whispered in her ear, telling her how beautiful she was, how desirable, how badly he wanted to be inside her, that he was going to make it wonderful for her. He wove his hands into her hair and kissed her again, holding her face steady while he nuzzled the high curve of her cheekbone, her ear, the slender curve of her throat. She trembled when his hands found the fastenings on her dress, releasing them, pushing the bodice down past her breasts and unlacing her corset. His lips brushed the pale globes and she nearly collapsed. He touched the tip of his tongue to an aching nipple . . .

No! Aimee bolted nearly upright in bed, her face bathed in sweat, shaking, remembering things she thought she had purged from her mind long ago, each aching detail a haunting memory that singed her conscience.

Dappled sunlight streamed through the window, and Aimee knew she had overslept. After she had left Nick the night before, she'd had a difficult time falling asleep. Usually Brand was the first one up, and she wondered why he wasn't in her room pushing her to get up, or why Savannah had allowed her to sleep so long. Sounds of activity floated up through the window from the yard below, and Aimee grimaced when she thought of the unwelcome guests occupying her property.

The delicious aroma of coffee enticed her from

the rumpled bed. Another of Nick Drummond's peace offerings? They hadn't had real coffee at Tall Oaks in ages. In fact, they no longer had parched corn or any other substitute. Her stomach rumbled. These past months Aimee had learned to live with the gnawing hunger that continually twisted her gut. She tried to exist on as little as possible in order that Brand have enough to fill his stomach.

Starvation had them backed into a corner when Nick Drummond rode to Tall Oaks yesterday. But it would be a cold day in hell before she would acknowledge that he had arrived just in time to save them. His arrival had made a shambles of her life despite the fact that his being here almost assured her of having food on the table.

Aimee paused at the bottom of the steps to gaze out the window. Numerous tents dotted the south lawn where men were busily engaged in all kinds of labor. She couldn't remember when there had been such a flurry of activity at Tall Oaks. Certainly not since the slaves had left. She started to turn away when something caught her eye, and she spun around again to peer out the window. She nearly fainted when she saw Brand standing on the lawn raising his arms to Nick, who was mounted on his horse. Then Nick bent down, lifted the lad, and swung him up before him in the saddle. He hugged the child and laughed in pure joy when Brand squealed in delight. Then Nick set his horse in motion, holding Brand with one hand while guiding his horse with the other.

Brand loved horses, but all of the decent stock at Tall Oaks had been confiscated at the beginning of the war. What the Confederate army left behind, the Union army quickly seized for their own. All that was left to them was one swaybacked mule fit only to pull the dilapidated wagon in which they rode to town when they still had money to pay for purchases.

"De captain seems mighty taken with Brand." Savannah had entered the foyer and stood behind Aimee, wondering what had captured her attention so thoroughly.

"Brand is a child; he doesn't recognize the enemy," Aimee said shortly.

Savannah bent her a measuring look. "I don't like dem Yankees any better dan you do, honey, but I sure appreciate havin' a full stomach. Captain Drummond, he don't seem a bad sort, as Yankees go, and you should see de food dem Yanks carted into de kitchen dis mornin' when de wagon from quartermaster done arrived. I don't think dey mean us any harm."

"Don't sing Captain Drummond's praises to me, Savannah," Aimee sniffed. She definitely wasn't pleased by Savannah's sage observations. In her eyes Nick Drummond was a devil. "And I don't want Brand becoming attached to that Yankee. Try to keep him inside as much as possible."

"Dere ain't no way to keep dat chile from goin' outside with all de activity goin' on," Savannah snorted.

"Nevertheless, we must try." Her voice was grim with determination and something else Savannah found puzzling. Aimee's light brown eyes were dark pools of rage as she opened the door and hurried outside.

"Where you goin', honey?"

"To get my son," Aimee replied over her shoulder as she slammed the door behind her.

Savannah clucked her tongue and wagged her head from side to side as she headed back toward the kitchen. "Dat chile sure is stubborn," she said to herself. She'd seen Aimee through many moods throughout the years, both good and bad, but never had she seen her so obsessed with a man was she was with Captain Nick Drummond.

Nick tightened his grip on Brand. The little imp was a joy to be around; someday he hoped to have a son just like him. It had only been since the war that he had even considered marriage and children. Seeing men die had instilled in him the need to leave a little bit of himself behind when he left this earth. Perhaps he would have children when he married Regina Blakewell, the daughter of General Andrew Blakewell. He had been more or less forced to propose to Regina since her father had caught them in a compromising position. In order to protect his career, which could be ruined by one word from the general, he had done the "gentlemanly" thing.

No date had been set for the wedding, since times were precarious at best, but Nick supposed they would marry after the war. No great love had emerged in his life, and since he despaired of ever finding Aimee Fortune, he had agreed to marriage out of hopeless remorse. Had he been able to find Aimee five years ago ... But that was another story, another time, and nothing could change the course of fate.

Nick's thoughts skidded to an abrupt halt when he saw Aimee heading straight for him. Her teeth were clenched, her stubborn jaw raised defiantly, and her eyes were dark with fury. He reined in his horse.

"Mama, look at me," crowed Brand, waving his chubby arms in the air. "Captain Drummond said I could ride Scout by myself when I get a little bigger."

"Would you please put my son down, Captain Drummond," Aimee demanded.

Nick obliged despite Brand's keen disappointment.

"Run into the house, Brand. Savannah has breakfast prepared."

"I already had breakfast, Mama. I ate with Captain Drummond."

Aimee ground her teeth in frustration. "Don't argue, Brand, just go inside. I want to talk to Captain Drummond in private." The little fellow looked hurt and puzzled but nevertheless obeyed his mother. She rarely spoke to him in that tone of voice, and when she did, he scrambled to do her bidding.

The moment he was out of earshot, Aimee rounded on Nick. "How dare you try to turn my son against me! I want you to keep away from him."

Nick's face grew stony. "He's a child, for God's sake. Why would I possibly want to turn him against you? Has it ever occurred to you that I genuinely like the boy? I'd never harm him."

"I don't trust Yankees. And cheating rogues are even more despicable."

Nick gnashed his teeth in vexation. "I didn't cheat you, Aimee, I won fair and square. You agreed to draw against me, knowing full well what I wanted from you if I won."

Aimee flushed, glancing around to see if anyone was listening. Except for Lieutenant Dill, who was eyeing them curiously, no one seemed to be giving them a passing glance. Just to be safe, she lowered her voice. "Don't remind me of my folly. That part of my life is over and done with. It ended the night you took . . . took everything from me. I had nothing left to give when you finished with me."

"Evidently Beau Trevor didn't find you lacking." Nick's lips curved into a wry curl. Aimee had sorely hurt him with her ridiculous accusation, and he wanted to lash out at her. But all he did was stoke the fires of her temper.

"Don't you dare say anything bad about Beau," she hissed. "The man was an angel compared to you."

Nick winced. Did she love her husband so much? "You don't even know me."

"I know all I want to know about you, and I don't like any of it. You're not fit company for my son, so keep away from him." She whirled on her heel and stomped away.

Unwilling to be bested by the acid-tongued little witch, Nick slid from his horse and grasped Aimee about the waist, swinging her around to face him. "Let's get one thing straight, Mrs. Trevor. You, your son, this house, and everything here are mine to command. I strongly suggest you obey me in all things and do nothing to invite my anger. If you behave, no harm will come to you. But I'm giving you fair warning—if you go too far, my good graces will end. Do you think I'm stupid? If not for me and my men, you would slowly starve to death. Be grateful I haven't ordered you to yield to me in . . . other ways. Some men I know wouldn't be so considerate."

"Considerate!" Aimee's eyes flashed indignantly. "Yankees aren't considerate, they're devils. They've raped our land and our women, and stolen our birthright. What can I hope to leave Brand when he's grown? A wreck of a house with no money to pay the taxes or feed a family? Land ravaged by war, and no one to work its fallow acres? A legacy of death and destruction? I haven't even begun to enumerate the wrongs you've personally done to me. Go away, just go away!"

Aimee's bitter recriminations stunned and bewildered Nick. He'd done nothing so terrible to her that he knew about. Nor had he asked anything of her that she wasn't prepared to relinquish to any other man to whom she owed a debt of honor. She had probably repaid many a debt in the same manner. That she'd been harboring a grudge against him all these years gave him pause. Was it because he had left her so abruptly the next morning?

"I'm sorry you feel that way, Mrs. Trevor, but I have an important job to do here that makes my presence necessary. As for your son, the lad seems to enjoy mingling with my men, and I'll not interfere with that enjoyment. He's had little enough pleasure in his young life, and he reminds my men of the children they left behind. No one would dare harm him."

Having said all he was going to on the subject, he turned on his heel and strode away, leaving Aimee fuming in impotent rage. Having Nick Drummond walk into her life again brought back bittersweet memories she'd rather forget.

Chapter 3

⚬⚬⚬⚬⚬

. . . *H*e touched his tongue to her nipple. She shivered in response. He told her that her body was made for love. He lowered the dress down her hips and legs and lifted her from the circle of cloth. Her petticoats and underwear followed in quick order. She stood before him clad only in shoes and stockings held up by frilly garters, shivering as his hot gaze slid over her. His eyes worshiped every place they touched—and they touched everywhere. Her shivering increased. He told her he wouldn't hurt her, that he only wanted to love her. Then he swept her off her feet and placed her on the bed.

Taking her foot in his hand, he slowly peeled the stocking from her leg, nuzzling the soft white inside of her thigh, her calf, her instep. He repeated the process with the other leg. Then he sat back on his heels and removed his jacket and shirt. The sight of his muscular chest captivated her, and she stared transfixed at the thick mat of curly black hair that disappeared into the waistband of his trousers. When he stood to remove his trousers, she tore her eyes away. But his husky, seductive whisper urging her to look at him brought her glazed eyes back to his magnificent body. He slid his trousers and underwear down his hips and legs in one *smooth motion and stood before her as God had created him—wonderfully male, arrogant, proud, fully erect. Her eyes paused briefly at the juncture of his legs, then opened wide in alarm and disbelief as they flew up to his face. He was so . . .*

"Aimee, are you all right, honey?" Savannah had walked into the parlor to find Aimee staring into space, her eyes unfocused, her body rigid.

Aimee started violently. Ever since that scoundrel Nick Drummond had intruded upon her life, she had had a difficult time controlling her thoughts. Though in the past she had thought about him upon occasion—how could she not when she had a living reminder of him?—it had never been to such an extent that she recalled every vivid detail of every minute they'd spent together. Previously, all she cared to remember was what a devil he was and the hatred she bore him.

"I'm fine, Savannah."

"What you doin' in here all by yourself?"

"I—I was thinking this room should be given a thorough cleaning."

"Why?" Savannah snorted. "Ain't no furniture in here to clean, so why bother? Most of de house ain't livable 'cept for de kitchen and some of de bedrooms. 'Sides," she added astutely, "you can't fool me, honey. Somethin's botherin' you. Ever since dem Yankees rode in, you ain't been de same."

"You're imagining things, Savannah. If I haven't been the same since the Yankees came to Tall Oaks, it's because I haven't forgotten that Yankees are responsible for Beau's death."

Savannah's dark eyes narrowed suspiciously. She wasn't fooled for a minute. "Dem Yankees been here for nearly two weeks, and dey ain't caused us no harm so far. I ain't sayin' I love dem, but at least we's eatin' regular. I'm thinkin' it's only one Yankee dat's botherin' you so much. You got a special grudge against Captain Drummond, and I ain't figured out why."

"There is nothing to figure out, Savannah," Aimee insisted stubbornly. "Stop trying to place any importance on my hatred for Captain Drummond. The man is an arrogant bastard who has taken over our lives without considering our feelings. Tall Oaks is mine; he has no business being here."

"C'mon, honey, why don't you come into de kitchen with me and help prepare supper. Dere's a brace of nice plump rabbits ready to be skinned and made into a tasty stew. Why, dere's even some sugar and flour to make Brand his favorite cookies."

Later, as Aimee rolled out sugar cookies for Brand, and Savannah put together the ingredients for the stew, a lone rider rode into the yard. His horse was lathered, and when he dismounted, his legs nearly gave way beneath him. He looked as if he had ridden fast and hard. Savannah joined Aimee at the back door as a soldier pointed out the man to Nick.

"Wonder what dat's all about," Savannah said curiously as the man placed a leather pouch in Nick's hand.

"Probably some kind of messenger," Aimee assumed. "I wonder ..." She shrugged and turned away.

Nick directed the man to the soldiers' mess, then walked slowly toward the house with the pouch. Aimee heard the front door slam behind him and his steps reverberating on the stairs as he sought the privacy of his room to peruse the dispatch from headquarters. It was the first time since the Yankees occupied Tall Oaks that a messenger had arrived. Though Aimee was curious, she deliberately refrained from speculating on the contents of the pouch. The war had caused her and her loved ones untold grief, and she had been able to cope with it by disassociating herself from its daily horrors. It might be cowardly, but it was her way of keeping her sanity.

The next day Nick led a patrol out at dawn. Aimee had been waiting for just such an occasion to defy his rule about leaving the confines of the house and yard. She knew the berries that grew in the nearby woods were ripe, and she planned to slip away at the first opportunity to gather them. There was still some sugar left, and they'd make delicious pies. She informed Savannah of her intention.

"You know what Captain Drummond said, honey," Savannah warned her. "Why not ask him if you could go? Dat way he can't say nothin' when he learned you went against his wishes."

Aimee bristled angrily. "I'm not going to let that man control my life! I've always picked berries this time of year, and I'm not going to let one of his silly rules stop me now. Please watch Brand while I'm gone; I'll be back long before Captain Drummond returns from patrol."

Savannah shook her head with misgiving as she watched Aimee walk toward the woods, a pail slung over her arm. "Stubborn," she muttered aloud. "She's de stubbornest little gal I ever seen."

"Where are you going, Mrs. Trevor?" Lieutenant Dill's challenge halted Aimee's progress across the yard. He greatly admired the petite, blond widow but was astute enough to know that Captain Drummond had some kind of prior claim.

"That should be obvious, Lieutenant," Aimee said sweetly. "I'm going to pick berries. Berry pie will make a nice treat for tonight's supper."

"Indeed it will," agreed Dill. "Has Captain Drummond approved your little excursion into the woods?"

"Of course," Aimee lied. "Otherwise I wouldn't be going."

"Then I won't stop you." Dill smiled, easily manipulated by Aimee's sherry-colored eyes and innocent manner. "I'll look forward with pleasure to supper tonight."

The woods was cool and dark. Aimee threaded her way around fallen trees and rotting vegetation as she headed directly toward the berry patch she had discovered years ago when she was still a new bride at Tall Oaks. Beau had enjoyed many a berry pie made from the fruits of that particular patch. Just as she suspected, the vines were heavy with large, succulent blackberries just waiting to be plucked from their thorny vines. She filled the pail in no time at all.

"Aimee." Her name rustled through the leaves like a disembodied specter. She heard it clearly but couldn't see its source. "Aimee, over here, behind the tall oak with the twisted trunk."

Whirling about, Aimee stared at the tree, unable to see through the massive trunk to the voice beyond. The fine hair at the nape of her neck stood on end and a frisson of fear curled down her spine. "Who—who are you? What do you want with me?"

Several tense seconds passed before the speaker stepped from behind the gnarled oak. Aimee gasped in recognition.

"God, Aimee, it's good to see you. You're just as beautiful as ever."

"Gar! Garson Pinder. I'd heard you'd been seriously wounded and were not expected to recover." Garson Pinder and his family were friends of the Trevors'. On occasion she and Beau had visited their lovely plantation, located a half day's journey from Tall Oaks. Only the burned-out hulk of their once magnificent house now stood. Garson's two sisters and mother were now living with relatives in Savannah. His father had fallen at Gettysburg.

Gar grinned impudently as his eyes raked Aimee from head to toe. He'd always been a cocky young man, and Aimee was surprised to see how little the war had changed him. On more than one occasion he had flirted openly with Aimee, but since he and Beau were such fast friends and no harm had come of his overtures, she had never mentioned the situation to her husband.

"As you can see, I'm alive and well. I'm attached to army intelligence now."

"What are you doing here? Don't you know Tall Oaks is swarming with Yankees?"

"At least they didn't burn it down like Rose Acres and other surrounding plantations," he said with a hint of accusation.

Aimee flushed guiltily, though in truth she had no reason to feel guilty. "I'm sorry. But you haven't answered my question. What are you doing in the midst of Yankee territory?"

"I followed a messenger here yesterday. I've been hiding in the woods ever since, hoping to have a private word with you. According to my information, Captain Nick Drummond is in charge of the blue-bellies billeted at Tall Oaks. Is that correct?"

"Your information is correct." Aimee wondered where this conversation was leading.

Gar moistened his slips, peered at her through hooded eyes, and asked, "Have they harmed you in any way?"

"No, they've not touched me. I'm in no danger as long as I abide by Captain Drummond's rules."

Gar nodded, apparently satisfied. "I need your help, Aimee. I desperately need to know what those dispatches the messenger delivered yesterday contained, and there is no way I can get inside the house without being caught. It's essential to the Confederacy that I learn the enemy's next move in the area. I have reason to believe that dispatches inside that pouch reveal the exact location of the North's next target."

Aimee didn't need an interpreter to know exactly what Gar was asking of her. "You want me to spy?"

"I'm asking you to do whatever is necessary to get that vital information to me. You're a beautiful woman, Aimee," he hinted crudely. "You should have little problem finding out what I need to know."

Aimee paused. Was he asking what she thought he was asking? "Just how far am I expected to go in order to get this information?"

Gar looked at her squarely, stripping her of everything but her pride. "I think you get the picture, Aimee. Do you think Beau would fault you if he knew how desperately the South needs your help? I don't care how you come by the information, I'm just telling you that without it, the war is as good as lost. You've been married; you know about men and how easy it is to beguile them."

Privately Aimee thought the Confederacy was headed toward defeat, but being as patriotic as the next person, she refrained from voicing her opinion. Perhaps Gar was right. Perhaps the dispatches Nick received would help the South win an important battle. But she had no intention of doing as Gar suggested in order to get that information. She hesitated so long that Gar began to fidget nervously. Fearing capture, he dared not linger in the area longer than necessary.

"Well, Aimee, will you help us? Or will you let Beau's death go unavenged? It's within your power to make a big difference in the course of the war."

With that, Aimee felt she could hardly refuse. "I'll try, but I can't promise anything," she said hesitantly.

Gar's lips curled in a slow smile. "I knew you'd see things my way. After all this nasty business is over ... well, you always knew you occupied a tender place in my heart. I was Beau's best friend, and I'll take care of you like Beau would have wanted me to."

Aimee had no illusions about Gar's halfhearted promise. "Gar, I'll help if I can, but—"

"Meet me here in one week, Aimee. At midnight. I'll be waiting. If you can't bring me the contents of the pouch, then at least read the dispatches and memorize their contents as well as any others that arrive for Drummond."

"I'll try, Gar, but . . ." Her sentence trailed off as Gar turned abruptly and disappeared into the dappled shadows of the forest. "Gar, wait!" But it was too late. He must have tethered his mount nearby, for she heard the horse prancing in the underbrush. Then absolute silence followed as they rode out of earshot.

Never had Aimee been so troubled. She was basically an honest person; spying went against everything she'd ever been taught. Yet Gar made it sound as if the future of the South depended upon the information in the dispatches Nick received. He had boldly intimated that she should do anything inside or outside the bounds of propriety to obtain that information. Her head spinning with terrifying visions of what Nick would do to her if he caught her spying, Aimee slowly made her way out of the woods. She had just stepped into the clearing when a lone horseman rode straight for her, hell for leather.

She tried to flee back into the protection of the forest, but the madman was off his horse and upon her before she could find a hiding place. "What in the hell are you doing out here when I specifically forbade you from leaving the yard?"

"I—I thought you were gone."

Nick bent her a disgruntled look. "My horse threw a shoe and I had to return. Are you going to answer my question?"

"I wanted to pick berries."

"So Lieutenant Dill told me. You deliberately

lied to him. You knew I never gave you permission to go into the forest by yourself."

Aimee held her ground despite his simmering anger. "I thought a pie would taste good tonight."

Grasping her arm, Nick gave her a vicious shake. "Forget the pie, Aimee; don't you know how dangerous it is traipsing through the woods by yourself? There are deserters and marauders out there who would make short work of you." Suddenly his green eyes narrowed suspiciously and he asked, "What are you *really* doing out here?" He peered around warily, his hand resting on his gun.

Aimee flushed, her eyes fearful as she followed the direction of Nick's gaze. She fervently prayed Gar was long gone by now. "I told you, I was gathering berries. Let me go!"

He released her so abruptly that she fell to her knees. "Where are the berries?"

His question startled her. "I—I must have forgotten them."

"You ventured into the woods specifically to gather berries and forgot them?" He stared at her doubtfully.

"My mind must have wondered and I walked off without them. I'll go back for them now."

"Not without me." He grasped her wrist and pulled her deeper into the woods, stomping around trees and underbrush until they came to the berry patch. The bucket sat on the ground, overflowing with plump blackberries.

"I told you so," Aimee crowed triumphantly.

"So you did," Nick said slowly. His vivid green eyes seemed to pierce into the very core of her, accusing, menacing—terrifying. "Pardon me if I don't believe you."

Aimee drew herself up to her full five feet three. "May I leave now? I should get started on the pie if we're to have it for supper."

A tense, awkward silence followed as they glowered at each other, each defying the other to make the first move.

Nick's control snapped first. He had deliberately kept his distance from Aimee during the past weeks, mindful of the hatred she bore him. But not a minute went by when he was not profoundly aware of her presence, of her icy disdain. He noted the difference three square meals a day had made on her thin body, and he was grateful he had arrived when he did. Her lovely face had grown softer. Her patched gown no longer hung askew on her slim frame. Now it hugged her curves provocatively. There was a fragile radiance about her that no other woman possessed.

She was incredibly erotic. Her eyelashes were dark gold and thick. Her sultry features exuded a potent sexuality that was almost palpable. The aching need that arose in him each time he looked at Aimee suddenly exploded as he spun her around to face him. His eyes darkened and he gave a long, moaning sigh as he pulled her close. Against the softness of her breasts Aimee could feel the rocklike fortress of his chest. Nick gave in to the devils driving him and kissed her. Like it or not, Aimee was quickly becoming an obsession with him.

Aimee was doomed. She felt trapped. She wanted to run from the comforting closeness of his big body, and from the unfamiliar lethargic feeling turning her legs into lumps of wood. Why did Nick Drummond affect her like this? she wondered resentfully. Why did the memory of Beau fade from her mind as if he never existed the moment this man took her into his arms?

His mouth was hard, hot, incredibly demanding, insulting—tempting. Too damn tempting as her arms suddenly developed a will of their own and crept upward to wind around his neck. She was drowning in his heat, his taste, his delicious masculine scent. Aimee's tentative response drew a groan from Nick's lips. When he broke off the kiss, a devilish grin settled on his roguish features.

"I told you before not to touch me!" said Aimee hotly.

"Are you going to tell me you didn't like that?"

"I hated it. I hate you!"

"Look at me, Aimee." When she shied away, he gripped her chin between forefinger and thumb and tilted her head up, forcing her to look into his eyes. They stared at each other breathlessly, neither willing to give an inch, before Nick said, "You're a liar, sweetheart. Don't you know that the eyes are windows to the soul? And yours, my beautiful Mrs. Trevor, are more expressive than most. You want me, sweetheart, as much as I want you. Why are you fighting me? Your husband has been dead a long time. There's nothing to keep us from satisfying our hunger for one another."

She shot him a scathing glance. Memories that refused to die lay like stepping-stones in her mind, leading her back to one inescapable fact. Nick Drummond had taken her virginity and had not even realized it. And he probably wouldn't have cared even if he did know it. She could forgive him for being a Yankee, pardon him for callously taking her virginity and giving her Brand, but never for thinking her a whore.

"You're despicable, Captain Drummond!" Those hours of incredible passion he had given her did not exist, she told herself firmly. They were visions from a dream that had no place in reality, over and done with years ago. "I want nothing to do with you."

"Tell me another lie." He carefully lowered her to the soft bed of leaves carpeting the ground. His hard mouth smothered her furious protests. She felt the breeze cool her heated flesh and knew he had worked her dress up her legs to her waist. And suddenly all the fight drained from her. She was tired of battling him.

"Very well, Captain Drummond," Aimee said, struggling for breath, "go ahead, do your worst, rape me. I can see you won't be satisfied until you get what you've been panting after since you walked back into my life. But don't expect me to enjoy it." Deliberately she spread her legs, offering him free access to that which he had been craving for longer than he cared to admit.

Nick uttered a sharp expletive and sat back on his heels. Though Aimee was tempting displayed before him, he hesitated. Rape? He abhorred rape—detested brutish men who felt the need to force themselves on women. The first time he had taken Aimee hadn't been rape, and he couldn't understand why she would think he would rape her now. He wanted to make love to her, to bring her the kind of pleasure she deserved. He was so certain of his ability to make her want him that he very nearly ignored her words. But the look in her eyes drained all the fire from his body. He leaped to his feet, turning his back while he adjusted his clothes.

His words were cruel as he lashed out at her. "Close your legs; you look like a whore."

Aimee blinked in disbelief. "Whore! That's what you've always thought of me, isn't it? No wonder I hate you."

"Go on back to the house," Nick ordered roughly. He didn't look at her. "I'll bring the berries." When she didn't move fast enough, he turned and shouted, "You heard me, get out of here before I change my mind!" Aimee took off at a run.

With ragged breaths, Nick rested his head against a tree, striking his fists repeatedly against the trunk until he drew blood. What was the matter with him? he asked himself bitterly. What had made him lash out at her like that? Why did her hatred pierce his heart like a dagger? Why did he have the feeling that if he couldn't thrust himself inside her, he would surely die? His own fiancée didn't affect him that way, and Regina was a passionate woman. Most women he had made love to were quickly forgotten after the first flush of passion was appeased. But after five years, his intimate hours with Aimee stood out in his mind in vivid relief.

Aimee hated him.

He closed his eyes, remembering . . .

He stood before her in all his naked glory, fully aroused and proud of his body, confident of his ability to please, eager to pleasure her as he had never pleasured another woman. He was hard and throbbing, his staff rising stiff and powerful from the dark forest be-

tween his legs. She looked at him then, and he nearly exploded on the spot. Her eyes were wide and incredulous, as if he were the first man she had ever seen in a state of full arousal. He knew it was all an act, but it pleased him. He dropped to his knees on the bed, worshiping her with his eyes. Then slowly he began to arouse her in all the ways, all the places, he knew women liked. With his mouth, his lips, the moist tip of his tongue . . .

"Captain Drummond, where are you?"

Lieutenant Dill crashed through the forest, his voice rousing Nick abruptly from his sensual journey into the past.

"Over here, Lieutenant," Nick called, struggling to control his turbulent emotions.

Dill soon came into sight. He seemed relieved to see Nick. "Mrs. Trevor returned to the house alone, and I grew worried. Are you all right?"

"No need for worry, Lieutenant," Nick said gruffly. "I decided to check the area before returning to the house. One can't be too careful in these times."

"Right, sir," Dill said skeptically. "Are you ready to leave now?"

"Ready, Lieutenant. Just as soon as I get the berries Mrs. Trevor gathered."

Aimee was panting by the time she reached the house. She couldn't believe how close she had come to submitting to Nick Drummond after the callous way in which he had treated her. To care for a man like him would destroy her utterly. On the heels of that thought came the terrible knowledge of all she stood to lose if she followed Garson Pinder's advice. He virtually asked her to sleep with the enemy in order to get the information needed by the Confederacy.

Aimee cast a furtive glance over her shoulder and spied Nick emerging from the woods. He looked thoroughly vexed, yet she instinctively knew that once she yielded to him, she'd be in a position to gain all the information Gar sought. But to yield to Nick now would cost her her pride, her honor—her very soul. In the end, her dilemma came down to one question: Did she want to spy? Did she truly want to search Nick's personal belongings in order to obtain the information for Gar?

The answer was more involved than she would have imagined. It was true she hated Yankees, was sickened by what they had done to the South. She despised Nick Drummond with an all-consuming passion. Her fierce patriotism demanded that she do her bit for the faltering Confederacy, but her thoughts stopped just short of placing herself in Nick's bed. If she used her wits, she felt confident of obtaining the information without resorting to such drastic measures. Feeling more optimistic, Aimee went to the kitchen to help Savannah with supper. She arrived just as Nick entered through the back door with the bucket of berries.

Savannah slid Aimee a questioning glance, curious as to why Captain Drummond was bringing the berries instead of Aimee. Aimee refused to acknowledge Savannah's unspoken query, turning her attention instead to Brand, who sat on the kitchen floor playing with a crudely carved wooden horse.

"Where did you get that, Brand?" Aimee asked.

She couldn't remember seeing that particular toy before. In fact, Brand had few toys.

"Captain Drummond gave it to me," Brand said proudly. "It looks just like Scout, doesn't it, Mama?"

Aimee hated the idea of Nick providing her son with a toy when she herself could give him nothing so fine.

"I hope it's all right, Mrs. Trevor," Nick said coolly. "Perhaps I should have asked you first, but it's such a small gift. I carved it in my spare time when I noticed the lad had so few toys."

For a moment Brand looked troubled. "It *is* all right, isn't it, Mama?"

Aimee didn't have the heart to deny her child so small a pleasure, even if it did come from Nick Drummond. "It's all right, darling." Her honey brown eyes settled on Nick. "But in the future I suggest Captain Drummond ask my permission before providing my son with trinkets."

"Self-righteous little bitch," Nick muttered to himself as he stomped from the kitchen. Aimee was quickly becoming a thorn in his side. He thought about her far too often for his own peace of mind. Of late he had begun to question his own sanity.

Why he should want such a contrary little vixen was beyond his powers of reasoning. She had never explained to his satisfaction exactly why she held a grudge against him all these years—and how she had disappeared so thoroughly when he returned to find her later. He was deeply troubled by her attitude, and the feeling persisted that she was deliberately trying to protect someone. He never really was convinced that she was a professional gambler, though Lord knows she was proficient enough at the game. There were so many things he wanted to know about her, just thinking about the situation gave him a vile headache.

Nick was walking toward the stable to see if Scout had been shoed yet when another messenger arrived. Once again Aimee watched from the window as the messenger pressed a leather pouch into Nick's hands before heading for the mess tent. She recalled Gar's words and his obvious desperation. It was common knowledge that the Confederacy was backed against a wall, and now it was within her power to help turn the tide of defeat. Squaring her narrow shoulders, Aimee reluctantly accepted the task Gar forced on her. She waited until Nick returned to the house and entered his bedroom before quietly following him up the stairs.

Walking to the window, Nick held the sheaf of papers up to the light and silently perused the dispatch from headquarters. General Sherman was concentrating all his power against Johnston's army in Georgia. Atlanta, Confederate General Johnston's base, was at the junction of four important railways. Its capture would be the death knell of the Confederacy. The dispatch set the date for Sherman's spearhead into Atlanta, a battle in which Nick and his men were expected to join.

Having read the dispatch through twice, Nick carefully refolded it, replacing it inside the pouch, intending to show it to Lieutenant Dill before destroying it. It contained dates, cities, and times that needed to be memorized by both officers in the event one fell in battle. He placed the pouch inside the small campaign chest that contained his spare articles of clothing. Then he quickly left the room. He had heard his patrol returning and was anxious to receive their report of enemy movement in the area.

Aimee waited until Nick left the house before entering his room. The first place she searched was the desk drawers. They contained nothing to rouse her suspicion. She turned her attention to the bureau, but that, too, held nothing of importance. Then she spied the small chest sitting beneath the window and quickly moved to inspect its contents. But to her chagrin, she was interrupted by Savannah, who entered the room carrying a stack of clean sheets in her arms. Aimee whipped around, her face flushed a guilty red.

Savannah was dismayed to find Aimee in Captain Drummond's room rifling his belongings. "What you doin' in here, chile? De Captain ain't gonna be pleased if he catches you goin' through his belongin's."

"I—I wasn't—I mean, it's none of your business, Savannah." Turning abruptly, she fled from the room.

Chapter 4

・・・ *b* *ig. He was so big, she feared he would split her in two. She must have conveyed her fright, for he whispered that he wouldn't hurt her, promised her delights beyond what she felt with other lovers, told her how he adored the way she responded to him. She felt consumed by white-hot lightning when he took her nipple into his mouth. She arched into him. He began to suckle.*

A warm knot formed in the pit of her stomach and she cried out. He turned to the other breast as his hand slid down between her thighs. She tried to clench her legs, but he wouldn't let her. She let out another shuddering groan. His naked flesh against hers was hot—so hot. He scalded her with his passion, fueling her own. His fingers rubbed the nub hidden between the tender folds of pink flesh until she was slick with moisture. His finger slowly eased up inside her, and she moved her hips in response.

Aimee jerked upright in bed. She was drenched in sweat, and her thrashing had caused her nightgown to slide up around her waist. Caught in the throes of the same erotic dream that had plagued her both night and day since Nick Drummond had ridden into her life, she pounded the pillow in frustration. Why? she asked herself in a fit of fury. Why did she have to relive those hours in his bed as if they had happened yesterday? Why did every lurid detail resurface after all these years to haunt her? Her body still tingled as if his hands and mouth had actually taken possession of her.

She had merely paid a debt five years ago, nothing more, Aimee tried to tell herself. Nick knew what he wanted from her even before that fateful draw of the cards. He had made his need perfectly clear. And she had accepted his challenge, knowing full well what he expected if she lost. But she had been so confident she'd win, so absolutely convinced, that she was stunned when Nick had drawn the high card. What followed was like a sequence in a dream. Then the rogue had left, making her feel like a common whore—left her with his child in her belly.

Now he was here at Tall Oaks, taunting her with his presence, making it clear as glass that he still wanted her, driving her crazy with his mocking smile and his kisses. And she had committed herself to spying on him. She had only a short time left before her meeting with Garson Pinder, and she still hadn't found the opportunity to read the dispatch that arrived for Nick. Savannah watched her like a hawk, afraid that she'd get into serious trouble with the Yank if she was caught in Nick's room searching his belongings. Aimee had mentioned nothing to Savannah about her meeting with Gar, thinking that the less Savannah knew about Gar's visit, the better off they'd both be.

Perhaps her chance would come today, Aimee reflected as she flopped over on her stomach. It was still too early to arise, but she was no longer interested in sleep. Somehow she had to get into Nick's room without being seen and obtain the information Gar requested.

Nick had awakened early. Too early to start the day but certainly not too early to slip into that semiconscious world where reality and dreams collided.

He wanted to be inside her so badly, he ached. His finger slipped inside her. She was hot—so hot. And wet. More than ready for him. She cried out. He told her he adored the way she responded to him, how desperately he wanted to thrust inside her in the same way his fingers were doing. How very much he needed to feel her tighten around him when she reached her pinnacle. He wanted her to forget her other lovers while she was in his arms. Then he was pushing inside her, stretching her, filling her. She stiffened and groaned and he pushed all the way inside her. She was tight, so damn tight he lost control of his senses, so consumed with passion, he knew nothing but the need to stroke them both to completion.

Nick groaned, reliving that incredible moment as if it were happening now. He had been awestruck by the wondrous heat of her, the tightness of her sheath. He remembered telling her she was as tight as a virgin, and laughing over that absurd observation. Then he flexed his hips, thrust forward, and embedded himself fully.

And thereby earned Aimee's undying hatred.

Yet if he had had it all to live over again, he knew he would have done nothing differently. The only part he would have changed was leaving her and letting Beauregard Trevor into her life. He should have caught another train for Chicago and stayed long enough to learn where he could find her when he returned. If he had, Brand might be his son. Suddenly his eyes narrowed thoughtfully. That same ridiculous notion he had when he first set eyes on Brand came back to haunt him. Was Brand really Beauregard Trevor's son?

Because both Aimee and Nick had awakened early, both left their rooms at nearly the same moment, meeting by chance at the head of the stairs. Aimee merely nodded, flushing as she recalled the dream that had jolted her awake at dawn's first light. Nick grinned, giving her the full benefit of his dimpled smile. His green eyes shimmered with secret knowledge. Aimee felt like slapping him.

"Good morning, Mrs. Trevor," he said with a hint of mockery. "I trust you slept well."

"Just fine, thank you," Aimee returned icily. She'd be damned if she'd tell him he haunted her dreams.

They descended the stairs side by side. "You're up rather early, aren't you?"

"I could say the same for you," Aimee countered. "Are you going on patrol today?"

"As a matter of fact, I am. Dare I hope you'll miss me?"

"Hardly," Aimee snorted. "I just wondered if you'd be back in time for supper."

He sent her a piercing look. Aimee tried not to flinch as his devil's eyes probed her innermost thoughts.

"I'll probably not return until after dark. Don't wait supper for me. In fact, the entire company, save for a few men left behind for guard duty, will ride out with me."

He watched closely for her reaction and wasn't disappointed by the barely perceptible glimmer in her eyes. He had no idea what it meant except for the fact that she was probably glad to be rid of him for a time.

"Captain Drummond!"

Both Aimee and Nick turned as Brand came bounding down the stairs. Aimee winced in dismay when Nick opened his arms and Brand leaped into them as if it were the most natural thing in the world to do. Then he placed the little boy on his shoulders and bounced down the stairs. He held him there until they reached the dining room. Then he plunked him into a chair and ruffled his hair in such an affectionate manner that Aimee cringed. Savannah entered the dining room almost immediately, carrying a platter of eggs from the chickens the Yanks has somehow found and installed at Tall Oaks. She placed them before Nick with a grin and a flourish.

"I hope you's hungry, Captain."

"I'm always hungry for your food, Savannah," Nick teased.

"Me, too," chimed in Brand. He looked expectantly at his mother, waiting for her to add her praise.

But Aimee was so distracted that the conversation barely registered. Foremost on her mind was the need to go to Nick's room and obtain the information needed by Gar. Fortunately Nick was going to be gone all day, affording her the much-awaited opportunity. She pushed her food around on her plate while the men ate. Lieutenant Dill arrived and the conversation returned to business. Aimee listened carefully, but nothing of importance was revealed in the rather brief discussion of their separate duties.

"Are you going away?" Brand asked worriedly.

"I'll be back," Nick assured him.

"Can I go with you?"

"Well, now—"

"No!" Aimee leaped to her feet, stunned by Brand's question. She felt betrayed by her own son.

Nick was surprised by Aimee's unwarranted outburst. Didn't she know he'd never place her son in danger? To Brand, he said, "That's not a good idea, son. I'd never take you where danger exists." Brand's face fell, causing Nick to add, "But tomorrow I promise to let you ride Scout."

"Really?" Nick nodded.

"If you've finished breakfast, Brand, you may leave the table," Aimee said tightly. She couldn't bear to see Nick and Brand getting along so famously. "Perhaps Savannah has a chore for you to do."

Brand looked askance at his mother but quickly obeyed. He couldn't wait to tell Savannah that he was going to ride Scout tomorrow.

"I would appreciate it, Captain, if you'd stay away from my son," Aimee said once Brand had left the room. "He's an impressionable boy who has lacked male companionship ever since Beau ... left. I fear he's far too trusting for his own good, and I don't want to see him hurt."

"And you think I'll hurt him?" Nick asked, frowning.

"Good Lord, Mrs. Trevor," Lieutenant Dill exclaimed, quickly coming to Nick's defense, "everyone is fond of the lad. You're accusations are unfounded as well as unjust."

"I can't be too careful where my son is concerned."

"Leave us, please, Lieutenant," Nick ordered. His eyes bored relentlessly into Aimee, but she held her ground.

Dill slid Aimee a compassionate look, then quickly departed. Nick stood behind Aimee, his hands resting lightly on her shoulders. Aimee flinched beneath the strength and heat of his touch.

"I think it's time you realized that I mean no harm to Brand. I won't contaminate the boy. He seems to enjoy my company. Whether it's because I'm the first male he's spent time with since his father ... well, you know what I mean, or because he genuinely likes me, makes no difference. I *enjoy* having Brand around. And until I leave Tall Oaks, you'll just have to accept the idea of a friendship developing between me and Brand."

"I don't have to like it," Aimee flung out.

His grip on her shoulders tightened. Aimee cried out, and Nick immediately apologized. "I'm sorry, I didn't mean to hurt you, but you do have a way of provoking me. I only wish ..." His sentence faltered. Aimee waited for him to continue, but he remained silent. Nick had started to say that he wished Aimee were half as friendly as her son. Instead, he turned away.

Aimee felt the warmth of his hands leave her shoulders, and a sudden feeling of abandonment seized her. She turned to look at him, her eyes hooded.

"I wish I knew what you're thinking," Nick said slowly. "I wish there was something I could do or say to make you stop hating me."

Aimee had no answer. They stood staring at each other, the tension between them so potent, she could almost reach out and touch it. She had never felt so alive, so vital, so profoundly moved, by another human being. Surely it was hate she felt, wasn't it? His devil's eyes singed her with searing flame, and she tasted his zest, his essence—his need. Enthralled by the flavor of his passion, Aimee stepped closer, inexorably drawn by the torrid warmth in his green eyes.

"Damn you to hell, Aimee Trevor," Nick groaned, surrendering to the devils driving him as he reached out and hauled her hard against his chest.

He was so hot for her, he shook with his desire. Tilting her face upward, he pressed his mouth down on hers. His action was instinctive, uncontrollable, primal. He couldn't help himself. Neither could Aimee as the extraordinary heat and force of his kiss made her momentarily forget her hatred. But before she could think, Nick broke off the kiss and shoved her away. Her breathing was ragged, her thoughts disjointed as she watched his angry strides carry him from the room. Dear God, how much more of this could she take?

She was so responsive, he nearly exploded the moment he shoved inside her! The mysterious lady gambler had no right to appear so naively innocent while driving him wild with all the practiced moves of a whore. He told her how wonderful she was, how perfectly she fit him. Then he thrust the rock-hard point of his erection deep—so deep. He felt her shudder, felt her mouth working wordlessly against his—he supposed in mindless passion. Then slowly, oh so slowly, he shoved himself in and out, to accustom her to the size of him—he couldn't ever recall being so hard. After a few minutes she began to move with him in instinctive rhythm as he whispered encouragement. He stroked with erotic precision as she undulated beneath him, shocking him with her heat and sweet response. His kiss caught her lips again and again as he rocked inside her. He panted. She cried out in response, and his answer was the hard, piercing thrust of his shaft deep inside her, touching her womb, her heart, her soul . . .

"Captain Drummond, there's nothing stirring out here; perhaps we should return to Tall Oaks."

Nick started violently. Once again he had allowed his thoughts to wander over forbidden territory. The years dropped in the face of such erotic memories, and now, with Aimee so close to him day after day, erotic recollections of that night so long ago made him wild for her. He wanted her. She knew it, knew it well. And passionate Reb that she was, she made it absolutely clear that she wanted nothing to do with a Yank who had made her his for one night and walked out on her the next morning.

"We may as well start back since there are no signs of Rebs in the immediate area, Lieutenant," Nick responded. "Nothing is moving out there, and though I told Mrs. Trevor we wouldn't return in time for supper, I do believe we could easily make it back in time."

The day was half gone when Aimee was finally able to slip off to Nick's room. Since she didn't expect him back from patrol until very late, she wasn't worried about the time. Savannah hadn't allowed Aimee out of her sight during the entire morning. Either she or Brand seemed to demand her presence most of the long, dreary day. Aimee knew Savannah feared for her safety, and she couldn't help but feel resentful. She was old enough to know where her duty lay and certainly responsible enough to accept full accountability for what she was doing. Besides, with Nick gone, being caught was a remote possibility. At the appointed time she'd simply sneak out of the house with the information she'd gathered and meet Gar. No one would be the wiser, and she will have done her bit for the Confederacy. It was the least she could do for Beau's memory.

Her opportunity came when Savannah went to the kitchen to start supper. Aimee volunteered to pick peaches from the tree in the yard for a cobbler, and she hurried off with a pail before Savannah could respond. Aimee hurried to complete her task so she could slip around the house, enter by the front door, and sneak up the stairs to Nick's room.

At her touch, the door to Nick's room opened silently and she slipped inside, closing it carefully behind her. Deep shadows cast the room into near darkness, but enough light filtered through the windows to make lighting a lamp unnecessary. Aimee set the bucket of peaches down by the door and moved immediately to the chest where she had last seen the leather pouch containing the dispatches Nick had received. Sifting though the assortment of clothing, she located the pouch immediately. Her hands shook as she removed the contents. She didn't dare steal the dispatches, for she knew Nick would suspect her at once.

Gar had told her to memorize the contents.

Aimee dragged in a shuddering gasp as she quickly read the bold pen strokes. Dates and places leaped before her eyes, each designating a targeted site for attack. Aimee realized immediately that what she held in her hands was indeed something of vital importance to the Confederacy. Those attacks could be repelled once the information was placed in the right hands. But instinctively Aimee knew she could never remember all the places and dates in so short a time. Her mind working furiously, she moved to the desk, drew out paper and ink, and quickly copied down all the pertinent information. When she finished she carefully folded the paper and slipped it into her pocket. Then she returned the dispatches to the pouch and replaced it inside the chest exactly where she had found it.

Aimee had just turned from the chest when the door opened and Nick stepped into the room. He had already removed his gun belt and holster before he saw her. She stood still as a statue, her face white, her eyes wide and frightened. They stared at each other for long, tense minutes. The sight of her white hand fluttering to her breast released Nick from his frozen stance as he moved more fully into the room.

"My God, Aimee, you gave me a fright! What in hell are you doing in here?"

"I—that is—I—" What could she say? That she was spying? That she was reading his dispatches so she might take the information to the Rebs? What would he do to her? Send her to prison? What would become of Brand and Savannah if she ended up in a northern prison? More than one women spy was incarcerated for spying, and the

Yanks wouldn't hesitate to lock her away for her crime—maybe even hang her.

"Spit it out, Aimee. What in God's sweet name are you doing here? Unless . . ." He bent her a narrow-eyed glance, clearly intrigued at finding Aimee in his room. To his credit, he only briefly considered that she might be spying. He hoped . . .

Do whatever is necessary to get that information to me.

Gar's words came back to haunt Aimee. She was horrified at the idea of sleeping with the enemy for the purpose of spying. But prison did not appeal to her, and Brand and Savannah needed her. Instinctively she knew that Nick was a conscientious military man who took his duty seriously. He'd never allow her to get away with spying. He was duty-bound to turn her over to a higher authority for sentencing. She was so lost in thought, she had no idea Nick was standing before her until the warmth of his breath brushed her cheek.

"I'm waiting, Aimee. What are you doing in my room?" His words were quiet, controlled—hopeful—and she sensed his unwillingness to believe her capable of spying. At that moment she hated herself almost as much as she hated Nick.

Do what you have to do.

Her mouth went dry. She licked her lips. Mesmerized, Nick stared at the tip of her pink tongue as it flicked out, and his control fled. Did she know what she was doing to him?

Her words were so low, Nick had to lean forward to hear them. "I came because I wanted to—to be with you. I was waiting for you return from patrol."

"You what! Excuse me if I don't believe you."

Sweet Lord, he wanted to believe her. "Until this moment you've given the distinct impression that you can't stand to be in the same room with me. Dare I hope your opinion of me has changed overnight? Why all of a sudden?"

Why was this so damn difficult? "I—I'm a widow."

"I'm well aware of that."

"It isn't right to—to want another man so soon."

"I understand your husband has been dead nearly two years." She nodded. "Now all of a sudden you want to be alone with me. Did your conscience suddenly leave you?"

"Dammit, why must you question my motives? Isn't it enough that I'm here? But I can see I made a mistake; I'll leave immediately." Anxious now to leave, she tried to step around him.

"Not so fast, sweetheart." He grasped her arm and swung her around to face him. "You came here to be alone with me, and I've never been one to deny a beautiful woman."

"I've changed my mind. Coming here like this was a mistake. I don't want to betray Beau's memory."

Nick went still. "Did you love him so much?" The thought of another man loving Aimee and giving her a child made him furious.

Hot color flooded Aimee's face. Love Beau? She had been fond of him, grateful to him, but love was an emotion she had never experienced with him. They had been married such a short time before the war started, and then he went off and was killed. But she'd never forget him for the unconditional love he'd given to her and Brand.

"Beau was a wonderful man."

"That's not what I asked you."

"I married him, didn't I?"

"Yes," Nick said softly, "you did marry Beauregard Trevor. And you had a son by him. But did you love him?"

Would he never be satisfied? "Yes. Dammit, I loved Beau. Does that answer your question?"

His eyes defied her. "You may have loved him once, but damn it, Aimee, when you're in this room with me, you'll think of no one but me. I swear I'll make you forget him. When you're with me, I'll make certain you think of nothing but how I make you feel. I'm going to love you, Aimee Trevor, love you so thoroughly that what you and your husband did in bed will seem like child's play."

Dismayed by his blatantly sexual language, Aimee gasped. She hadn't planned on this encounter when she entered Nick's room. He wasn't supposed to be here. But she couldn't deny the fact that his words had a profound impact on her. A surge of raw hunger shot through her as his green eyes settled on her lips. He was going to kiss her, she knew it, and nothing short of sudden death could have stopped her from leaning forward into the lure of his lips. His mouth was fire and heat and passion, demanding, relentless, claiming her completely. She whimpered in futile protest as he swept her up in his arms and laid her down on the bed.

She felt the wetness of his kisses again, his tongue seeking hers as he parted her lips and tasted her sweetness. She lost herself in the erotic hunger of his kiss, surrendered to his heat, his fire, his need. Her bodice was loosened and then his lips were at her breasts, tugging at her nipples, the heat of his wet mouth drawing them into taut, aching points. Suddenly her skirt was swept upward, and Nick caressed the naked curve of her hip, her buttocks, the inside of her thigh; at the same time he suckled her nipples with ever-increasing vigor. Shimmering waves of sweet fire jolted through her body, soaking her with the moistness of desire.

Then he touched her. Touched that part of her where her hunger centered. Stroked her where she longed to be stroked. Stroked her until she undulated to the erotic rhythm of his hand. Her eyes closed, soft gasps exploded from her, and she arched her body into his bold caress. In one of her few lucid moments she realized she was enjoying this too much, that she shouldn't have succumbed so easily to his seduction, and she made a feeble effort to escape. But Nick had no intention of letting her go. He had waited much too long for this moment.

"Don't fight it, sweetheart," he whispered raggedly. "Let it happen. You can't begin to imagine how long I've dreamed about this. About you."

He held her tight and continued his sweet torture. His fingers were magical, demanding, drawing forth feelings she didn't know she possessed. She couldn't stop the climax. It came in great shattering waves of raw primal bliss, crashing like foaming surf upon the rocks and dashing her into tiny fragments.

The world was still spinning when Aimee floated back to reality. Nick was removing her clothes. "Did you like that, sweetheart?" He grinned wickedly. "That's only the beginning. I've waited so long for this moment, it's difficult to believe you're here now, in my bed, in my arms."

"Wait! Stop!" Aimee grasped the edges of her bodice, pulling it together. "I didn't mean for this to happen."

"Nothing happened yet, but it's damn well going to. Do you know how badly I want to be inside you? You were mine once, Aimee; I'm going to make you mine again. Having you come to my room like this is a miracle I never thought would happen. I'm not even going to ask you how or why you changed your mind about me, I'm just going to thank God you did."

Aimee groaned. Was she such a good actress that Nick didn't suspect her of spying? And if she didn't want to end up in prison, she had to continue the charade.

But was it really a charade? Or did she want this as much as Nick did? Had she secretly yearned to savor Nick's love one more time?

The question stormed through her mind like a winter gale. The answer nearly blew her away. She had relived those hours spent in Nick's bed so often, in such lurid detail, that she wanted to experience his lovemaking again.

Lord help her!

The timid knock on the door startled them both. "Captain Drummond, have you seen Aimee? I haven't seen dat chile since she went out to pick peaches, and I'm worried 'bout her." Savannah's voice was fraught with concern.

"Savannah! Oh God!" Aimee's voice trembled. What would Savannah think of her?

Nick stared deeply into Aimee's eyes and replied, "Aimee's in here with me, Savannah; no need for worry."

"Damn you, Nick Drummond!" Aimee hissed through clenched teeth. "Was that necessary?"

"There's no sense in lying to Savannah; she's smart enough to figure things out for herself."

There was silence on the other side of the door. Aimee thought Savannah had left until she said, "Aimee, honey, dat cobbler ain't gonna get made if you don't bring dem peaches."

"I—I'll be right down, Savannah." The blush in her voice told a story all its own. Savannah's retreating footsteps had all but disappeared when Aimee rounded on Nick. "You Yankee bastard! What are you trying to do to me? No wonder I hate you."

"Can't you be honest for once in your life? We're both adults, doing what we want, what our hearts dictate."

"Let me up! You heard Savannah; she needs me to help with supper."

"She'll manage. Dammit, Aimee, I'm so damn hot for you, if I'm not inside you soon, I'll explode. You owe me, sweetheart."

"Please let me go now, Nick," Aimee cajoled.

He began tugging at his clothes.

"Wait! If—if you're adamant about this, can't it wait until later?"

A ragged sigh left his lips. "Very well, Aimee, until later. Will you come to my room or shall I come to yours?"

Aimee swallowed past the lump in her throat. "I'll come to your room after I put Brand to bed and Lieutenant Dill retires for the night."

Reluctantly he moved aside to allow her to rise.

Then, ignoring her protests, he helped her smooth out her clothes. When she turned to leave, he laid a hand on her arm. "Aimee, I'll be waiting. Don't disappoint me. I want you, sweetheart. You may not believe me, but I've always wanted you, even before I knew who you were or where to find you. And if you'd allow yourself time to think about it, you'd realize you want me, too. Otherwise you'd not be here now."

Then he kissed her, kissed her so thoroughly, with such raw passion, it left Aimee dazzled. She turned and fled from the room, stopping only long enough to retrieve the bucket of peaches.

Oh, God, she thought, sobbing in frustration. What had she done? Loving Nick Drummond could destroy her.

Chapter 5

The house was quiet. An air of expectancy pervaded the stillness as Aimee entered her bedroom after putting Brand to bed. She started violently when she saw Nick sitting calmly on the bed surrounded by a pool of lamplight, waiting for her.

Aimee chose not to appear at supper that night, pleading a headache. Not only could she not bear Savannah's reproachful glances, but being with Nick was too painful, given her knowledge of what he expected from her later tonight. The thought of surrendering to Nick again really did give her a headache. Only this time she had no debt of honor to repay and no intention of keeping her word. The first time she ended up in Nick Drummond's bed, she did so to preserve her honor, but there was no honor involved this time. Quite the contrary. She had spied, lied, and fully intended to renege on her promise to present herself at Nick's door after the household was sleeping. She had obtained the information requested by Gar but felt no obligation to bed with Nick Drummond.

Her intention had been to slip into her room

and lock herself in, only Nick had astutely prepared for that. When Aimee failed to show up at supper, intuition warned him that she intended to break her promise to come to his room when everyone was sleeping. So he had sneaked into her room while she was busy with Brand.

"What do you want?" Aimee gasped, shocked to find Nick sitting on her bed in a pool of lamplight.

"Why are you avoiding me? Were you going to break your word?" Aimee shook her head in vigorous denial. "Then I'm going to love you, sweetheart," he continued, "and nothing short of death or an enemy attack is going to stop me. It's what you want, too, isn't it?"

Her body screamed yes while her mind rejected the idea utterly. But no matter how desperately she tried, she couldn't purge her memory of that night Brand was conceived. Conceived in lust, not in love.

Earlier, waiting for Aimee to come to him, Nick had paced his room like a caged tiger. He burned, he ached, he wanted Aimee with a need that went far beyond lust. He could still taste her kisses, smell the musky odor of her passion, feel her trembling flesh beneath his fingertips. If it wasn't lust he felt for Aimee, what was it? Unfortunately Aimee's hatred for him made it impossible to explore his feelings for her. But tonight ... tonight she had admitted she wanted him, had come to his room to be with him. At first he was skeptical, then puzzled, then inordinately pleased. Finally he could wait no longer. Assuming Aimee was putting Brand to bed, he had quietly entered her room to wait for her.

"I—told you I'd come to your room," Aimee hedged. "What if Brand should awaken and come in here?"

His answer was to sweep her up in his arms and carry her out the door the short distance to his room. He set her on her feet. "Is this better?" he teased. His voice was low and evocative. "I always aim to please a lady. I'd rather have you in my room anyway."

Aimee quickly took a step backward, his heart nearly overpowering her. "I—didn't Savannah tell you I had a headache?"

A lazy smile hung on the corner of Nick's mouth. "You're not getting off that easily. Do you really have a headache? Or are you fishing for excuses now that the moment we've both been yearning for has arrived?" Suddenly his face grew thoughtful and he looked at her probingly. "Could there possibly be another reason you came to my room?"

Hot color flooded Aimee's cheeks. Did he suspect? "No, no other reason. I meant what I said."

Nick's smile deepened, making his dimple even more prominent. "Good. And I meant what I said. God, Aimee, you don't know how long I've waited for this moment. I couldn't bear your hatred."

He stepped forward. He was close—so close the heat emanating from him seemed to scorch her. She could almost smell the acrid scent of his arousal, taste the delicious flavor of his need. Her expression must have conveyed her thoughts, for his response was immediate and overwhelming.

"Take off your clothes, sweetheart; I want to see all of you."

Aimee's mouth went dry. "Perhaps we should wait."

"No, I've already waited too long. You've bewitched me, Aimee; I'm like a kid with his first woman. I want you, now."

The wanting within him moved her in a way she couldn't explain. When he drew her into his arms, the taste of his kiss was bittersweet. So many nights she had lain awake tortured by memory. So many times she had dreamed about him when she knew they would never meet again. And now here he was, as handsome as ever—no, more handsome—more demanding, his need for her just as great as it had been the first time. His devil's eyes still tormenting her.

He was her son's father, the man she had vowed to hate forever. The only man who had the power to arouse her sleeping passion.

His lips upon hers were fervent, ardent, swiftly igniting the passion between them. She returned his kiss, eager for it, responding with a fervor nearly as great as his. Their tongues met, dueled, retreated, then met again as the kiss deepened. Panting for breath, Aimee broke away, staring at him.

His tongue moved over her throat, slowly, teasingly, gliding down the length of it, spreading fire in its wake.

She closed her eyes, reveling in his touch, gasping in delight when his wet mouth closed over a taut nipple, making a damp circle on the worn material of her dress. She heard him curse, then heard the rending of fabric. Impatient to bare her flesh, he ripped the gown cleanly so that it fell open, exposing every delicious inch of her to his devouring eyes.

"Nick!"

"Don't worry, sweetheart, I'll buy you another. This one doesn't do you justice."

Then she felt the slow, burning touch of his lips on her breast. He drew hot, wet circles on her breasts, caressing, licking, the roughness of his tongue like an aphrodisiac. Dropping to his knees before her, he continued the hot slide of his tongue downward to her stomach, pausing to sip hungrily at her navel before the searing hot moistness of his mouth moved down, down, until she wanted to scream. Sweet, hungry agony seized her as his tongue invaded a place so sensitive, she wanted to cry out.

Suddenly he was on his feet, lifting her from the ruins of her clothing, bearing her down to the softness of the bed. He knelt beside her, making love to her with his eyes. Then he was flinging off his clothes, pressing her down with his nakedness, his lips hot and hungry, smothering the tiny sounds of ecstasy that escaped from between her parted lips. His body was taut, sleek, covering hers in a way that made her aware of every magnificent inch of flesh that came into intimate contact with hers. Her entire body awakened, hungry, hot, needy, wanting what only Nick could give her. The bitter-sweet agony of her wanting brought with it the shattering knowledge that she had waited five years for this moment.

A soft murmur of desperation came from her lips and she arched against him. She felt the throbbing head of his shaft separate the sensitive folds between her legs and she pulled him tightly against her, molding herself to his hard, hot length. He balanced himself on his elbows and looked into her eyes as he slowly invaded the moist tightness of her body. Deep—deeper— deeper still. A shattering sensation burst through her. A cry welled up inside her, but Nick took it into his own mouth, where it mingled with his groans of bliss.

Never had Nick known such an intense agony of sublime emotion. He'd had sex with dozens of women in the five years since he'd taken Aimee to his bed, but never had he felt such a tremendous outpouring of ecstasy.

"My God, Aimee, I can't believe what I'm feeling," he groaned against her mouth. "You're so tight, so hot, so—so damn *good*. Don't move, not yet. Not until I'm in control."

Then she felt him move inside her, possessing her body, demanding her soul. He was moving so slowly, it was more like torture, drawing forth every sweet nuance of his possession, watching her as he thrust in and out with exquisite patience.

Then suddenly his eyes burned with wicked intention as he abandoned his slow seduction. His muscles rippled, his hips flexed, as he hastened the tempo, whirling, grinding, sweeping her into the maelstrom of unparalleled passion. In sweet desperation she clung to him, lost in his kisses, tasting him, his face, his shoulders, slick and warm.

"Nick! Oh, God, Nick!"

"I know, sweetheart, I feel it, too. Sweetheart, I want you to come with me. Now!"

He moved like lightning, then slowly, slowly, touching all of her, inside and out, stroking, coaxing, the pulsing shaft of his body sinking deep inside her. Suddenly he went rigid, and Aimee felt the hot molten core of him splash against her womb. Then all thought ceased as her own climax rushed over her in great waves of sensation, making her oblivious to all but his warmth and the liquid heat of fulfillment.

She hadn't felt that sublime rush of ecstasy in any of those brief intimate moments she had shared with Beau.

It was wrong.

"Oh, God." Her words came out as an anguished sob.

She felt a flush of heat as his eyes searched her face. "Did I hurt you?"

"I—no. This is wrong. Lying with you is defiling my husband's memory. You're a damned blue-belly, for God's sake! And—and—"

Nick's eyes narrowed. "And what?" He rolled to his side and pulled her against him.

Aimee clamped down on her bottom lip until she drew blood. She wanted to scream at him, to tell him she hated him for thinking her a common whore the first time he had taken her, but she didn't. What good would it do? He'd only deny it just as he had denied cheating at cards. After five years he had probably forgotten half of what had happened that night.

"And we're enemies," she finished lamely.

"We're lovers, sweetheart," he reminded her.

His rakish grin sent an arrow straight to her heart. Enemies by day, lovers by night. She hoped the information she had stolen for the Confederacy was worth all the anguish she was suffering.

"It can't happen again. It *won't* happen again."

"Look at me," he told her.

With great reluctance she met the searing green of his eyes.

"You came to me, remember? I tried my damnedest to keep my hands off you."

She turned away, but his hand shot out to hold her chin in place. "Don't turn away from me. Look at me and tell me you didn't come to my room because this is what you wanted. Be honest and admit you wanted me as badly as I wanted you."

Aimee blanched. The truth would send her to prison and separate her from her son. "I—I—suppose that's the way it was. But it was a moment of madness; I shouldn't have . . ."

"But you did. Now be quiet and let me love you again."

"Damn you!" Tears stung her eyes. Moments ago she had lost her will to him. What would he demand next?

He demanded her soul.

He wanted to erase the touch of a dead man. He had no idea the memory of Beauregard Trevor's timid loving had fled from Aimee's thoughts the moment Nick Drummond touched her.

He took her again, slowly building the fire in her blood. By the time he lifted her to straddle him and thrust into her, no war separated them. They were one, moving together in perfect harmony, the subtle scent of love's juices spurring them on. He moved constantly, exquisitely, faster, harder, with each thrust, urging her toward climax with hoarse cries.

The delicious thrill of fulfillment came upon her suddenly and she threw her head back and screamed as searing pleasure consumed her. Nick continued thrusting a few moments longer, until she had given everything she had to give, then plunged one last time, held it, and spilled his seed. It was several minutes before either of them could speak or move.

"I don't know exactly what happened, sweetheart, but that was the most wonderful loving I've ever had," Nick admitted wryly. He tried to disguise his awe and confusion, but his trembling voice betrayed him. "Go to sleep; we'll talk in the morning." Nick's emotions were too raw to test his power of reasoning. He needed time to come to grips with what he might or might not have discovered about his feelings this night.

Aimee waited until Nick's even breathing indicated he was asleep before slipping from his arms. Quickly gathering her clothes, she tiptoed from his room. Remaining with him a minute longer than necessary was dangerous. He had caused her too much grief and anguish to fall victim to his seduction. Just being around him had taken a toll on her. She had sacrificed her integrity to the Confederacy, and her pride and her honor to Nick Drummond. Deep in her heart she knew the threat Nick Drummond presented to her placed her in great danger. The danger lay deep in the torrid depths of his green eyes, in the heat of his arms, in his bed . . .

Nick awoke suddenly, then smiled at the memory of Aimee coming alive in his arms, turning to him in her need, wanting him, loving him. He reached out to bring her back into his embrace and found her gone.

Pale streaks of crimson barely lit the eastern sky, yet he realized Aimee must have left him hours ago, for the bed beside him was cold. He couldn't blame her. It wouldn't do for Brand to find his mother in another man's bed when he so obviously revered his father. Dammit, he wished with all his heart he were Brand's father! And the longer and harder he thought, the more he became convinced that his wish might be the truth. The problem lay in getting Aimee to admit it.

Rousing himself, Nick left the bed, his body still tingling with a sweet languor. Loving Aimee had been more pleasurable than anything he had experienced in recent years. He'd had many women in those five intervening years since he'd first seen her, yet when he thought back, none of them had satisfied him as Aimee had aboard the *Dixie Belle* when she had responded to him with the artful innocence of a practiced whore.

Nick dressed quickly, then suddenly recalled that he hadn't destroyed the latest dispatches from headquarters. Both he and Lieutenant Dill had memorized the message the day before yesterday, and instead of taking the time to destroy the papers, he had replaced them inside the pouch and returned them to the chest. Since he had plenty of time before mustering the men, he moved briskly toward the chest beneath the window. The dispatches were too important to allow them to fall into the wrong hands. Not that he suspected anyone here of spying, but one couldn't be too careful in times of war.

Opening the chest, he rummaged through his clothes until he located the leather pouch. With great care he drew forth the dispatches, intending to destroy them, something he should have already done. Suddenly his expression hardened and his heart slammed painfully against his chest. Someone had tampered with the dispatches! One of the sheets of paper bore a stain. Holding it to the light, he recognized the clean imprint of a thumb. And he quickly identified the substance that made the stain as peach juice. He wanted to scream, to shout his rage—to cry. With a certainty that tore at his gut, he knew why Aimee had come to his room last night. And it wasn't because she felt the same driving need he had. The foolish little chit. Did she have no idea what a charge of spying would do to her and her loved ones?

Placing the dispatches in the washbowl, he set a flame to them and watched them burn. He didn't welcome the dilemma he faced, nor the position in which Aimee placed him. Spying was serious business, and as an officer in the Union army, he had a responsibility to his government and his men. He was fighting for a belief, for the unity of his country, for equality for all men regardless of race or color. He turned away, knowing there would be no rest for him until he came to grips with what his duty demanded and what his heart dictated.

In the end, duty prevailed.

Aimee carefully avoided Nick that day. Which wasn't difficult considering the fact that he had ridden out with his men very early and hadn't returned until after supper. She saw him briefly just before she retired, and the strange, hooded look he sent her frightened her. Did he expect her to come to his room tonight? she wondered. If he did, he was certainly going to be disappointed. Tonight was the night she was to meet with Gar and give him the information for which she had sold her soul. And after that, she vowed never to spy again. She had too much to lose. She couldn't be separated from Brand. And Nick was too astute not to realize what was going on.

Suspecting that Nick might be waiting for her in her room again, Aimee had moved her night-clothes to Brand's room earlier that day, intending to spend the night in her son's bed. Nick certainly wouldn't demand her presence in his bed while Brand looked on, would he? And just to make certain, she locked the door. When the household was asleep, she'd sneak down the stairs, out the door, and into the woods. She'd be back long before anyone stirred.

Nick had come to a decision concerning Aimee before he returned to the house that evening. If she was spying, it stood to reason that she had an accomplice or a contact. There had to be someone nearby to receive the information she gathered. Since the only time she had left the house or yard had been when she went to the woods to pick berries, he assumed it was then that she had met her contact. And since, to his knowledge, she hadn't left the yard since, he knew she would sneak out very soon in order to pass on the information she had stolen. In order to catch them red-handed, all he need do was play the waiting game. So he didn't insist she come to him tonight—he had to give her every opportunity to meet her contact.

Sweet Jesus, could he send her to prison?

She was a spy.

Dousing the lamp in his room, Nick waited for Aimee to make her move. If not this night, then the next—or the next. He hesitated telling Lieutenant Dill about his suspicions, but since Dill was second in command, he felt duty-bound to do so. Dill was appropriately shocked; he had held Aimee in high regard. He should have known, once a Reb, always a Reb.

Nick stood at the window. He was to keep watch while Dill listened for footsteps in the hall. The clock in the foyer struck midnight. Just as the last chime reverberated through the stillness, Nick saw a vague movement outside in the shadows at the corner of the house. His attention sharpened. He was rewarded when he saw a wraithlike figure detach itself from the shadows and glide toward one of the sturdy oak trees lining the driveway. The figure was clothed in white, and Nick gave a snort of disgust. Aimee was obviously so inept at spying, she didn't realize how easy it was to spot a white object in the dark.

Fearing the sentry would challenge her, she remained concealed behind the huge tree trunk until he passed by. She had no inkling that the sentry had been instructed to ignore her in order that she might lead them to her accomplice. When Nick was satisfied that she was heading toward the woods, he moved swiftly. Fully armed, he sped from his room, stopping only long enough to summon Lieutenant Dill, who had failed to hear Aimee's light tread when she traversed down the hallway on her secret mission. Together they moved noiselessly through the house and out the door. They followed Aimee's path, gliding from tree to tree, keeping enough distance between them to prevent discovery. They entered the woods only moments behind her.

Once inside the protection of the trees, Aimee

paused only long enough to catch her breath. She had made it! She uttered a quick prayer that Gar would be waiting for her so she could return to the house before her absence was noticed. Since she no longer felt the need to conceal herself, she hurried through the trees and underbrush toward the meeting place. Her slippers moved softly across the spongy earth, the brilliant moonlight lighting her way. The hoot of a night owl startled her, but she gathered her wits and continued onward. She had been in these woods many times during the years she had lived at Tall Oaks, and had never found anything to frighten her.

She approached the gnarled old oak cautiously, her eyes darting about, on the lookout for Gar. She saw nothing, heard no one. The crash through the underbrush of a nocturnal animal sent her heart racing, but it quickly subsided when nothing menacing appeared from out of the darkness. The sturdy oak was directly in front of her now, and she stood fearfully beside it, waiting, listening. Her fingers clenched the scrap of paper bearing the information she had copied from the dispatches Nick had received, and she grew more desperate by the minute.

Suddenly a twig snapped and she started violently. Spinning on her heel, she saw a dark, specterlike figure emerge from behind a huge tree trunk. Her hand fluttered upward to still her wildly racing heart.

"Gar! You frightened me. I thought you weren't coming."

"I've been here all along, Aimee. I didn't want to show myself until I was certain you weren't being followed."

Aimee peered behind her. "No one followed me; I'm certain of it. But I must get back before my absence is noticed."

Gar nodded. "Were you able to get the information for me?"

"I got what you requested," Aimee said with such bitterness, Gar's interest sharpened immediately.

"Was there a problem?"

No problem, she wanted to scream. Unless you call sleeping with the enemy a problem. "I managed," she bit out. "Here." She thrust the scrap of paper into his hand. "I copied the information down just like you asked. I think you'll find it of vital importance to the Confederacy."

Gar palmed the paper, slipping it inside his jacket pocket. "The Confederacy is grateful, I'm grateful. And if you'll let me, I'll show you how much." The meaning of his words failed to register until he reached out and dragged her into his arms. She gasped in outrage. "You're a beautiful woman, Aimee Trevor. Beau's been dead a long time; I reckon you must be real lonely by now. I can remedy that before I leave."

His lips came down on hers; his audacity shocked her. Aimee struggled free of his kiss, her eyes fiery with anger and disgust. "Gar, stop that! How dare you assume I'd welcome your attentions."

Gar slid her a sly glance, his arms tightening around her. "Maybe you're not as lonely as I thought. Just how far *did* you go to get to those dispatches?"

Nick stood behind the gnarled oak, having just stepped a bit closer so that he could hear the two talk. He managed to understand Garson Pinder's last sentence. Intense anger seethed through him when he realized just how far Aimee had gone to spy for her beloved South. She displayed no remorse over making him believe she came to his bed because she wanted him as badly as he wanted her. It hurt, dammit, hurt bad. And he was the biggest fool God ever created.

"She went too far—much too far," Nick said bitterly as he stepped into full view.

Gar's hands fell away from Aimee and went for his pistol. His effort proved futile as Lieutenant Dill materialized from the thicket of trees. "I wouldn't do that if I were you, Reb." When he realized he hadn't a snowball's chance in hell of escaping, Gar's hands fell limply to his side. He gave Aimee a withering glance.

"Did you bring the blue-bellies with you?" asked Gar.

Stunned, Aimee couldn't speak, couldn't move, could only drag one shuddering breath after another until the need to faint had passed. Nick! How did he know? When did she give herself away? How? Questions without answers tumbled one upon another as she stared from Nick to Gar. Nick took it upon himself to answer Gar's question.

"Your little Reb whore didn't bring us, not intentionally anyway. She's good, very good. She used great imagination in order to bring you the contents of the dispatches," he said crudely. "I thought—I hoped—never mind what I thought, it's not important. You're both spies, and I'm placing you under arrest."

"Spies?" Gar said, managing a nervous laugh.

"You've got me wrong, Yankee, I'm no spy. Since when is it a crime for a man to meet his lover in the woods?"

Aimee gasped in dismay. Events were taking a turn she hadn't counted on. "No—it's not—"

"Bind their hands, Lieutenant," Nick ordered crisply. "I'm sure we'll find incriminating evidence somewhere on the spy." He thanked God it was dark. He'd hate like hell for Aimee to see how deeply she'd hurt him. In the few weeks he'd been at Tall Oaks, Aimee had come to mean more to him than he cared to admit. "You're in civilian clothes, carrying secret information. Need I continue? Your name, Reb!"

Dill used the rope he had brought along to tie both Aimee's and Gar's hands behind them. Gar glared at him insolently while Aimee began to weep softly. The sound tore at Nick's heart.

"How long have you been in the area spying?" Silence. "How long has Mrs. Trevor been supplying you with information?"

More silence.

"Very well, have it your way; we'll get the information out of you one way or another." He shoved his pistol in Gar's back to start him moving while Dill prodded Aimee forward, careful not to hurt her. He didn't trust Nick with Aimee. His captain was too damn angry right now to think straight. He had been watching Nick's feelings for Aimee grow during the past weeks and knew how badly this betrayal had affected him.

Aimee's weeping continued unabated as she stumbled toward the house. Nick said nothing to her, not a word, his expression unreadable. How he must despise her. Truth to tell, she despised herself at this moment. The sentry met them at the perimeter of the property.

"Is everything all right, sir?"

"Everything went just as planned, Simpson. Lieutenant Dill has a prisoner to see to. Lock him in the tool shed until I decide what's to be done with him. Then awaken one of the men to stand guard outside the shed."

"And Mrs. Trevor?" Dill asked. "Is she to be locked in the shed also?"

"The Union army doesn't mistreat women," Nick bit out. His tone indicated that he had every intention of disregarding the way the Union army treated women as far as Aimee was concerned. He looked as if he wanted to wring Aimee's neck and to hell with gentlemanly behavior. "Mrs. Trevor will be confined to her room until I decide otherwise."

Dill saluted and shoved Gar rudely forward. Then Nick grasped Aimee's arm roughly and dragged her toward the house.

"Nick, please, let me explain."

"What's to explain?"

"Garson Pinder isn't my lover. He's merely a family friend who has visited our plantation frequently."

"You could have fooled me. Actually, I don't give a damn what he is to you. You made a fool out of me, Aimee Trevor, and for that I can't forgive you."

"You can't send me to prison, Nick. Brand needs me. What will happen to him if I'm not around to provide for him?"

His face was cold, remorseless, as if her problems were of little concern to him.

"You should have thought of that before you turned to spying, Aimee." His words were fraught with quiet menace.

Chapter 6

Kicking the door open with his foot, Nick placed a hand in the middle of Aimee's back and shoved her inside. She stumbled into the room, bruising her hip against the bureau before her balance returned. Tears sprang to her eyes and she stifled the cry of pain that trembled on her lips, refusing to act a coward before Nick Drummond. She spun around to face him.

"You Yankee bastard! Untie me."

His lips thinned, but he said nothing, turning her roughly to tug at the ropes binding her wrists. She saw the fury of betrayal in his eyes, and hot accusation. When her hands were free, he whirled on his heel and strode angrily toward the door.

"Nick—Captain Drummond, wait!"

He paused, fighting the urge to turn and look at her. "I'm in no mood for conversation." She could tell by his tone of voice that he was teetering on the edge of his control.

"What will happen to me?"

"That's for those higher than me to decide."

"Brand! What about Brand? My, God, I—"

"I suggest you get some sleep, Mrs. Trevor. Right now I can't think beyond the fact that you used sex to manipulate me. Whose idea was it to sleep with me?" He hurled the words at her like stones. He didn't wait for an answer as he opened the door, removed the key from the inside, and closed it noiselessly behind him. Aimee's bravado crumbled when she heard the rasp of the key in the lock.

She rushed to the door. "Nick, please, you can't keep me from my son. He's all I have."

Nick leaned against the door, desperately trying to blot out Aimee's pleas and curses. When they dissolved into heartrending sobs, he pocketed the key and slowly walked away. He felt old and tired. Tired of war, sick of killing, disgusted with subterfuges and betrayals. He wanted to go to sleep and wake up fresh and clean, finished with the terrible business of war.

He didn't sleep at all.

He imagined he could still hear Aimee sobbing. He wanted to go to her, hold her in his arms, tell her everything was going to be all right, promise her he'd let no one hurt her or Brand.

He couldn't.

Could he?

He drifted to sleep toward dawn and awoke later to the certain knowledge that someone was staring at him. Instantly alert, he reached beneath his pillow for his gun. He drew in a ragged sigh when he saw Brand standing beside the bed. The boy's hazel eyes were large and troubled. Nick could tell that the child was trying his best to fight back tears, and failing miserably. He rose on his elbow, reaching out to draw Brand down beside him. The lad resisted.

"Mama can't get out of her room."

Nick cursed beneath his breath, calling Aimee every vile name he could think of. Why would she deliberately put her child through such anguish?

"I know, son."

"Did someone lock her in, sir? I can't find the key."

Nick closed his eyes and inhaled deeply. "I locked your mama in her room, Brand. It was necessary."

"Why? Was she bad?"

"Yes, she was very bad."

"Are you going to punish her?"

Nick flushed. "She deserves to be punished," he hedged, not wanting to frighten the child.

"I could hear her crying. I think she wants out."

"That's impossible. I can no longer trust her. I know you don't understand any of this, Brand, and I wouldn't have hurt you for the world, but some things can't be ignored."

Brand's bottom lip trembled and Nick cursed, dragging the boy close and hugging him tight. Stiffening his shoulders, Brand pulled away. "I want to see Mama."

Nick sighed. How could he separate mother and son? Aimee might be a spy and whore, she might be rash and reckless, but he couldn't accuse her of not loving her son. Instinct told him she was a true southern zealot who, in a moment of weakness, had allowed her lover to talk her into spying.

"Run along, Brand; I'll see what I can do. Perhaps I can arrange it so you'll see your mama for a specific period of time each day." It was the least he could do for the fatherless little boy who stood in danger of losing his beloved mother.

Aimee's tears gave way to impotent rage when

she found her door still locked the next morning, preventing Brand from entering. What harm could a small boy do? She called Nick every vile name she could think of, wishing him straight to hell. She rushed to the window, hoping to attract him in order to alert him to her plight. What she saw brought a shudder of terror to her slender form. Garson Pinder, his hands bound behind his back, was being led to one of the outbuildings. Nick entered the building a few minutes later, looking grim and determined. She preferred not to think about what would probably take place in that shed.

Just then the door to her room opened and Brand rushed into her outstretched arms. Sergeant Jones, a grizzled soldier, followed, carrying a tray containing Aimee's breakfast.

"The captain said it's all right for the lad to visit for a spell," Jones said, his gaze sliding away from hers. He never would have suspected her of spying, such a sweet, pretty lady. But the captain had caught her red-handed.

"Thank you," Aimee said with quiet dignity. "How long may he stay?"

"An hour, and he's allowed to visit again before bedtime. I brought your breakfast." He set the tray down on the small nightstand.

"Where's Savannah? Am I allowed to visit with her?"

"Sorry," Jones muttered, making a hasty exit. He couldn't bear the wounded look in Aimee's eyes. "The captain thought it best to keep the two of you apart, if you get my meaning."

"Perfectly," Aimee said tightly. Her control was

slipping, and all she wanted now was to be alone with Brand for her allotted hour.

"Captain Drummond said you were bad, Mama," Brand said as he hugged Aimee tightly. "Why were you bad? I don't want you to be locked in your room."

"I wasn't bad, Brand," Aimee tried to explain. "I did something Captain Drummond didn't like, and for punishment I'm being locked in my room. You can come visit me twice a day."

"I don't like Captain Drummond very much," Brand pouted sullenly. "I thought he liked us."

Aimee was at a loss for words. What could she say to a five-year-old that would explain the cruel complexities of war? Instead, she hugged him close, offering the comfort he seemed to need. But Brand wasn't so easily appeased.

"I'm going to ask Captain Drummond to let you out."

"I'm afraid it isn't going to help, darling. Captain Drummond isn't the type of man to let sentiment interfere with duty."

"I suppose it will be all right as long as I can see you twice a day," Brand compromised.

Aimee gulped back her tears. She had no idea how long she had before Nick shipped her north to prison. But until then she intended to make every moment with Brand count. If it actually came to separation from her son, there was an alternative, one that would virtually ensure that Brand wouldn't suffer in her absence. She could always tell Nick that he was Brand's father. But she would save that bit of information until the last possible moment.

Nick returned from interrogating Garson Pinder

in a vile mood. The man had refused to divulge one pertinent piece of information, nor would he elaborate on his involvement with Aimee Trevor except to smile knowingly when asked if he and Aimee were lovers. Maybe intelligence could persuade the spy to talk, he reflected as he made his way slowly back to the house. He made immediate plans to send Pinder to headquarters, where they had the means and patience to break the man. In any event, Pinder would spend the rest of the war behind bars.

That line of thinking led him to Aimee and the fate that awaited her if he sent her north to prison. A shudder of revulsion passed through his body when he recalled the horror of visiting one of the facilities that housed women spies. A woman as frail and sensitive as Aimee wouldn't survive long in the squalid conditions that existed in most of those prisons. As beautiful as Aimee was, she'd surely be raped by guards who considered women spies fair game. That terrifying notion brought him to an abrupt decision. He motioned to Lieutenant Dill that he wished to talk with him privately. Dill dropped what he was doing and followed Nick inside to the small study.

"You wished to see me, sir?"

Nick nodded grimly. "Prepare the prisoner for transportation to headquarters. I'll leave first thing in the morning with a squad of six men. I want you to remain at Tall Oaks and see that our other prisoner remains safely behind locked doors."

Dill was stunned. "You're not taking Mrs. Trevor to headquarters along with the other spy?"

"I—no, she'll remain at Tall Oaks under supervision."

"Do you think that's wise, Captain? What will headquarters say about withholding a prisoner?"

"Have you ever seen the inside of a prison, Lieutenant? How long do you think a woman like Mrs. Trevor would last in that kind of squalor and misery? Not long, I'd wager. I'm certain this is Mrs. Trevor's first offense, and I fully intend to argue the case against sending her to prison. I'm convinced she'll be no danger to the Union now that her contact has been apprehended. What would it serve to separate her from her son at this point in the war? The South is all but defeated. I may be a bastard, but I'm not totally without compassion. No, Lieutenant, if I have anything to say about it, Aimee Trevor will remain under house arrest, under my jurisdiction, until such a time that I'm ordered elsewhere. By then, command will have forgotten about her."

Dill did not question Nick's judgment, but he did wonder at his motives. He knew Nick had strong feelings for Aimee, but he assumed those feelings had died a natural death when Aimee was caught spying. He suspected that intimacy was involved somewhere along the line, which would explain Nick's wounded pride, but he could prove nothing.

"I hope you know what you're doing," Dill observed before he left Nick sitting deep in contemplation. "You know headquarters might decide against your request. They hold little sympathy for spies." Having said his piece, he quietly departed.

Somehow Nick managed to get through the day, his mind consumed with thoughts of Aimee, how ardently she responded to his touch, how wonderfully alive she became in his arms, how easily she had beguiled him—how eagerly she had used him and lied to him. She didn't want him. All she'd wanted was the classified information headquarters had sent him. It rankled him to realize how far she was willing to go for those dispatches.

Supper was a dismal affair. Savannah's reproachful looks were enough to turn the food to sawdust in Nick's mouth. Brand was sullen and uncommunicative. Restricted to her room, Aimee was eating in solitude. It was too much. Abruptly he leaped to his feet, knocking the chair over in his haste, and strode from the room.

Aimee stared at her food, unable to swallow a bite. She wanted to know what Nick had decided to do with her. She needed to learn how long it would be before she was separated from her son. She wanted to see Nick but was too proud to ask. Then she heard the solid thread of his footsteps on the stairs and grew tense. Would he stop and let her know what her fate was to be or would he ignore her? She listened intently as his footsteps slowed when they reached her door. She held her breath, then let it out when he continued on. She didn't know whether she was relieved or vexed. Then her breath stopped when she heard him halt and return. The key scraped in the lock and the door flung open. Nick stood in the doorway, his face set in grim lines, shoulders squared, big, powerful, menacing. So handsome he took her breath away. She winced when he slammed the door behind him.

"I hope your solitude has been productive. You've had plenty of time to contemplate your crime."

"It's the punishment I've been thinking about."

Her expression was guarded. "Have you come to tell me when I'm to be sent to prison?"

"I haven't decided," Nick said sourly. She didn't sound the least bit contrite. Why should she? She was a true defender of the South.

"Why have you come?"

"Damned if I know."

. "What have you done to Gar?"

"Nothing that he didn't deserve. Your lover is a spy; he'll be dealt with accordingly."

"Are you going to torture me, too?"

Nick flushed, enraged that Aimee would think he'd stoop to torture. "Perhaps, if that's what you're expecting."

"I always expect the worst from you."

Nick sent her an oblique look. "It's taken me all day to calm down enough to speak with you without wringing your beautiful little neck. You certainly have a way of destroying a man's ego, Mrs. Trevor. You must have had a lot of practice at seduction, for I could have sworn there was something special between us."

Aimee lowered her eyes. Oh, yes, Nick Drummond, she thought. There was indeed something special between us. You demanded my soul, and I gladly, happily, ecstatically, surrendered it to you. With a note of constraint in her voice, she said, "You're much too fanciful, Captain. I did only what was necessary, and I'm not sorry. I'd do it again if it helped the Confederacy."

"I'm sorry for you, Aimee Trevor," Nick said, "but it's Brand who truly has my sympathy. You should have thought of him before spying for a Confederacy that is all but defeated."

"Damn you, Nick Drummond, for being a heartless Yankee blue-belly!"

Consumed by anger and frustration, she flew at him, sobbing and pounding his chest with small fists, cursing the day he had arrived at Tall Oaks, cursing their first meeting five years ago. Against his better judgment, Nick's arms closed around her, holding her close while she poured out her rage and frustration. For a brief moment he wanted to lift her chin, smother her lips with his, feel her passion build as he claimed her body in the most basic way. But in the nick of time he remembered how she had lied to him, used him, betrayed him, and he shoved her away, fighting the lust that shuddered through him.

Aimee gasped in dismay as Nick flung her away from him, leaving the room in angry strides. She hadn't even realized she had been clinging to him with almost frantic desperation, or seeking comfort where none was forthcoming. For one blissful moment she felt so secure in his arms, she never wanted to leave them. The comforting warmth of his big body made her forget that Nick Drummond was the man responsible for some of the most traumatic moments in her life. A man she had vowed to hate.

The following morning Aimee watched from the window as Garson Pinder was loaded in a wagon and taken from Tall Oaks. Nick and a small group of mounted soldiers served as escorts. She supposed Gar was being taken to prison, and wondered why she had been left behind. She knew it wasn't because he felt sympathy for her, for there wasn't a sympathetic bone in Nick Drummond's rather impressive body. And since she was still under lock and key, she suspected that he had no intention of freeing her. Just what exactly did he have in mind for her?

Nick was gone for a week. Lieutenant Dill was left in charge of Tall Oaks, and his orders differed little from his superior's as far as Aimee was concerned. Her meals were brought to her three times a day. Brand was allowed to visit morning and evening, and she wasn't mistreated in any way. She was even allowed to bathe in the big brass tub upon request. Sergeant Jones was usually the one who carried in the tub and filled it with hot water. When she asked to see Savannah her request was denied. But Savannah was a resourceful woman and Aimee prayed her companion would find a way to bend the rules.

Nick reached headquarters with his prisoner and turned him over immediately to intelligence. Then he reported to Colonel Brooks, his superior. Brooks sat back in his chair while Nick explained the circumstances leading to Garson Pinder's apprehension.

"Good work, Captain," Brooks said. "We've been after this man for a long time. You say there was a woman involved? Where is she?"

"Yes, sir," Nick replied, his tension mounting. What if Brooks denied his request? "She's under house arrest at Tall Oaks."

Brooks's shaggy eyebrows rose askance. "Why haven't you brought her here for questioning along with Pinder?"

"I didn't think it would serve any purpose," Nick explained. "Mrs. Trevor is a widow and mother of a young son. I'm convinced this is her first offense, and I'll personally vouch for her if you'll allow her to remain under my custody for the duration of the war. I—I knew Mrs. Trevor before the war, Colonel, and I feel prison is too harsh a punishment for her."

Brooks gave Nick a severe look. "You say you knew her before the war? Fraternization is frowned upon, Captain Drummond. Are you and the lady intimately involved?"

"I hope you won't insist I answer that question, Colonel. Suffice it to say that my relationship with Mrs. Trevor, whether intimate or not, has no bearing on my duty. I wouldn't recommend sending any woman to prison given the same set of circumstances. I don't believe she is a danger to the Union. Her lo—Garson Pinder coaxed her into spying, and I personally guarantee she'll not be afforded another opportunity to do so again. It's her young son I'm concerned about. The lad is only four years old, and he lost his father early in the war."

"Hmmm," Brooks mused, drumming his fingers on the desk. "You plead quite eloquently for the lady's life. You're right about prison, though; it's a vile place for a lady." Fortunately Brooks was a compassionate man with a family of his own. "And you say there is a small child involved?"

Nick nodded. "I doubt Brand would survive without his mother to see to his welfare. They were both near starvation when I showed up at Tall Oaks."

"Very well, Captain, you've convinced me. But I'll expect you to make damn certain this woman never spies again. Your career is at stake in this one. You're right about the war nearing its conclusion, and Sherman's sweep through Georgia is the beginning of the end of the Confederacy. I'm convinced that only months remain till the ultimate defeat of the Rebels."

"You have my word, sir; Mrs. Trevor will cause no further trouble."

Nick arrived back at Tall Oaks in a bleak mood. He had won Aimee's freedom from a northern prison, but by so doing, had condemned himself to being her keeper. By rights he should despise her for the calculated way she had seduced him, but deep down inside the hidden chambers of his heart, an emotion that had nothing to do with hatred took root and refused to die. He recalled the sweetness of her kisses, the heat of her body, the incredible passion she was capable of. Lord help him!

Nick received a tepid welcome from Brand when he returned to Tall Oaks. Obviously the lad blamed Nick for keeping his mother locked in her room. Savannah said little, though her accusing eyes spoke volumes. Nick motioned Dill to accompany him into the study.

"Any problems, Lieutenant?" he asked crisply.

"No, sir," Dill responded. "Everything went smoothly. What about you? Did you turn in the prisoner?"

"He's in good hands. Let's hope by now intelligence has gleaned some information from him."

"And—er—the lady, sir? What about Mrs. Trevor?"

"She's been released into my custody. Colonel

Brooks agrees with me that no purpose would be served by imprisoning her this late in the war."

"Is she to be kept under lock and key?"

"For the time being."

"She's barely eating enough to keep a bird alive. Why not give her the run of the house?"

"I'll consider it when the time is right."

Aimee knew Nick was back when she heard his deep voice echoing through the hallway. She wished he would come and tell her what was to become of her. Did he derive some perverse pleasure from deliberately keeping her in the dark about her fate? Later that night she heard him pass her room, pause briefly, then hurry on by. Damnable provoking Yankee!

Aimee lay on the bed, but her eyes refused to close. Sleep eluded her most nights, due to her intolerable position as Nick's prisoner. The house was quiet. Presumably everyone was sleeping. Suddenly Aimee became aware of a strange sound at her door and flipped over on her side. With a sense of foreboding she watched the door slide open on noiseless hinges—then she recognized the slightly stooped figure of Savannah.

"Savannah, how—"

"Shhh, honey, you know I'd find a way to see you. Are you all right? Dem Yankees ain't hurt you, have dey?" She pushed the door shut, but in her haste, it failed to latch properly.

"Oh, Savannah, how glad I am to see you!" Aimee cried, flinging her arms around the older woman's bent shoulders. "How did you get in? Does Captain Drummond know you're here?"

"One question at a time, honey. I found another

set of keys. I knew dey were around here somewheres, and it took me a while to find dem. I reckon Captain Drummond would have my hide if he knew I was here."

"Tell me what's going on, Savannah. Has anyone mentioned what's to become of me?"

Savannah shook her head sadly. "I ain't heard a word. But somehow I don't think de captain wants to send you to prison. If he did, he would have taken you away with Mr. Garson. Why did you do it, honey? I done tole you not to interfere."

They spoke together quietly for a spell, unaware that Nick, alerted by a sixth sense, was awake. Something compelled him to walk out into the hall and pause outside Aimee's door. The soft murmur of voices captured his undivided attention. A spurt of anger shot through Nick when he noticed the door wasn't completely latched, and he eased it open a tiny bit, wondering how Aimee's visitor had obtained entrance when the key rested in the pocket of the pants he now wore.

"Dere's somethin' between you and Captain Drummond, ain't there?" Nick heard Savannah ask Aimee.

"You're imagining things," Aimee scoffed softly.

"I've been doin' a heap of thinkin' lately, 'bout Brand's papa, and lots of things are fallin' into place."

Aimee froze. If Savannah had figured out the identity of Brand's real father, sooner or later so would Nick.

"What exactly is falling into place, Savannah?" Nick demanded.

Savannah started violently.

Aimee groaned in dismay.

Nick walked boldly into the room and lit a lamp.

"Well, Savannah, do you want to tell me about this great discovery you have just made?"

"No, sir," Savannah gulped, shaking her head. "I don't reckon I do."

"Then perhaps you can explain how you got in here."

Silence.

"Savannah!"

"I found another key. It ain't right dat you should keep Aimee locked up like an animal. She's only one small woman amongst all you Yankees. Look at her, Captain. She looks right peaked to me. And Brand is so upset, he cries himself to sleep every night."

"That's enough, Savannah; you can leave now." His expression was so grim, Savannah feared for Aimee's life.

"Don't you dare hurt dat poor chile!" Savannah threatened, refusing to budge. "She's already suffered more dan a woman should oughta."

Nick's tone softened. "Don't worry, Savannah, I'm not going to harm Aimee. Go on to bed; we'll talk about this tomorrow."

Her head held high in defiance, Savannah reluctantly left the room. Nick closed the door behind her and turned to face Aimee.

The nightgown she wore was no more than a veil covering the creamy contours of her body. Unconsciously his eyes settled on her breasts, and Aimee could feel her nipples distend, the small buds pushing wantonly against the cloth. Her arms flew over her chest in a purely protective motion. Nick grinned knowingly. With lamplight dancing over his face, his devil's eyes glowed with unholy green fire.

"Don't act coy with me, Aimee." His voice was dangerously quiet. "We both know you're no angel. I imagine Pinder is spilling his guts about you right now. How sad that your lover didn't consider the consequences to your child when he involved you in spying."

"You're despicable!" Aimee spat. "Gar isn't my lover—he never was! I saw him for the first time in years that day I entered the woods to pick berries. If you had asked me, I would have told you, but you were ready to believe the worst."

Nick's heart soared in sudden elation. Could Aimee be telling the truth? "Your love life has little bearing on what I think. It only became my concern when you seduced me in order to steal secret information. I might never have known you read those dispatches if I hadn't discovered a peach stain on one of the papers. You were picking peaches the day I found you in my room, weren't you, Aimee?"

Aimee groaned. Foiled by a damned peach stain! She'd wondered how Nick knew she was spying. "I—I wondered how you knew."

"What?" He wasn't listening. He was occupied elsewhere, thinking of her opulent lips and gorgeous eyes. Of the creamy expanse of skin visible beneath the thin material of her nightgown. His head began to pound, and a rush of hot blood swelled his loins. He forced his thoughts past the dull pounding in his head and his aching loins to the matter at hand, but he couldn't recall what he was going to say.

All he could think about was a defiant little chin,

pouting red lips, a small, elegant nose, skin as pale as a white carnation. Eyes as warm as molten honey, aslant under arched blond brows fringed by thick lashes. The truth slammed into his gut like a steel fist. No matter what she was or what she did, she had become a sickness in his blood.

He wanted Aimee Trevor.

He wanted her now.

Forever.

He wanted Brand to be his son.

Aimee gazed into his eyes and quickly read his desire. When he looked directly at her in that special way, she almost forgot to breathe.

"Colonel Brooks placed you in my custody, Aimee. I talked him out of sending you to prison. I did it for Brand's sake and ... and because I couldn't bear the thought of you dying in a northern prison. For the duration of the war you'll remain under house arrest. But if you deliberately provoke or defy me, I'll have no recourse but to send you away. And I also expect you to be properly grateful."

Aimee's temper flared. She knew Nick expected her gratitude, and she *was* grateful, but not enough to let him use her for sexual gratification.

"Did you hear me, Aimee? You're not going to prison."

She gave him a hostile glare. "I heard, damn you. Does that mean I'm required to bed with you?"

Nick grew rigid. Clenching his fists, he declared, "You were more than willing to bed with me when your precious Confederacy demanded it." Then he turned abruptly and marched from the room. Unfortunately for Aimee, he wasn't angry enough to forget his duty. He locked the door behind him.

Chapter 7

Aimee was shocked the following morning when Brand flung open the unlocked door to her room and bounded inside. Excitedly, he told her that Captain Drummond said his mama could leave her room, but not the house. And she'd still be locked in her room at night.

Aimee was elated. It was a small concession, but enough to send her spirits soaring. Being confined to one room had led her to depression and crushing boredom. Freedom of movement, no matter how small, offered a slim hope of somehow escaping from this intolerable situation.

Savannah was ecstatic when Aimee appeared downstairs after Nick had left the house that morning. They hugged and cried and talked for hours. Savannah scolded her fiercely for getting involved in the nasty business of spying, but Aimee was too happy to allow Savannah's scolding to dampen her spirits. Being prevented from seeing Brand whenever she pleased had been bitter punishment, and being released from the stifling prison of her room was wonderful.

"Maybe you oughta thank Captain Drummond

for lettin' you outta your room," Savannah suggested.

"If it wasn't for him, I wouldn't be in this position," Aimee snapped bitterly. "I'll be damned if I'll thank that Yank for taking over my home."

"We ain't starvin'," Savannah ventured.

"I'd rather starve than rely on Yankees for my well-being."

"You don't mean dat, honey. I ain't seen Brand look so fat and sassy since he was a babe."

Aimee knew Savannah was right, but she'd be damned if she'd grovel before Nick Drummond. The man already had a profound and compelling hold on her senses. What more did he want from her?

Nick Drummond wanted Aimee body and soul, wanted her with a need that was staggering.

He wanted her in his arms and in his bed. He wanted to believe that Garson Pinder wasn't her lover, that she had responded to him in a pure outpouring of emotion. He wanted to believe Brand was his son.

Each night, a feast of sensual visions tormented his dreams. The innocent act of walking past Aimee's bedroom door before retiring was an exercise in self-control.

One night, driven by a force that had battered him relentlessly both day and night, his control snapped. He had tried, Lord knows he had tried, to stay away from Aimee, but he was a flesh-and-blood man, not some damn saint.

He burst into her room without knocking, startling her awake. He closed the door with his foot, holding the lamp high so the light fell on her.

Aimee sat up in bed, rubbing the sleep from her eyes.

"Is something wrong? Is it Brand? My God, Brand is sick!"

"Brand is fine, Aimee," Nick said, carefully setting the lamp down on the nightstand. "Nothing's amiss."

Aimee eyed him warily. His shirt was wrinkled and unbuttoned to the waist, his hair was mussed, and he looked as if he'd been engaged in some kind of struggle. But it was his eyes that held her captive. They glowed with a savage inner fire. Devil's eyes.

"If everything is all right, then what are you doing in my room this time of night?"

"Surely you have some idea."

Two red flags of anger bloomed high on her cheeks. "No!"

"I see you understand. I promised myself I'd stay away from you, but—I can't. Dammit, Aimee, I can't even put a name to what I feel for you."

"How about lust," Aimee returned sarcastically.

"Lust has a lot to do with it, but I think it goes beyond."

Aimee uttered a squawk of protest as he settled down on the bed beside her and gathered her into his arms.

"Don't touch me!"

"I can't think of a single reason why I shouldn't make love to you. You enjoyed it the last time, I know you did, even though your purpose was to seduce me into believing you innocent of spying. Dammit, Aimee, I can't even think straight anymore."

"There are many reasons why I should resist

you," Aimee protested. "The first and foremost is that we are enemies."

"Enemies by day, lovers by night. So be it; I can live with that. What I can't live without is the sweetness of your response, the heat of your body. Let me love you, sweetheart. And in case those aren't reasons enough, just remember that I have the power to send you to prison."

She felt his heat, his passion, his raw desperation and determination. The need in his green eyes made her blood sizzle. She was hot, she was cold, she was both at once. And to her everlasting regret, she *did* want him.

When his mouth pressed down on hers and his tongue parted her lips, she could reason no more. She absorbed the moist warmth of his kiss and felt the rough journey of his hands over her body. She felt her nearly threadbare nightgown drifting downward past her shoulders and hips, and the sensitive peaks of her naked breasts brushing against the thick mat of black curls covering his chest. She felt as if she'd been struck by lightning when he took her nipple into his mouth and began to suckle. She groaned. He turned to her other breast as his hand slid down between her thighs. She didn't react against the intrusion but let out another groan louder than the first.

"I love to touch you like this." His fingers rubbed against the hidden nub between her legs until she was slick with moisture. "And I adore the way you respond to my touch despite the fact that you profess to hate me." One finger eased up inside her. "You're all passion and fire, sweet and hot. I hope your husband appreciated you."

Beau never knew me like this, she thought. Only

you have the power to move me, and it frightens me.

The tension inside her was driving her wild. She rotated her hips against the pressure of his fingers and felt him slide deeper inside.

"I know you want me, Aimee." His fingers moved in a circular motion until she was moaning nearly nonstop. "Tell me, Aimee, tell me you want me."

She gritted her teeth, burying her head in his shoulder. "You—bastard—"

He reached out and caught hold of her hair, bringing her face close to his. "Tell me." His fingers moved with greater urgency, piercing her deeply, withdrawing, returning again, and all the while his thumb did wonderful things to that sensitive, throbbing place between her thighs.

"Yes, dammit, I want you! Are you happy now?"

"You'll never know how much." Raw desire roughened his voice. He paused only long enough to fling off his clothes before moving atop her. But instead of thrusting into her as she expected, he bent and kissed the fragrant valley between her breasts. Then his mouth slid slowly downward, skimming over her belly and thighs to press moist kisses on that exquisite place where his fingers had been only moments before. His tongue parted the tender folds, and Aimee arched upward, exploding with sweet agony.

"Nick! You can't!" His response was to grasp her hips and hold her in place while his mouth feasted upon her. Her protests turned into soft whimpers of delight as his lips and tongue drove all thought from her mind. Her hands touched his shoulders, urging him on as she arched into his mouth, demanding more and receiving it.

Aimee teetered on the edge of ecstasy, driven by the wet heat of Nick's tongue. The fever of passion raged inside her, hot and wild. She cried out his name, relinquishing her hold on reality as she dropped into a pit of splendor and agony.

Nick waited until the final tremor left her body before sliding upward to cover her. She was slick with sweat, and he licked the salty moistness from her nipples as he thrust deeply inside her. He moved slowly, languidly, wanting their lovemaking to last forever.

"Put your legs around me." His voice was harsh with desire, thick with urgency.

When she did, he let out a low growl, sliding even deeper insider her. Her tight heat surrounded him, squeezed him, made him want to splash his seed inside her immediately.

"Oh, God, don't move! Not yet."

It took several minutes of deep breathing before his control returned and he could fully savor their joining. When he found he could continue without erupting, he thrust into her again and again. Aimee felt her body responding to his rough passion, answering it with a renewed hunger that left her dazed. Pleasure curled her insides. Like a wild animal she clawed his back with her nails as heat spread upward from her toes to her loins.

Then she felt Nick's belly tighten and the hot rush of his seed as it splashed against her womb. His last thrust brought her the release she sought, and she screamed his name. Nick's kiss absorbed her cry, mingling it with his own growl of completion. He collapsed on top of her, too weak to

move, too content ever to let her get away from
him. His head rested in the sweet hollow of her
neck. His breathing was still ragged and shaky. So
was hers. That gave him profound satisfaction.

As soon as her hold on him slackened, he rolled
to his side, taking her with him. Aimee's soft
curses brought his mood to a skidding halt.

"What is it? Did I hurt you?"

"You damn blue-belly bastard!" Aimee snarled.
Sudden, remorseless fury replaced her euphoria.
"You've taken over my home; must you demand
my pride? You've left me nothing, nothing . . ."

"God help me, Aimee, for I can't help myself.
What does it matter whether I'm wearing blue or
gray? If you'd allow yourself to think about it,
you'd realize that what we have just experienced
goes beyond hatred. The war is nearly over; it's
time to let go of prejudices."

"Prejudice? You think what I feel for you is
merely prejudice?" She laughed harshly. "You
have a short memory, Nick Drummond. Have you
forgotten the *Dixie Belle?* Or what happened that
night?"

For a moment Nick looked puzzled. "My memory hasn't failed me, sweetheart." He flashed her
an impudent grin, hoping to diffuse her hatred.
"How could I forget the *Dixie Belle*, or the magnificent way in which you repaid a gambling debt? It
was an extraordinary experience, one that lingered
in my memory far longer than I would have
liked."

Aimee shook with indignant fury. "You Yankee
bastard! I was a virgin! Did it never occur to you
that I might be innocent?"

"Dear God, how can that be? I would have known if you were an innocent."

"You were so consumed with lust that my state of innocence escaped your notice," Aimee accused hotly. "You took me with callous disregard for my feelings. Then you left the next morning without a word."

"I assumed that was what you wanted. Lord knows it was difficult leaving you, but you were a professional gambler, for God's sake, and I never expected to find an innocent in my bed. I thought your naïveté quite charming, but considered it an inborn trait of—"

"A whore," Aimee spat, completing his sentence. "You thought me a whore."

"Perhaps I did at first," Nick admitted, "but that's not what I was going to say. I was going to say an inborn trait of a very good actress. That was a long time ago. Don't you think it's time to forgive? You could have told me you were an innocent."

"Would it have made a difference?"

"I'd be lying if I said yes. Five years is a long time to recall details, but if I remember correctly, I was so hot for you, I'd probably have taken you no matter what you said. But can't you put aside your hatred for me? I'd be loath to leave here knowing your hatred followed me wherever I went."

"You're still a Yankee, but if you left here tomorrow, I might not hate you so much," Aimee suggested hopefully.

Nick sighed. "That's impossible, and you know it. I'm here until my superiors decide to send me elsewhere."

"Then keep away from me until that happens."

"That's impossible." His voice was faintly apologetic but determined. "I sincerely wish I could honor your wishes, but to do so would take more control than I'm capable of. I'm going to keep on making love to you, Aimee Trevor, until I've sated myself with your sweetness—which might take forever—or I'm ordered to leave. And since I have the power to send you to prison, I suggest you submit to the inevitable."

A shudder passed through Aimee's slender form. "Am I to be your whore?"

Nick frowned. "I'd much prefer to think of you as my lover."

"And I prefer to think of you as a bastard."

Nick smiled ruefully. "Now that the air is clear between us, we can settle down to what's important." He grasped her roughly, pulling her into the hard contours of his body. "God help me, but I want you again, Aimee Trevor."

His hot kisses seared her lips, her throat, the peaks of her breasts. Frightened by the response he never failed to incite in her, Aimee tried to pull away, but he quickly subdued her. His kisses fell like searing brands over her body, his tongue finding sensitive places she never knew existed, suckling, stroking, until she writhed beneath him. She could feel the core of her winding tighter and tighter, ready to spring at any moment. Suddenly she was mounted atop him and he was spreading her legs, sliding inside her and urging her to ride him as she would a wild stallion. Throwing her head back in sublime surrender, she rode him furiously, teetering on the crest of sensation, hovering between sanity and madness as she sped recklessly to her final destination.

She recalled nothing after that. The words she screamed when waves of ecstasy broke over her might have escaped her memory, but Nick placed them inside his heart to take out and examine at leisure.

Life went on at Tall Oaks. Nick rode out on patrol nearly every day. Though Aimee could hear the thunder of guns, the line of battle did not approach Tall Oaks. Sometimes Nick remained out overnight, and when he did, he nearly always left Lieutenant Dill in charge. The good lieutenant treated Aimee with the respect due a lady, but he didn't trust her. Nick's orders that Aimee be restricted to the house had remained in force, and no amount of pleading had swayed either him or the men left to guard the house. New dispatches arrived at Tall Oaks frequently, and they were too important to fall into enemy hands. But something Nick mentioned during supper one night lifted Aimee's spirits as well as reinforcing her resolve to escape the devastating hold Nick had on her senses. Enemies by day, lovers by night. No statement had ever been closer to the truth.

Nick had mentioned to Lieutenant Dill that the Rebs, under General Hood, were setting up defenses in Atlanta, and Sherman's army was poised to cross Peach Tree Creek, the only natural obstacle between the Chattahoochee and Atlanta's northern defenses. Grant believed that capturing Atlanta would mean the death knell for the Confederacy. The city was full of arsenals, foundries, and machine shops, and it was also the junction of four major railways, which were needed to supply the Union army.

The conversation that night made Aimee more determined than ever to escape her prison. With the Confederate army nearby, she, Brand, and Savannah could easily reach the safety of Confederate lines. Once behind friendly lines, she'd no longer be subject to Nick Drummond's sensual control. His almost nightly visits to her bed left her confused and bitter. His powerful hold on her senses had made her life a shambles, nearly destroying her in a maelstrom of passion that reduced her to mindless ecstasy.

She hated him.

She wanted him.

Aimee discussed her plans to leave Tall Oaks with Savannah one night while they were preparing supper. She was surprised when Savannah showed little enthusiasm.

"What you want to leave for, honey?" she asked. "We ain't been mistreated, and Brand is eatin' more than he can hold. If we go to Atlanta, we'll starve along with everyone else livin' there."

"I have to get away from Captain Drummond, Savannah," Aimee persisted. "You can't begin to understand how much I hate that man."

Savannah slanted Aimee an oblique look. "I understand more dan you give me credit for, chile."

Aimee panicked. "What do you mean?"

"I done figured out why you fear Captain Drummond. He's de gambler, ain't he? He's Brand's papa. And you been sleepin' with him."

"My God, Savannah, he—he forced me!" Her voice was quivering, her eyes wild as she dug her fingers cruelly into Savannah's shoulders. "Please don't tell him about Brand. If Nick found out, I could lose my son. And I'm only sleeping with him because he'll send me to prison if I refuse."

Savannah fixed her with a reproachful glare. "Are you sure dat's how it is, chile? I ain't condemnin' you, but I think you oughta tell Captain Drummond he's Brand's papa. I'm think' he'd be mighty pleased."

"If you love me, Savannah, you'll not mention this again."

"If dat's de way you want it, honey, then course I won't say nothin'. But I think you're makin' a big mistake."

Nick read the latest dispatch from headquarters, then burned it immediately afterward. Colonel Brooks suspected a strong Reb buildup across Peach Tree Creek, and Nick was ordered to take a patrol behind enemy lines for a closer look. He'd be away from Tall Oaks for two or three nights. Though Nick was eager to perform his duty, leaving Aimee for so long gave him an uncomfortable feeling. Even though Lieutenant Dill would be in charge at Tall Oaks, he knew Aimee wouldn't hesitate to flee at the first opportunity. He fully intended not to give her that chance. Aimee had quickly become an obsession with him. Not a night went by that he could trust himself to pass her bedroom door without entering and making love to her. And though she protested vigorously, her body told him she wanted him as much as he wanted her. She was just too damn stubborn to admit it. She had never forgiven him for taking her virginity, and when he had arrived at Tall Oaks to claim her home in the name of the Union, her hatred had intensified.

That night was no different from previous ones as far as Aimee was concerned. Once the household was asleep, Nick quietly entered her room. She couldn't have latched the door against him even if she'd wanted to, for he locked her in every night after she put Brand to bed. That was the rule he had laid down when he allowed her the run of the house, and it meant that he could come and go from her room as he pleased.

Aimee was sound asleep. Nick was later than usual, having remained in the study until nearly midnight formulating plans with Lieutenant Dill for Union infiltration into enemy territory. After Dill sought his bed, Nick allowed sufficient time for him to fall asleep before going to Aimee. He realized that both Dill and Savannah must know what was going on, but keeping away from Aimee would be more difficult than cutting off his right arm.

The room was dark but for a ray of moonlight that fell across Aimee's face. His mouth curved in a smile, briefly detracting from the brooding expression he normally wore. A strand of black hair flopped carelessly over his forehead, giving him a curiously boyish look. But there was nothing boyish in the predatory expression in his green eyes. Aimee had called them devil's eyes on more than one occasion, and at the moment, he felt like a devil.

He stared at her with appreciation, marveling at her beauty. His hunger for her was enormous, a savage beast that ruled him utterly. He undressed and slid into bed beside her. She felt his breath against her cheek and sighed, coming slowly awake. He was naked, hot and hard, and she felt his arousal. Attuned by now to his need, Aimee moved against him in a provocative manner, forgetting for a moment that this was the man she hated. What she had always perceived as hatred had grown to an obsession as powerful on her part as it was on his.

"I don't ever want this to end, Aimee. Love me, sweetheart, love me like there's no tomorrow. I go on a dangerous mission tomorrow, and only God knows what fate has in store for me."

Aimee's attention sharpened. "You're leaving tomorrow? For how long?"

"I'm not certain. Two or three days. Will you miss me?"

Aimee's mind seized on his words. "Who are you leaving in charge?"

Keen disappointment brought a frown to Nick's face. He had hoped Aimee would admit to missing him just a little. "I intended to leave Lieutenant Dill in charge, but my second in command should accompany the patrol in the event I'm—er—incapacitated. Sergeant Jones will remain at Tall Oaks along with three enlisted men. Try to behave, sweetheart."

Aimee held back a sly smile. Together she and Savannah should have no problem finding a way to get the key to her room from Sergeant Jones. Then suddenly her thoughts stopped as Nick's hands and mouth set fire to her blood. Her body felt as if it were ready to hurl itself from some high mountain. She tried to retreat from the edge, but he held her tight against him, refusing to allow her a moment's respite. When his fingers explored the slick crevice of her womanhood, he found her wet and ready.

"Touch me, sweetheart," he gasped raggedly. "Please touch me."

Hesitant at first, Aimee realized this was probably the last time she'd be so intimate with Nick, and so she succumbed to his erotic words. Her fingertips followed the rippling muscles of his waist and hip, down one thigh and up again. She stopped briefly to draw courage before brazenly curling her fingers around the throbbing staff of his manhood. She heard him gasp over the pounding of her heart. Her hand moved hesitantly in a purely instinctive motion.

He endured for several agonizing minutes before groaning, "Oh, God, enough!"

The next instant he was atop her, parting her thighs and thrusting inside. The end came much too swiftly, and when Aimee opened her eyes, she found Nick's startling green gaze on her. There was something profound and sincere in his eyes, something she'd rather not confront. She had her own personal demons to battle without battling those that plagued Nick Drummond.

"Is Brand ready to leave?" Aimee whispered to Savannah as she helped carry out the supper dishes. Nick had left early that morning, and Aimee wanted to leave as soon as the men guarding her had retired for the night. Sergeant Jones had taken supper with them and was now in the parlor waiting for the coffee and cake Savannah had promised.

"He's ready, chile, but I think you oughta think twice about this. Brand ain't been feelin' good all day, and I'm afeared he's comin' down with somethin'."

"I can't wait, Savannah; I have to leave Tall Oaks before Nick figures out that Brand is his son. I'm sure it's just some upset; you know how children are. Do you have the laudanum to put in Sergeant Jones's coffee? Thank God I remembered it being in Captain Drummond's medicine chest. It was easy to sneak into his room and take it after he left."

"I got it right here," Savannah said, pulling the small vial from her pocket.

"Give him a large dose; I want him to sleep all night. We'll be halfway to Atlanta before the sergeant awakens and discovers us gone."

"I hope you ain't gonna be sorry for this," Savannah said cryptically.

Chapter 8

Aimee's plan did not go as expected. When she brought the laudanum-laced coffee into the parlor for Sergeant Jones, he inexplicably decided he had wasted enough time in the house and declined the coffee and cake. He bid her a hasty good night and left immediately.

"What was dat all about?" Savannah asked when Aimee returned to the kitchen with the untouched pot of coffee.

"Sergeant Jones suddenly decided he'd spent too much time over supper and not enough time on duty," Aimee retorted. She was furious over the unexpected delay.

"If dat don't beat all. Does dat mean we ain't goin' tonight?" She sounded almost pleased at the unexpected turn of events.

"We'll try again tomorrow night," Aimee said, far from ready to give up. Staying in the same house with Nick Drummond was too dangerous for her peace of mind. "Only this time we'll make certain Sergeant Jones drinks the coffee. Instead of inviting him to the house, we'll take coffee and dessert out to the mess tent so he can share it with his men. Then all three Yank soldiers can join the good sergeant in a long, deep sleep."

Savannah rolled her eyes, shocked by Aimee's deviousness. Was she so anxious to escape Nick Drummond she'd use potent drugs without giving a thought to the consequences? Savannah couldn't help but wonder just what Aimee wanted to escape from. Did Aimee really fear what Nick would do if he learned Brand was his son, or did she fear coming to grips with her own feelings for the man?

"What if Brand ain't no better tomorrow?" Savannah asked.

"As long as he's not any sicker, we're leaving." Aimee's face was grim, her voice desperate. "I pray he's just coming down with a cold. I have to leave, Savannah, for Brand's sake as well as for mine."

Rather than appearing disloyal, Savannah didn't dispute Aimee. But in her heart she hoped Captain Drummond would return. Remaining with a known quantity was far better than facing the unknown. She recalled how it had been before Captain Drummond pulled them from the brink of starvation. It wasn't herself, but Brand she was thinking about. He had a full life ahead of him and didn't deserve to starve to death, which was what would have happened had they tried to survive on their own in a strange place. At least at Tall Oaks they had a roof over their heads and food in their bellies.

Brand seemed somewhat improved the next day, instilling Aimee with hope that their venture would succeed. Their meager belongings were packed in pillowcases and concealed in the wagon with a packet of food and a jug of water. Once the Yankees drank the laudanum-laced coffee and fell asleep, Aimee intended to hitch a horse to the wagon and ride away from Tall Oaks and not return until the blue-bellies left her home. The once magnificent plantation house might be falling down around her, but at least it was hers—or it was until the damn Yanks had arrived.

The day crawled by with annoying slowness. Aimee was nearly beside herself with worry. She feared that Nick would arrive home before expected and that Brand, who still wasn't himself, would become too ill to travel. She watched him closely all day. Besides being listless and lacking appetite, he was slightly flushed and cranky. But since there were still no symptoms of a serious illness, Aimee saw no reason to cancel her plans. With amazing composure she carried a pot of coffee and a luscious cake out to the mess tent when she knew the men would be eating their supper.

The soldiers' enthusiastic welcome and appropriate gratitude was nearly her undoing. Guilt swept over he when she thought of how she was going to drug these unsuspecting men. But she quickly overcame her initial reluctance when she considered that men just like these had invaded her home and deprived Beau of the full life he was meant to lead. One Yank in particular had a hold on her senses that both frightened and dismayed her. She had no choice, she must leave, using any method available in an effort to keep Nick from learning about Brand and destroying her life.

An hour later, Aimee snuffed out the only lamp left burning in the house and turned to Savannah. "Do you think they're asleep yet?"

"If dey ain't, dey ain't human. I mixed enough laudanum for ten men in de coffeepot. De'll sleep like babes till mornin'."

"You get Brand and put him in the wagon while I make sure. Nothing must go wrong. I'll meet you in the stable."

Aimee needn't have worried. The laudanum had done its work. Two men were slumped over the table where they had fallen into a deep sleep, one man lay across the bed, and Sergeant Jones was stretched out on the floor next to the door, as if he knew what had happened and was trying to summon help. After making certain the men were sleeping peacefully, Aimee hurried away, eager to put as much distance as possible between herself and Nick Drummond.

Since there was little need for stealth, Aimee and Savannah quickly and silently hitched a horse belonging to one of the cavalrymen to the wagon. She hated to have stealing added to her list of crimes, but if she didn't take the horse, she'd be forced to hitch the old mule to the wagon. Brand didn't awaken when Savannah laid him on the blankets she had placed in the bed of the wagon.

"Brand feels mighty feverish, honey," Savannah said. Her misgivings over this reckless venture grew more pronounced by the minute.

Aimee gnawed her lower lip as she anxiously gazed at Brand. He *did* look flushed. And his sleep seemed more drugged than peaceful. "It's too late now to change my mind, Savannah. Once we're safely behind Confederate lines, we'll find a doctor."

Aimee took up the reins and slapped the horse's rump. Unaccustomed to being hitched to a wagon, the horse balked, but through perseverance and raw determination, Aimee managed to make him move. An enormous cavern of blackness swallowed them as they rode down the long, oak-lined driveway, leading away from Nick Drummond and the almost fatal hold he had upon Aimee.

The going was slow. Too slow for Aimee's liking, but the night was so dark, it was difficult even to follow the thin strip of road. What was even more frightening was the fact that she wasn't even certain which direction to take. Tall Oaks lay northwest of Atlanta, so she headed southeast, or what she thought was southeast. Until the sun came up, she could only pray her sense of direction hadn't failed her.

Brand woke up crying. Aimee left it to Savannah to soothe him, afraid to take her eyes off the strip of road she was following. He settled down quickly enough but continued to whimper in his sleep. Aimee was more worried than she'd let on to Savannah. Brand had suffered his share of childhood illnesses during his five years of life, and she was concerned now that something more serious might be involved. Perhaps he had caught something from one of the Yanks staying at Tall Oaks, she reasoned, and it would quickly pass.

The next time Brand awoke, Aimee handed the reins to Savannah and crawled into the wagon bed with him. She cried out in alarm when his tiny body convulsed with chills while still releasing enormous amounts of heat through his pores.

"What is it, honey?"

"You were right, Savannah, we should have never left Tall Oaks with Brand ill. He has a fever."

"You want me to turn back?" Savannah asked hopefully.

"No, not now, not when we've come so far. Have you forgotten that we've drugged four men and stolen a horse? I'll be sent to prison for sure. It would kill me to be separated from Brand."

Shortly after dawn they met a Union patrol. Fortunately for Aimee, it wasn't Captain Drummond's patrol. Their wagon was stopped and Aimee was questioned closely about their destination. Batting her eyes in a helpless manner, Aimee blandly informed them she was taking her sick son to the next town to see a doctor. One look at Brand's flushed face convinced the captain in charge to allow them to continue. He issued a well-meant warning before waving them on.

"I suggest you obtain a pass next time you wish to travel through Union territory. Spies are known to employ devious methods in order to smuggle messages through enemy lines. They wouldn't hesitate to use a sick child. The next patrol you meet might not be so eager to let you proceed without written permission or proper identification."

Aimee hoped no one could hear the wild pounding of her heart as the men rode away. A pass! Why hadn't she thought of that? She could have easily forged some kind of official paper using Nick's name.

"What we gonna do if we meet up with more Yankees?" Savannah asked anxiously. "You heard de captain; de next patrol might turn us back."

"No one is going to turn me back," Aimee said, her eyes blazing defiantly.

"We's in Yankee territory."

"I know." She grew thoughtful. "The obvious solution is to travel by night until we cross into Confederate territory. And I know the perfect place to hide."

"Where's dat, chile?"

"The Pinder plantation. I understand that nothing remains of the grand house except charred ruins, but it's the last place anyone would look for us. And it's far enough off the main road to discourage searchers."

Less than a hour later, Aimee guided the wagon down the dusty track leading to the Pinder plantation. Brand was fully awake now and complaining loudly of various aches and pains. He was flushed, his eyes were glazed, and beads of sweat dotted his forehead.

The Pinder house was in worse shape than Aimee had supposed. There wasn't a wall standing that offered shelter or a hiding place for the wagon. Aimee's hopes plummeted, until her gaze wandered beyond the charred hulk to the stable. She noted with glee that a large section of the structure stood virtually intact.

"Look, Savannah!" Aimee cried, pointing at the stable. "We can spend the day there, and no one will be the wiser. It will give us a chance to see to Brand and rest up before setting out again at dark."

Once the wagon was concealed and the horse unhitched, they ate sparingly of the food they had brought along. Brand ate nothing, requesting only water. Aimee ventured out of the stable once to inspect the pump in the yard, grateful to find it still in working order. They used the cool water to bathe Brand, but it seemed to do his fever little good. The heat of his body felt as if it would singe her fingertips. When darkness arrived, it was apparent to both Savannah and Aimee that they could not continue without endangering Brand's life.

"What we gonna do, chile?" Savannah asked fearfully. "Brand needs his own bed to lie in, soothing broth to give him strength, and medicine to ease his fever."

"I should have heeded your warning, Savannah," Aimee admitted. Guilt plagued her. She would never willingly endanger Brand's life. "I never meant to place Brand's life in danger. You must take him back to Tall Oaks at once."

"Ain't you coming with us?"

Aimee flushed. "I can't, Savannah. I'd die in jail. No, you take Brand back. I trust you to care for him. And as much as I hate to admit it, Nick will see to Brand's welfare. He's become quite attached to the boy."

"I can't just leave you out here on your own," Savannah protested. "What you gonna do?"

"Exactly what I intended in the first place. I'll continue on to Confederate territory. I'll come back to Tall Oaks when the blue-bellies leave. Go now, Savannah; get help for Brand. If you leave now, you'll reach Tall Oaks before sundown."

As if in challenge to her words, a roll of thunder reverberated through the countryside with ominous foreboding, followed by a brilliant flash of lightning.

"Not now, chile; it's fixin' to rain. Brand is sick enough without givin' him a good soakin'."

Shortly afterward a curtain of steady rain lashed the stable; a sufficient amount poured through cracks and rotting timber to make the occupants cold and uncomfortable. Crawling under the wagon for protection from the elements, Aimee cuddled Brand, giving him the added heat of her body, meager though it was. The rest of the day and night crawled by with agonizing slowness. By first light the downpour had slowed to a steady drizzle, and Aimee placed Brand inside the wagon bed, covered him with blankets they had brought along, and kissed him good-bye.

"Aren't you coming, Mama?" Brand asked when Savannah climbed into the wagon seat and took up the reins.

"I'll come later, darling," Aimee said, holding back tears. "Be a good boy for Savannah; she'll take good care of you."

"Captain Drummond's going to be mad at you again," Brand frowned, "and lock you in your room."

"No, Brand, he'll never lock me in my room again," Aimee assured him. "I love you, darling."

She kissed him one more time, frightened by the heat rising from his pores, then signaled to Savannah. Immediately the wagon jerked forward, the creak of the wheels filling Aimee's heart with a desolation that nearly tore her apart. Tears streamed down her pale cheeks, and the only thing that saved her from being utterly destroyed was the thought that she was doing what was best for Brand. Nick Drummond might be a damn Yankee, but she knew instinctively he wouldn't let Brand suffer because of her mistakes.

It was still raining at dusk when Nick rode back to Tall Oaks. His mission was hugely successful.

He and his patrol had penetrated deep into Reb territory and had gotten a fairly accurate estimate of the strength of the enemy army Sherman would encounter in his march to Atlanta. Nick had sent one of his men to headquarters with the information and rode hell for leather back to Tall Oaks. He'd missed Aimee and Brand, missed them dreadfully. If that was a hint of what life would be without them, he didn't like the feeling.

Drenched to the skin, Nick stabled his mount and approached the house, eager to see Aimee and Brand. His stomach rumbled from hunger and he wondered what delicious concoction Savannah had cooked up for supper. Perhaps another of those savory stews accompanied by biscuits and pie for dessert.

A strange premonition seized Nick as he entered the house. Normally at least one lamp was left burning in the foyer as evening neared, but tonight the foyer was dark. When he noted the absence of cooking odors, an odd coldness seized him. Aimee! He knew she was gone even before he received Sergeant Jones's report. How or why made little difference; her departure left an aching void in his heart.

"Sergeant Jones!" Nick bellowed the name at the top of his lungs. It echoed ominously through the house and into the yard beyond. Within minutes the guilt-stricken Jones was standing at attention before Nick.

He didn't wait for Nick's first question. "I know what you're thinking, sir, but it wasn't deliberate. I guarded the lady just like you said, but she tricked us."

"One fragile lady tricked four burly soldiers?"

Nick repeated dully. His tone clearly conveyed his disbelief.

"Yes, sir, that's just how it was. Mrs. Trevor drugged a pot of coffee she brought out for us two nights ago, and—and when we fell asleep, she and her servant hitched one of our horses to that dilapidated wagon and took off."

Nick, spit out an oath that turned the air blue. "What kind of a drug did she use?"

"Must have been laudanum, sir. There was a good deal of it in the medicine chest in your quarters, but when I checked later, it was gone. I never suspected—that is, I didn't think Mrs. Trevor was so eager to leave. She's not been mistreated here."

"No, not mistreated," Nick concurred. What he didn't say was that he was forcing her to his bed with threats of prison if she didn't comply. Though he liked to think she wanted him as badly as he wanted her, it was highly unlikely she really felt that way. He wore a blue uniform and he was the enemy. "I assume you searched for her."

"Yes, sir, me and two men went out the next day but saw nary a sign of the wagon or its occupants. It just don't make sense. How could she have disappeared into thin air? Traveling by night isn't easy, and they couldn't have made very good time, yet the roads were deserted but for several patrols in the area."

"They have to be headed for Confederate territory," Nick mused thoughtfully. "Pick two men to accompany me tomorrow. I'll leave at first light and search for them myself. I gave my word to Colonel Brooks that if he placed Mrs. Trevor in my custody instead of sending her to prison, I'd accept full responsibility for her actions. When I find the little witch, I'll personally wring her neck. She doesn't realize the danger that exists for a woman and child alone."

"Deserters have been seen in the area, Captain. They're mean and desperate enough to attempt anything. That wagon and horse will look mighty tempting to men with no means of transportation. And the lady is beautiful enough to bewitch a saint."

"Don't I know," Nick muttered beneath his breath. Aloud he said, "I'll find her, Sergeant." His mouth was set in grim lines; his eyes looked bleak. If it was the last thing he did, he'd find Aimee and bring her back to Tall Oaks. Then somehow he'd force her to admit that Brand was his son.

Nick had thought quite a bit about Brand lately. The first time he'd seen the lad, Nick was reminded of someone; he'd finally figured out who—himself at the same age. Aimee told him Brand was four years old, but he seriously doubted that. Brand was too big and too smart for a four-year-old. He figured the boy's age was closer to five than four. If that was so, then Brand was his son.

When Aimee admitted she had been a virgin the night he took her five years ago, the pieces all fell neatly into place. If he hadn't been so damn hot to be inside her, he would have realized he had taken a virgin, but at the time he was so consumed with lust, he didn't feel the slight resistance to his penetration. Nor did he stick around long enough the next morning to inspect the sheets. He simply thought he had bedded a professional gambler who didn't mind paying gambling debts with her body. Time and maturity had altered that opinion.

Nick took time to bathe and change before joining the men in the mess tent. He was walking
across the yard in the drizzle when he noticed a
wagon approaching in the distance. He frowned as
he watched its slow progress from the avenue of
tall oaks lining the driveway. When he recognized
Savannah driving, his heart thudded painfully in
his chest. Where was Aimee? Why were they returning? Had something happened?

By now others had noticed the wagon and stood
around gaping. Jones and Dill joined Nick as he
walked down the gravel drive. Nick grabbed the
harness when they drew abreast.

"Thank the good Lord," Savannah said as she
all but collapsed in the seat. She was drenched to
the skin and shivering, ill clad in ragged remnants.

"What happened, Savannah? Where's Aimee?"
Worry overrode Nick's anger. Something disastrous must have happened to bring Savannah back
alone.

"Look, Captain, in the wagon bed!" Dill had
heard a noise coming from the back of the wagon
and moved to investigate. He threw aside a blanket and discovered Brand lying beneath the covering. He was soaked to the skin and shivering
violently.

Nick moved quickly to Dill's side, praying he
wouldn't find two dead bodies. What he saw filled
him with fear. Brand looked so ill, Nick thought
him beyond help. A glad cry escaped his throat
when he noticed the steady rise and fall of his tiny
chest.

"For God's sake, what happened?"

"He's sick," Savannah wailed. "My baby's sick."
Having dismounted from the wagon with the help

of one of the men standing nearby, she now hovered over Brand, moaning and wringing her hands. "You gotta help him, Captain."

With more gentleness than he knew he possessed, Nick picked up the small boy and started briskly for the house. "We have to get him out of the rain, Savannah." Intense heat pouring from Brand penetrated the thick material of Nick's uniform, and he feared for the boy's life.

Once Brand was tucked snugly in bed, Nick rummaged through his medicine chest and carefully spooned a concoction made especially for fevers down the lad's throat. Throughout the war, Nick had learned that traveling without a doctor meant he had to be prepared to treat many minor ailments. Before being assigned to Tall Oaks, he had stocked his medicine chest with every kind of medication that one of the doctors at headquarters had suggested. He thanked God he had the foresight to do so, for the medicine might save Brand's life.

Savannah hadn't left Brand's side, not even to change her damp clothes. She merely stood quietly, waiting for Nick's anger to explode, as she knew it must.

"How did this happen, Savannah?" Nick asked quietly after he had done what he could for Brand. "Why didn't Aimee return with you? Where is she now?"

"I—I don't rightly know, Captain. Brand wasn't feelin' well when we left Tall Oaks, but by then it was too late to turn back."

"Too late!" Nick hissed between clenched teeth. "What kind of mother would endanger the life of her son? I thought Aimee loved her child. Go

157

change, Savannah. When you return, I want a full explanation."

Savannah stood her ground. "I promised Aimee I'd look after Brand."

"Don't worry, I'll see to Brand. Besides, if you get sick, you'll be useless to the lad. By the looks of you, you've ridden hours through the rain."

Brand woke up once while Savannah was gone. His eyes fell on Nick and he tried to smile but failed. "I'm glad we came back, Captain. I didn't really want to leave."

Nick smoothed the dark hair back from the searing heat of the boy's forehead. "I know, son. I'm glad you returned. You'll have to get well, though, if you expect to ride Scout again."

His lids lowered sleepily, then flew up, his eyes troubled. "Where's Mama? She knows how to make me well when I'm sick."

"She's not here right now. But don't fret, she'll be here before you know it."

Satisfied, Brand drifted off.

Sergeant Jones entered the room. "Is there anything I can do, sir? I have children of my own; perhaps I can soothe the little lad."

"Sit with the boy, Jones, while I question Savannah. If he awakens, spoon some more of this medicine down his throat. I'll return shortly."

Nick found Savannah in the kitchen. "Very well, Savannah, out with it. Why did Aimee decide to leave, and where is she?"

"I tried to talk her outta it, Captain, I purely did. But you know how stubborn she can be."

He did indeed know. "Does Aimee care so little for her son?"

"Aimee is a good mother," Savannah said defensively. "If she wasn't desperate, she wouldn't have left."

"Desperate?" Nick's insides tightened. "In what way? She wasn't being mistreated." Savannah's lips tightened, and she refused to divulge any more information. "You may as well spit it out; I know you've got something to say."

"I know all about you, Yank! You're de man what ruined my chile. And now you's forcin' her to bed with you or go to prison."

Nick blanched. Put that way, he sounded like a despicable bastard. But it wasn't that way at all. "I have deep feelings for Aimee, Savannah. I hoped she'd changed her opinion of me."

"Harumph, that ain't likely. Not as long as you's here threatenin' those she loves."

Nick looked puzzled. "I've threatened no one that I know of."

"She's worried that you might—" Suddenly she realized what she was about to divulge and stopped in midsentence. "I ain't sayin' no more."

"Is Aimee worried that I might suddenly realize that Brand is my son? Is that why I'm a threat to her? Does she think I'll take Brand away from her?"

Savannah sent him a startled glance, then looked away, refusing to answer or acknowledge Nick's questions. "Look at me, Savannah! I'm right, aren't I?"

"It ain't my place to say what's right or ain't right. If you're done with me, I'll go to Brand now."

"Not quite, Savannah. Where is Aimee now?"

"I don't know."

"Why did she send Brand back to Tall Oaks?"

"She knew you'd take good care of him for her."

That admission sent his heart soaring. Aimee thought enough of him to entrust him with the care of her son. "Where is Aimee going?"

"Somewhere behind Confederate lines," she said after a long pause.

"Does she have a mount?"

"No. No mount, no food, just plain guts. Which is more than you got, Yank. If you love my chile, why didn't you tell her how you feel instead of beddin' her and makin' her feel like a whore?" Lifting her grizzled head at a defiant angle, she brushed past Nick with a twitch of her ragged skirt.

Nick stared after her, his thoughts in a turmoil. Love? Was love the confusing emotion that had been turning him inside out ever since he had arrived at Tall Oaks and found Aimee again? He told Savannah that he cared for Aimee, but in his heart he knew those feelings went deeper and were more firmly entrenched than he had been willing to admit. But how could he love a woman who repeatedly told him she hated him? Though in the many weeks he'd been at Tall Oaks, he had done little to make Aimee love him. She responded to his touch in a way that gave him hope, but he astutely realized he was spinning dreams. Imagining Aimee in love with him was a fantasy that had no place in real life. He was a Yankee, and she hated everything he stood for. And if Brand was truly his son, as he suspected, she had another reason for hating him. He'd planted his seed in her and abandoned her.

"Captain Drummond, come quick!"

A greatly agitated Sergeant Jones stood in the

doorway, motioning to Nick. The man turned abruptly and sprinted up the stairs, Nick in hot pursuit. Nick's heart pounded against his ribs in a wild tattoo, and the blood froze in his veins. Was it Brand? Had something happened to the lad?

He rushed into the bedroom prepared for the worst. Savannah was bent over the boy, making clucking sounds deep in her throat. She moved aside to make room for Nick as he dropped to his knees beside the bed.

"Oh, God, I thought . . ." His eyes filled with tears. He couldn't ever recall weeping since he was a small child the size of Brand. This time, however, his tears were those of gratitude.

Brand's face was covered in small red eruptions.

"It's measles, sir; I'd recognize them anywhere," Sergeant Jones said with a conviction that came from experience. "His whole body is covered with them. Give him a week or two and he'll be right as rain."

Chapter 9

The weight of Aimee's muddy skirt dragging along the wet earth slowed her down considerably. The misty rain continued, but it barely touched her beneath the dense canopy of tall trees. Her clothes and shoes were thoroughly soaked from her earlier dousing, and she felt the dampness clear to her bones. She shivered, wondering how much farther she had to travel before reaching Confederate lines.

But her discomfort was nothing compared to her concern for Brand. She worried about the illness that had prompted her to send him back to Tall Oaks. Though she hated to admit it, she knew Nick would care for Brand and see that he received proper medical attention. Parting from Brand had wrenched her heart dreadfully, but she had done what she thought was best. Brand's well-being was Aimee's paramount concern. She knew Nick wouldn't harm Brand, that he would care for him and treat him kindly. Savannah would be on hand to make sure he did. Aimee knew that returning to Tall Oaks herself was out of the question.

Nick Drummond had treated her with callous

disdain from the day they first met, bedding her and leaving her with his child in her belly, and now she had become little more to him than his whore. It didn't help any to realize that she was beginning to care for him when her heart told her she should hate him. The fact that he was a Yank soldier made him despicable in her eyes. If she lost her heart to him, she would hate herself even more than she hated Nick Drummond.

The day wore on as Aimee made her way through the woods. She deliberately avoided the road for fear of meeting another Yankee patrol, and if her estimation was correct, she figured she'd reach Confederate lines soon. When she grew tired, she hunkered down beneath a tree, wrapping her cloak around her and nodding off to sleep almost immediately. The sound of voices brought her abruptly out of a sound sleep.

"Will ya look at that!"

"Purty, ain't she? What do ya reckon she's doin' out here?"

"Who cares? I never was one to look a gift horse in the mouth."

The light in the forest was so muted, all Aimee could see were two dim figures hovering over her. She sat up abruptly, clutching her cloak tightly around her. "Who are you?"

"We could ask ya the same, little lady," a snickering voice replied.

Suddenly a breeze shifted the leaves of a nearby tree, and a shaft of waning daylight filtered through the branches. Aimee could clearly see two men leering down at her. The ragtag remnants of the uniform they wore were gray, and a thrill shot through her. She had reached Confederate lines!

"You're Confederate soldiers!"

"Who said?" one of the men asked sullenly.

"Am I close to Confederate lines?" Aimee asked. "Thank God; I was afraid I'd wandered in the wrong direction."

The men exchanged glances. The taller and younger of the two frowned and said, "We ain't soldiers no more."

A warning bell sounded in Aimee's brain. "I—I don't understand."

"The South already done lost the war even though it ain't official. We ain't stickin' around to see the end. There's more than one way ta make a livin', and we aim ta get our share of the spoils."

"You're deserters!"

"I reckon ya could say that. Me and Cullen been livin' in these woods fer quite a spell, visitin' farms and plantations occasionally when our supplies run low. Ain't that right, Cullen?"

"Right as rain, Rolly," Cullen agreed. "And we ain't seen nothin' like you in a long time."

Goose bumps skipped along Aimee's flesh. She had dealt with deserters before, but it was easier with a gun in her hand. This time she had nothing with which to stop them from doing whatever they pleased with her. All she had was words, and her mind worked furiously as she sought a way to make them let her go unharmed.

"I'm a widow; my husband died defending the South."

"So what?" This from Rolly, who was already picturing Aimee spread beneath him.

"Will you let me go on my way unmolested?"

"We ain't gonna let her go, are we Rolly?" Cullen asked, rubbing his crotch in an obscene manner.

"Naw, we ain't gonna let her go," Rolly replied, grinning lewdly. "We're gonna have us our own personal whore, that's what we're gonna do."

"No!" Aimee cried, staggering to her feet. "You can't do that! I'm a Reb just like you are. I've been held prisoner by the Yankees and finally managed to escape. Why would you hurt one of your own?"

"This ain't our war, little lady," Rolly sneered. "It don't make me no difference who dies or who lives. The only people this war will benefit is all them rich plantation owners wantin' to keep their slaves. I ain't never owned a slave in my life."

"Me neither," said Cullen.

"So we figure we might as well get as much outta this war as possible," continued Rolly.

"Can I have her first?" Cullen asked. "When you get through with them, they ain't worth much."

"Ain't nobody havin' her yet," Rolly said. "That Yankee patrol we seen earlier is nearby, and I ain't takin' no chances of gettin' caught. There might even be a Reb patrol in the area. We ain't too popular these days with Rebs or Yanks."

"Why don't you just let me go?" Aimee asked. "I'll probably be more trouble than I'm worth."

Rolly laughed, a harsh sound deep in his throat that sent chills down her spine. "Not damn likely. I ain't had a woman in quite a spell."

"Not since that little darky we caught hidin' in the woods," Cullen recalled, licking his lips. "It'll be a treat pokin' a white woman."

Aimee decided she wasn't going to hang around

to become a victim. Turning on her heel, she fled into the woods, hoping to lose herself amidst the trees and growing darkness. Gasping for breath, Aimee could hear Rolly and Cullen thrashing through the woods behind her. Panic-stricken, her legs trembling from exhaustion, she searched frantically for a hiding place from the two vile creatures chasing her. She nearly fainted from relief when she saw a huge fallen tree limb that appeared to be hollow. Dropping to her knees, she pushed and squeezed until she was completely encased in the dank, dark hollow space.

Forcing her mind from dwelling on the crawling, creeping creatures inhabiting the rotting limb, Aimee brought her harsh breathing under control. Lying still within the confining darkness was agony for her.

Minutes later Cullen and Rolly passed so close to the fallen limb, she could hear their footsteps. Aimee lay still long after they had passed, fearing to leave her hidden sanctuary lest the men return and find her.

Why had she ever left Nick? she wondered dismally. Whatever made her think she could forget him by leaving him? Why hadn't she considered the possibility of encountering deserters and low-life scum who preyed on innocent people? Was it her fate to be ravished and killed in the prime of her life when her son still needed her? Aimee thanked God that she had sent Brand back to his father. If he had been captured by these desperate men, they might have killed him outright so as not to be bothered by him. Finally exhaustion claimed her and she fell into a fitful sleep.

* * *

Meanwhile, back at Tall Oaks, Nick stared at Brand, so relieved to learn he had merely broken out with measles that he laughed aloud. He had imagined all sorts of terrible diseases the little tyke could have been infected with, and not once had he thought of so common a childhood ailment as measles. Of course, that wasn't to say that the boy was out of danger. But with the proper care, Nick expected him to recover fully. It had frightened him badly when Savannah had returned to Tall Oaks with Brand, sick and burning with fever. Having concluded that Brand was his son, Nick feared he would lose him before he really had much of a chance to know him.

Nick raked his fingers through his black hair. His displeasure with Aimee was evident in his scowling features. He wanted to wring her neck for endangering the boy. At Tall Oaks he was safe, contented, and well fed. Didn't Aimee know he'd never let anything happen to the lad? Furthermore, why had she left in the first place? He hadn't mistreated her; he only wanted to love her, not earn her hatred. Unfortunately the fact that he was a Yankee was enough to earn her hatred. And it hadn't helped any that he had left her over five years ago with his babe in her belly.

Dear God, he would never forgive himself for taking her virginity and then walking out on her after their one night of incredible rapture. Even though he had looked for her afterward, that thought did little now to comfort him. He had still abandoned her. And once he had found her again at Tall Oaks, he had earned her hatred once again by becoming a threat to her and her son—his son. By God, Brand *was* his son! He felt it in every pore of his large body. Someday, he vowed, he'd get Aimee to admit it.

"He's gonna be all right, Captain, my baby is gonna be just fine," Savannah said when she saw Nick standing beside Brand's bed. "I just wish I could say de same about Aimee. Dat chile's in big trouble; I can feel it in dese old bones."

Nick's attention sharpened. "What are you saying, Savannah? Do you know something I don't?"

Savannah shook her head in vigorous denial. "I just know what dese old bones tell me."

A worried frown furrowed Nick's brow. "I fear you may be right, Savannah. A woman alone is at the mercy of deserters, raiders, and all kinds of desperate men. Aimee couldn't have been thinking clearly when she left Tall Oaks."

"No, sir, she surely wasn't. Her thinkin' ain't been right ever since you showed up at de front door." She flashed him a baleful look, filled with accusation.

Nick flushed, silently agreeing with Savannah. "I'll find her, Savannah. Now that I know that Brand isn't seriously ill, I can leave immediately. Will you be able to care for him if I leave?"

"Don't you worry none about Brand; he'll be just fine. It's Aimee I'm worried about. I been tending her since she was a babe; she's all I got left in de world."

"I'll find her, Savannah," Nick said with conviction.

Turning on his heel, he left the room. He spent the rest of the day issuing instructions to Lieutenant Dill, then caught a few hours of much-needed sleep before leaving Tall Oaks at dawn the next morning. Since every man was needed to make up the patrols that probed deep into Reb territory, Nick chose to travel alone. He had no idea how close to Reb lines Aimee had traveled, and he thought it best not to endanger the lives of his men on a mission that was important only to him. Although he did promise the colonel he'd keep Aimee safely incarcerated, his primary reason for finding her had to do more with her safety than with the colonel's wishes. He couldn't bear it if anything happened to her.

Nick cursed the rain that had turned the road into a quagmire. Though it had stopped raining and the sun was shining brightly once again, thick mud and deep ruts hindered his progress. He thought of Aimee trudging through the mud without benefit of a horse, and he spurred his mount to greater speed. Thus far he had seen nothing to indicate that Aimee had traveled along this road. He considered the notion that she might have taken to the woods, but decided to follow the road until he neared Reb territory. Since he had been on patrols over this very same ground recently, he knew from experience just where those lines lay.

Around noon he met a Union patrol. He recognized the captain in charge immediately, and they greeted each other warmly. "Bruce Birch, what are you doing out here so close to Reb lines? I thought you were with General Sherman."

"Good to see you, Nick," Birch returned. "I've recently been reassigned. My duty now is to bring in Reb deserters. They've been plaguing the farmers hereabouts with their unprovoked raids and killings. Less than a week ago two deserters killed a farmer and raped his wife while their two small children looked on. I want those men, Nick, I want them bad."

"Have you been in the area long?" Nick asked.

"Several days," Birch allowed. "And we're not leaving until those men are caught."

"Have you seen a woman in the vicinity?" Nick asked hopefully. "A beautiful young woman with blond hair and soft light brown eyes?"

Birch rubbed his chin thoughtfully. "I can't be sure it's the same woman you're looking for, but I did see a woman yesterday. Only she wasn't alone. She had a servant and a sick child with her. Going to the doctor, she said. What's she done?"

"She's been in my custody for several weeks," Nick said, carefully refraining from mentioning the fact that Aimee was a spy. "She left without my permission, and I'm anxious to find her. She sent her sick child and servant back to Tall Oaks, where I'm quartered, and went on alone."

"Alone?" Birch repeated, shaking his head in obvious disapproval. "That was a foolish move on her part. There are dangerous men loose in the area."

"I've got to find her, Bruce, before harm comes to her. Are you certain there are deserters in the area?"

Birch nodded. "We caught a glimpse of them yesterday, but they slipped away from us in the woods. I was just about to order the patrol into the woods again when I spied you."

A sudden premonition seized Nick. "Do you mind if I join you?"

"Not at all." Birch gave the order, and the patrol melted into the covering of thick trees. Birch and Nick rode side by side. "What's this woman to you, Nick? I heard you were engaged to General Blakewell's daughter."

"It's a long story, Bruce. Suffice it to say that Aimee and I have a rather complicated relationship. As for Regina Blakewell, I rather doubt we would suit one another."

"So that's the way it is," Bruce said astutely. "Your Aimee must be some woman to make you give up the daughter of a general. I assume she's a southerner."

"Remind me to tell you the whole story after the war," Nick said, unwilling to talk about Aimee while his feelings for her were still so raw. "All I want to do right now is find her."

Aimee awoke with a sense of being slowly suffocated. She could see light ahead of her, and with a jolt of panic recalled that she had wedged herself into a fallen log to escape Cullen and Rolly the night before. Slowly inching forward toward the light, she stuck her head out of the log and peered cautiously in all directions. No one was in sight, so she emerged, attempting to get her bearings as she stood on wobbly legs.

Frowning in consternation, Aimee tried to recall in which direction Confederate lines lay. Deciding she was hopelessly lost, she resolutely trudged forward, keeping a sharp eye out for Cullen and Rolly. Having spent a miserable night in a hollow log, she had no intention of being caught again. Unfortunately, fate willed otherwise. She was still trying to find her way out of the woods when she was caught by the hair and tugged backward.

"Gotcha!" Cullen crowed, bringing Aimee to an abrupt halt.

Aimee screeched in pain, only to be silenced by Rolly's grubby hand across her mouth. "Shut up, bitch! Do ya want the Yanks breathin' down out necks?"

At that particular moment, Aimee would have welcomed Yankee soldiers.

"Move," Rolly ordered, pushing her before him. "Did ya think ya could escape us?" Since it was full daylight, Aimee was able to get a good look at her captors.

Rolly, the younger man, was tall and lanky. He looked mean, with shifty eyes the color of slate. A blue-black stubble covered his chin; his hair clung to his neck in dirty strands, and his clothes were a ragged combination of gray and tan. Cullen looked to be about ten years older than his companion, yet obviously under the control of the younger man. Of medium height, Cullen was thin as a rail and wiry. His graying hair stood nearly straight up on his head, and he wore a scruffy beard. His clothing was as tattered as Rolly's, and his worn boots were held together with strips of cloth.

Aimee's mouth went dry. Somehow she had to persuade these despicable men to let her go. "Please don't hurt me. Where is your conscience? I'm a Rebel the same as you. My husband died for the cause."

Placing his filthy hand on her back, Rolly shoved her forward. "Shut up. Ya ain't goin' nowheres. Cullen and me are randy as goats. We had all night to think about ya."

"You both smell like goats!" Aimee shouted back. She wasn't going to make raping her easy.

"You're a disgrace to the good citizens of the South."

Aimee stumbled through the woods, prodded ruthlessly by Rolly, until her legs felt like wooden poles. When they entered a small clearing, Rolly called a halt. "This should be far enough." He flung Aimee to the ground, knocking the breath from her lungs.

"Go ahead, Cullen," Rolly sneered, sending Aimee a baleful glare, "stick it in her. Ya might have ta slap her around some, but don't take too long, I'm fair ta burstin' myself."

"Bastards!" Aimee gritted from between clenched teeth.

"Who ya callin' bastard?" Rolly growled. Deliberately he bent, flipped her dress up, and ran his hand down her thigh. "Did ya ever see such purty white skin, Cullen?"

Saliva dripped down from one corner of Cullen's gaping mouth. He swallowed several times before he was able to speak. "Never in my borned days." He rubbed his crotch, staring at Aimee.

"Are ya gonna do it or are ya gonna stand there starin'?" Rolly asked disgustedly.

Cullen crouched beside Aimee, shoving her legs apart as he fumbled with the fastening on his trousers. Aimee managed one shriek before Cullen clapped a hand over her mouth.

"Do you hear that?" Nick halted beneath a large maple tree, instantly alert.

"Sounded like an animal," Birch said.

"Or a woman," Nick argued.

"By God, do you suppose . . ."

Nick didn't wait around for Birch's answer as he

spurred his mount. Scout leaped forward, attuned to his master's slightest command. Intuition told Nick that Aimee was nearby, and that she needed him. Keen instinct pointed him in the direction of the sound. But the going was slow, too slow to suit Nick. The forest was thick and dense. Finally, in desperation, he dismounted, tethered Scout to a nearby bush, and continued on foot. Birch was close behind him. They burst into a small clearing to a scene straight from hell.

Cullen had managed to pull down his trousers but was having difficulty holding Aimee. She was fighting furiously. Rolly hovered over them, laughing at Cullen's efforts to tame her. Seeing Cullen's thick, dirty fingers touching Aimee's tender flesh made Nick wild with rage. He let out a trumpeting roar and lunged forward. Rolly reacted instantly, but Cullen was too consumed with lust even to notice.

Gathering his wits, Nick flew into action. He leaped at Cullen, knocking him aside. His eyes wide with shock, Cullen went sailing off Aimee. She sat up immediately, pulling down her dress.

"What the hell!" said Rolly, who reacted by drawing his gun from his holster and aiming at Nick. Suddenly Birch burst into the clearing, drew his weapon, and fired at Rolly. The gun flew out of Rolly's hand, the impact of the bullet shattering his wrist. Birch hadn't intended to kill the traitor; he wanted him to hang for his crimes.

Cullen merely sat on the ground, his pants still down, staring at Nick in confusion. But Nick had no time for Cullen; he went straight to Aimee and helped her to her feet. She was sobbing—her body shaking—and her eyes were squeezed tightly shut.

Nick uttered a violent curse when he saw the scratches on her arms and face. By now Birch's men, having heard the shot, were emerging from the woods into the clearing, taking charge of the deserters. Nick noticed none of it.

"It's all right, Aimee, they can't hurt you anymore," Nick crooned as he cradled Aimee in his arms. "Shhh, sweetheart, don't cry, you're safe now."

The intimate scene drew the attention of more than one man, and Birch immediately ordered his patrol back to the road with their prisoners. Reluctantly they melted away, leaving Birch, Nick, and Aimee behind in the clearing.

"Is she all right?" Birch asked. His voice was filled with concern for the beautiful woman Nick held so tenderly in his arms.

"I think so." Actually, Nick wasn't so sure Aimee hadn't already been ravished. He had no idea how long she had been held by the deserters or what they had done to her while she was in their custody. But he did know she was in no condition right now for further questions. Besides, he didn't want to embarrass her in front of Birch.

"Will you be all right if I leave you now? I want to get those bastards back to headquarters as soon as possible."

"We'll be fine," Nick assured him. "I'll be taking Aimee back to her son at Tall Oaks as soon as she's able to travel."

Birch nodded, aware that Nick was perfectly capable of protecting himself and Aimee if the need arose. "I'll be off then. Look me up after the war, Nick, if I don't see you sooner." He turned, walk-

ing back through the woods to where he had tethered his mount.

Through all this, Aimee had kept her face carefully hidden against Nick's shoulder, sobbing
softly. She knew what the Yankee patrol had seen
and was consumed with shame. She hated appearing weak and vulnerable before Yankees, but she
was grateful they had arrived when they did.

"Aimee, look at me," Nick ordered softly. She
shook her head. "Please, sweetheart, I have to
know how badly they hurt you. Should I take you
to a doctor? There's one at headquarters."

Aimee found her voice. "No! No doctor, I'm
fine."

Nick looked skeptical. "Are you certain? Did—
did either one of the deserters rape you?"

She shook her head in vigorous denial, but still
he didn't believe her. Gently he raised her chin,
looking deeply into her soft amber eyes. A flicker
of raw emotion was clearly visible in Nick's expression as he searched her face. "It's all right,
Aimee, you can tell me the truth."

"First tell me about Brand," Aimee asked anxiously. "Is he well? Did Savannah get him back to
Tall Oaks in time? Please, Nick, don't keep me in
suspense."

"Brand is fine, Aimee, truly. I stayed with him
until I was certain he was going to recover. He has
measles. Savannah is caring for him."

Aimee seemed to collapse inwardly and she
sobbed in relief. "I was so frightened for him." She
dropped her face in her hands, then gazed back
up at Nick, tears streaming from her eyes. She was
crying in relief for Brand and for being saved by
Nick. Also, the aching pain of hating Nick all these

years had nearly torn her apart. Did she still hate him? she wondered curiously. For years she'd fed off that hatred, nurtured it. Dear God! A flash of insight into the complicated workings of her heart nearly undid her. No! It couldn't be love ... it wasn't possible! She wouldn't allow that to happen.

"Aimee, you haven't answered me," Nick said with concern. "What did those men do to you?"

Aimee gulped and replied, "Nothing, they didn't harm me. I escaped from them yesterday and spent the night hiding in a hollow log. They caught me again this morning, but you arrived in time."

A certain watchfulness in his eyes left her with a disquieting sensation of vulnerability. But when her eyes didn't waver from his, he finally seemed to believe her.

"Thank God. When I saw that man ... abusing you, I was so afraid ..." A glimmer of moisture appeared at the corners of his eyes, looking suspiciously like tears, but Aimee quickly discounted the idea of a strong man like Nick weeping. Men didn't cry.

"Can you walk?"

"Yes," Aimee replied, leaning heavily on Nick.

He searched her face, wondering if the bruises had come from wedging herself into the hollow log or if those scum had struck her. Her hair was a tangled mass, and her skin and clothing were covered with pieces of rotted wood and grass stains.

There's a stream nearby where you can bathe before we return to Tall Oaks," he suggested with concern. "I've been all through these woods in the past few weeks and know them by heart. Would you like that?"

"Yes."

"I'm glad you trusted me enough to send Brand to me," Nick said after a pause. "What I truly don't understand is why you felt the need to leave Tall Oaks in the first place."

"Can't you guess? I had to." The words were torn from deep inside her tormented soul.

Chapter 10

The stream was closer than Aimee had realized. She knew, of course, that it was an offshoot of the Chattahoochee River, which flowed through Tall Oaks plantation, but she had become disoriented while being dragged through the woods by Rolly and Cullen.

"Let's see your wrists," Nick said. He held out his hands palms up, and she placed her bruised wrists in them. He inspected them carefully, his face taut with rage.

"They don't hurt much."

"Like hell! There's a first aid kit in my saddlebag; when you're finished bathing, I'll put some salve on them and bind them."

Before Nick had taken her to the stream, he had retrieved Scout, who was tethered nearby, and led him through the woods.

"That's not necessary," Aimee muttered. She turned toward the stream, uncertain what to do when she felt Nick's hands on her shoulders.

"Do you need help getting out of your dress?" He didn't wait for an answer but started unhooking her dress at the back.

"Nick, wait; what if someone should discover

us? What if there are more deserters hiding in the woods?"

"Don't worry, sweetheart, I'll keep watch. But I seriously doubt we'll be bothered. Birch and his patrol have been in the area several days now, cleaning out pockets of deserters. The scum who attacked you were probably the last. It's unlikely any others remain in these woods."

Nick's confidence seemed to reassure Aimee as she slid the dress from her shoulders, removed the ragged petticoat, and slipped into the water wearing her thin shift. She waded in up to her waist, dipped briefly below the surface, and came up sputtering.

"It's cold."

"It will refresh you before our ride back to Tall Oaks."

It did feel wonderful, Aimee had to admit, and soothing to her bruised flesh. For a few moments she forgot all the horror of the previous hours and the reason she felt compelled to leave Tall Oaks as she lifted her face to the sun and splashed in the cool water.

Nick couldn't take his eyes off the sea nymph cavorting in the middle of the shallow stream. Beneath her shift, her breasts were high and softly curved, and he vividly recalled how perfectly suited they were to the palm of his hand. He wanted to throw caution to the wind and dash in after her, lift her high in his arms and press her down onto his manhood.

He wanted to throttle her for placing herself and Brand in danger.

He wanted to love her until she was giddy with desire.

He wanted . . .

Aimee.

He wasn't aware that he spoke her name until she turned to look at him, her eyes wide and questioning. She didn't speak, merely stared, as if in response to his unspoken request. He didn't wait for her to come to him, he went to her. In moments his clothes lay in a heap next to hers. Aimee stood still as a statue as he waded out to meet her, unable to move even if she had wanted to. The blue-green of the water was reflected in his vivid eyes. But that's not all Aimee saw in his intense gaze. She saw desperate need and smoldering desire, and something else—something that went much deeper.

Then he was standing beside her, the coolness of the water warmed by the heat of his body. She felt his breath against her face, inhaled deeply of his scent, and closed her eyes against the pain of what her heart was trying to tell her. Then her conflicting thoughts skidded to a halt as his mouth came down on hers with a fierce plundering heat. He kissed her endlessly, her mouth, her neck, her eyes, then her mouth again, ravishing her with tender kisses until he was breathless and had to stop.

"My God, Aimee, do you realize I could have lost you? I should spank you for leaving like you did, but all I want to do is love you. I haven't been the same since I found you again. I don't know what it is you do to me, but I do know that making love to you gives me more pleasure than I ever thought possible."

Aimee stared past his shoulder, saying nothing, fearing the words that she might utter, fearing the loss of her pride, her spirit, her soul. Yet when she was in Nick's arms, she was afraid of nothing. If those conflicting thoughts frightened her, the next one terrified her. Love and hate—might not one be confused with the other?

"Say something, Aimee, say anything," Nick begged, confused by her silence. Was she still in shock due to her recent ordeal?

She looked at him then, her eyes soft and luminous. She wanted to tell him that she had to leave Tall Oaks, that she couldn't allow herself to love him, that her son was his son, but she couldn't admit it for fear of losing Brand. She opened her mouth, and what came out was so shocking and in such contrast to her thoughts that she began to question her sanity.

"Make love to me, Nick."

Nick groaned, his response to her request instant and compelling. His groin was throbbing, painfully full with his need.

"Aimee." He kissed her, pulling her tightly against him, bringing her to her tiptoes, stripping the thin shift from her and tossing it to the grassy bank. When she responded, arching against him, he trembled with the force of his need.

She was no longer pliant and unresponsive in his arms. She was frantic and wild, throwing her arms around his neck, nearly choking him in her fervor to get closer to him. Grasping her by the waist, he lifted her until her breasts dangled above him and he could take her nipples into his mouth, suckling vigorously, making her cry out. She thrust herself against him. The water churned around them, waist-deep, as he set her back on her feet, parting her legs and stroking his hands up the slick insides of her thighs.

When his fingers found her, she cried out, her legs trembling uncontrollably. She clutched his shoulders, her breathing shallow, her head thrown back, her long blond hair trailing in the water.

"Hush, sweetheart," he said, his breath hot on her flesh. "I know what you want; I want it, too."

Underwater, his fingers slipped inside her, and he felt the rippling spasms, took her wrenching cries into his mouth, feeling himself grow and swell. Then he was lifting her, urging her to wrap her legs around his waist as he came inside her powerfully, deep—so deep, she felt him touch her womb. As he braced his feet against the sandy bottom of the stream, Nick's thrusts were hard and fast and deep, setting up such a clamor in her body, she was nearly driven frantic with it.

The buoyancy of the waist-deep water added to her pleasure as Nick drove into her relentlessly, wanting to bring her to climax before surrendering to the fury of his own. Suddenly he pulled out of her. It was going too fast, much too fast, and he was in danger of losing control. Aimee cried out in protest as he carried her, still wrapped tightly around him, toward shore.

"The pleasure is just beginning, sweetheart," he promised her as he carried her ashore and lay her down on the grassy bank beneath the shade of a large oak tree.

She lay there in a daze, staring up at the sunlight filtering through the oak leaves, unable to focus her splintered thoughts. Then he came over her, parting her knees, nuzzling her belly, his hands stroking up and down the insides of her trembling thighs. When his mouth touched her, she lurched wildly and cried out. It was beyond anything she had ever felt before.

Nick supported her thighs, holding them apart, feeling the sleek muscles tense and tremble as his mouth plundered her soft woman's flesh. She screamed, jerking spasmodically as he held her down with a hand on her belly until the force of her climax abated and she lay quiescent beneath his touch.

"Open your eyes, sweetheart," Nick said as he poised above her. "I want you to watch us coming together. I want you to know who is making love to you. I don't ever want you to think of your dead husband while I'm loving you."

Aimee looked confused. Think of Beau while making love with Nick? The thought had never occurred to her. Beau was a dear, sweet man, but elicited little passion from her body. Nick was her lover, the flame that burned inside her—her enemy. Then her thoughts shattered as he thrust powerfully, lifting her hips, sending himself deep inside her. Never had Aimee felt herself so much a part of another human being.

He buried his face against her neck, breathing heavily, lost now in the pursuit of his own climax but not too enmeshed to be aware of Aimee's escalating passion. She was quick to respond, and he strained to control his release until Aimee had reached hers. Then he was kissing her, thrusting his tongue into her mouth, loving her taste, her heat. Her small cries pleased him enormously and he groaned in response, so near to bursting, he thought he would die. Suddenly he felt her stiffen, felt her muscles quiver, felt the tension in her body release itself and burst forth in an outpouring of incredible heat. Only then did he allow his own climax to explode. And for several minutes he knew no more.

He lay atop her as his thundering heart slowed its furious pace. Never had he felt so at peace, so incredibly content. He reared up on his elbows, staring down at Aimee. Her eyes were closed, her face unreadable, making it impossible for Nick to tell what she was thinking. He eased off her, settling down beside her on the grass.

"What are you thinking?" he asked her, once his heart had slowed to a steady beat.

Aimee's eyes opened slowly. She blinked several times, nearly blinded by the brilliant sunlight filtering through the leaves. "I'm thinking of nothing," she lied.

"Don't lie to me, Aimee. After what we just shared, I assumed you'd forget the hostility between us and tell me the truth for once. You were the one who begged me to make love to you."

A dull red stained Aimee's cheeks. "I must have been mad."

"I love it when madness strikes you," Nick teased. His words brought no answering smile. "Aimee, why do you continue to resist? You want me as much as I want you. Can't you forget I'm the enemy?"

"Some things are impossible to forget. Being a Yank is just part of it."

Nick sighed in weary exasperation, then turned on his side to face her. But Aimee still lay on her back, refusing to look at him. Gently but firmly he pulled her around until he could look into her eyes.

"Tell me what you're thinking, Aimee. Tell me why I'm a threat to you." He thought he already knew, but he wanted to hear her say the words.

Her expression held such abject fear, Nick was almost sorry he asked.

"Aimee, I won't hurt you. You ought to know that by now."

"You've hurt me before," Aimee said defiantly.

"Not knowingly."

"What do you want from me?" Her cry was like a knife thrust to his heart. He had no idea she was referring to Brand, that she feared he would take her child from her if he learned he was his father.

Nick frowned, wanting to tell Aimee about his suspicions concerning Brand, but astute enough to realize that now was not the time. Her feelings were still too raw, and she was too stubborn to admit the truth. One day, he told himself, one day soon Aimee will realize that he meant no harm to either her or Brand. If Brand was indeed his son, he wanted to provide for him. And he wanted to do more—much more. Convincing Aimee of his good intentions would be difficult because this senseless war made him her natural enemy. Yet her question bothered him. Exactly what did he want from her?

He wanted her to admit Brand was their son. He wanted her to stop thinking of him as the enemy. He wanted her . . . love.

"Sweetheart," he said, "I don't think you'd like the answer to your question. Instead, I'll pose a similar one. What do you want from me? You seem to enjoy my lovemaking, yet you profess to hate me."

His question sucked the breath from her lungs. "I do hate you. I've always hated you."

"You don't hate it when I love you. Were you so starved for a man's affection that any man would do? You've been a widow a long time."

"You take too much for granted!" Aimee shot back in sudden anger. "I don't need a man to make my life complete. I have Brand."

"What about your dead husband? Did you love him so much that no one can take his place?"

Aimee's flush deepened. "Of course I loved Beau; he's the father of my son."

"Is he?"

A frisson of panic shuddered through her body.

"Are you cold?"

"No."

"Then answer my question. Is Brand really Beau's son?"

"You bastard! Just because you've made me your whore doesn't mean I was unfaithful to Beau."

"That's not what I'm suggesting, Aimee, and you know it."

She tried to rise, but Nick placed a hand against her stomach to hold her down.

"Please, Nick, don't do this to me. Your questions are leading nowhere."

"Do you think of Beau while I'm making love to you?" He had no idea where that question came from, but he couldn't help asking it.

He felt her stomach clench against the palm of his hand. "I—no." Why couldn't she lie to him?

He wanted to believe her, but she had lied about so many things, he was hesitant to put much faith in her words. But suddenly it didn't matter anymore, for the flesh beneath his hand was warm to his touch, the blond hair between her legs moist and inviting. He wanted her again. Wanted her with a desperation that gnawed at his gut.

"It doesn't matter," Nick said in a strangled voice. "Even if you do think of Beauregard Trevor during our most tender moments, I'll make you forget him somehow. I'm going to love you again, and when I finish, my name will be the only one on your lips and in your mind."

Grasping her hips, he rolled her atop him. He was already hard and throbbing as he probed her softness. Nick couldn't recall when he had been ready to perform again so quickly. Only Aimee had the power to reduce him to raw need and gnawing hunger.

"Spread your legs, sweetheart." She hesitated only a moment before straddling his loins. Then he grasped her hips and shoved her down hard, stretching her, filling her, bringing a gasp of profound pleasure to her lips.

Aimee lost all track of time as she rode Nick, abandoning herself once again to the frantic burst of wild rapture only this man had the power to give her.

Her enemy.

Her love.

"Nick!" Nick smiled a secret smile. His name trembling from her lips was like sweet music to his ears. For the very first time he was absolutely certain no other man filled her thoughts.

They started back to Tall Oaks a short time later. Aimee rode in contemplative silence mounted before Nick on Scout's broad back. She had much to think about, though none of her thoughts were comforting. She had acted the wanton with Nick, saying one thing while meaning another. She had begged him to love her when what she really wanted was to get as far away from him as possible. That *was* what she wanted, wasn't it? To get far enough away from Nick Drummond until he no longer filled her mind and her body. Until he posed no threat to her and her son. But instead, she mindlessly offered herself to him, responded to him in ways that left her breathless with wonder and behaving like a whore.

Nick guided Scout back to the road, seeing no need to keep to the woods, where the going was much rougher and slower. With any luck they'd be back at Tall Oaks not too long after nightfall. But as luck would have it, rain began to fall shortly before darkness arrived, forcing them to seek shelter. Aimee mentioned their proximity to the Pinder plantation, where she, Brand, and Savannah had spent one night, and Nick wheeled Scout in that direction. They sheltered that night in the ruins of the ramshackle stable. Aimee didn't protest when Nick pulled her shivering form into his arms, where she warmed immediately.

"Go to sleep, sweetheart; you must be exhausted."

She was. But not too exhausted. "Nick, what do you really want from me?" she asked.

His eyes glowed a brilliant green. Devil's eyes. "You, Aimee, I want you."

They reached Tall Oaks at noon the next day. The camp was in an uproar. Lieutenant Dill was the first to reach them.

"Thank God you've returned. I was about to organize a search party. We've received orders from headquarters."

Nick dismounted first, then reached up to lift Aimee from the saddle. "What kind of orders?"

"We're moving out."

Nick was instantly alert. "We're leaving Tall Oaks? What is our destination?"

Dill gave Aimee a wary glance. Nick realized immediately that Dill no longer entirely trusted Aimee. "I imagine Brand is waiting anxiously to see his mother, Aimee. Why don't you go to him?"

Aimee couldn't blame either man for distrusting her, but it hurt to be held in such blatant contempt by a Yankee. On her way to the house, she passed Sergeant Jones. He said nothing, merely giving her a scathing look that spoke volumes. After all, she had drugged him and the other men left behind to guard her. She tried to ignore the sour looks cast her way as she hurried into the house.

Brand was still a sick little boy, but it was obvious he was going to recover. She entered his sickroom to find Savannah hovering over him. When she approached the bed, he perked up immediately.

"Mama!" He held out his arms. "Where were you? I told Captain Drummond you knew how to make me well. I'm so glad he found you."

"I'm glad, too, darling," Aimee said, meaning every word. How could she have ever thought that leaving Brand with Nick would solve anything? She must have been desperate as well as foolish to send him back to Tall Oaks without her.

"I hope you done learned your lesson," Savannah grumbled. "Captain Drummond was mad as a wet hen when he learned you were gone. He wanted to look for you right away, but he wouldn't leave until he knew what was wrong with Brand. He loves dat chile like he was his own."

"Savannah! Watch your tongue."

"Well, it's true," Savannah said sullenly. "And you'd realize it if you wasn't so darn stubborn. I don't think de man means you any harm, honey. Why not tell him?"

"I don't know what you're talking about," Aimee insisted. She turned back to her son, discouraging further conversation.

"Mama, did Captain Drummond bring you back?"

"Yes, darling, he did."

Brand managed a weak smile. His face was covered with so many red spots, he looked like a painted clown. "I itch, Mama."

"I'll have Savannah mix a paste of baking soda and water to spread on your skin. That should stop the itching. Meanwhile, try not to scratch, darling."

"I want to see Captain Drummond."

Aimee's mouth turned down into a frown. "I'm sure he has better things to do than amuse a sick child."

"Don't put words into my mouth, Aimee." Nick strode into the room in time to hear Aimee's remark.

"I'll go get dat bakin' soda," Savannah said. She scurried from the room, unwilling to become a party to the tension crackling between Nick and Aimee.

"How are you feeling, Brand?" Nick asked as he approached the child's sickbed.

"Not too bad, sir." His voice quivered from the sickness that still ravaged his body.

"Your mother is here now; she'll take care of you."

His words sounded too much like a farewell to Brand. "Are you leaving, sir?"

Nick was amazed at the child's astuteness. "Yes, Brand, I'll be leaving soon, but I want you to concentrate on getting well."

Brand appeared on the verge of tears. "I'll try, sir. Will you come back?"

"You have my promise, son, that I'll return." He looked straight at Aimee when he spoke. "It may not be until after the war, but I *will* come back to Tall Oaks."

"Don't make promises you have no intention of keeping," Aimee hissed.

"I always keep my word." There was no flicker of emotion in his cool green eyes, only the confidence of a man who knew what he wanted. "Now, if you will excuse me, I have some dispatches to read."

Lieutenant Dill awaited Nick in the study. "The orders arrived just this morning," Dill said, handing the packet of official papers to Nick. Nick opened them immediately and scanned the contents.

"We're to join part of Sherman's army at Jonesboro, south of Atlanta," Nick said slowly. "It's the junction of four important railroads, and their capture is vital to the defeat of the Confederacy. General Sherman believes that once the railroads are disabled, disrupting the flow of supplies and arms, the fall of Atlanta and other major cities will quickly follow."

"When do we leave?" Dill asked.

"At dawn tomorrow. The attack is set for August thirtieth. We'll just have enough time to meet up with the main army before the skirmish begins. While we're attacking Jonesboro, another flank of Sherman's army will surround Atlanta and force the Rebs to surrender the city."

"The end is near, isn't it, sir?"

"God help the South, Lieutenant, for I fear the end is very near. Not only the end of the war but of an entire way of life. See that the camp is dismantled in orderly fashion and prepare for our departure at dawn. I want all our spare supplies left behind for Mrs. Trevor."

It was very late when Aimee tiptoed down the stairs. She knew Nick was leaving Tall Oaks, but knew no other details. She hadn't seen him since that scene in Brand's bedroom. Nor had she heard his footsteps pass her room. When she reached the study, she noted the light shining from the space beneath the door. She didn't bother knocking but turned the knob and entered on silent footsteps. Nick was bending over a map, deep in thought. Yet somehow he sensed her presence and looked up.

"Come in, Aimee."

"Is it true? Are you really leaving?"

She wore a flowing white gown that revealed more than it concealed. Nick nearly lost his train of thought when he recalled every vivid detail of her lush body beneath the thin cloth.

"Dare I hope you'll miss me?"

She deliberately ignored the question. "Will there be a battle?"

"That's something I'm not allowed to divulge."

"What will become of me when you leave? Will someone arrive to take me to prison?"

"Is that what you fear? Being taken to prison?"

"Brand needs me."

"I'm aware of that."

"If you have any compassion in your soul, you'll let me remain at Tall Oaks. I'm not a spy; I'm no longer any danger to the Yanks."

"I'm well aware of that also. Is that why you're here, to persuade me to let you stay at Tall Oaks?"

"I know the condition of my release. I was to remain in your custody until you leave Tall Oaks. But nothing was said about what happens to me when you leave."

"Nothing happens to you, Aimee. By now no one will have remembered your name. I've already convinced the colonel you are no longer a threat to security. I never intended that you should go to prison."

"You never . . ." Aimee's temper flared. "You bastard! You led me to believe I'd be sent to prison if I didn't become your—your—"

"Lover."

"—whore."

"Aimee, I meant what I said about returning after the war. There's too much between us for us to consider parting without ever seeing one another again. We share too many memories. Then there's Brand. I know you're reluctant to admit it, but in my heart I feel as if Brand could be my own son."

"No! Don't even think such a thing! Brand is Beau's son."

"I don't have time to argue about it now, but one day I'll learn the truth. If it turns out that Brand belongs to me, you can damn well believe I'll want to raise my own son."

Aimee froze, all her fears returning. If Nick knew Brand was his son, he'd take him away from her. He recognized her terror and was puzzled by it. Did she hate him so much she'd refuse to marry him so they could raise their son together? Unable to face the prospect of losing her child, Aimee turned to flee.

"Aimee, wait!" He caught her at the door. "There's a good chance I won't survive the battle. I've made a new will. It's in the desk drawer. In the event of my death, take it to my lawyer in Chicago; his name is on the envelope."

"I care nothing for your will." The thought of his death was too painful to contemplate.

"Nevertheless, I want your promise you'll see that my will reaches my lawyer."

"I—very well." She stared at him, wanting to throw herself into his arms, beg him to love her, tell him that Brand was his son. But she feared the consequences. He'd made her his whore, stolen her heart, and she vowed he'd not have her son.

"Is that all, sweetheart? No tender good-bye, no words of remorse should I die in battle?"

"I don't wish your death, Nick." Her words were spoken with such profound conviction, Nick believed her.

"Then kiss me, sweetheart. Kiss me for all those wasted years before we found one another again; kiss me and make me believe you really care what happens to me."

She stared at his mouth, at those full, sensual

lips that gave her such pleasure. He waited. Then slowly, oh so slowly, she leaned forward, touching her lips to his. The shock of their meeting sent a tingle down her spine. She memorized the contours of his lips with her tongue, savoring his taste, committing it to her memory to last a lifetime.

A long, agonized groan sounded from Nick's throat as his control snapped. He seized Aimee, dragging her against the solid wall of his chest. He returned her kiss with all the fervor in his huge body, crushing her against him, the heat of him scorching her through the thin material of her gown. Scooping her into his arms, he flung the door open with his foot and took the steps two at a time. When he reached her room, he flung her on the bed, too aroused to bother with clothes. He released himself, shoved her skirt over her hips, and drove himself into her. Surrendering to his fury, Aimee cried out and lurched upward to meet his thrusts.

He was gone the next morning before she awoke.

Chapter 11

～ᴑᴑ～

Two days after Nick and his Federal soldiers left Tall Oaks, the ominous thunder of cannon could be heard rumbling over the countryside. For Aimee it meant only one thing. The battle for Atlanta had begun in earnest. Sherman was determined to drive the Rebs from that city, and his march was sweeping through the area, taking everything in its path. She prayed that since Nick was no longer at Tall Oaks to protect it from destruction by Union soldiers, those invading forces would be occupied elsewhere and her home considered too trivial to bother with.

As for Nick, she realized now that he had been ordered to join the battle for Atlanta and may even now be lying dead. That horrible thought sent a shudder of dread through her body. She didn't wish Nick dead. She only wanted him to leave her son alone. She felt burdened by a tremendous guilt for not telling Nick the truth about Brand at a time when his life was in jeopardy. A man had a right to know he had fathered a child, yet deep down the fear that she might lose Brand kept her from admitting the truth even when Nick pressed her.

Nick said he would return, and she didn't doubt for a moment that he would, if only to plague her with questions she didn't want to answer. He'd as much as said that he expected to raise his own child. If he learned that Brand was his son, it would threaten her very existence. Where did that leave her? Aimee wondered dismally. Not once had she heard the word "love." He made love to her as if he truly cared for her, but nothing was said of marriage. At least a marriage between them would allow them both to raise Brand.

But you hate Nick Drummond, a little voice whispered.

Aimee made a derisive sound deep in her throat. How could she hate a man, yet love him to distraction? How could she yearn desperately for his touch yet despise him?

When had her hatred turned to love?

In the final days of August 1864, stragglers began showing up at Tall Oaks. All were Rebs evacuating the city with General Hood's army. Some were wounded, some merely dazed by the three-pronged attack waged by Sherman's army against the railroads and the city, and some were just plain tired of death and destruction. Most came in search of water and food on their way to an unknown point to regroup to fight another day. Yet nearly every man Aimee spoke with seemed convinced that the South was doomed. After conversation with a Reb captain and his aide, Aimee learned just how far the South had sunk in its battle to remain a separate unity. She also had some vague idea where Nick had been sent to fight.

"The battlefield is littered with dead," Captain Feldon said when questioned by Aimee. The faraway look in his nearly expressionless blue eyes frightened Aimee. His face was as gray as his tattered uniform, and he appeared weary beyond endurance.

"Is the Confederate army in retreat?" Aimee asked.

"Sherman withdrew his entire army from the trenches surrounding Atlanta and moved against the railroads at Jonesboro," Feldon replied in a voice fraught with anguish. "The day still could have been saved if General Hood, who replaced General Johnson, knew what was happening. But Hood thought Sherman was retreating north. The Federals could have been routed if Hood had attacked while they were changing positions.

"But it wasn't until Sherman sliced across one railroad and on to another that Hood learned where the Federals were. Hood sent two corps south to stop the Federals. Losses were heavy and the attack unsuccessful. The next day Sherman counterattacked and mauled us dreadfully. To avoid being cut off and trapped, Hood ordered Atlanta evacuated."

"Were casualties heavy on both sides?"

"The casualties were severe at both Atlanta and Jonesboro, but Confederate forces suffered the greater loss. I heard Atlanta was set on fire and a large part of it burned. Most of the civilians had already left, but the military casualties were enormous. Both Confederate and Union soldiers lay dead or dying in the streets."

After partaking of the food and drink she offered, Captain Feldon and his aide continued on their way, leaving Aimee deep in thought. Was Nick at Jonesboro or Atlanta? Was he dead or alive? She was unable to dispel the feeling of dread that lingered in her heart.

Brand recovered from his bout with measles and, for some unexplained reason, spent hours each day sitting on the porch staring down the long driveway toward the main road. When Aimee asked him what he was looking for, his response startled her.

"I'm watching for Captain Drummond, Mama. He promised he'd return. You don't suppose anything happened to him, do you?"

Aimee was at a loss for words. She knew Brand was fond of Nick, but when had the Yank come to mean so much to her son? Though they were joined by the common bond of blood, she had no idea Brand would recognize those ties. If Nick perished in the war, Brand would have been denied his natural father as well as his surrogate father. Nothing in life was fair.

On the second day of September, Brand, perched on the porch railing, spied a wagon moving slowly down the driveway. "Mama, someone's coming!"

Assuming it was more refugees from Atlanta, Aimee joined Brand on the porch. The food Nick had left was nearly gone, and she worried that she had nothing but water to offer the poor men stopping by for rest and nourishment. What little was left must necessarily be conserved for Brand.

When the wagon ground to a halt, Aimee was surprised to see it driven by a Federal soldier. Until now, everyone who had stopped by had been a Reb. Then she recognized Sergeant Jones, and her heart thumped furiously. Was it Nick? Had Sergeant Jones brought back Nick's dead body? She was running toward the wagon before it stopped.

"What is it, Sergeant Jones? Is it Captain Drummond?"

"No, ma'am," Jones said, refusing to look her in the eye. "It's Lieutenant Dill. Took a bullet at Jonesboro. The makeshift field hospital is so crowded, I brought him here. It's not serious, but I feared gangrene would set in if the bullet isn't taken out soon."

"Bring him inside," Aimee ordered crisply. "Put him in his old room upstairs. I'm no doctor, but between Savannah and myself, we should be able to get the bullet out. Where was he hit?"

"Left thigh. He lost a lot of blood, but I got it nearly stopped."

Dill groaned as Jones lifted him out of the wagon. "I'm sorry to be a burden, Mrs. Trevor, but I was afraid I'd lose my leg if I lay on the ground until the doctors could get around to me."

"It's all right, Lieutenant. A wounded man is a wounded man no matter the color of his uniform." To Jones she said, "Get his clothes off while I help Savannah assemble the things we'll need to extract the bullet."

"Have you seen Captain Drummond?" Brand asked. His small voice startled Aimee, who had forgotten he was there as she took charge of the situation. But now she turned to Jones, waiting breathlessly for his answer. She had wanted to ask the same question the moment she saw Sergeant Jones.

"Yes, Sergeant, what about Captain Drummond?"

"He led us at Jonesboro, Mrs. Trevor," Jones

said, choosing his words carefully. Every man in Nick's company knew of the curious relationship between the widow Trevor and their captain. "We were part of General Howard's forces, intending to join up at Atlanta later with the rest of Sherman's army."

"Then he's all right!" she said, elated.

"I ... well, that is ... I'm not sure."

"What!"

"Lieutenant Dill saw him fall in battle."

"And you left him?" Aimee was aghast. "How could you do such a thing?" Suddenly she froze. "He's not dead, is he?"

Beside her, Brand began to wail, bringing Savannah rushing from the house.

"What is it? What's wrong with Brand?"

"It's all right, darling," Aimee said, taking the child in her arms. Truth to tell, she wanted to cry herself. To Savannah she said, "Lieutenant Dill saw Nick fall in battle. Please take Brand inside while I speak further with Sergeant Jones. Lieutenant Dill is wounded. Boil some water and prepare instruments to take the bullet out of his thigh. When they're ready, bring them upstairs."

Brand put up a fuss, but when Aimee assured him that no one said Nick was dead, he went quietly with Savannah.

She didn't question Jones again until he had carried Dill upstairs and placed him in bed. "Now, Sergeant, tell me all you know about Captain Drummond."

"I don't know much, Mrs. Trevor. Lieutenant Dill was the one who saw him fall."

"Why didn't you look for him?"

"I did, but you can't imagine the carnage out

there around Jonesboro. I even checked the field hospital, but he hadn't been brought in."

Suddenly Dill opened his eyes and gasped out words that sent Aimee's heart plummeting. "I was nearby when he fell from his mount. From the looks of him, the wound was mortal. I'm sorry, Mrs. Trevor. I wasn't able to get to him before I took a bullet myself, but Sergeant Jones walked through the dead and wounded without finding him."

"If he's not on the battlefield, what could have happened to him?" Aimee asked.

His eyes downcast, Jones said, "We think he was picked up by a burying detail before I could find him and shipped out with the dead."

"No, I don't believe you!" Aimee cried. She couldn't believe that Nick was dead.

Just then Savannah arrived with the boiling water and a sharp knife which would serve as a scalpel to remove the bullet from Dill's thigh. There was no ether. Dill was given a piece of wood to bite on, and Sergeant Jones held him down while Savannah probed for the bullet. After the first few minutes Dill passed out, making it easier on all concerned. Though he had lost a considerable amount of blood, he was strong and likely to recover. The bullet was lodged against the thigh bone, and once it was removed, Jones magically produced a small bottle of whiskey from inside his jacket and offered it to disinfect the wound. One of Aimee's petticoats provided the bandage. Afterward, Aimee spoke privately with Jones.

"Savannah thinks Lieutenant Dill will recover."

"When the lieutenant is himself again, I'm sure he'll thank you."

"I'm not looking for thanks, Sergeant," Aimee said brusquely. "I want your help." While they had been working over Dill, Aimee had come to a decision. It might not be a wise decision, but she had to take action.

"Help, ma'am?"

"What are your plans, Sergeant?"

"As soon as Lieutenant Dill is able to travel, I intend to take him back to the field hospital, where he'll be sent to a northern hospital to recover."

"He won't be fit to travel for several days."

Jones looked puzzled. "I realize that."

"Take me to Jonesboro, Sergeant; I want to look for Captain Drummond."

Jones looked astounded. "I can't do that, Mrs. Trevor; it's too dangerous."

"The battle is over, isn't it?"

"The battle is over, but the war goes on."

"If you don't take me, I'll go alone. Don't you understand? Nick could be lying wounded out there somewhere."

"No, *you* don't understand, Mrs. Trevor. There's still fighting in the area. Atlanta has fallen, but Hood's army is out there regrouping. We may run into some of his men anywhere between here and Jonesboro."

"You can't stop me," Aimee said defiantly. The stubborn tilt of her chin made Jones realize she'd do exactly what she said whether or not he accompanied her. For the sake of his dead captain, who he knew harbored tender feelings for the widow, he decided to honor her request.

"Very well, Mrs. Trevor, I'll take you. But first you must promise that if we don't find the captain's body on the battlefield, you'll return home without a fuss."

"I promise," Aimee said, having no intention of keeping her word. Once in Jonesboro, she wouldn't be content until she found Nick alive or had definite proof of his death. Even if she had to go to Atlanta, she'd learn what happened to the man who had stolen her heart without her realizing it. Intuition told her that Nick was alive and needed her. Other than that, she couldn't explain the urgent need that drove her to attempt such a dangerous journey.

They left early the next morning. It wasn't a long trip. Tall Oaks was actually closer to Jonesboro than to Atlanta, but traveling by wagon was considerably slower than by horseback. If a wagon weren't necessary to transport Nick back to Tall Oaks should they locate him, she would have insisted on the faster mode of travel. And to her credit, Aimee never considered the possibility that Nick was dead. It was late afternoon when they reached Jonesboro.

"Shall we go to the field hospital first, Mrs. Trevor?" Jones asked as they approached the juncture of the railroads where the battle was fought.

"No, take me to the battlefield," Aimee answered without hesitation.

They had arrived too late. Most of the Federal wounded had already been gathered by medical orderlies and taken to the hospital. Only a few wounded remained amid the many Reb and Federal casualties. The stench was appalling, but Aimee was undaunted, merely covering her nose with her handkerchief and proceeding forward. She walked among the dead, forcing herself to look into their bloated faces, asking Sergeant Jones to turn over a man when she couldn't see his face. She thought of all the mothers who would never see their sons again, and sweethearts waiting for lovers who would never return from war.

As an eerie dusk settled over the ravaged land, Sergeant Jones suggested they leave.

"Maybe he was brought to the field hospital after I left," he said hopefully. "It's getting dark; there's nowhere else to look out here."

Aimee stared around her, seeing the carnage, the destruction, and fearing Jones was right. They had been searching for hours, and Nick wasn't among the dead. "Very well," she acquiesced wearily. "Take me to the hospital; we'll continue to look there."

A thorough search of the field hospital proved just as fruitless. Nick wasn't among the wounded, nor was there any record of him having been brought in with the dead.

"Shall we return home now, Mrs. Trevor?"

Aimee couldn't say yes. Something deep inside her refused to surrender to the inevitable. "No, not yet. Please, Sergeant Jones, take me back to the battlefield. I have a feeling that Nick is alive and needs me."

Jones shook his head. "For a Reb, you sure have a strange way of showing your hatred for the enemy." He recalled hearing Aimee say she hated Nick on more than one occasion.

"I—I don't hate Nick," Aimee said in a strangled voice. "You—don't understand about us. I don't even understand myself. I just know that I have to keep looking."

Aimee looked so distraught, Jones didn't have

the heart to deny her. "We've still an hour or two before dark. But if we find nothing by then, we're going back to Tall Oaks."

Aimee nodded miserably.

She felt like a scavenger as she and Jones walked among the dead again. She peered closely into faces stiffened by death, and vomited into the dirt time and again from the sight of maimed bodies and blank eyes. She prayed constantly even though these men were already in the hands of God. They encountered an orderly with a pair of stretcher bearers and learned little beyond the fact that nearly all the wounded had already been carried to the field hospital.

"We've inspected every body left on the battlefield, Mrs. Trevor." Jones's voice was filled with pity.

Unable to talk, Aimee merely nodded. Admitting defeat was the most difficult thing she had ever done. Resolutely she turned to follow Jones from the battlefield. Abruptly she stopped, her eyes mysteriously drawn to the forest a short distance beyond the railroad tracks.

"Sergeant Jones, wait. Has anyone searched the woods?"

Jones spun around to stare at her. "It's unlikely any men, either dead or wounded, remain in the forest."

"Unlikely but not impossible," Aimee persisted.

"I reckon not," Jones grumbled, "if you put it that way." That's all Aimee needed to hear. "Where are you going, Mrs. Trevor?"

"Call it intuition, call it foolishness," Aimee threw over her shoulder, "but I'm not leaving here until I search the woods."

Jones raced to catch up with her. "You promised, Mrs. Trevor. Why torture yourself? It's nearly too dark to see, let alone search for bodies. Why can't you accept it that Captain Drummond is dead?"

"Because he's not!" Aimee said, turning on him ferociously. "Go back if you wish, but I'm remaining until I've searched the woods."

"Deliver me from stubborn females," Jones muttered to himself as he followed Aimee into the dense cover of trees. "I've heard love makes people daft, and now I know it's true."

Nothing Jones said could dissuade Aimee from venturing deeper into the woods. Neither darkness, the threat of unknown danger, nor Sergeant Jones's dire predictions called a halt to her frantic search through the forest. Exhaustion finally forced her to leave—and Jones's threat to pick her up and carry her back to the wagon.

If anyone had asked her later, Aimee couldn't have said what had made her turn to the right and stumble into a small clearing. She saw Scout first, his muzzle lowered, calmly grazing on the succulent grass that grew in abundance. As if recognizing her, he raised his head and snorted in welcome. Aimee opened her mouth and shouted Jones's name.

Assuming Aimee was close behind him, Jones spun on his heel. He was shocked to find her nowhere in sight. "Where are you?"

"I'm in a small clearing to the right of you. Come quickly!" He was beside her almost instantly.

"What is it?"

"Isn't that Scout?"

Due to the encroaching darkness, it was difficult to tell, but Jones was nearly certain the stallion belonged to his captain. "Looks like him, right enough."

"If Scout is here, then Nick can't be far away."

For the first time since Aimee had insisted upon this ill-fated search, Jones became excited. Thank God she had insisted upon not giving up. They both began a search of the clearing, scrabbling on the ground so as not to miss a single clue. They found him at the far edge, partially concealed by a bush. He looked dead.

"No!" Aimee screamed when she saw the ominous blotch of blood congealing on the ground beneath him.

"He's still alive, Mrs. Trevor," Jones said in a voice that held little hope for his survival. He carefully peeled open the flaps of Nick's jacket, wincing at the grievous wound in the center of his chest. "If he isn't seen to immediately, he'll die."

"Can we take him to Tall Oaks?"

"No time," Jones grunted. "The field hospital is closer. Can you hold him on Scout if I lift him up before you in the saddle?"

Aimee nodded, unable to speak. Her mouth went dry with fear. What if she had given up when Sergeant Jones insisted they leave? Nick would surely have died out here all by himself with no one to help him. Scout made no objection when Jones lifted her aboard his broad back. Then he pranced impatiently, seeming to understand the gravity of the situation as Jones carefully lifted Nick and sat him in the saddle before Aimee. It was all Aimee could do to hold his limp body in place. Still unconscious, he moaned once, then fell silent.

Grasping the reins, Jones led Scout out of the forest. When they reached the wagon, he removed Nick from Aimee's arms and lay him down in the wagon bed. Aimee scrambled up beside him, holding his hand and whispering that she wouldn't allow him to die, that she had something important to tell him concerning Brand.

The field hospital was in chaos. Not only were the wounded from Jonesboro being treated in the makeshift arena, but those from around Atlanta as well. The wounded, both Federal and Confederate, lay in rows outside the operating tent waiting to be treated in order of the seriousness of their wounds. Those with no hope for survival were set apart and made as comfortable as possible until the end. Jones summoned an overworked orderly while Aimee sat in the wagon holding Nick. Jones held a lantern high in the air as the orderly examined Nick. Aimee was so distraught, she didn't see the look the two men exchanged over her head.

"Take him over there, Sergeant," the orderly directed. He pointed to a group of wounded lying apart from the others. "He'll be made comfortable until . . ." His words fell off.

Suddenly Aimee seemed to come alive. "He needs help immediately! Can't you see how serious his wound is? I demand that a doctor treat him immediately."

"The doctors are working as fast as they can, ma'am," the orderly said kindly. "There are other men just as seriously wounded as the captain."

"I don't care about other men; it's Nick I'm concerned with. Don't you understand? He'll die without immediate attention."

"Mrs. Trevor, I think what the orderly is trying to say is that it may already be too late for the captain."

Aimee sent him a look so filled with venom, he drew back. "What kind of place is this? I thought doctors saved lives. There's a wounded man here; now, save him."

"What's the trouble out here?"

"Sorry, Major Bellows, but this lady is insisting you treat this wounded man before the others."

"Are you the doctor?" Aimee asked, ready to do battle with anyone in order to get help for Nick.

"I am."

"I brought a man who desperately needs your help. We found him in the woods. If you don't treat him immediately, it will be too late."

"See here, young lady, the orderly decides in which order the men will be seen. You'll have to abide by his wishes. But if it will ease your mind, I'll have a look at him." He climbed into the wagon, made a cursory examination, and came to the same conclusion the orderly had. His face was sad as he said, "There are men whose chances of survival are far greater. It's those men I must concentrate on. I'm sorry."

"Are you God?" Aimee cried, utterly shattered by the doctor's words. "I won't allow it!"

Her next move so startled the three men bending over Nick's nearly lifeless body that they seemed to react in slow motion. Her face was set in grim lines as she grabbed Jones's gun from his holster and pointed it at the doctor. "I can play God, too."

"Mrs. Trevor, put the gun down." This came from Jones, who felt responsible for this shameful display.

"Not until the doctor treats Nick." She waved the gun from side to side, her finger poised on the trigger. "I've used a gun before, you know."

Aimee was so distraught that each man thought her perfectly capable of firing. Owing to the darkness and state of upheaval around them, no one noticed the desperate scene being played inside the wagon bed. Suddenly the doctor came to a decision. Arguing with a maniacal woman wasn't saving lives, and there were still many to save this night.

"Carry him inside."

"Are you sure, Doctor?" the orderly asked.

The doctor nodded brusquely and leaped from the wagon. Aimee followed, the gun, hidden in the folds of her skirt, still trained on him. But the doctor, having already made up his mind to treat Nick, paid little heed. He was all business now, snapping orders to his assistants while they readied the operating table for yet another patient. Besides, if he had a woman as concerned for him as this woman appeared to be about the wounded captain, he'd consider himself lucky. Few men were blessed with the kind of selfless love exhibited by the beautiful woman who was willing to kill to see her man cared for.

Standing at the rear of the operating tent, Aimee observed the operation from a distance that allowed her to keep tabs on the proceedings without actually witnessing the doctor's skilled hands probing Nick's torn flesh. The operation seemed to go on forever. At one point Sergeant Jones entered the tent and removed the gun from her limp fingers. He urged her to accompany him outside for a brief respite, but she refused. If Nick was in danger of dying, she wanted to know.

Two hours later, the doctor stepped back and glanced over at Aimee for the first time since he began the operation. "It's done; he's in God's hands now."

"How serious is it?"

"There was considerable damage to the lungs. The bullet tore a hole the size of a walnut in fragile tissue. I removed the bullet and repaired everything that was damaged. He may live if he doesn't die from infection. It's difficult to keep a wound as grievous as this sterile in the crude conditions of a field hospital. Of course, he'll be sent North to recuperate if he survives the next several days."

Aimee moved then to Nick's side. He looked pale as death and so still, she feared he had expired while the doctor spoke. The doctor noted her worried look and tried to reassure her.

"He's not dead, just pale from loss of blood. Is the captain your husband?"

Aimee considered her answer carefully. "Captain Drummond is the father of my son."

There was no time to question her further, for already Nick was being carried out of the operating tent and replaced by another wounded man. Aimee turned and followed the stretcher. Sergeant Jones fell into step behind her.

"I've found a place for you to sleep, Mrs. Trevor. One of the orderlies offered his tent since he'll be on duty tonight."

"I'm staying with Nick."

"You're too exhausted to be of any help tonight." Did the woman never take anyone's advice? Jones wondered. No wonder she clashed wills with his captain constantly.

"Nevertheless, I'm staying with Nick."

Jones sighed and ended the argument. She may not be tired enough to sleep, but he certainly was.

Aimee sat the night beside Nick's cot in a large tent containing several other wounded men. Only one orderly was on duty, and he welcomed her assistance. Not only was she on hand should Nick need her, but she answered more than one sick man who cried out in the night for water or just plain comfort. Nick regained consciousness just once during those long hours, and she was beside him instantly, offering water. When he opened his eyes and saw her, his eyes cleared for a brief moment.

"Aimee? Where am I?"

"In a hospital, Nick. You were wounded at Jonesboro."

His brow furrowed in painful concentration. "Scout. The last thing I recalled was Scout dragging me into the forest."

"So that's how you got there. Sergeant Jones and I found you the next day."

"I don't understand. What are you . . ." The effort was too great for his fragile condition. His thought was disrupted and he drifted back into the dark, fuzzy void of unconsciousness.

Aimee hovered over him, wringing her hands. "Oh, Nick, please don't die."

Suddenly he opened his eyes again and whispered, "Don't leave me."

Chapter 12

Nick clung to life with a tenacity that amazed even the doctor. Dr. Bellows felt strongly that Nick's will to live was due entirely to the lovely blonde who showered him with tender care. Aimee rarely left Nick's side. Sergeant Jones had returned to duty, leaving her virtually friendless in the Federal field hospital. But her compassion for both Yankee and Confederate soldiers being treated for wounds by Union doctors soon earned her their respect. To Nick she was his guardian angel, beside him during his brief lucid moments, comforting him when pain took his senses from him.

Dr. Bellows couldn't help but be impressed by the young widow's obvious devotion to the Yank captain. By now he had learned most of Aimee's history from Sergeant Jones before he had left. And though Jones's knowledge was far from complete, it was enough for Bellows to know that no woman would devote herself so selflessly to a man unless she loved him. Thus when Aimee asked if it was possible to take Nick back to Tall Oaks, where she could care for him in the comfort of her own home, Bellows readily agreed.

"I think he can travel if you take it easy, Mrs. Trevor," Major Bellows said. "Captain Drummond is still grievously ill, but as you can see, we are overcrowded here and it's unlikely to improve. Besides, I'm not certain he would survive if we ship him north at this time."

"What about Lieutenant Dill? Did Sergeant Jones tell you he's at Tall Oaks right now recuperating from a wound?"

"He told me. He said Tall Oaks isn't all that far from the field hospital. Before long we'll be moving to Atlanta to a more permanent facility. When we do, I'll send someone after both Lieutenant Dill and Captain Drummond. Meanwhile, when I send my report to headquarters, I'll mention that both men have been wounded and are recovering at Tall Oaks plantation."

"Thank you, Doctor; you won't regret this," Aimee said gratefully. "I left my son at Tall Oaks over a week ago, and I'm sure he's growing anxious."

"Can you handle the wagon by yourself?"

"I can manage," Aimee assured him.

"Then if Captain Drummond fares well today, you can leave tomorrow. I may be extending my authority in this, but I feel it's in the captain's best interest to allow him to go with you. Don't prove me wrong, Mrs. Trevor. You did say Drummond is the father of your son, didn't you?"

Aimee flushed a dull red. "It's a long story, but I didn't lie. I have a five-year-old son fathered by Captain Drummond. He'll come to no harm at my hands."

Bellows nodded, satisfied. "I'll send along medicines necessary to his treatment. Do you have sufficient food at Tall Oaks?"

Aimee hated to admit that food was scarce for fear the good doctor wouldn't allow her to take Nick home with her, but she realized she couldn't lie about something as important as nourishment for Nick. "There is little left at Tall Oaks but for the end of summer's bounty from our small garden."

"I'll send along what I can spare, but it won't be much. But then, I doubt the captain will be with you long. As soon as a proper hospital is established in Atlanta, I'm certain headquarters will send someone after both officers."

Later that day when Nick awoke and looked at her with more clarity than he had in days, Aimee tried to explain what she intended to do.

"I'm taking you to Tall Oaks, Nick. It's quieter there and more conducive to your recovery. I need to get back to Brand, but I didn't want to leave you here."

"Is—this all right with the doctor?" His voice was raspy from weakness, but he appeared to understand what she was saying.

"I have his permission. You're still very ill, but I'm certain I can care for you at Tall Oaks as well or better than the overworked orderlies can tend you here."

"I—trust you," Nick said. Then he slid back into a stupor, his meager strength taxed by the brief conversation.

Nick wasn't entirely lucid when he was carefully loaded into the wagon early the next morning. Under Aimee's supervision he was placed on a straw mat in the wagon bed and covered with blankets for the trip. A small amount of fresh meat and staples were packed around him before Aimee climbed onto the driver's bench. Dr. Bellows handed her a packet of medicine and a letter of permission allowing her safe passage to Tall Oaks. Then she slapped the reins against the horse's rump and left the stench and horror of the field hospital behind.

Aimee kept the pace deliberately slow, ever aware that each bump in the rutted road added to Nick's already considerable pain. The sun beat down relentlessly. Although it was September, the Georgia clime had not yet accepted the fact that summer was spent. She stopped frequently to offer Nick water and medicine. They were only three miles from home when she crossed the path of a Federal patrol. She recognized the captain in charge immediately. It was the same man who had helped Nick rescue her from the Confederate deserters.

"Mrs. Trevor, I hadn't expected to meet you again so soon. Who do you have in the wagon bed this time?"

"A friend of yours," Aimee said. "Nick was seriously wounded at Jonesboro. I have permission to bring him back to Tall Oaks to recover."

Captain Birch's heart lurched as he rode back to peer at the wounded man reclining in the wagon bed. "By God, it's Nick Drummond! How serious is it? He doesn't appear to be conscious."

"He has a long way to go, but Dr. Bellows seems to think Nick will recover. The doctor gave me written permission to take Nick to Tall Oaks until a permanent hospital could be established at Atlanta." She handed him the pass.

"Everything seems to be in order," Birch said as he looked over the pass. "I don't think we've been properly introduced, Mrs. Trevor. I'm Bruce Birch. Nick and I have been friends for many years. I'm glad I was able to help him rescue you from those deserters a while back."

"No, Captain, I'm the one who's grateful. If everything is in order, I'll be on my way. I haven't seen my son in over a week."

"Bruce, is that you?"

Nick opened his eyes, recognizing his friend immediately.

"Didn't anyone ever teach you how to dodge a bullet?" Birch joked. Nick looked so pale, it alarmed him.

"It happens to the best of us," Nick said, attempting a weak smile but failing.

"You're in good hands, Nick." He glanced significantly at Aimee. "The next time I see you, you'll be back in the thick of things."

"Not anytime soon," Nick allowed, "but I'd rather be at Tall Oaks than anyplace in the world." The brief conversation had drained him utterly and he closed his eyes.

"Best be on your way, Mrs. Trevor," Birch said, eyeing Nick worriedly. "We'll give you escort to Tall Oaks."

It was dusk when they drove beneath the stately oaks leading to the house. Brand flew out the door to meet them. Savannah was hard on his heels.

"Mama! We were so worried about you."

"De chile's right, honey, we were powerful worried. Did you find Captain Drummond?" She eyed the Yank patrol accompanying Aimee with misgiving. "What's dem Yanks doin' here?"

"Nick is in back of the wagon," Aimee said, sliding down from the driver's bench and gathering Brand in her arms. "He was seriously wounded at Jonesboro, and I brought him back to Tall Oaks to recover. Captain Birch and his men gave me escort."

"Is he going to die, Mama?" Brand's distress tore at Aimee's heart.

"Not if I can help it, darling." She turned to Captain Birch. "Can your men carry Nick upstairs and put him to bed? I fear it's beyond our capabilities."

"Of course." Within minutes Nick was eased out of the wagon and carried upstairs to the room he had occupied previously.

Hearing the commotion, Lieutenant Dill appeared in the doorway of his room, leaning heavily against the jamb to steady himself. Seeing Nick, he cried, "He's alive!"

Startled to find another wounded Union officer in residence, Captain Birch went immediately to Dill and helped him back into bed. "What are you doing here, Lieutenant?"

"I was brought here after I fell in battle," Dill said, easing his throbbing thigh into a more comfortable position. "I fell at Jonesboro, and when I saw the deplorable conditions at the field hospital, I realized it would be hours before I could be treated. The threat of gangrene frightened me, so I ordered Sergeant Jones to take me to Tall Oaks. Mrs. Trevor and her woman removed the bullet from my thigh, and so far there have been no complications."

"I'll report the fact that both you and Captain Drummond are recovering from wounds at Tall

Oaks," Birch informed him. "We're on our way to Atlanta now."

Birch spoke briefly with Aimee before he left. "I realize this is highly irregular, Mrs. Trevor, but both Nick and the Lieutenant seem satisfied with their treatment, so I'll not complain."

"You and your men are welcome to camp on my property if you'd like," Aimee offered.

"We're due back in Atlanta tonight, so I dare not linger. I'll report the whereabouts of both officers to officials in Atlanta, and the fact that they are receiving adequate care."

"I believe Dr. Bellows mentioned that he intended to report to headquarters concerning Nick and Lieutenant Dill."

"Then I'll be on my way." He paused, then added, "Take good care of Nick. He's a good friend; I'd hate to lose him."

"He's more than a friend to me, Captain; we won't lose him."

During the following days, Brand hovered at Nick's bedside, unwilling to leave in case Nick died while he was absent. Aimee tried to reassure the child that Nick was in no danger of dying, a fact she wasn't herself certain of, but Brand stubbornly refused to leave Nick's bedside.

Nick rallied for brief intervals during this time, comforted to find both Aimee and Brand hovering nearby whenever he opened his eyes. His thoughts were still confused and disorganized, but he did know that Aimee couldn't hate him and still tend him with such loving care. Nor would she have insisted on bringing him back to Tall Oaks to care for him instead of leaving him in the field hospital in danger of dying from infection or lack of care. But

what truly amazed him was the fact that she had
risked danger and even death to go to Jonesboro
to find him. If only he could persuade her to admit Brand was his son.

Aimee thought long and hard about telling Nick
he was Brand's father. Despite the fact that she
had vowed to tell him the truth once he was well
enough to hear it, she still hesitated. She couldn't
help but recall his words before he left. He already
suspected that he had fathered Brand, and told her
he expected to raise his son if his suspicions
should prove correct. Where did that leave her?

Nearly losing Nick had been the catalyst that
jolted Aimee's heart into admitting she loved him.
Losing him forever had been so painful a thought,
she had risked her life to go to Jonesboro to find
him. And when she found him, after refusing to
give up and return to Tall Oaks, she couldn't leave
him to die with the rest of the hopeless cases
deemed too serious to treat. She knew she had
taken a risk pulling a gun on the poor overworked
doctor, but she had to make the doctor take her seriously.

Fortunately Major Bellows was a compassionate
man who didn't insist she be thrown in prison for
daring to play God with his patients. Convincing
him to allow her to bring Nick back to Tall Oaks
hadn't been all that difficult once she pointed out
that she could give him better care than the overworked orderlies in the field hospital. She had no
idea how long she would be allowed to keep him
at Tall Oaks, but even a few days could mean the
difference between life and death.

Several days after Aimee had brought Nick to
Tall Oaks, he awoke and was completely lucid for

the first time. He knew exactly where he was and had brief recollections of falling at Jonesboro, being carried to the field hospital, and being cared for by Aimee. He even recalled the trip to Tall Oaks in the back of the wagon and the appearance of Captain Bruce Birch.

Brilliant sunlight poured through the window, and Nick blinked repeatedly against the intrusion. He glanced around the room, looking for Aimee, and saw Brand's serious little face staring down at him. The expression was so like his own that his breath caught painfully in his throat. It suddenly came to Nick that this wasn't the first time he had awakened to find Brand staring at him. He tried to smile but ended up grimacing in pain. Suddenly Brand turned and fled from the room. Within minutes he was back, tugging Aimee by the hand.

"See, Mama," he crowed delightedly. "I told you Captain Drummond was awake."

"How are you feeling, Nick?" There was so much Aimee wanted to say, but she could think of little beyond the fact that he appeared in complete control of his faculties for the first time since he'd been wounded.

"Like I've been to hell and back." His voice was thin and raspy, as if he hadn't used it for a long time. "How long have I been here?"

"Nearly a week. This is the first time you've given any indication that you were aware of your surroundings. Are you hungry?"

"Famished."

Another good sign, Aimee thought jubilantly. "Savannah has some broth simmering on the stove. Doctor Bellows was good enough to send some provisions home with us." She turned to

Brand. "Tell Savannah to bring up the broth while I change the dressing on Nick's wound." He scooted off without complaint.

"Aimee, I—I don't know how to thank you. If not for you, I'd be dead by now."

He looked at her closely, then seeing the purple shadows beneath her eyes and the tired lines around her mouth, he realized he owed her more than just his life. "How did you get the doctor to treat me so fast? I know how field hospitals work. Those whose chances for survival are good are treated first; the hopeless cases are left until the last. I knew from the beginning my wound was serious."

Aimee's face turned a dull red. "Lie still while I change your bandage."

He stopped her with a hand on her wrist. "Aimee, I asked you a question. What did you do to get the doctor to treat me so swiftly?"

"I did what I had to do, Nick. You would have died if you weren't treated immediately. The bullet struck you in the chest and tore your lung. If Dr. Bellows hadn't operated immediately, you wouldn't have lived, so I—I held a gun on him until he agreed to treat you before any of the others. Then I stood inside the operating tent and watched while he performed surgery."

"My God, you did that? I'm surprised he didn't order you disarmed and thrown in jail."

"Dr. Bellows is a compassionate man, Nick. I think he realized that I was desperate."

Nick searched her face. "Were you, Aimee? Were you desperate?"

Aimee dropped her eyes. "More than you know."

He smiled then, a real smile, not just a hollow motion. But Aimee saw that this conversation had cost him energy. His face was gray and drawn, and Aimee placed a finger against his lips, cautioning him to conserve his strength for eating. As if on cue, Savannah came into the room carrying a bowl of steaming broth. Brand was close on her heels. The child sat quietly and watched while Aimee changed the dressing on Nick's chest, then spooned broth into his mouth. When Nick ate as much as he could hold, Aimee herded Brand from the room so Nick could rest.

"No," Nick protested, "let him stay. His presence comforts me."

"I'll be quiet, Mama," Brand promised as he climbed into the chair Aimee had vacated and settled back.

But Nick wasn't ready yet to go to sleep. He preferred to talk to Brand. The child's youthful voice gave him the will he needed to get well. When the bullet had struck him down, he feared he'd never see Brand or Aimee again.

"You don't have to sit with me, Brand. It must be difficult for an active youngster like yourself to sit still for so long."

"I don't mind, sir," Brand insisted. "I'm used to it now. I sit here every day when Mama and Savannah are busy."

"You don't need to call me 'sir,' Brand. For the time being just call me Nick. Later . . ." His sentence fell off. He couldn't discuss "later" until he had spoken with Aimee and convinced her to tell him the truth about Brand. She was the only one who knew for sure who had fathered Brand.

"Were you going to say something—Nick?"

"It will have to wait, Brand. I think your mother is right, I am tired."

When Nick woke up again, Lieutenant Dill was occupying the chair where Brand had perched. Nick was more than a little startled to see him. "What in God's name are you doing here?" he asked.

Dill smiled. "Same as you. I fell at Jonesboro and had Sergeant Jones bring me here."

"I had no idea Aimee was nursing two invalids." His admiration for her escalated by leaps and bounds. Not that he wasn't already utterly besotted by her. "Thank God your wound isn't serious."

"I fully expect to join the war again soon, if it isn't over before I return. Have you heard? Atlanta has fallen and Sherman has vowed to march to the sea. The end is in sight."

"No, I didn't know. I fell before I learned what happened in Atlanta."

"I doubt you'll have to worry about the war, Captain. Your wound is serious; you'll be shipped north to recuperate. Captain Birch said he would inform headquarters that we are at Tall Oaks, and I assume someone will come for us soon."

Dill left shortly afterward, shooed away by Aimee, who had cautioned him about remaining overlong and tiring Nick.

The sun playing hide-and-seek through the leaves of the huge oak tree on the front lawn made dappled shadows on the porch steps. Nick sat in a dilapidated rocker on the wide veranda, enjoying the fresh air and waning days of summer. A week had slipped past since Nick opened his eyes and was welcomed back to the world by Aimee and Brand. Since then his slow but steady progress had heartened Aimee. He was able now to descend the stairs with her help and walk to the porch. He was still weak and would require many weeks of rest and care for his lung to heal properly, but he was well on his way to a full recovery.

Aimee appeared on the porch, and Nick smiled at her. "Sit beside me."

"I'd think you'd be tired of seeing so much of me," Aimee teased.

"Never. Aimee, I'll always be grateful to you."

"There's no need, Nick; I couldn't let you die. No more than I could turn Lieutenant Dill away when he needed help."

"If I didn't know better, I'd think you no longer hated me."

Aimee grew quiet. Her voice was barely audible when she said, "I never hated you, though Lord knows I tried."

"You could have fooled me. I wasn't exactly endearing. I hope you believed me when I told you I never realized you were a virgin that first time I took you aboard the *Dixie Belle*. And I did try to look for you afterward, but you had disappeared from the face of the earth. I truly believe it was fate that brought us together again."

"I—I've forgiven you for that night on the *Dixie Belle*."

"And for taking you against your will during the time I was at Tall Oaks? I wanted you fiercely, sweetheart. So fiercely I made you believe I'd send you to prison if you didn't let me make love to you."

"I hated you for that."

"Is that why you ran away from Tall Oaks?"

"That's one of the reasons. But nevertheless, I enjoyed making love with you. But in truth, I really don't hate you. I still don't like the idea that you are a Yankee, but I can no longer find it in my heart to hate you."

"What *do* you feel for me, Aimee?"

Aimee wasn't ready to admit yet what was truly in her heart. She had to be certain first how Nick intended to use the information. If he was fishing for an admission that Brand was his son, he'd have to wait until he proved he wasn't interested in taking Brand from her.

"You know I care for you—otherwise I wouldn't have gone to such lengths to find you on the battlefield."

"You care for your pet, or a friend. I hoped for more than that."

"I'm sorry, Nick, I—I'm not prepared yet to give you more than that."

"I don't believe you, Aimee, but for now I won't press you. What I truly want is for you to tell me the truth about Brand. By now you must surely realize that I have reason to suspect he's my son, conceived that night aboard the *Dixie Belle.*"

Conflicting emotions warred inside Aimee. She wanted to blurt out the truth, to admit that Nick was Brand's father, but the burden of not knowing how Nick would use that information was too great. For now it was enough that she considered telling him in the near future.

"Nick, I—" Her words were cut off when Brand came running from the house and perched beside Nick's chair.

"How are you feeling, Nick?" he asked cheerfully.

"Better, now that you're here," Nick replied, meaning every word. A bond had been established between him and Brand. A bond that would never have been severed no matter whose son Brand was. Couldn't Aimee understand that? But if Brand was his son, he wanted to be responsible for him, provide for him, raise him to be a Drummond.

"I'll leave you two," Aimee said, grateful to be relieved of answering Nick's query. One day she'd be ready to admit the truth, but not yet, not before she had Nick's promise that he wouldn't take Brand from her.

Aimee's biggest worry during the following days was the swift depletion of provisions. The flow of Confederate soldiers stopping at Tall Oaks had ceased, but Aimee had generously shared their food until little remained. The supplies that Dr. Bellows had sent home with her were nearly gone, and she wondered how she would feed Nick, Brand, and Lieutenant Dill.

Dill took some of the burden from her when he proclaimed himself well enough to rejoin the war. Three weeks after he had been brought to Tall Oaks suffering from a bullet wound, he left for Atlanta. He still limped somewhat, but the wound had healed sufficiently for him to ride.

Unfortunately his leaving did little to alleviate the shortage of food. Aimee and Savannah barely touched what they prepared, leaving most of it for Brand and Nick. Nick made amazing progress. He was now able to walk completely around the house before shortness of breath forced him back to bed. Finally one night, he asked Aimee to sleep in the bed beside him, but she promptly refused.

"Nick! You can't believe you're well enough for—that!"

"I merely want you beside me, sweetheart. Is that asking too much?"

"Much too much," Aimee said adamantly.

"Please, Aimee, I'll rest much easier with you beside me. Besides, we have no idea when someone will come to take me to Atlanta."

That was true. Aimee was surprised no one had showed up yet to escort Nick to a hospital in Atlanta. For him the war was all but over, and they both knew it. Once in Atlanta, he would be promptly shipped north to recuperate. That might well mean they would never see each other again. It was that thought that finally made her give in to his demand.

Careful of his wound, Aimee slipped into bed beside him. Brand was already asleep, and Savannah had merely stared at her in disapproval when she told the former slave she would be spending the night with Nick. To make certain Brand wouldn't burst in on them in the morning, Aimee carefully latched the door to Nick's room. Nick's arms went around her immediately. It felt wonderful. She snuggled down comfortably, perfectly satisfied to spend the night in companionable closeness. She closed her eyes, willing her body into slumber. She was nearly asleep when she felt Nick's hand stroking her breasts.

Her eyes flew open and she flipped over to look at him. "Nick, you're in no condition for this."

"I'm not going to do anything, sweetheart," he promised. Concealed by the darkness, the green devil in his eyes danced with wicked delight. Satisfied, Aimee settled back down. When Nick's hand slid down to her stomach, she quivered in anticipation of his next move. She knew she would never allow him to make love to her, but it had been so long since she had felt his hands on her that she savored the caress.

"Take off your nightgown, sweetheart; I want to feel you naked next to me."

"I don't—"

Even as she spoke, he inched the nightgown upward over her breasts and held it there until she raised her arms so that he could lift it off. "There, that's better. I wish you'd left the lamp burning." As it was, he had to be satisfied with the pale moonbeams bathing her body in shades of silver and gold.

When his hand slid down between her thighs, Aimee gasped and said, "What are you doing?"

"I know I can't love you properly, but I'm still capable of giving you pleasure."

"No, Nick, it's not necessary; my pleasure can wait until you are well."

"Let me do this for you, sweetheart." His finger eased inside her, and her protest was lost as he carefully raised himself above her and kissed her hungrily. "I've wanted to kiss you ever since I opened my eyes and saw you bending over me in the field hospital."

He kissed the damp corners of her mouth, her ears, her chin, the sensitive hollow of her throat. Though he hadn't his usual stamina, he still had the power to turn her insides to mush.

"You'll hurt yourself," Aimee said, fearing he'd do himself irreparable damage.

"Don't fret over me; just lie back and let me love you. There are many ways to love a woman, and I promise this won't hurt me in the least."

His mouth continued downward to the tips of her breasts. Taking the throbbing peaks in his mouth, he suckled her as he were a babe, taking great pleasure in her response. Another finger slid inside her while his thumb massaged the tiny bud of femininity nestled within tender folds of moist flesh.

"Nick!"

"Do you like that, sweetheart? Don't hold back; enjoy what I can do for you."

"But you—"

"Don't worry about me; it makes me happy to give you pleasure."

His fingers slid deeper, stretching her as he worked them inside her. He felt her wetness against his fingers as they slid effortlessly in and out. The rhythm of his thumb and thrust of his fingers drove her higher and higher, until she was gasping for breath, until stars filled the room and she soared to reach them, until she shattered into a million pieces and cried out with the force of her climax. Nick didn't remove his fingers until she lay quiescent beneath his stroking.

"Go to sleep, sweetheart. Dream of the day I'll join you in that world where I've just taken you. Maybe one day soon you'll learn I mean you no harm, and tell me the truth about Brand."

His words fell uselessly into the darkness. Aimee was already asleep.

Chapter 13

⌒◯⌒

Two days later, visitors arrived at Tall Oaks. It was midafternoon. Nick and Brand were both napping. Aimee was in the garden scrabbling in the dirt for the last of the potatoes and beets, and Savannah was in the kitchen lamenting the lack of fresh meat. She had shot a rabbit yesterday, but it was small and had already been consumed. Today's dinner was to be a meatless stew of whatever vegetables Aimee was able to scrounge from the garden. If they had money, Savannah thought glumly, she could hitch the old swayback horse to the wagon and ride to Atlanta. But chances were food wasn't any more obtainable in the city than here at Tall Oaks, with or without money.

Savannah heard the riders first. She rushed to the back door, warning Aimee. Grabbing the shotgun and handgun kept always in readiness, Savannah joined Aimee, and together they walked around to the front. About a dozen mounted men rode down the driveway. They wore blue uniforms. Aimee watched in dread as they halted a few feet away. No officer was among them, the highest-ranking man being a sergeant. Were they sent to fetch Nick? she wondered, somehow doubting it. If they had been sent from Atlanta, they should have known Nick couldn't have ridden a horse after sustaining such a serious wound.

"Are you the owner of this here plantation?" the sergeant asked. He stared down at her from the height of his mount, eyes narrowed, grinning at her with slow relish. Aimee cringed at the way he was undressing her with his eyes.

"I'm Mrs. Trevor," Aimee said. "What is it you want?"

"We've orders to burn everything left standing. I reckon that includes this here house. You have five minutes to get your family out."

"No, wait!" Aimee cried. "You can't do that. There's a Union officer upstairs recovering from a serious wound."

He hacked and spat with a crudeness that disgusted Aimee. "You expect me to believe that?" He turned to his men ranged behind him. "All right, boys, hop to it."

The men dismounted. One produced torches from a canvas bag while another lit them with a sulfur match. "You've been warned, lady; you'd best get your family out of the house."

Her eyes blazing defiance, Aimee raised the shotgun while Savannah took aim with the pistol. "Move and you're dead. There's a small child inside the house, and one of your own captains. No one is going to fire Tall Oaks."

The sergeant grinned malevolently. "Says who? Maybe we'll have a little fun with you after we're through since you're so disagreeable." Then he lunged, catching the shotgun by the barrel and shoving it aside. It discharged harmlessly into the air. Savannah suffered the same fate. But Aimee's shot succeeded in awakening Nick.

"Maybe we'll have fun first and fire the house later," the sergeant said as he grasped Aimee and held her immobile against him. The feel of her soft body prompted another more urgent need. Several of his men nodded avid agreement.

"Don't touch dat chile!" Savannah shouted as she struggled with her captor. She was rewarded with a clout to the head that knocked her senseless.

"Savannah!" Aimee was terrified when Savannah fell to the ground. Even if Nick had been awakened by the commotion, what could one man do against so many?

"She ain't hurt none, lady," the sergeant said. "And neither will you be hurt if you give us what we want. You sure are soft." His huge hands kneaded her breasts, then moved lower to probe her belly.

"Take your filthy hands off her."

A dozen heads turned toward the voice. Nick stood in the doorway, pistol drawn, his expression fierce. Somehow he had put on his uniform, and only Aimee realized what the effort must have cost him.

"Who in the hell are you?"

"Captain Nicholas Drummond, Federal army. Who are you?"

"Sergeant Wayne Purdy, Federal army. How do I know you're telling the truth? You could have stolen the uniform off a dead soldier."

"Unless you want to face a court-martial, I suggest you and your men withdraw. Mrs. Trevor has given succor to wounded Federal officers and doesn't deserve to have her home burned."

"Orders are orders, Captain, if that's what you are. We're to leave nothing standing. Sherman believes that before the war can be won, the spirit of the people must be broken, and that means burning their homes and crops."

"Not this home, Sergeant Purdy. I have orders in my chest upstairs preserving this house from destruction as long as it's occupied by Union troops."

"I don't see no troops," Purdy said sullenly.

"What do you think I am?" Nick returned coolly. His face was drawn and ashen, and Aimee feared he'd collapse before he could persuade the soldiers to leave.

"Aimee," Nick continued. His voice was strong even though she knew his energy must be depleted. "Go upstairs and bring down the orders I mentioned to Sergeant Purdy. They're in my chest in a leather pouch."

Purdy made no objection when Aimee sidled around him and scurried inside the house to do Nick's bidding. The man might doubt Nick's claim, but obviously he had enough sense to look at the proof. Disobeying an officer was no light offense, and harming one was enough to send him before a firing squad.

Aimee returned a few minutes later, having found the pouch with the orders. Nick removed them and handed them to Purdy. "You can read, can't you?" Nick asked disparagingly.

Purdy slid Nick a baleful glance, then frowned in concentration as he perused the orders. Truth to tell, his education was sadly lacking, but he could make out enough words to know that Nick had been telling the truth. Tall Oaks plantation was to be spared the torch. At least as long as troops were still in residence. Whether or not one man constituted a troop was debatable, but Purdy decided not to force the issue.

"If you're really Captain Drummond, I'm sorry for doubting you," Purdy said, not entirely convinced.

It wasn't so much the burning of the plantation, but Purdy sure as hell wanted the woman. He and his men could easily overpower the man claiming to be a Union officer, but it was bound to come out sooner or later that he and his men had harmed an officer. Purdy planned on a career in the army, and one little incident like this could destroy that career. The woman wasn't worth his hide.

Nick leaned against the doorjamb, at the end of his tether. Beads of cold sweat broke out on his forehead, and he fought desperately to conceal the weakness that was slowly draining his body of what little energy remained. Only Aimee recognized Nick's struggle to remain upright and in control. One inkling of weakness and the men confronting him might decide to challenge him.

"I suggest you mount up and ride out," Nick said tightly. "When you return to Atlanta, you can mention my name at headquarters and I'm certain they'll confirm my identity."

"Yeah, well, maybe we made a mistake," Purdy acknowledged, shifting uncomfortably.

"Tell them I'm recovering from my wound as well as can be expected," Nick added for good measure.

The moment they mounted up, Aimee was on her knees beside Savannah, who was just beginning to stir. There was a knot the size of an egg on her forehead, but otherwise she appeared unhurt. Aimee helped her to her feet and steadied her as the men mounted and rode away.

"I'm all right, honey," Savannah said groggily. "Are dey gone?"

"Nick convinced them to leave," Aimee replied. She glanced over at Nick and gasped in alarm. "Nick!"

His head was bowed, the gun held loosely in his fingers, his arm extended downward as if he could no longer bear the weight. His body was slumped against the doorjamb and he was perspiring profusely. "I'm all right, Aimee; just let me rest here a moment." She watched fearfully as he slowly fought for control of his weakened body. She breathed a sigh of relief when, after several moments, he pushed himself away from the doorjamb.

"Let me help you upstairs," she offered, moving to his side. He leaned on her heavily as they slowly made their way upstairs to his room. She helped him off with his uniform and into bed.

"I nearly died when I saw that man's hands on you," Nick said. His voice was low and strident and filled with barely suppressed rage. "You were very brave to challenge so many men."

"It was you who was brave," Aimee observed. "They could have killed you when they saw how weak you were."

"They were Federal soldiers; I seriously doubted they'd challenge an officer."

"But they didn't believe you."

"Forget it, sweetheart, it's over and done with. The men are gone; they won't bother you again as long as I'm here."

"You won't be here forever," Aimee said in a forlorn voice.

"No," Nick agreed, "but I'll come back. There's so much I want to say to you, so many things to ask you. Surely you know how I feel about you."

"Nick, you need your rest. We'll discuss this another time. You're exhausted, and I don't want you to have a relapse; you've come so far."

Aimee needed time to think. She knew what Nick was referring to. He hadn't pressed her about Brand in several days, but she knew he hadn't given up. Perhaps she was being overly cautious, or just plain stubborn. Perhaps the time had arrived to tell him that he was Brand's father. He might suspect the truth, but she was the only one who could confirm it. Though he hadn't actually said he loved her, he had told her many times over that he cared for her. She wondered if Nick cared enough about her to propose marriage once she told him about Brand. And would he do so because he wanted her or because of Brand?

The dilemma wasn't easily solved, but in the end Aimee decided to tell Nick the truth and pray that it all worked out the way she hoped it would. Selecting the right moment presented another problem. Since Nick was still weak from facing the Union soldiers who came to burn Tall Oaks, she thought it best to wait a few days until he was recovered from the ordeal. Perhaps she was just trying to delay the inevitable, but now that she had made her decision, her mind rested easier.

Nick slept the rest of that day and through the

entire night. When he awoke the next day, he seemed much improved and in a good humor. His good spirits were somewhat tempered when Nick took careful note of Aimee's thinness and her fragile appearance. He questioned her closely when she brought up his lunch later that day.

"Are you well, sweetheart?" he asked worriedly. "You look so pale and thin. Are you sure you're eating enough?"

"I'm fine, Nick; you're imagining things."

"Have I been too much trouble for you? Nursing both myself and Lieutenant Dill couldn't have been easy."

Aimee bit her bottom lip and hoped Nick wouldn't realize she had been skipping meals so that he and Brand could have enough to eat. "You haven't been much trouble at all," she insisted.

"Something's wrong." Suddenly his face brightened as a thought occurred to him. "You're not—not breeding, are you? You could be expecting my child."

"No! I mean, I'm not expecting. It's just—" Lord, what could she tell him?

"What, Aimee? You'd better tell me, for I'll find out sooner or later."

Indeed he would, Aimee surmised. One day soon there would be nothing for any of them to eat. "I—I haven't been eating regularly."

"Why not?" Her face turned a dull red, and the answer came to him. "Of course; there isn't enough food left to feed us all! How stupid of me. Do you have any money?"

Aimee shook her head. What little coin they had had been spent long ago.

"Why in the hell didn't you say anything to me?

There's money in my belt. Not a great deal, but enough to buy food. Savannah could go to Atlanta for supplies. Bring me my belt."

Aimee retrieved it from where it hung over a chair and handed it to him. He drew forth a sheaf of bills and placed them in her hands. "I have little use for money; the army provides all that I need right now."

The need for provisions was desperate, and Aimee didn't refuse Nick's generous offer. "Perhaps I ought to go to Atlanta myself."

"No, send Savannah. It's not safe for you in the city alone. I can well imagine the chaos that exists now." Aimee nodded and turned too leave.

"Aimee." His brilliant green eyes regarded her gravely. "Please sleep beside me tonight. I have this strange feeling that I'll be leaving soon."

After a moment's hesitation, Aimee nodded; she harbored the same feeling. Besides, tonight would be a perfect time to tell Nick about Brand. She had waited long enough, and come what may, he should know Brand was his son.

A single lamp burned in the room when Aimee slipped into bed beside Nick. She thought he was sleeping and tried not to awaken him, but his arms slid around her and pulled her close. He was naked beneath the covers.

"I thought you'd be sleeping."

"I was waiting for you."

"I'm here now; you can go to sleep."

"I slept almost all day yesterday and all night last night. Sleep isn't what I crave right now." One hand eased upward to caress her breasts. He stroked her slowly, his hand exploring each curve, his fingers examining every hollow. He rolled her nipples between thumb and forefinger and grinned when they became hard nubs.

"If I suspected you had anything other than sleep in mind, I would have refused your bed. You're still not well enough for what you have in mind."

"I'm going to prove you wrong, sweetheart." He leaned over her, his mouth hard and demanding on hers. There was nothing of the invalid in the force of his kiss. Her mouth opened, her tongue met his, inviting him into her moist heat.

Nick groaned into her mouth. He was definitely in pain, but not from his wound. It had been so long—too damn long—since he'd made love to her. "Touch me, sweetheart. Feel how much I need you."

She could not resist. Her hands splayed across the wide expanse of his chest, savoring the heat and hardness of him. Slowly her hands descended to the taut planes of his belly, over narrow hips, then almost shyly to the strength rising from a forest of crisp curls.

"Oh, God!"

Emboldened by his cry, Aimee grasped his member in her two hands, stroking upward, then down in instinctive rhythm. She kept it up a few moments before Nick grasped her wrists and cried, "Stop!" He had been too long without a woman for that kind of torment. "Take off your nightgown, sweetheart." He helped her pull the threadbare garment over her head and tossed it on the floor.

"I don't want to hurt you." Her voice shook with the need he evoked in her.

"You won't hurt me, not if we do this right."

When his hand slipped down between her thighs, she cried out softly and pressed against his fingers. He found her moist and ready for him.

"Part your legs. That's it. Ahhh, you're so warm and wet. Wider, sweetheart."

She obeyed blindly as his finger slid inside her. Bending over her, he licked the ripe tips of her breasts, then nipped them hard enough for her to cry out. Then he suckled them to soothe away the sharp pleasure-pain. Each tug of his lips seemed connected to that secret place between her legs where Nick's fingers drove her wild with urgent desire.

"Nick, oh please."

"Yes, sweetheart, soon. I want this to be wonderful for you." When the pad of his thumb teased the exquisitely sensitive nub of flesh nestled amid blond curls, the blood roared in her ears.

A shivering, convulsive release shuddered through her as Nick's fingers continued their tender torment. "You're so responsive," he groaned in satisfaction.

She was still trembling with the aftershocks of her release when Nick rolled her onto her side, placed her leg over his hips, and thrust himself into her hot tightness. Her body convulsed around him, and her climax began anew as he drove himself to his own shattering release. Loathe to separate their bodies, Nick remained deeply embedded, astonishingly hard for a man who had just glimpsed paradise.

"You make me feel strong, even when I'm weak from loving you."

She was still panting softly when she replied, "You are strong, Nick. I can still feel you inside.

Your strength is incredible." She made a jerking motion with her hips, and Nick responded by growing even harder.

"I can't believe I want you again so soon. I'll always want you, Aimee, always."

His words sent her spirits soaring. They removed the remaining doubts she had concerning Brand. Surely Nick must love her if he'd always want her, didn't he? "Nick, it's time I told you about Brand,"

"I'm fairly certain I know what it is you're going to say, sweetheart, but at the moment I can't think beyond the fact that I want you again. I'm going to love you again, Aimee, then you can tell me about Brand."

Still lying on their sides facing each other, he moved his hips, moaning in delight when Aimee parried his thrust with a subtle motion of her pelvis. He found her lips and kissed her repeatedly, deeply, demanding her full attention. And she responded in kind, returning his kiss full measure, opening her mouth to receive his tongue. She loved his taste, his scent, everything about him.

"Am I hurting you?" she asked worriedly when moan after moan continued to slip past his lips. "Perhaps we should stop."

Nick rallied enough to say, "Stop? Good God, to stop now would kill me."

Aimee tried to protest further, but by then Nick had driven her beyond the bounds of reason. She was soaring. She was trembling. She was hot and cold at the same time. Her mind and thoughts were controlled by the thrust and withdrawal of Nick's hardness inside her softness. Then suddenly she reached that place where rapture dwelled and she screamed. Nick covered her mouth with his own, swallowing her cries, replacing them with his own harsh grunts.

It was a long time before either of them could move or speak. Carefully Aimee removed her leg from atop Nick's hip, hoping he had spoken the truth when he said she wasn't hurting him. He didn't move. In the dim light cast by the lamp, she saw that his eyes were closed. She studied his relaxed face for a moment, never more aware of her love for him. He looked so much like Brand that her heart clenched painfully, and she recalled that she still hadn't told him he was Brand's father.

"Nick, I know you suspect Brand is your son, and it's true that I've continued to deny it, but it's time you learned the truth," Aimee began hesitantly.

Nothing.

"Nick. Do you hear me? It's true. Brand was conceived aboard the *Dixie Belle* over five years ago."

No shout of joy. No words of reproof for her reticence on the subject up till now. Nothing. Nick was sleeping soundly. Making sweet love to Aimee hadn't hurt him, but it had exhausted him beyond his meager endurance. He had fallen into a deep slumber within seconds after their coupling.

Aimee hummed to herself as she skipped down the stairs to prepare breakfast. She had arisen quietly, leaving Nick in bed sound asleep. He hadn't stirred once during the night, so complete was his exhaustion. Since there was no reason for him to arise, she hadn't disturbed him.

Savannah was already in the kitchen lamenting

over their lack of provisions. "We got mush, honey, and dat's about all. And some of dat fatback to fry. Don't know what we's gonna do once dat's gone. If we's lucky, a rabbit of squirrel will wander into the yard for our supper."

"Nick gave me money, Savannah. One of us can hitch the old horse to the wagon and go to Atlanta. I hope there's still food to be bought in the city."

"I'll go," Savannah offered. "You already proved it ain't safe to go traipsin' over the countryside by yourself."

"It's not safe for you, either."

"I'm an old colored woman; no one's likely to bother me. I'll leave tomorrow mornin'."

That settled, Aimee began slicing fatback. Brand came down a short time later, famished as usual. He made a face at the mush but managed to wolf down his portion before Aimee shooed him outside to play. It was nearly noon before Nick stirred himself and came downstairs. Aimee was nearly beside herself with excitement. There was nothing stopping her now from telling Nick about Brand. Savannah astutely sensed her mood and left the kitchen, offering to do some hunting. She took the shotgun from the corner and promptly left.

"I didn't mean to sleep so late," Nick said, sliding into place at the oak table. "Or fall asleep so quickly last night."

"You needed the rest."

"I'm fully awake now and ready to listen to what we never got around to discussing last night."

Aimee dished out his portion of mush and fatback and took a seat across from him.

"Aren't you eating?"

"I've already eaten," Aimee insisted. She had allowed herself a bite or two of mush but little else.

"Why don't I believe you? You're far too thin to have been eating regularly. Here." He shoved half his portion into a saucer and placed it in front of her. "I'm not very hungry this morning."

Aimee picked at the mush, not really tasting it. She had far more important things on her mind. "Nick, about Brand . . ."

Nick searched her face. She had his full attention now. "What about Brand, Aimee? Is he my son?"

"Mama, Nick, someone's coming up the driveway!" Brand burst through the door into the kitchen.

"Oh, God," Nick said, leaping to his feet. "Not again."

"What did you see, son?" Aimee said. Were the Yanks coming again to burn her house?

"They're Yanks, Mama. But that's not all; there's a carriage, too."

Aimee and Nick exchanged glances. "Perhaps they've come for you from Atlanta," Aimee suggested.

"Perhaps, but I'm not taking any chances. I must be getting careless. I left my weapon upstairs."

"I'll get it," Aimee offered, realizing she could make the trip upstairs and back much faster than Nick. She turned and raced from the room.

Nick walked through the house to the front door, stepping out on the porch just as the group of six Union soldiers escorting a rather grand carriage halted before the steps. Nick knew immediately he'd have no need for his weapon, for these men were from his own company, including Sergeant Jones. Then the door to the carriage was flung open and a vivacious redhead appeared in the opening. She spied Nick standing on the porch, and a wide smile spread over her lovely features.

"Nick! Thank God you're all right!"

Daintily raising her skirts to reveal a pair of well-turned ankles, she held out her hand. Two privates leaped forward to help her alight. His mouth gaping, too stunned to move, Nick watched in a daze as the woman glided toward him.

"Regina! What are you doing here?"

While the men stood by grinning foolishly, Regina Blakewell reached Nick and flung her arms around his neck. Nick had no recourse but to embrace her in order to keep them both upright.

"I accompanied Father to Atlanta and just recently learned you were wounded. When Father found out you were at Tall Oaks plantation and that you were to be brought to the hospital in Atlanta, I offered to come along and see to your welfare. I'm quite knowledgeable about nursing, you know. I've performed many hours of volunteer work at the hospital in Washington."

Aimee chose that unfortunate moment to burst from the house, Nick's gun in hand, ready to defend her home and family.

Nick did not see her. To Aimee it appeared that Nick was too involved with embracing the curvaceous redhead to pay heed to anyone or anything. He was holding her so tenderly, gazing at her with such dazed passion, that she felt as though she was intruding upon a very private moment. It wasn't until Sergeant Jones cleared his throat that the couple remembered that they weren't alone. Abruptly Nick pulled away, carefully removing Regina's arms from around his neck.

"You shouldn't have come, Regina. There was no need."

"No need? Of course there was a need. You're my fiancé; we're going to be married when this wretched war is over."

Aimee stood absolutely still, too stunned to move, too hurt to speak. How could Nick have made love to her with such passion if he had a fiancée waiting for him up North? How could he not have told her? Was he only pretending to care for her in order to take her son from her once she admitted he was Brand's father? Her first impression of him had been correct. He was a cheat and a scoundrel. A man who could leave a woman broke and pregnant without a thought to her welfare.

A total bastard.

A Yankee.

The man didn't deserve a son like Brand. Thank God she hadn't told him the truth yet.

Suddenly Regina noticed Aimee standing behind Nick, and her blue eyes widened as she took careful note of her threadbare dress and painfully thin figure. It was obvious from her contemptuous expression that she thought Aimee unworthy of her attention.

"Is that the widow who has been caring for you? Papa said a woman had taken you from the field hospital. I wondered why she had been allowed to do so. I must admit I was worried that your affections had tuned from me, but now that I've seen her, I realize I had nothing to worry about." She turned her brilliant blue gaze back to Nick. "You look wonderful for a man so close to death."

Nick turned slowly, fearing the damage Regina might have done to the fragile relationship blossoming between him and Aimee. He groaned when he noted the bleak expression in her amber eyes. Why hadn't he told Aimee he was engaged to Regina? he wondered regretfully. At first, before Aimee had come to mean so much to him, he saw no need to reveal his private life. And later, he hoped to be able to tell Regina in person that their engagement was a mistake. It was Aimee he loved, always Aimee. But now, Regina showing up was the worst possible thing that could happen at the worst possible time.

"Aimee." His green eyes dimmed with remorse. "I didn't mean for it to happen this way."

"Whatever are you talking about?" Regina asked. Her narrow gaze slid over Aimee, then back to Nick. "Is there something between you and this—this dismal creature that I should know about?"

Aimee bristled indignantly. At one time she had dressed every bit as fashionably as Nick's fiancée. "Nothing that matters." Her flippant remark made Nick wince.

"Perhaps we should go inside," Nick suggested, "where we can speak in private."

Without waiting for a reply, he led the way into the kitchen. Suddenly weary, he sank down heavily into the nearest chair. Aimee and Regina stood over him, glaring at each other.

"Aimee, this is Regina Blakewell. She is—was—my fiancée."

Chapter 14

Regina bristled indignantly. "This is the first I've heard of a broken engagement."

"I intended to write, Regina, though I would have preferred to tell you in person. Truth to tell, I had no idea where you were. You accompany your father on all his assignments, and I had no idea how a letter could reach you."

"You are breaking our engagement for this—this person?" She thrust a hand in Aimee's direction, obviously unimpressed by what she saw.

"Definitely not," Aimee interjected. "There has never been any indication of love or marriage between Nick and myself. We met five years ago. I hated him then and I hate him now."

Regina's brow cleared immediately. It wasn't as bad as she had thought. Evidently Nick wasn't enamored of the woman.

Nick sucked in his breath and let it out slowly in a long, painful sigh.

"Then I see no problem," Regina proclaimed. "Are you ready to leave, darling? Father is waiting anxiously in Atlanta for us. I wouldn't be remiss in saying there's a promotion waiting for you."

Suddenly Savannah burst through the back

door, the shotgun in one hand, two rabbits in another. "Who are dem Yanks, honey? What do dey want?"

"It's all right, Savannah," Aimee said quietly. "They've come for Nick."

"Where's Brand?"

"He's with Sergeant Jones," Nick answered. "No harm will come to him."

"Who's dat?" Savannah asked, motioning toward Regina with the gun.

"Don't point that thing at me," Regina warned indignantly.

"The lady is Nick's fiancée," Aimee said before Nick had a chance to reply.

Savannah regarded Nick with the intensity of her black eyes. "I declare, if dat don't beat all." Realizing she was intruding, she said, "I'd best skin dese rabbits." Then she turned and stomped out the door, but not before sending Nick a look that left no doubt about her opinion of him.

Reluctantly Nick realized he had no choice but to leave Tall Oaks with Regina and the escort sent on his behalf. It was a miracle that he had been allowed to remain this long. He knew he still had many long weeks of recuperation before he was fit enough to return to duty, and he desperately wished he could have stayed at Tall Oaks with Aimee and Brand while he regained his strength. Regina's arrival had been completely unexpected and unwelcomed. Nick knew by the stubborn set of Aimee's chin and her unrelenting stance that she had been hurt, and he couldn't blame her. He should have told her about Regina and explained that once he found Aimee again, he had no intention of marrying the general's spoiled daughter. Aimee and his son were all that mattered now.

"Regina, please wait outside; I'd like to speak to Aimee in private."

"There's no need for private words, Nick," Aimee said. Her voice was flat, her face devoid of all emotion. "We've already said all there is to say."

"Please, Aimee. There is still something between us that needs clarifying."

"I can't imagine what it is."

"You heard her, Nick, there's nothing more to gain by remaining here," Regina said, placing her hand possessively on Nick's shoulder. "There will be proper doctors where you're going who will supervise your recovery."

Nick shrugged her hand away. "I asked you to wait in the carriage, Regina." His voice was implacable, his green eyes cold and remorseless. Regina glared at Aimee, gave a careless shrug, and walked out the door.

"That wasn't necessary," Aimee said in an accusatory tone. "Do you enjoy hurting women?"

"I never meant to hurt anyone, Aimee. I realize it was remiss of me not to write Regina of my intention to break our engagement, but these are precarious times, and it isn't always convenient to do what one wishes."

"You could have told me you were engaged to be married."

"Would it have made any difference? We were destined to be together, sweetheart; it's as simple as that."

"It isn't simple at all, Nick," Aimee returned shortly. "You've just proven that my original opinion of you was correct. You're a cheat, a liar, and a womanizer. The sooner you get out of my life, the better off I'll be."

Nick paled. "You don't mean that."

"Every word. I suggest you not keep your fiancée waiting."

Nick rose painfully to his feet. "What about Brand?"

"What about him?"

"It's time you admitted he's my son."

"I can't admit something that's not true."

"Dammit to hell! I *know* Brand is my son. I can feel it in my gut. I want him, Aimee; I want to raise my son. I want him to know his real father. He's at an impressionable age where he needs a man's influence."

"Perhaps one day I'll remarry," Aimee said, hoping to hurt Nick in the same way he had hurt her. "And Brand will have a father. But if I do marry, it will be to a man nothing like you."

Nick leaped to his feet, groaning as shards of pain stabbed through his body. Beads of sweat broke out on his forehead as he struggled to control his body's weakness. Aimee's first inclination was to rush to him and offer comfort, but she held her ground, refusing to fall victim to his wiles again. He was slick and practiced in the art of seduction; she had learned that the hard way. Not once in all these weeks had he mentioned a fiancée.

"You're mine, Aimee; you were always mine," Nick gasped as he fought the remorseless pain. "Since I never intended to marry Regina once I came to care about you, I saw no need to mention her."

"Your lack of consideration appalls me. Please leave, Nick; your escort awaits."

He grasped her arm before she could turn away, his grip strong despite his obvious physical limitations. "I won't leave like this, Aimee."

"You have no choice."

"Damn you!"

"No, Nick, damn you! You never wanted me. I was just a means to an end. You'd do anything to get me to admit Brand is your son. Well, you can't have him. Brand is mine. I'm sure Regina will give you several sons, so you don't need mine."

Nick shook his head sadly, wearily. Fatigue etched deep lines around his eyes and mouth, but Aimee hardened her heart.

"You're mistaken if you think all I want is Brand. It's true I've come to love the boy, but what I feel for you is—"

"Lust."

She tried to shake free of his grip, but he was too strong for her. He pulled her closer, closer still, until their faces were inches apart. "Perhaps that was true at first, but lust has nothing to do with my feelings now. I have to leave whether I want to or not, but you've not seen the last of me. I'll make Regina understand that marriage between us is out of the question."

"It doesn't matter."

Oh, Nick, why couldn't you have confided in me? Why couldn't you have loved me?

Then he was kissing her, his mouth slanting over hers in almost desperate need. He kissed her long and deep, trying to convey all that she had come to mean to him in that one last kiss. He forced his tongue past the barrier of her teeth, savoring her taste, her scent, her warmth, stroking her back and hips, painfully aware of the fragile bones beneath her thinness. When he broke off the kiss, they were both panting. Aimee backed away, wiping her lips with the back of her hand, but it didn't help; the special essence that was Nick was etched upon her brain forever.

"Are you ready yet?" Regina appeared in the doorway, tapping her foot impatiently. "Father has a room reserved especially for you at the hospital. You'll remain until you are fit to travel and can be sent north to recuperate properly. I took the liberty of sending Sergeant Jones upstairs for your belongings. He said he knew which room was yours."

His face contorted in pain and anguish, Nick nodded. He took a step, faltered, and Regina rushed to his side. "Oh, you poor dear, let me help you."

Aimee turned away, unable to watch the possessive way in which Nick's fiancée took control, as if the right were hers alone. How fortunate for Nick that his fiancée just happened to be the daughter of a general. In Aimee's opinion, Nick Drummond was an opportunist who took unfair advantage of every situation. Nick hesitated at the doorway, turned as if to speak to Aimee, thought better of it, and continued through the door.

Nick, Regina, and their escort were gone a full ten minutes before Aimee moved. It might have been longer if Brand and Savannah hadn't come into the kitchen. As usual, Brand was full of questions.

"Why did Nick leave, Mama?"

"Because he had to. You knew he would leave one day."

"Did he want to leave?"

"He needed proper care by a proper doctor."

"Who was that lady?"

Silence.

"Mama, I didn't like her; who was she?"

"The woman Nick is going to marry, darling."

Brand chewed on that for a while, then said with the innocence of a five-year-old, "Nick likes you better. Why can't he marry you? Then he would be my father."

Aimee tried to speak past the lump in her throat. How do you tell a child that the man he adores is a liar and a scoundrel? The answer was simple. You don't.

"Nick and I . . . well, Regina Blakewell is more suited to him."

"Nick said he would come back. Do you think he will?"

"No, son, I don't," Aimee said, not wishing to give hope where none existed.

"I'm sorry, Mama."

"So am I, darling, so am I." Subdued, Brand left the kitchen.

"I ain't gonna say nothin', honey," Savannah said. "You're already sufferin' enough. I thought dat man truly cared for you."

"Nick had no choice; he had to go with Regina. He had orders stating he was to report to the hospital in Atlanta." Why was she defending him?

"Uh huh, but he shoulda told you he was gonna marry up with another woman."

"I had no hold on him."

"What about Brand? De man suspects he's Brand's papa."

"He can speculate all he wants. No one will ever know Brand isn't Beauregard Trevor's child."

Nick dozed most of the way to Atlanta. He was exhausted both emotionally and physically. No explanation he had offered seemed to placate Aimee. How easily she had reverted back to her old opinion of him, he thought bitterly. The fact that they had come to care for each other during these past months seemed to make little difference to her. His small omission concerning Regina had all but destroyed what he'd accomplished thus far with Aimee. Though she had little reason to trust him after the disaster of their first meeting, he had brought her to a place in their relationship where he thought she had forgiven him. He had intended to ask her to marry him once he'd broken his engagement to Regina.

And he wasn't proposing because he suspected Brand was his son. No, indeed. He wanted Aimee even if Brand were Beauregard Trevor's son. When had he fallen in love with Aimee? he wondered bleakly. The answer came to him in a flash. He'd always loved Aimee. He loved her the moment he saw her seated at the poker table, he loved her when he went back later to search for her, and he loved her all those years when he thought he'd never see her again. He'd only proposed marriage to Regina to save his career—and no hope existed of ever finding Aimee again.

"We're almost there, Nick," Regina said, nudging him gently. "I know you're in pain now, but Father has arranged for you to have the best care available. I'll even accompany you north when you're well enough to travel."

"Regina, we must talk. There isn't going to be a marriage. We should have never become engaged. When your father discovered us, I took the coward's way out and proposed. I realized that one word from him could make or break my career. I wasn't marrying you out of love. Someday you'll find a man who truly loves you."

"You're talking nonsense," Regina scolded. She sounded annoyed but not overly concerned, which puzzled Nick.

"Don't you understand what I'm telling you? Our engagement is off. It wouldn't be honest to marry a woman I don't love."

"Oh, pooh, Nick, I'm not taking anything you say seriously. I know the strain and stress you've been under since being wounded in battle, but in time you'll recover and realize it's in your best interest for us to marry. I'll make a wonderful wife, and Father can do wonders for your career."

"Of course you'll make a wonderful wife, Regina, but not my wife."

The carriage made slow progress down streets strewn with rubble, and Nick's attention strayed to the terrible destruction wrought by the war.

"I had no idea it was this bad," Nick said when he noted how few civilians remained in the devastated city.

"Food is scarce," Regina revealed, "but Father said trains are arriving sporadically with supplies to feed our troops left behind to hold the city."

The carriage ground to a halt before a large building. "We're here at the hospital," Regina said. Then the door opened and Sergeant Jones helped

Nick down from the carriage. "I'll see you inside, darling."

"No need, Regina. Thanks for your trouble, but I'll be all right now."

"Trouble? Since when is it trouble to help someone you love? I'll be by to see you tomorrow."

Too weary to argue, Nick merely nodded.

General Blakewell beamed down at Nick. "I hope you didn't mind Regina going along with the escort yesterday. Women in love and all that nonsense. You know how it is. But seriously, Captain, we're just glad to have you among the living. Dr. Bellows tells me your wound was one of the most serious he's ever seen. Thank God you were treated promptly."

"Thank God and a woman named Aimee," Nick muttered.

"What was that?"

"Nothing, sir, I was just agreeing with you."

"Harumph. In any case, you'll be traveling north soon to recuperate. There is an excellent hospital in Washington; does that suit you?"

"As well as any."

"Good, good. I'm due back in Washington myself soon. Regina and I plan to travel with you. I don't suppose it will come as any shock that you've been promoted to major. No one deserves it more. Regina couldn't be happier."

Nick cleared his throat. "About Regina, sir. I don't believe marriage—"

"Now, now, Cap—er—Major, Regina told me about your little stubborn spell. You'll feel differently once you're hale and hearty again. Illness is a damn bore, especially for a man like you. Well,

I must be off now. It's nearly time for my conference with Colonel Watson."

Dismayed, Nick fell back against the pillow. The journey from Tall Oaks to Atlanta had sapped his meager strength, and he had barely moved from his hospital bed since arriving yesterday. Though his body was weak, his mind worked overtime fretting over how Aimee and Brand would fare in his absence. Aimee had the money he had given her before he left, but how long would that last? Nick had no idea when he could return to Tall Oaks, and any number of things might happen to a beautiful woman all alone but for a small boy and an elderly black woman.

Owing to General Blakewell's personal interest in his welfare, Nick was scheduled to be sent north for convalescent leave in a few days. He would ride aboard the special train taking General Blakewell back to Washington. To Nick's chagrin, Regina made plans to travel with them, but he had little say in the matter. In any case, Nick hoped that during the train ride, he would be able to persuade Regina that breaking their engagement was in her best interest.

"Honey, we gots to go to Atlanta to buy food." Savannah had been trying to rouse Aimee from her lethargy since Nick had left several days ago. "Now dat we gots money, dere ain't nothin' stoppin' us. I'll go first thing in the mornin'."

Her words barely made an impression.

"If dere ain't no food for Brand, he'll starve to death."

That did rouse her.

"What did you say?"

"Captain Drummond left money, didn't he? I'll drive de wagon into town tomorrow and see what's available."

Aimee nodded her approval and slipped back into her dark thoughts. The thought that Nick only wanted her to satisfy his lust did little for her self-esteem. Perversely she wondered if he had thought about his lovely fiancée when he had made love to her. She felt that his suspicions that Brand was his son prompted him to tell her that he cared for her. She should have listened to her conscience and never let him breach her heart.

The next day Savannah was unable to rise from bed. She'd always had a touch of rheumatism, and the cooler weather they were having these past few days played havoc with her poor old joints. The medicine the doctor had given her for the ailment had been used long ago, but now that they had a bit of money, Aimee decided to replenish the supply at an apothecary in Atlanta. Of course, that meant she must now make the trip to Atlanta herself.

Aimee left early the following morning. Since she feared leaving Brand with an ailing Savannah, she took him along. The old nag plodded along at a snail's pace, but eventually they reached the city, this time without mishap. Aimee prayed the nag wouldn't collapse before they made it back to Tall Oaks that evening. When they passed by the railroad station, Brand let out a shriek and pointed to a group of passengers boarding the train.

"Mama, look!" Aimee slowed the nag and looked in the direction Brand pointed. "It's Nick, Mama! He's getting on the train with that woman."

Aimee's heart lurched painfully. It was indeed Nick. He still looked pale and somewhat shaky, but he was navigating on his own two feet—with the help of his flame-haired fiancée. So much for his insistence that Regina Blakewell meant nothing to him, Aimee thought furiously. She had known him for a liar and cheat for more years than she cared to count; why did she expect him to change now?

"Can we say good-bye to him, Mama?" Brand asked. "I think he would like that."

"I think not, darling. It's best we go on. I want to reach Tall Oaks before dark."

In his enthusiasm Brand paid no heed to Aimee's answer as he leaped from the barely moving wagon and ran toward the train, shouting Nick's name at the top of his voice. Miraculously Nick heard him above the confusion of boarding passengers. A brilliant smile lit his face as he knelt on one knee and held his arms out to the small boy. Aimee watched in mute fury as Brand leaped into Nick's arms. She had no recourse but to rein in the nag and look on as her son and Nick spoke earnestly together.

"What are you doing in Atlanta?" Nick asked, hoping they had come to see him.

"We came to buy food and get medicine for Savannah's rheumatism. Are you leaving, Nick?"

His woebegone little face tore at Nick's heart. He glanced over at Aimee, recognizing her unrelenting anger, her absolute belief that he had used her ruthlessly. Obviously she had no idea how much she meant to him.

"We mustn't tarry, Nick," Regina urged, annoyed by the unwelcome appearance of Widow

Trevor and her son. "The train is due to leave momentarily."

Nick hugged Brand tightly and whispered in his ear, "Take care of your mother for me, son. Tell her—tell her I'll be back." Then he rose and quickly boarded the train.

"Ain't that the same captain who kept us from burning that plantation a while back, Sergeant Purdy?"

Purdy and his mounted patrol were riding past the train station when they happened to see Nick boarding the train for Washington. "Sure is, Corporal," Purdy said thoughtfully. "Since the captain is leaving, I don't suppose it matters now if we go back and burn the place. Our instructions were to fire everything left standing in and around Atlanta."

"What about the widow who owns the place?" the corporal asked, licking his lips in avid anticipation. "She sure is a fine-looking woman." They had spied Nick boarding the train shortly after Brand had climbed back into the wagon with his mother, so they did not see Aimee in the crush of people.

"She's a feisty little witch, all right," Purdy mused. "Mayhap we'll find out just how feisty." His lascivious grin needed no interpretation.

Purdy's statement reflected Sherman's belief that his troops weren't only fighting hostile armies but hostile people as well, and that the Union armies must destroy the capacity of the southern people to sustain the war. Their factories, railroads, farms—indeed, their will to resist—must be torn apart. So Sherman's soldiers put the torch to everything of military value—and much having nothing to do with the military—in and around Atlanta that Hood had left standing.

It didn't take Aimee long to discover that food was scarce in the city. Men had left their farms to take up arms, depriving the population of the products they grew. Few truck gardens still produced crops this late in the year, and Sherman had burned fields of cotton and grain in his march to the sea. A few intrepid sea captains had run the blockade successfully, and it was the result of their bravery that stocked the shelves in the stores still operating in the city. Northern goods had just begun to trickle into the impoverished city, going primarily to feed the troops Sherman had left behind to defend Atlanta.

After spending more time than she would have liked trying to purchase staples and medicine for Savannah, Aimee didn't start back to Tall Oaks until much later than planned. She had been obliged to spend nearly all the money Nick had given her to buy provisions at outrageous prices. But at least she had cornmeal, flour, a bit of sugar, salt, fatback, and some canned staples. She had even found shells for the shotgun. At least now they could continue to hunt for fresh meat. She was a tolerable shot, and so was Savannah.

A crash of thunder rattled the wagon, and Aimee hoped she'd reach Tall Oaks before rain pelted them. At this time of year the rain would be bone-chilling. Thank God she had thought to bring a blanket or two to cover herself and Brand should the need arise.

She saw the eerie glow illuminating the overcast sky a good two miles before they reached Tall

Oaks. Her cry of dismay awoke Brand, who was sleeping in the back of the wagon.

"What is it, Mama?" he asked groggily.

"N-nothing, son; go back to sleep." Though Aimee knew immediately what the glow meant, she didn't want to alarm Brand. But she had seen fire light up the sky too many times in the past not to recognize its terrible portent.

The last time she had seen the sky a fiery red, the Yanks were burning the Pinder plantation house. Before that, it had been the Belfour place. She uttered one prayer after another on Savannah's behalf. Had the old woman escaped from the inferno engulfing Tall Oaks? she wondered desperately. Or had she perished in the flame? If she and Brand hadn't been in Atlanta, Savannah's fate might have been theirs.

It began to rain almost immediately. Not a misty sprinkle, but hard and pelting. Aimee could only hope the rain would douse the fire consuming Tall Oaks. The pop and crackle of dying flames filled the damp air as Aimee stopped the wagon a short distance from the burning house. The fire was almost out, but most of the house had already been destroyed before the rains came. Two front pillars stood in eerie welcome, looking curiously unscathed against a backdrop of charred wood. Though the walls still remained upright, the roof had fallen in several places and the insides were gutted.

There was no sign of Savannah, and Aimee feared the worst. She stumbled from the wagon, peering through the misty twilight at the ruins that had been her home since the day Beauregard Trevor had made her his wife. She was in shock, recalling the countless times she and Savannah had defended

Tall Oaks against Confederate deserters, scavengers, and Union soldiers called "bummers." These were the scourge of the South—men who destroyed anything they could not eat, burned homes, cotton, and gins, plundered railroads, and generally raised hell, all under the guise of warfare.

"What are we going to do, Mama?" Brand's question released Aimee from her dazed state. For her son's sake she would do whatever was necessary to survive.

"We have food in the wagon, darling; somehow we'll survive."

Suddenly Aimee saw a lone figure emerge from the back of the house. She pulled Brand behind her and reached into the wagon for the shotgun she had taken to Atlanta for protection. Savannah had kept the ancient pistol.

"Aimee, is dat you, chile?"

"Savannah! Thank God you're alive!"

Her steps were slow and measured, as if walking was pure agony. When she reached Aimee, she had to be supported to remain upright. "De Yanks done burned de house, honey. I couldn't stop dem nohow. It was dat ornery sergeant Captain Drummond sent packin' not too long ago."

"He must have realized Nick was no longer here and came back to finish the job. Did they hurt you?"

"No, honey, dey just burst up de stairs and gave me five minutes to get out. I was barely able to gather up our clothes before de flames shot up de stairs and I had to leave. I'm sorry, chile, dat I couldn't save Tall Oaks for you."

"It's all right, Savannah; it was only a house. We still have our lives."

"Dey was disappointed you weren't here, honey. Lord only knows what dey would have done to you had you been here when dey came."

"I—I don't want to think about it." Aimee shuddered, aware of the fate that would have been hers had the soldiers found her at Tall Oaks.

"I'm tired, Mama, and hungry," Brand whined. He clung to Aimee's skirt, confused and troubled by the abrupt change in their lives. "If Captain Drummond hadn't left us, this wouldn't have happened."

Aimee had no answer for the child.

"I took our belongin's to one of de slave cabins still standin' out back," Savannah said. "I know it ain't much, but at least it's a roof over our heads. And it's snug and dry. I even scrounged a couple of cots and some furniture dat ain't too badly damaged."

"It will do just fine, Savannah," Aimee said. For Brand's sake she attempted a brave smile. It did little to soothe him.

"What's going to happen to us, Mama?"

"We'll manage, darling. You'll see; we'll be fine in the cabin."

"Winter's comin' on," Savannah said with ominous portent.

"I said we'd manage," Aimee repeated crossly. "Neither you nor Brand will suffer, no matter what I have to do to provide for you."

When winter winds howled through the rafters and snow filtered down upon them through holes in the roof, when their food was gone and Brand cried himself to sleep at night from hunger, Aimee found the courage to take the necessary steps.

Chapter 15

~~~❦~~~

Snow drifted lazily down on the city, covering Washington in a new coat of pristine white. Outside his frosted window, Nick saw a few brave souls braced against the storm as they trudged along icy streets to reach their various destinations. It was the first day of December, and he had been in the convalescent hospital nearly six weeks. A congestion in his lungs had slowed his recovery when he first reached Washington, but his will to recover had never deserted him. He fought the setback with the same grit and determination that made him the kind of man who rarely accepted defeat.

Now, when his health had improved to the point that he no longer needed hospitalization or convalescent care, the weather had turned nasty. Nick had left the hospital three days ago and checked into bachelor officer quarters while awaiting reassignment. It came through just hours ago. He had been assigned to a prestigious job in Washington as adjutant to General Blakewell. He should have known Regina would have her fine hand in here somewhere.

Regina. Lord, just thinking about her hit a raw

nerve with him. The woman refused to accept the fact that their marriage was never going to happen. She lived in a world all her own, marching to her own drummer. If plans did not go her way, she tended to ignore them. At the time, proposing to Regina had seemed necessary to his career. She had all the right connections, and if he had balked, her father could have ruined his chances for advancement. But that didn't seem to matter any longer.

Then Aimee Trevor had come back into his life and made him realize that marriage to Regina was impossible. As usual when Nick had extra time on his hands, his thoughts turned to Aimee and Brand. He worried that they weren't getting enough to eat and fretted because he had no way of knowing if they were still at Tall Oaks trying to eke out a meager existence.

The moment he had received his new assignment, which allowed him two weeks leave before requiring him to report for duty, Nick made immediate plans to travel to Atlanta, find Aimee and Brand, and bring them back to Washington with him. But the weather turned blustery, and the train between Washington and Atlanta, which had been running sporadically since the Rebs began blowing up railroads, wasn't due to leave for another two days.

A knock on the door interrupted Nick's reverie. He was pleasantly surprised when he opened the door and found Captain Birch standing before him covered with fluffy flakes of snow and shivering from cold.

"Bruce! Don't stand there, man, come in out of

the cold. What the devil are you doing in Washington?"

"I was slightly wounded and given a leave to recuperate. Since I had business in Washington anyway, I thought I'd look you up." He ran a critical eye over Nick's imposing form. "Except for being unnaturally pale, you look hale and hearty for someone who was just recently knocking at death's door. I can only assume your recovery is due to the care you received at Tall Oaks by that lovely blonde you're so fond of."

"I not only owe my recovery to Aimee, but my life," Nick said. His lips slanted upward in a wistful smile. "I'd be dead if Aimee hadn't taken matters in her own hands at the field hospital."

"Seems to me I heard something about that. I also heard that Regina Blakewell brought you back to Atlanta and then accompanied you to Washington. Does that men your engagement to General Blakewell's daughter is still on?"

"That depends on whom you speak with. If you asked Regina, she'd tell you our marriage is still set for sometime after the war. But if you asked me, I'd tell you there will be no marriage between me and Regina. I think you know how I feel about Aimee Trevor."

Birch nodded sagely. "Quite a fix you've gotten yourself into. What do you intend to do?"

"I'm taking the first train I can to Atlanta. I must find Aimee and her son. They must be desperate for food by now, and Lord only knows in what condition I'll find them."

"Have you been reassigned yet?"

"It just came through today. I'm to act as aide to General Blakewell. Regina's doings, I suppose. But

I intend to make good use of the two weeks allotted me before I report for duty, if the weather cooperates."

"Fortunately I arrived in Washington before the weather turned bad. I assume you've heard that Atlanta is a ghost town. Sherman returned to Atlanta, and before he marched out on November fifteenth, he ordered all civilians out of the city and burned everything of military value. The only public buildings left standing are those being used by Union forces left behind to occupy the city. Of course, you'll find the usual number of whorehouses deemed necessary to uphold morale, a few homes, and some shops."

"I'd heard it's bad," Nick said grimly. "Is it true that Yank soldiers are starving in the fields and trenches?"

"That's a pretty good assessment of the situation. Sherman is marching toward Savannah while Hood and his army are moving toward Tennessee. Rebel cavalry and Georgia militia attacked Union infantry and suffered enormous casualties on November twenty-second."

"It's all pretty grim," Nick said, "but what you've told me only makes me more determined than ever to go to Atlanta."

"What about Regina? Perhaps I ought to console the lady in your absence."

"She's all yours, Bruce. Take her with my blessings. When I find Aimee, I fully intend to bring her to Washington with me as my wife."

Brand had been coughing for several days. Now it had become worse, and Aimee pulled the blanket from her own shoulders to add to the one covering Brand. Snow filtered into the dilapidated cabin through the cracks in the walls, making dappled wet spots on the dirt floor. Wind howled down the chimney and drove additional snow through holes in the roof. The occupants of the tiny one-room cabin were silent and subdued, except for the sound of Brand's hacking cough and occasional sneezes.

Aimee moved listlessly toward the small fire in the hearth, seeking its meager warmth. Savannah dozed in the charred rocking chair that had been salvaged from the big house after the fire. Aimee poked into the flames with a stick, realizing that their firewood was nearly gone and she'd have to leave soon to find more. Fortunately there was sufficient wood from the partially destroyed slave cabins and the big house to keep them from freezing to death. But food was another matter entirely, and their shotgun shells were nearly gone, making their situation even more desperate. They had existed almost entirely these past weeks on what small game could be shot or snared.

"Mama?" Brand's voice was hoarse from coughing, his eyes overbright from fever.

"I'm here, darling."

"I'm still cold."

"I'll lie down with you and keep you warm." She moved to the narrow cot, slid in beside him, and gathered him in her arms. "Is that better?"

"Much better."

"Are you hungry? There's still a piece of rabbit left from yesterday. And perhaps a bit of cornbread."

Brand shook his head. "You eat it. I know you

and Savannah have been going without so I could eat."

How perceptive he is for one so young, Aimee thought, hugging Brand fiercely. He was indeed a special child. Nick Drummond might be a bastard, but his son was everything a mother could ask for.

Nick Drummond.

The name dredged up evocative memories. She hoped Nick was happy with Regina Blakewell, for she knew that a woman as beautiful and determined as Regina would have no trouble convincing Nick that marriage to her was what he wanted. And to think that she, Aimee, had very nearly fallen victim to Nick's lies. Not that she regretted saving Nick on the battlefield. He was her son's father, after all. But she tried to convince herself that was the only reason that she'd risked her life to save him.

While Aimee lay beside Brand, listening to his harsh breathing and thinking about the man who had fathered him, Savannah stirred in the rocking chair and rose painfully to her feet. The cold dampness played havoc with her rheumatism, and her medicine had run out days ago. Her stomach rumbled, but she ignored it, accustomed now to the empty feeling deep in the pit of her stomach. But Aimee heard it and could no longer ignore the fact that they were slowly starving to death.

"I fear there's not much left in the larder," Aimee said softly so as not to awaken Brand. He had finally fallen into a restless sleep.

"I ain't hungry, honey," Savannah lied. "I think dere's enough left for Brand when he wakes up."

Aimee scooted out of bed and joined Savannah as she rummaged around in the basket that held their supplies. "Something has to be done soon, Savannah; we can't go on like this. Both you and Brand need medicine, and if we don't find food soon, we'll all starve. We're worse off now than before Nick—" Her words skidded to a halt. Why must Nick be constantly in her thoughts? Why couldn't she accept the fact that Nick Drummond had walked out of their lives for good?

"Dere's still a few shells left; I'll go huntin' soon as de snow stops. Maybe I'll be lucky and bring back a plump rabbit. A rich broth will make Brand feel better."

"Bagging a rabbit is only a stopgap remedy, and you know it," Aimee said angrily. She knew her anger was misplaced, but couldn't stop it. It wasn't fair that she and her family were starving while people in the North were enjoying a hearty meal in a warm house before a blazing fire. Yankee soldiers had cruelly raped her land, and nothing would ever be the same again.

Nick was a Yankee soldier.

She hated him and his kind for the injustice done to the people of the South.

Savannah had no answer to Aimee's furious comments. She knew Aimee was right, that it was only a matter of time before they starved to death. And the sad part was that she saw no solution. "I know, chile, I know."

"I absolutely refuse to stand by and let my loved ones starve!" Aimee spat the words with such vehemence and determination that Savannah was momentarily taken aback.

"What you gonna do, chile?" Savannah was well aware of Aimee's impetuous nature and had stood helplessly by while Aimee landed in precarious fixes time and again. She hadn't been able to stop Aimee the first time she plunged headlong into danger when she became a riverboat gambler, and she feared she'd have no say now in Aimee's decision.

"I'm going to Atlanta."

"What for? Ain't nothin' dere but burnt-out buildings and Yankees."

"I'm going to find work."

"Work! What kind of work? De last word we had from Atlanta was that it was a ghost town, except for de Yanks and a few—" She paused, looked over at Brand, then hissed in Aimee's ear, "You know, dem places where women pleasure men. Besides, I ain't certain dat old nag can get you to Atlanta."

"He'll get me there, Savannah. If not, I'll walk. I won't allow my son to starve. I won't! Don't try to dissuade me, for my mind is made up. I'll leave when the weather clears. Atlanta rarely receives enough snow at one time to hinder traveling."

"I don't like it, chile."

"I see no other solution, Savannah." Though Aimee's face was set and her resolve staunch, she felt a certain amount of fear. But she was prepared to do whatever was necessary in order to buy Brand and Savannah food and medicine.

A cold wind shifted debris in the deserted streets as Aimee entered Atlanta. The nag had gotten her here, but Aimee seriously doubted whether he would get her back to Tall Oaks. Since winter, he'd had to forage for food, and had not fared well. His ribs were touching his backbone, each one plainly defined on his skinny carcass.

Few civilians were on the streets, though it was only early afternoon. Aimee tried to ignore the men who ogled her curiously, but found it difficult to disregard the leers she was forced to endure. She had no idea that few women besides whores remained in Atlanta.

To Aimee's disappointment, she found most of the stores abandoned by their owners. Shopkeepers who remained open for business turned her away with amused laughter when she informed them that she was looking for employment.

"Did Miss Mona turn you out?" one shopkeeper asked pointedly.

"Miss Mona?" Aimee repeated. "I'm sorry, but I don't know a Miss Mona."

When the man grinned at her as if he didn't believe her, Aimee turned and walked away, a puzzled look on her face.

The next shopkeeper was more blunt. "Are you one of Miss Mona's girls?"

"No, should I be?"

"That depends. You're pretty enough, but not quite the type I'd expect to find in a—er—house of pleasure. But nowadays it's the only job available for a female in Atlanta. More than one girl from a good family has ended up working for Miss Mona. Besides, all the civilians have been ordered out of Atlanta."

Abruptly Aimee turned and made a hasty departure, aware now of the meaning behind the strange looks aimed at her by Yank soldiers on the street. They thought her a whore!

Deep in thought, Aimee led the nag down the street, fearing he'd collapse if she tried to mount him. She shivered as a cold draft crept beneath the skirt and single petticoat of her threadbare dress, chilling her legs and backside. She led the nag directly toward Yankee headquarters, having asked directions from one of the soldiers she passed in the street. By now all her options were exhausted. Clearly there was no work available for her in Atlanta, and she had no alternative but to ask the Yankees for help. It went deeply against everything she stood for, but her pride was nothing in comparison to the life of her son. Brand needed food and medicine, and if the Yanks wouldn't supply them, her family would perish.

Squaring her narrow shoulders, Aimee pushed open the door and stepped inside. She welcomed the rush of warmth that greeted her and stood motionless a moment, envying the soldiers who had nothing to do but sit before a fire toasting their backsides. Several moments passed before she was noticed by a corporal sitting at a desk, bent over a sheaf of papers.

"Can I help you, miss?"

Gathering her courage, Aimee said, "I'd like to see the officer in charge."

"Do you have an appointment?"

"No, I've just arrived in Atlanta. But the life of a small child depends on my speaking with him."

"I'm sorry, miss, but Major Tanner is a busy man. Haven't you heard that all civilians were ordered out of Atlanta? I suggest you return to where you came from."

"Not before I've seen your Major Tanner." Her chin rose to a defiant angle and her amber eyes narrowed stubbornly. She eyed the closed door to the right of the desk, wondering if she could get past the corporal before being stopped. The two other men in the room said nothing; they merely ogled her with more than a little curiosity.

She made up her mind instantly, dashing past the corporal and flinging open the door.

"What's the meaning of this?"

The corporal was hard on her heels. "I'm sorry, sir. I tried to tell this young lady that you were too busy to see her without an appointment, but she wouldn't listen."

Major Tanner glared at Aimee, and she knew instinctively that she'd receive little help from the stern-looking officer. "Very well, Corporal Little, I'll speak with her."

Corporal Little nodded and closed the door behind him as he backed out of the room. Major Tanner turned icy blue eyes on Aimee, and she shivered in response.

"Well, young lady, this had better be important. Are you from Miss Mona's? Or one of the other houses in town?"

Flustered, Aimee stammered, "I—I'm not—not from a house of pleasure. I live with my small son and companion in a slave cabin at Tall Oaks plantation not far from Atlanta. My home was burned by your soldiers on their sweep through Atlanta."

"I'm sorry, miss, but what has that got to do with me?"

Aimee bristled angrily. "Because of you Yanks, my son is starving! He needs medicine, and there's no money with which to purchase any."

Major Tanner had the grace to flush. "If I tried to provide for every family that's been burned out of their homes, there would be nothing left for my own men. And God knows they have little enough to see them through the winter. These are desperate times; you'll just have to survive the best you can. Now, as you can see, I'm busy. Be so good as to leave."

"You don't understand! Without proper food and medicine, my son will die. Do you want that on your conscience?"

Tanner looked up at her, and Aimee thought she saw a hint of compassion in his blue eyes. But it lasted only a moment as a curtain seemed to drop over his expression, deliberately blocking out all the horrors of war. "See Miss Mona if you need work. I'll wager she'll take you in if you explain your need. If you're not so inclined, you'd best leave town immediately. It isn't safe for civilians in Atlanta presently."

Aimee's lips tightened into a thin white line. "Where will I find Miss Mona?"

His expression did not soften as he said, "At the end of Peachtree Street. You can't miss it; it's the only house on the block left intact."

Aimee stared at the fence surrounding Miss Mona's large, rambling house on Peachtree Street. In fact, she couldn't take her eyes off the fence. It seemed so commonplace and functional in a street where most houses had been destroyed beyond repair. The paint was worn thin in places, and some of the stakes were missing, but it looked so normal amidst chaos that Aimee forgot for a moment exactly why she was standing there staring at an insignificant little fence.

"Well, honey, are you going to come in or just stand out there in the cold all day staring at my fence?"

Aimee started violently, breaking off her contemplation to look at the woman beckoning to her from the doorway of the house. She was tall and voluptuous, clad quite elegantly in green brocade. She had the most garish shade of orange hair Aimee had ever seen.

Aimee swallowed the lump in her throat. "Are you Miss Mona?"

"In person, honey. It's warmer in the house; would you care to join me?"

Aimee nodded in response, pushed open the gate, and started up the front walk. She hesitated briefly when she reached the door.

"Don't be shy, honey. You've come this far; you might as well come all the way."

"Yes," Aimee said as she preceded Miss Mona inside. "Thank you." She had indeed come this far, and Brand's welfare was more important to her than her pride. Before she left Tall Oaks, she had made a vow to do whatever was necessary to obtain funds for food and medicine. She intended to keep that vow.

The household was just beginning to stir. As she passed the parlor, Aimee peeked in and saw young women in various degrees of undress talking and laughing with one another as if they hadn't a care in the world. They returned Aimee's stare but didn't appear disturbed to see another woman being introduced into their midst.

"We can talk in the study, honey," Mona said as she led Aimee to a room down a short hallway from the parlor. Aimee followed her inside and perched nervously on the edge of a chair. Mona didn't seat herself behind the desk; she merely balanced one hip against the edge and looked down at Aimee. Her expression was neither critical nor censuring, merely curious.

"What's your name?"

"Aimee Trevor."

"Who sent you here?" Mona didn't believe in beating around the bush.

"No one sent me. I was told you'd give me employment, so I came of my own free will."

Mona studied Aimee through intelligent eyes neither green nor blue. More like the color of the sea during a storm. "You know, of course, that the women I employ must be willing to pleasure men, don't you?"

A dull red crept up Aimee's neck. "I'm aware of what goes on here."

"Have you worked in a house of prostitution before?"

Aimee's mouth worked noiselessly until she found the courage to answer. "No."

"That's what I thought. You don't look the type. But you're willing to do so now?"

"Yes."

"Obviously my house wasn't your first choice of work," Mona observed dryly. "Would you like to tell me what brings you here?"

"I'm in desperate need of money," Aimee confided. "My home was burned by Yanks, and my son and I are forced to live in slave quarters."

"What about relatives?"

"We have none. My husband and his parents are dead, and mine have been gone many years. I believe there are some Trevors in France or England, but little good that does me now. I need money immediately to purchase food and medicine. Without them, we won't survive the winter."

"And you're willing to sell yourself in order to buy food for your son." It wasn't a question but a comment.

"I'd do anything, even compromise my morals, to save my son from starvation."

"You look as if you could use a good meal or two yourself," Mona said, casting a critical eye over Aimee's thin frame. "My customers like their women plump; they want no reminders of the war going on around them. And your clothes are in deplorable condition. It would probably take several days of grooming before you're presentable enough to introduce to my clients."

"Several days! I—I need money now. I could start immediately.

"You wouldn't last the night," Mona scoffed. "A half-starved waif like you wouldn't have the stamina necessary for this kind of work. No, honey, if you want work, you'll have to let me fatten you up a bit before you can begin. And find you clothes suitable for this profession. Look at your hair; it's a mess. I have a tradition to uphold; the men who come here expect to find the best, and I've never failed them."

Aimee wrung her hands. "What can I do? I need the money now."

Mona's expression softened. She was not nearly as heartless as one might expect from a woman of her calling. She had once been in the same position as Aimee, and wouldn't have made it this far in life without a helping hand.

"I can loan you the money, honey, though I doubt you'd find food for sale anywhere in Atlanta."

"But how do you survive if no food is available? All your girls look healthy and well fed."

"Of course. The Federals see that I receive food and medicines necessary to keep my girls in good health. We're essential to the well-being of their troops."

Aimee flushed, embarrassed by Mona's frank words but determined to persevere.

"Tell you what, honey. I'll give you what food I can spare, and you can pay me from your first earnings."

"You'd do that for me? How do you know you can trust me to return once I leave here?"

Mona's steady gaze did not waver. "I just know. I'll even loan you a horse to carry you back to your home. Your nag looked done in. You can leave in the morning. I'll expect you back before dark. Is it a deal?"

Not only was Mona keenly perceptive when it came to judging character, but she was an excellent businesswoman. She saw Aimee's potential, saw through her gauntness to the fragile beauty concealed beneath the unattractive dress she wore. Mona knew at a glance that Aimee Trevor possessed an innate beauty and vulnerability that men found endearing. She fully expected Aimee to become a favorite among her clients and earn more than enough money to compensate her for the loan.

Aimee swallowed several times before she could reply. She knew that once given, her word was inviolate. Just as she had once risked her honor on a game of cards and paid in a way that changed her life forever, she must be prepared now to compromise her morals if she accepted Mona's generous offer.

Her pride for the life of her son. There was no contest. It was a small thing to surrender when so much was at stake.

"It's a deal, Miss Mona. If you provide me with provisions to last several weeks, I'll take them to Tall Oaks and return immediately, fully prepared to fulfill my duty to you. You may take the cost out of my earnings."

"Is there someone at Tall Oaks to care for your child in your absence?"

Aimee nodded, suddenly fearing Savannah's response when told she was going to work in a whorehouse. "My old nanny. Savannah loves Brand as much as I do."

"Then it's all settled, honey. You can sleep undisturbed here tonight. Tomorrow you'll go home with supplies, and when you return, I'll groom you to take your place with my girls. Don't worry, honey, you'll do just fine."

"You're what!" Savannah looked at Aimee as if she'd just told her the world was going to end tomorrow. That at least would have been easier to accept.

"I found a job, Savannah; what difference does it make what kind of work I'll be doing? Miss Mona is a good person. She gave me all this food to bring to you and trusts me to return to Atlanta."

"You ain't gonna do it." Savannah's dark eyes glinted dangerously.

"This discussion is unnecessary, Savannah. I've

already given my word. I'm returning to Miss Mona's."

"Over my dead body."

Aimee sighed wearily. "I'll bring out additional food whenever I can get away. And more medicine. Miss Mona sent me to her doctor, and he gave me medicine for both you and Brand. I have a debt to repay, and my honor demands that I return to fulfill my promise."

"How can you talk about honor when what you're doin' is dishonorable? Why, if Captain Drummond knew about this, he'd—"

"Savannah! I'll hear no more about Captain Drummond or what he would do. He's not here, and we're unlikely to see him again, so it can't matter to him what I do or don't do. You'll just have to accept the fact that I'm determined to save you and Brand no matter what it costs in terms of pride."

"I hate it, chile, I surely do, but if you're dat determined, den dere's nothin' I can do to stop you. I'll take good care of Brand for you. Ain't nothin' gonna happen to dat child while you're gone."

"I'll come back often, Savannah. As often as I'm allowed," Aimee amended.

"Take care of yourself, honey," Savannah sobbed as she turned away. "It just ain't right. A fine lady like you shouldn't have to lay with Yanks for money."

Unable to come up with a response that would placate the old woman, Aimee turned to leave. "I'll say good-bye to Brand before I leave. I love you both, Savannah."

Chapter 16

Nick stepped off the train to a scene as desolate as any he had ever seen. Except for bluecoats, few people were out on the streets of Atlanta. Much of the railroad station had been demolished, and Nick noted that workers toiled to repair the tracks leading out of town. An occasional painted whore drove by in a buggy, alone or accompanied by a Union protector, but even though some civilians had begun returning to their homes, few were in evidence.

The trip from Washington had been a tedious one, delayed by work crews repairing tracks that had been destroyed by Rebs. Sherman had decided to abandon the railroads and its supply lines, placing Union General Thomas and his sixty thousand men in charge while he marched to the sea, smashing everything along the way. It seemed as if nothing could stop Sherman's relentless pace of a dozen miles a day. Georgia militia wrecked bridges, burned provisions, toppled trees, and planted mines on the roads ahead of the Yankees, but this accomplished little except to make them more vengeful.

The cold temperatures and blustery winds of

only days before had suddenly warmed into Indian summerlike weather, and Nick welcomed the change from the winter he had left behind in Washington. He made his way directly to headquarters, requesting billeting for a few nights. He was given a room in a hotel that was being used by the army to house its men. Since he hadn't slept well on the train, he lay down to rest for a few minutes, and instead fell into a deep sleep. When he awoke, it was too late to start out for Tall Oaks, so he decided to check on his horse. Sergeant Jones had promised Nick he'd see that Scout was taken care of at the livery, while Nick stayed in Washington.

Nick indeed found Scout well cared for. He paid the livery owner for Scout's keep but left him in the man's charge until morning, when he planned to leave for Tall Oaks. He ate dinner at the officers' mess and declined an invitation to visit Miss Mona's, the best of the local whorehouses. Making love to any woman but Aimee did not appeal to him. Instead, he downed a stiff whiskey and went directly to bed, dreaming of his reunion tomorrow with Aimee.

Would she be glad to see him? he wondered anxiously. Or was she still angry with him? Had she and Brand been getting enough to eat, or would he find them starving? Tomorrow couldn't arrive soon enough.

It was an exceptionally warm December day when Nick mounted Scout and rode off in the direction of Tall Oaks. Stuffed in his saddlebag were treats for Brand, a colorful embroidered shawl for Savannah, and a length of silk for Aimee. He knew an embroidered shawl and length of silk were frivolous gifts, but practical ones would come later. He wasn't a poor man, Nick reasoned, and he could well afford to give the woman he hoped would be his wife some pretty things.

Since his father had died nearly ten years ago, Nick had been the head of the family, acting as sole support of his mother and sister, until his sister's marriage several years ago. His father's munitions plant had always made money—more so now than ever. When he went to war, he left Cliff Wayland, his sister's husband, in charge, and the man was doing an excellent job of running the family business in his absence. So good, in fact, that Nick seriously considered selling it to Wayland, taking the money, and investing it in some other enterprise more to his liking.

Nick turned off the main road and nudged Scout down the long avenue of oaks toward the house. His eagerness must have been catching, for Scout danced beneath him excitedly. It was as if the horse recognized the path down which they traveled and was eager to return home.

Home.

Strangely enough, Nick had come to think of Tall Oaks as home. He had grown to love the place nearly as much as Aimee did. Nick pictured how it would be after the war, assuming help could be hired to run the vast acres. He envisioned it in all its former glory, with ripe cotton waving in the breeze, their pods bursting and ready for harvesting. He saw animals grazing on the hillsides, and the orchards producing bumper crops of fruit.

When he came within sight of the house, Nick saw only the tall front pillars left unscathed by the fire. Nothing seemed amiss. But that initial impression was shattered when he noticed the charred, blistered walls and remains of the roof fallen in upon itself.

"Sweet Jesus, no!"

Leaping from the saddle, Nick ran toward the gutted wreckage of the house, sobbing and calling Aimee's name. His answer was an ominous silence. Like a madman he began tossing aside boards and charred debris until his hands were bleeding and he was grimy and blackened with soot. When he realized that the house had been burned weeks ago and was unlikely to yield a clue to Aimee and Brand's fate, he sat down on a stump and stared dazedly into the rubble.

Were Aimee and his son alive? he wondered bleakly. Or had they perished in the fire? What about Savannah? Had the house been burned by Union soldiers or Reb deserters? When he learned who was responsible for such wanton destruction, he'd personally see that the men were punished.

"You're too late, Captain Drummond."

Leaping to his feet, Nick spun around. He had recognized Savannah's voice immediately, and relief surged through him. Until he considered her words. "What are you talking about? Why am I too late?" Lord, don't let it be what I think, he fervently prayed.

"Aimee's gone."

"Oh, God, no." The cry ripped past his lips, the agony tearing him apart. Without Aimee, life wasn't worth living. And then he remembered Brand. Had his son perished also?

"What about Brand? Is he—is he . . ."

"Brand is just fine. We're livin' in one of de

slave shacks out back. It ain't much, but it keeps us warm and dry."

"Oh, God, I'm so sorry, Savannah, so damn sorry. How long ago did it happen?"

"Right after dat woman took you to Atlanta."

"Thank you for keeping Brand safe for me. It couldn't have been easy. How did you manage?" He didn't want to think about Aimee. Not now, not when the pain was still so raw.

"We used up de money you left, and when dat was gone ..." She grew quiet and lowered her head to stare at a big toe peeking out from the rags she had tied around her feet when her shoes wore completely through. "It ain't right, Captain, it ain't right dat my chile should suffer." He thought she was talking about Brand.

"You need worry no longer about Brand, Savannah; I'm taking you both back to Washington with me, where you'll be properly cared for. Though Aimee has never admitted it, I know Brand is my son."

Suddenly Savannah turned belligerent. "I ain't goin' nowhere without Aimee, and neither is Brand. She'd have my hide if she knew you was takin' Brand away."

Tears gathered in Nick's eyes and he hastily brushed them away with the back of his hand. "Aimee wouldn't want her son to starve. I loved her, too, Savannah, but we must think of Brand. Somehow we'll survive."

"We'll survive, but I ain't so sure about Aimee," Savannah replied glumly.

Her remark stymied Nick. He thought about it for a few seconds before her meaning became clear. His heart leaped in unfettered joy and he grasped Savannah by the shoulders, the intensity of his green eyes frightening her.

"What are you saying, Savannah? I thought you said Aimee was dead."

"Dead? Lordy, no." Her eyes rolled heavenward until only the whites were visible. "She ain't dead, Captain, just gone."

"Gone where?" His hands tightened, making Savannah wince in pain.

"To Atlanta. I done told her there was no work for her in Atlanta, but she couldn't let us starve, could she? It ain't like she's doin' it 'cause she wants to. Or dat she enjoys it. We was all starvin', Captain; it was de only way."

"What in the hell are you babbling about?"

"Nick! You're here! I knew you'd come, but Mama said you'd never return to Tall Oaks."

Nick caught up the little boy as he leaped into his arms. He groaned in dismay when he felt the lad's thin frame beneath his hands; he could count every rib beneath his narrow chest. With a pang of guilt Nick imagined all the suffering and hardships they had been forced to endure in his absence. He vowed then and there that neither Aimee, nor Brand nor Savannah would ever experience hunger or deprivation again. And as soon as he learned where Aimee was working, he'd make it all up to her.

"Where is your mama, son?" Nick asked, setting Brand down on his feet.

"In Atlanta. She brought us food and medicine and left again."

"Were you sick?"

"He had a congestion in de chest," Savannah replied. "Aimee couldn't bear to see him suffer. Dat's why she did it."

"Did what?" Nick was becoming more impatient by the minute.

"It ain't for me to say."

"Just tell me where to find her."

"She's at Miss Mona's," Brand piped up. "I heard her telling Savannah that she was going to work in a warehouse."

Nick nearly choked. "She what!"

"Oh, Lordy," Savannah moaned, shaking her head in dismay. "Aimee would have a fit if she knew Brand was listenin' to our conversation."

Nick's face was like thunder. Never had Brand seen him so angry, not even when Aimee had run away from Tall Oaks and was locked in her room as punishment. His small face screwed up as he bravely fought back tears.

"Did I say something wrong?"

Nick bent and scooped the lad up in his arms. "No, son, you didn't say anything to make me angry with you. I'm just worried about your mama. Why don't you look in my saddlebags; I've brought you some gifts."

"Gifts? For me?" His eyes danced with curiosity. "I can't remember when I last received a gift. I know, I think it was that horse you carved for me." Bursting with excitement, he squirmed out of Nick's arms and bounded over to Scout, where he proceeded to dig into the saddlebag. While he exclaimed over the treasure trove he found stashed inside, Nick conversed quietly with Savannah.

"How long has Aimee been at Miss Mona's?" His voice sounded as if it were stretched taut.

"A week."

A soft groan slipped past Nick's lips. "Have you heard from her since she left?"

"No. She brought enough food to last us two or three weeks and said not to expect her for a while."

"Why in the hell didn't you stop her?"

"I tried. The good Lord knows I tried, but you know how stubborn Aimee is." He did indeed. "She hoped to get respectable work, but dere wasn't none available. She couldn't let Brand starve, and dat's what would have happened if she hadn't gone to Miss Mona's."

"Pack up your things and Brand's. I'll be back."

His face a mask of fury, Nick turned abruptly and walked over to where Brand was still rummaging around in his saddlebags. The lad was sucking on a peppermint stick. Never had Nick seen an expression of such delight on the face of another human being.

"I have to leave, son, but I'll return soon with your mother. Then we'll all go to Washington."

"Leave Tall Oaks?"

"For the time being." He turned to Savannah. "Take care of Brand, Savannah." Then he remembered the gift he had for her, removed it from his saddlebag, and tossed the package to her. She caught it neatly. "This is for you."

"Don't you be angry with Aimee," Savannah warned, shaking a finger in his face. "She done what she had to do."

Nick mounted up. "Don't lecture me, Savannah. Aimee is the one you should have scolded. When I find her I'll try to contain my anger. If it's any consolation, be advised that I won't harm her."

As he rode off, he wasn't certain he could live

up to that promise. He was angry enough with Aimee to wring her beautiful neck. Imagining her spread beneath men who would use and abuse her rattled him so badly, he couldn't think straight. Even though he knew she was doing it for Brand's sake, the knowledge still threw him into a rage. He loved her, for God's sake!

Aimee stared at herself in the mirror, seeing a strange woman who bore her little resemblance. The woman who stared back at her had pouty lips painted a ripe red, and cheeks artfully rouged. Her eyes were outlined in black, the lids highlighted with subtle color that gave them a sensual glow. She wore a sheer peignoir that floated about her body but concealed little. A hip-length chemise beneath revealed long, shapely legs, nearly all of her breasts, and the tiny span of her waist.

Though Miss Mona had stuffed Aimee with rich food for an entire week, it had accomplished little except for filling out the hollows beneath her cheekbones and collarbone. Her body was still painfully thin but nevertheless all woman, with curves and indentation in all the right places. A pair of high-heeled slippers completed Aimee's costume.

Aimee's greatest fear was that she wouldn't be able to do what was expected of her tonight.

The nearer the time came to walking down those stairs and mingling with Mona's girls, the more panicky she became. She had tried to separate herself from everything that would take place tonight, but nothing short of death would make her forget that the moment she let the first man bed her, she would become a whore.

Think of Brand, she told herself sternly. Think of the two lives she was saving, not about her silly pride or honor. What possible good would her honor do her when those she loved were dead? A soft knock on the door jerked Aimee from her mournful thoughts. The door opened and Mona entered without waiting to be invited.

"You look marvelous, honey," Mona gushed delightedly. "But then, I knew you would. Still a mite thin, but I'm sure my customers will be as pleased with you as I am. You're not nervous, are you?"

"I—yes, of course I am. This doesn't come easily to me."

"It will get easier with time," Mona said, her tone brusque and businesslike. "You know the rules, don't you? You let me do the negotiating. After the details are worked out and a price agreed upon, you are free to take the client upstairs. I keep careful accounting of the earnings of all my girls. Rest assured you won't be cheated. I don't allow any rough stuff here, either. If a man gets rowdy or tries to hurt you, you have only to call out and one of the bouncers will come to your aid."

"I trust you, Miss Mona; that's not what's bothering me. I just don't know if I can go through with it."

"I'm not holding you here, honey," Mona reminded her. "If you had any other means of feeding your child, I'd let you go now, even if you do owe me money. I'd trust you to pay it back."

"You took me in and gave me food to take to Tall Oaks; I'll not let you down. Besides, we both know there is no other work available to me in Atlanta. A bargain is a bargain; I'll live up to my part of it."

"I knew you'd feel that way. What you're doing here has nothing to do with honor, it's survival. You aren't the only woman driven to prostitution by starvation and circumstances beyond her control. Thank God you had the good sense to come to me, for I take care of my girls. Now then, honey, the other girls are already assembling downstairs. Men have already begun to arrive. Come down whenever you're ready."

Aimee remained in her room a few moments longer. She felt like vomiting but managed with difficulty to swallow the bitter taste of bile that rose in her throat. Her knees were weak and her head hurt. Yet Aimee knew she could not linger. With shaking hands she opened the door and stepped out on the landing overlooking the crowded parlor below.

A sea of blue uniforms intermingled with scantily clad girls offering drinks on trays. Some men openly ogled the girls; others were much bolder, squeezing and stroking private parts of their anatomy. None of the girls being openly caressed seemed to mind. Aimee watched as one of the men seized a girl by the hand and led her over to Mona, where a friendly bargaining commenced. Once the man explained what he wanted, a price was agreed upon and Mona wrote it in a book. Payment was tendered, and the girl led the man up the stairs. Taking in a deep, steadying breath, Aimee waited for the giggling couple to enter a room, then started down the stairs.

Nick rang the bell at Miss Mona's house of pleasure with great impatience. His stark, intense face effectively conveyed the anguish he was suffering. He still found it difficult to believe he'd find Aimee in a whorehouse, but desperation drove people to do things they might never consider in less difficult times. According to Savannah, Aimee had been at Miss Mona's an entire week. He shuddered, thinking of what Aimee had been forced to endure before he arrived in Atlanta.

The door opened, and declining to hand over his hat and coat to the maid, Nick strode into the parlor. It was already crowded with soldiers and a few civilians attached to the government. Nick recognized one or two of the officers present, but most of the men were strangers, which suited him just fine. The fewer acquaintances who knew his future wife was a—good Lord, he couldn't call Aimee a whore!

Then he saw her, poised at the top of the stairs looking frightened and lost. Her face was heavily painted, and she was dressed—or undressed, as was the case—most provocatively. He stopped just inside the door, staring at her, noting that her thinness served only to enhance her fragile beauty.

Aimee failed to notice Nick in the crush of blue uniforms. She looked at no one in particular, keeping her eyes trained on a point above everyone's heads. Nick watched her descend the stairs, saw the stir she created among those men present who had the good fortune to notice her, and his eyes glazed over with the fury of his knowledge that other men wanted to bed her. Suddenly staunch willpower was no longer enough to keep him from doing what his conscience demanded he do from the moment Savannah had told him where Aimee could be found.

Aimee had reached the bottom of the stairs now, pausing to gather her courage before taking that last step. Once she joined the other girls in the parlor, she had no control over what must necessarily follow. She was wild with panic, her gaze sweeping the room. Then she saw him; he was pushing rudely through the throng of men and scantily clad women to reach her. His face was stark with fury. His fists were clenched at his sides, and his eyes were so dark a shade of green, they were nearly black. Truly devil's eyes. Aimee felt a shaft of raw, naked fear shudder through her.

Nick stopped scant inches from her, staring at her with his astonishingly level gaze for the space of a heartbeat. "Playtime is over, sweetheart; you're leaving with me."

Aimee's eyes widened; her jaw worked noiselessly, but no words came out. With an efficiency of effort, Nick pulled off his overcoat, placed it around Aimee's shoulders, swept her off her feet, and threw her over his shoulder like a sack of potatoes. "You're mine, Aimee Trevor; I'll be damned if I'll let another man have you."

"What's going on here, Major?" Mona appeared at Nick's elbow, flanked by two burly bouncers. "If you've made your choice, you must make arrangements with me first."

"The hell with arrangements," Nick said tightly. "Aimee belongs to me; I'm taking her with me. Any fool can see she doesn't belong here."

"Aimee is here of her own free will," Mona said in an effort to disarm the potentially volatile situation. "I hold no girl by force."

"Let me go, Nick Drummond!" Aimee

screeched, pounding at Nick's back. "I belong to no man."

"You heard her, let her go, Major." The two bouncers took a menacing step forward.

"Look here," Nick said with exaggerated patience, "Aimee and I need to talk privately. I'll gladly pay for her time."

Mona's eyes sparkled in understanding. Since Aimee seemed to know the major, and the major sure as hell knew Aimee, she saw no harm in letting Nick have his way—up to a certain point. "If you want to 'talk,' you have to do it in my house. I take care of my girls, and I don't let them leave unless I know for sure they want to go. Providing you pay for her time and promise not to hurt her, I see no reason to deny your request."

"I don't know the going rate for the entire night, but this ought to cover it," Nick said disgustedly as he dug in his pocket with his free hand. He removed several bills and tossed them at Mona. She caught them deftly, then motioned for the bouncers to let Nick pass.

"Third door on the left. And remember, no rough stuff."

"I don't want to go with him," Aimee said in a muffled voice as she continued to struggle. What right did Nick have coming in here like this and making a fool of her? No doubt he was already married to Regina Blakewell and came to Miss Mona's to escape her cloying possessiveness.

"Shut up," Nick said as he sprinted up the stairs before Mona could change her mind.

Mona watched them thoughtfully. She didn't know everything, but she did know men. Nick Drummond was a determined man who knew

what he wanted. He had emerged from somewhere out of Aimee Trevor's past to claim the
woman he considered his. No doubt remained in
Mona's mind that Aimee's career in her house had
ended before it ever really began. Mona wondered
if the impetuous major knew this was to be
Aimee's first night of entertaining clients. She
wished she could witness the fireworks that were
bound to result when those two temperaments
clashed, but she'd put her money on the major
coming off the winner.

Nick slammed the door to Aimee's room with
his foot, wrinkling his nose in disgust at the osten-
tatious furnishings and gaudy wallpaper. He
threw her roughly onto the soft surface of the bed,
returned to lock the door, then came back to stand
over her. His face was like a thundercloud, dark
and menacing.

"Where in hell were your brains, coming to
work in a whorehouse? Do you enjoy having several men a night? Wipe your face; you look like a
whore."

"Don't judge me, you bastard! You have no idea
what brought me here or why I did what I did."

"I have some idea," Nick said, his expression
softening. "But it doesn't make it any easier for me
to swallow. Why didn't you get in touch with me?
You could have asked the commanding officer to
send word to me. Or written."

"If you're talking about Major Tanner, forget it.
I did go to him, but he refused to help me."

"Did you ask him specifically to contact me?
Did you tell him my son was sick and starving?
I'll wager you never even mentioned my name."

"Your son! I never told you Brand was your son."

"No, but you're going to tell me now. I've been extremely patient with you, Aimee, but the time has come to tell the truth." He glared down at her with a look that told her there was no sense in pretending any longer.

"Yes, dammit, Brand is your son! Are you happy now?"

Nick smiled. "Exceedingly happy."

"What are you going to do about it? Don't think that you and Regina are going to raise my son, for you can't have him."

"What's Regina got to do with anything?"

"She's your finacée. Or are you already married? She was quite determined to have you."

"I am not going to marry Regina Blakewell. And I *will* have my son."

Aimee inhaled sharply. It was just as she feared. Nick would take her son from her, and she'd never see him again. "You can't have Brand, Nick. Please, can't you see that it would kill me if you took him away from me?"

"We'll talk about Brand later. First tell me what made you seek work in a—a—"

"Whorehouse," Aimee finished since he seemed to have such difficulty with the word. "I did what was necessary to save Brand and Savannah. Brand was ill. They both needed food and medicine. I made a bargain with Mona, and I intend to live up to my end of it."

"By sleeping with men?"

A dull red crept up Aimee's neck. "We do what we have to do for our loved ones."

"My God, Aimee, I wanted to throttle you when

I heard what you did! I'm still not sure you're safe from me, which is why I haven't touched you since coming into this room. I told you I'd come back to Atlanta. You know how much I care for you."

"You didn't care enough about me to tell me you were engaged," she accused hotly.

"Truthfully, I never gave it a thought. Once I found you again, Regina no longer held any interest for me. I intended to break the engagement at the earliest opportunity, but one can't always do what one wants in times of war."

He dropped down on the bed beside her, suddenly weary of argument. He didn't care what she had done, or with whom. He'd never bring up the past to her; it was their future that mattered. How many men could she have had in a week, anyway? Even one was too many, a little voice whispered. But he quickly put the thought out of his mind.

"What makes you think I'd ever care for a bluebelly?" Aimee bit out. "Your kind has devastated the South, subjugated our people, raped, destroyed, and pillaged at will. I hate you, and I hate all you stand for. Why couldn't you leave us in peace?"

Nick's eyes turned brilliant green. "You don't hate me, sweetheart. We have a child together, remember?"

"How could I forget? For years I lived in fear that someday, somehow, you'd learn about Brand and take him from me. It was a preposterous idea given the fact that you apparently didn't care what happened to me after you collected the debt of honor I owed you. Yet it happened. We did meet again, under less than favorable circumstances, I might add, and you do intend to take Brand from me. How do you explain that?"

"Fate, sweetheart. It was meant to be. Just as our loving one another was preordained. I won't take your son from you. You, Brand, and Savannah are coming with me to Washington."

Aimee struggled upright on the bed. "What! Absolutely not. I'll never set foot in that Yankee stronghold. As for loving one another, why don't you admit it's lust you feel for me? You're asking me to go to Washington with you only because you want your son, not because you have tender feelings for me."

"You're wrong, sweetheart. Yes, I want Brand, but not without you. I admit I lust for you, but it goes deeper than that. If you're afraid I'll think less of you for—for coming to this place, rest assured I'll never bring it up again. I don't like it, but I accept that you acted out of desperation and need."

"How gallant of you," Aimee said bitterly. "But quite unnecessary. I've bedded no one since you left Tall Oaks with Regina."

Joy bubbled up inside him, causing his heart to overflow with happiness. It was almost too good to believe. Aimee had been at Miss Mona's for an entire week. How could she not have been intimate with anyone? Aimee saw his happiness, and then the curtain of disbelief that tempered it.

"I don't expect you to believe me, but it's true. Mona didn't rush me. She said I needed rest and food. She stuffed my belly for a week, and tonight was to be my debut."

"It was?" Nick said. The devil in his green eyes

danced with mischievous delight. "Well, I'm the one you're going to spend the night with. Love me, Aimee. Surrender to the fury that was uniquely ours. Tomorrow we leave for Washington, but tonight belongs to us.

"Like hell!"

Chapter 17

"Shut up and kiss me."

Aimee groaned in dismay. Didn't Nick understand? She was going nowhere with him. Nor could he have her son. He wasn't the kind of man with whom she wanted to spend her life. Besides, the only reason he wanted her was because he wanted Brand. She wasn't stupid. There was no possible way for him to prove Brand was his son, was there?

"Why must you keep up this pretense?" Aimee asked.

He looked at her with intensity—far too determined to give her peace of mind. "You're not getting away from me again, Aimee. Why is it so difficult to believe that I care for you? Deeply."

She looked away, visibly shaken. How easily the lie came to his lips. "Don't patronize me, Nick."

"Is that what you think I'm doing? Think again, sweetheart. I rushed to Atlanta the moment I was free in order to bring you and our son to Washington. We'll be married as soon as arrangements can be made. For weeks I've suffered the pangs of hell thinking about you and Brand in this war-ravaged land, starving perhaps, or even worse."

305

An uneasy silence settled between them as Nick continued to stare at her. His head bowed toward her. Aimee tried to turn away, but he grasped her face and held it in place between his hands. She stared at his mouth, remembering the moist heat of his full lips pressed across hers in passion, tasting her in places that made her forget her undying hatred.

Nick smiled, and she watched in fascination as the moist corners of his mouth tilted upward. Suddenly the thought occurred to her that he knew exactly what she was thinking, and hot color flooded her cheeks. A low chuckle rumbled from his chest.

"I remember, too, sweetheart." His voice was sensual, seductive, and wildly erotic.

Dear God, was he a mind reader?

"You can't possibly know what I'm thinking," Aimee said.

"You're remembering how magnificent it was between us when we made love. You're recalling the wanton way in which you responded to the touch of my hands and mouth, and how tightly you held me inside you. We can have that again, sweetheart. Every night if we want."

She grew breathless at the thought. "Nick, please, I can't think straight when you're confusing me like this."

"Don't think, Aimee, just feel." Then his mouth, so close to hers that she could feel his warm breath on her lips, closed the gap between them.

His mouth covered hers completely. She felt his hunger in the furious pressure of his lips and in the hot, stabbing length of his tongue as it forced itself past the barrier of her teeth to fill her with his need. He moved upon her until her body had no choice but to accept his weight and press upward against him in self-preservation. His hands touched her everywhere, her breasts, her hips, the soft place between her legs, and still he kissed her, forcibly pressing her mouth open with his as his tongue continued to plunder her sweetness.

It wasn't until her tiny fists beat repeatedly against his chest that he allowed her respite. They were both panting erratically when he drew his mouth away from hers.

"You're hurting me."

"I'm sorry, sweetheart, but it's been so long, so damn long."

"Evidently Regina wasn't very obliging."

"I've not bedded Regina since I rode to Tall Oaks that day and met a woman from my past whom I've never been able to forget. In fact, I've bedded no other woman since fate brought us together again."

"I was handy; there was no need to bed another woman."

Nick groaned in frustration. Suddenly he stood up and began stripping off his clothes. Aimee lifted herself to her elbows. "What are you doing?"

"What does it look like? Since you're 'handy,' I may as well take advantage of the situation. Besides, I paid dearly for the pleasure of your company."

Aimee opened her mouth to fling back a scathing retort, but when Nick pulled off his shirt and she saw the vivid red scar, she sucked in her breath and stared at the healing wound in mute dismay. Seeing the direction of her gaze, Nick paused.

"Does it disgust you?"

Aimee looked puzzled. Disgust her? Far from being disgusted, she recalled the suffering he had endured because of it. "Why should it disgust me? I've seen it often enough when I was caring for you. Does it still give you discomfort?"

Nick's green eyes glinted wickedly. "Not enough to keep me from loving you." Then he slid his trousers down his legs and sat on the bed to remove his boots.

"I don't want to make love with you, Nick."

Nick's smile vanished, replaced by a ferocious scowl. "You were willing enough to do it with a stranger."

Aimee had the grace to flush. "I—had no choice."

"You have no choice now," Nick said as he rolled to his side and pulled her into his arms. "Since you won't believe me when I say I care deeply for you, I'll just have to show you by my actions. Before we leave this room, you'll have no reason to doubt me or resist my efforts to make you my wife."

"I'm not stupid; I know it's Brand you want."

"You stubborn little fool! Of course I want my son. But I also want my son's mother. Now, shut up and let me love you."

There was no tenderness in his kiss. It was penetrating, hard, and desperate. While his mouth worked to dissolve her resistance, his hands skillfully removed her clothes—what little she had on. The filmy robe went first, then the thin chemise. When she lay nude and vulnerable beneath him, his mouth left hers, sliding down the slope of her breast to its hardened point.

Aimee shivered at the feel of his warm, moist lips against her sensitive flesh. She closed her eyes and moaned when his calloused fingers slid up the inside of her thigh.

"Open your eyes, sweetheart. I want you to know who's making love to you. I'm not your dead husband, or a faceless man who paid for your favors."

Slowly Aimee's eyes opened, clashing immediately with Nick's mesmerizing gaze.

"Who am I, Aimee? Say my name, darling."

"Oh, Nick!" His name came from her lips in an exclamation of mounting passion.

Then Nick's lips, so insistent upon her breasts, began sucking vigorously at an engorged nipple as his hand explored the moisture between her legs.

His mouth closed over hers as his finger slipped inside her, the tormenting plunge of his tongue mimicking his motion below. Her head rolled back and forth. Her hands wound themselves in the tousled sleekness of his hair as his mouth returned to her ripe, sweetly swollen nipples. He nudged her knees, and to her own dismay, she found herself opening her legs wider, lifting herself against the subtle pressure of his hands, writhing to the rhythm of the awful pain he was creating there. When he slid down the length of her body, she tried to stop him, but was powerless to halt the spiraling surge of wanton hunger he had unleashed inside her.

He looked at her and grinned knowingly before spreading her open for the sweet torment of his mouth and tongue.

"Nick, please!"

"Are you going to marry me?"

"No."

Lowering his head, he flicked his tongue out to tease her mercilessly. Then he tasted and tormented her, driving her wild with a need that went beyond anything he had ever done to her before.

She pleaded, but it did absolutely no good as he continued to lick and bedevil her with his lips and tongue. Every sensation was centered between her legs. The feeling grew and throbbed and grew until—

She screamed.

The release came like an eruption, shattering her soul. She was still vibrating when Nick slid upon her body and thrust the hot, throbbing shaft of his being into her. Incredibly, the feel of him filling her, stretching her, touching the very center of her soul, revived the hot spiral of bliss that gripped her body, and the splendor intensified.

"Ah, sweetheart, you never cease to amaze me. You're body is so responsive to mine. How can you deny what we have together?"

Suspended in the grip of passion, Aimee could not reply. But Nick did not need one. He felt it in the way her body expanded to accommodate his, in every tiny tremor that squeezed him inside her with gentle pressure, in every shudder that made her body his to command, in the way she called his name when she climaxed around him. Then Nick's own release came upon him and he no longer had the ability to think.

Unwilling to separate their bodies, Nick clung to Aimee, holding himself inside her as he rolled to his side, taking her with him. More content than she was willing to admit, Aimee rested her head against his chest and counted his heartbeats as they slowed to a steady rhythm.

"Tell me now that we don't belong together," Nick said breathlessly. "I'll wager your husband didn't make you feel like that."

"I don't want to talk about Beau."

"Then let's talk about us. And our son. I'm going back out to Tall Oaks tomorrow to bring Brand and Savannah to Atlanta. Our train leaves at seven o'clock tomorrow evening."

"I just can't leave Miss Mona like that. She won't understand. I—I owe her for the loan of food and medicine I took out to Brand and Savannah."

"I'll pay her," Nick said, gnashing his teeth in frustration. "I have a feeling Mona understands more than you give her credit for. Don't worry, sweetheart, Mona won't be cheated."

"I'm not going to marry you, Nick."

"Since you have few decent clothes, pack whatever you deem appropriate from those provided by Mona," Nick continued, paying little heed to Aimee's protests. "Surely Mona furnished you with something other than nightwear, didn't she? I'll pay her handsomely for whatever you take from your wardrobe. When we get to Washington, I'll buy you and Brand whatever you need. We'll be married as soon as arrangements can be made."

"Nick, do you love me?" The words tumbled from her lips before she could bite them back.

"What in the hell kind of question is that? What do you think this is all about? Of course I love you. You're the mother of my son."

Aimee's heart sank. Nick loved her because she was the mother of his son. Could she settle for his passion and live her life being loved for that reason only?

"Oh, God."

"What's that supposed to mean? What in the hell did I say now to upset you?"

"If you don't know, I'm not going to tell you."

"Women! The only time I can satisfy you is when I'm doing this." He flexed his hips and thrust forward, revealing that he was still hard inside her.

Aimee felt him throb against the walls of her tight sheath as he grew and expanded, making her aware that his hunger had been momentarily appeased but not sated. He still wanted her.

"Feel what you do to me? We've all night, sweetheart; let's make the most of it. I've yet to hear you say you love me."

"I don't love you. I—I hate you. I hate the fact that you're a Yankee. I hate the way you left me aboard the *Dixie Belle*. I hate—"

He grasped her buttocks and held her in place while he thrust in and out, setting up a clamor in her blood.

"I love you," Nick said. "I love the way you respond to me. I love the way you look at me and call my name when you climax. I love the way you hate me."

Then he was lifting her atop him, pressing her down onto his erection, filling her deeply—so deep.

"Kiss me, sweetheart."

She did, filling his mouth with the incredible taste of her.

"Ride me, Aimee. You're in charge; do whatever you like."

Closing her eyes and throwing her head back, Aimee took control, already lost in a world of sensual pleasure. When Nick lifted his head and took her nipple into his mouth, she exploded. Vaguely she heard him cry out, felt the hot splash of his sperm, then knew no more.

"One day you'll admit you love me, sweetheart," Nick whispered before he joined her in slumber.

She was awakened once during the night by hot kisses falling randomly over her face and body. At first she thought she was dreaming, until Nick's lips and hands became so aggressive, she could no longer ignore the pounding of her blood or furious beating of her heart. Then he was thrusting inside her, bringing her the special kind of rapture only he was capable of. When she fell asleep again, she didn't awaken until the sun streamed through the window and Nick was gently shaking her.

"Aimee. Wake up. It's time I left for Tall Oaks."

Aimee stirred, flipped on her stomach, and said, "Go away."

Her buttocks rising beneath the single sheet was too tempting, and he stroked them absently as he spoke. "Aimee, I'm going to speak to Mona before I leave. I'll take care of everything, sweetheart. Sleep as late as you like. All you need do is pack and meet me at the train station before seven o'clock tonight. I'll have Brand and Savannah with me."

His words succeeded in chasing the last vestiges of sleep from her. "What! What did you say?"

"Our train leaves at seven o'clock. You have all

day to make yourself ready. I expect you to be at the station on time."

"What if I choose not to go?"

His lips thinned. "I don't recall giving you a choice. But should you foolishly decide not to join me and Brand in Washington, we'll somehow manage without you. It's your choice, Aimee. Me and your son, or a life of spreading your legs for every man who meets your price."

Her reply was a sharp intake of breath. God, how could he be so cruel? Did he have no compassion? Nick was a Yankee officer, and she was a southerner with no authority. Who would come to her defense if she complained that Nick was taking her beloved son away from her without her permission? The South was in chaos, and the damn Yankees were too busy with winning the war to concern themselves with one Reb woman's claim against one of their own kind. Nick's offer of marriage was obviously a sham; his words of love were meant only to soothe her wounded pride. How could she marry Nick when she suspected that his proposal was meant simply to appease her—when what he really wanted was custody of their son?

Nick watched the play of emotion on Aimee's face, realizing he had come down hard on her, but deeming it necessary in order to shock her into realizing that her life was with him.

"Seven o'clock, Aimee. Be there." Turning on his heel, he stalked out the door.

Mona didn't appreciate being roused from sleep so early, but she pulled herself together and listened to Nick's explanation. When he finished, she accepted payment for the clothes, provisions, and medicine Aimee had taken out to Tall Oaks without too much protest. Then she wished them both good luck and went back to bed. Girls came and went, and she wasn't the kind to hold them back when another opportunity came along. Nor did she begrudge anyone happiness. Life had taught her invaluable lessons, one of which was to take love when and where you found it. The great love of her life had been killed early on in the war, and she had never found another to take his place. Though Lord knows it wasn't from lack of trying.

Nick rented a wagon to drive to Tall Oaks. He seriously doubted that Brand and Savannah had much baggage between them, but a wagon had been all that was available for rent. He wasn't certain if Savannah could ride a horse, so he had to make do with the slower conveyance. Not that it mattered greatly; they had plenty of time to return to Atlanta by seven o'clock to catch the train to Washington. Would Aimee be there to meet him?

He had to hope she loved her son enough to want to be with him. He couldn't imagine any situation in which Aimee would willingly agree to be separated from Brand. He had pinned his hopes on her fierce love for her son. Marrying a Yankee might go against everything she believed in, but following Brand to Washington was something Nick could count on. Once she was with him, he had faith in his ability to convince her to marry him.

God, he loved her. He admitted freely that he hadn't always behaved like a gentleman to her, but Nick nevertheless realized that he had loved her forever—even when he mistook her for a whore aboard the *Dixie Belle*.

Nick had been so obsessed with finding the lady gambler known as Aimee Fortune that he finally had to confess the cause of his obsession to his mother, who was thoroughly shocked that her jaded son had finally found a woman worthy of his consideration. Though the good woman had commiserated with Nick, she had finally convinced him that the reason Aimee Fortune hadn't been found was that she didn't want to be found. When the war came, he finally gave up the search and concentrated on staying alive.

Then he found Aimee again.

And learned he had a son.

And found love.

Brand sat on a stump staring down the avenue of oaks, waiting for Nick. When he saw the wagon turn off the main road, he jumped up and ran for Savannah. Both Brand and Savannah were standing in front of the charred remains of the house when Nick arrived a few minutes later. Brand could hardly contain his excitement.

"We're ready, Nick!" he called as Nick climbed down from the wagon. "Where's Mama? You found her, didn't you?"

"I did indeed." Nick grinned, swinging the boy into his arms and placing him on the high seat of the wagon.

"How is she?" Savannah asked anxiously. Her face wore all the signs of a sleepless night—many sleepless nights. "She ain't been hurt, has she?"

"Aimee is fine, Savannah." He looked pointedly at Brand then said, "I'll tell you all about it later.

Suffice it to say that it isn't as bad as you thought. Now then, are you packed and ready to leave?"

"We ain't got much," Savannah said, holding out a modest bundle neatly tied in a square of cloth. Nick took it from her and placed it in the wagon. "I also packed what food was left. Thought it might come in handy before we reached Atlanta."

"That it will, Savannah. I didn't have time for breakfast. Up with you now." He helped her climb into the wagon bed, then settled himself beside Brand on the driver's seat. "Are you ready, son?"

"I'm going to miss Tall Oaks," Brand said wistfully as Nick drove the horse down the avenue of oaks. "Do you think my papa will know I'm no longer here?"

Nick swallowed painfully. He wanted so badly to tell Brand that Beauregard Trevor wasn't his father, but he knew that now wasn't the time, that Aimee was the one who should tell him.

"I think your papa will know that it has become necessary for you and your mother to leave Tall Oaks. Perhaps one day you will return. When the war is over and all is peaceful once again."

"I don't remember my papa," Brand said sadly, "but I'd want him to be just like you."

Nick's heart burst with gladness. "Doesn't it bother you that I'm a Yankee?"

Brand grew thoughtful. "It did at first. I knew how much it bothered Mama and that she seemed to hate you, but you never really hurt us."

"I'd never hurt you, Brand."

"I know that. What about Mama? You've hurt her."

"Not intentionally. The worst I did was to lock

her in her room, but she did a bad thing and I had no choice."

Lies, he told himself. All lies. Of course he had hurt Aimee. He hurt her by taking her virginity without realizing it and leaving her to bear his son in shame. He hurt her when he forced her to submit to him by convincing her he'd send her to prison if she didn't. He hurt her by not telling her about Regina.

"What would you think if I married your mama?" Nick asked with sudden inspiration.

Brand chewed on that for a while. "Like Mama and Papa were married?"

"Well, yes, something like that."

"Would you and Mama have a son like me?"

"We might have children. I hope we would, anyway. But they'd never take your place in our hearts. We have room in our hearts to love many children."

"I'd like brothers and sisters. It gets kind of lonesome sometimes with no other children around. Would you be my papa?"

"You can't imagine how desperately I'd like that."

"Then I guess it would be all right if you married Mama," Brand decided emphatically. "I always wanted a papa I could remember. You must promise, though, that you won't try to turn me into a Yankee."

Laughter bubbled up from Nick's throat. He was so delighted with Brand, he wanted to stop the wagon and hug him. The thought that he had missed out on the first five years of this precious child's life made him sad. From this day forward he vowed to be the father Brand needed. And nothing Aimee could do or say would ever change that.

They reached Atlanta in plenty of time to scour the stores still open for business for proper clothes for Brand and Savannah. It was going to be much colder in Washington, and it was obvious that neither Brand nor Savannah had suitable clothing. Savannah's shoes were beyond redemption, and Brand's were two sizes too small. It was close to seven o'clock by the time Nick had purchased everything they needed from the meager supplies available. Shoes for Savannah presented the biggest problem. They ended up settling for a pair of men's boots and were glad to get them.

Since Nick had already made arrangements with the livery to put his horse aboard the train, he only needed to drop off the wagon at the livery and walk the short distance to the railroad station. A great puff of steam and black soot bellowed forth from the engine as they approached, warning all passengers of its imminent departure. Nick purchased the tickets and waited with Brand and Savannah by the boarding steps for Aimee.

"I don't see Mama," Brand said as he peered anxiously into the crowd of people boarding. Most wore blue uniforms; few civilians were visible in the nearly deserted city.

"She'll be along," Nick said with more certainty than he felt.

He had counted heavily on Aimee being unable to let her son go off without her. He prayed he hadn't been wrong in that assumption.

"The train is going to leave." Brand was now truly concerned that his mother wouldn't arrive in time.

"She'll be here."

* * *

Aimee spent the entire day alternately cursing Nick and finding reasons to love him. On one hand was the fact that he was a despised Yankee who wanted to take her son from her. On the other was his declaration of love for her. Were his words merely lies uttered in a moment of weakness, or did he truly love her? To a man like Nick, lies seemed to come easily when they served his purpose. Aimee never truly believed he had looked for her after their night together aboard the *Dixie Belle*. And what about Regina Blakewell? If he loved Aimee, why hadn't he told her he had a fiancée?

Yet all the conjecturing in the world wouldn't solve her dilemma. Nick was going to take Brand to Washington whether or not she chose to accompany them. He wanted his son badly enough to snatch him from her loving arms, so to speak. Then he had the unmitigated gall to tell her he loved her.

As the day wore on, Aimee made a halfhearted attempt to pack some of the more appropriate articles of clothing given her by Mona. She chose two day dresses that weren't too revealing, some underclothing, and two pairs of slippers. She was grateful to add a warm cloak, for she'd heard the North could be bitterly cold this time of year.

By six o'clock Aimee was sitting on the bed still trying to decide whether she should appear at the train station and try to talk Nick out of taking Brand to Washington or do nothing in hopes that he'd relent and leave Brand behind when she failed to appear. Knowing Nick as she did, she seriously doubted he'd consider either alternative. He'd probably leave Atlanta as planned, taking her son, and promptly forget she ever existed. He had done it years ago, so why not now?

Aimee was still wallowing in indecision when Mona appeared at the door a few minutes later.

"Are you almost ready, honey? If you need any help with your bag, one of the bouncers can carry it to the station for you."

"Thank you, but the bag's not heavy. Besides, I haven't made up my mind whether or not I'm going with Major Drummond."

"Seems to me you have no choice," Mona observed. "Before he left, the major told me he's the father of your son and that he's taking the boy to Washington."

"The man is a damn Yankee and a scoundrel to boot!"

"You must have liked him well enough at one time." Mona's sly wink left no doubt as to her meaning.

"It's a long story, Miss Mona."

"And it all boils down to whether or not you love your son enough to marry the father."

"Did Nick tell you we were going to marry?"

"He sure did, honey. I assumed it was what you wanted, too. You're still welcome to stay on with me if you've a mind to."

Aimee shook her head in vigorous denial. "No, I don't want to stay on here. It was a mistake coming here in the beginning. I'm not certain I could have gone through with it if Nick hadn't showed up when he did."

Mona nodded sagely. "I kind of thought that,

but I was willing to give you the benefit of the doubt."

"I'm still grateful to you, Miss Mona. I'm certain the food and medicine you provided saved Brand's life. You offered help when I needed it most."

"My pleasure, honey, though your man paid generously for my services. Are you sure you don't love him just a little? He certainly is a handsome devil."

"Love him a little?" Aimee asked, astounded. "I love him more than I ever thought possible for a woman to love a man."

"It's time to board, Brand," Nick said as he guided Brand toward the boarding door.

Nick's face was set in grim lines. He had gambled on Aimee loving her son more than she hated him, and he had lost.

"Mama's not here yet." His voice was shrill with panic.

"She's had plenty of time, son. If she was coming, she'd be here by now."

"She'll be here, I know she will," Savannah said staunchly. "She ain't gonna let you take Brand away from her."

"That's what I thought, Savannah, but I guess we were both mistaken. But don't you worry, I'll be a damn good father to the boy. And he still has you."

"It ain't de same," Savannah grumbled as she stepped aboard the train.

Nick lifted Brand aboard and then followed. He glanced over his shoulder one last time to scan the now-deserted station, then turned away in bitter disappointment. Suddenly, from the corner of his eye, he caught a movement. Someone was hurrying down the length of the train. His heart jumped erractically in his chest. Aimee!

The train whistle gave an earsplitting blast, then the train jerked forward. Slowly at first, then gaining momentum, its wheels churned into motion and they began moving.

"Aimee! Hurry!"

She saw him then, hanging with one hand on the door rail, the other extended out toward her. She stumbled and nearly fell, then righted herself and reached out for his hand. The train gained speed, widening the gap between them. She wasn't going to make it. But she hadn't counted on Nick's determination. When he disappeared from the door, Aimee thought he had left her, when suddenly he appeared on the platform of the caboose. Leaning out over the rail, he reached out, grasped her about the waist with one long arm, and swept her up beside him.

Chapter 18

❦

Aimee hated Washington. The dirty blanket of gray slush that covered the streets was depressing, and she couldn't seem to shake the penetrating cold that seeped into her bones. She knew Savannah felt the same way about the dismal city even though the old woman said little about their circumstances. As for Brand, he was still too excited about his new surroundings to notice his mother's aversion to them.

Somehow Nick had managed to rent them a suite in a fairly decent hotel in the crowded city. Aimee would have moved into the same room with Savannah and Brand, but Nick told her in no uncertain terms that her place was with him. Then he took them all out and purchased clothes suitable for northern climes. When he informed Aimee that he was going to make arrangements for their wedding, Aimee stubbornly refused to take part in the ceremony, insisting that she would never consent to marry a damn Yankee. Her words had forced Nick to postpone the wedding.

They had been in Washington nearly a month when Sherman presented the city of Savannah to Lincoln as a Christmas gift. Hood's army had dug in around Nashville, waiting for Thomas to attack. When the attack came, it was a devastating knockout that almost annihilated the Rebs. It took but two winter days before the collapse finally came during a drenching rain and a gathering darkness. Christmas came and went with little celebration.

By the first of the year 1865, the remnants of Hood's army, decimated by nearly half, and most of the troops without shoes, fetched up at Tupelo, Mississippi. Heartsick and broken, Hood resigned his command on January 13, a Friday. Aimee took the news hard. Bitter disappointment made her even more determined than ever not to marry Nick. Nick seemed to take her refusal in stride, as if so confident of his ability to change her mind that a few days delay mattered little.

Nick's position as aid to General Blakewell kept him busy. So busy, in fact, that had Aimee given consent to their marriage, he doubted he'd find the time to appear at the ceremony. It was obvious to all that the war was nearly over and the South beaten to their knees. Rumor had it that the last meat ration was issued to Lee's army, and not a pound remained in Richmond. The South had expended all its resources and energies. The price of gold rose and the Confederate dollar slipped to less than two percent of its 1861 level. In contrast, the Union had inexhaustible resources to do the job and the largest navy in the world. They also had more men available to them now than they had when the war began. In effect, the North had gained strength while the South was barely able to struggle on. Incredibly, the war had boosted northern economy to new heights of productivity.

During this time Aimee came face-to-face with

Regina Blakewell. Aimee and Brand were just leaving a restaurant where they had stopped to warm themselves with a cup of hot chocolate when they bumped into Regina. The attractive red-head was wrapped in fur, wore a pert hat atop her bouncing curls, and looked stylishly elegant. She had just entered the restaurant with two other women who were dressed just as elegantly. Aimee thought of the poor starving women and children in the South and added another grievance to her growing list of reasons to hate Yanks.

"Why, Mrs. Trevor, imagine bumping into you like this," Regina said in a loud voice meant to attract attention. Nearly all within hearing distance swiveled their heads in Aimee's direction.

"Hello, Miss Blakewell," Aimee replied coolly.

"I'd heard Major Drummond brought a mistress to Washington," she said with sly innuendo. Aimee winced, aware that they were being observed by everyone in the crowded restaurant. Aimee's southern drawl made her sound conspicuously out of place.

Grasping Brand tightly by the hand, Aimee said, "Please excuse me, I must take my son home."

"What's the matter, Mrs. Trevor, does the truth hurt? If Nick was serious about you, he would have married you by now." The two women with Regina snickered behind their hands. "Thank goodness I learned what kind of man he was before we married. Fortunately I broke our engagement before it was too late," she continued, speaking loudly enough to carry across the room. By now people in the restaurant had stopped eating and were staring at them. "It's uncanny how much your son resembles Major Drummond."

Aimee had heard enough. It enraged her to think that Brand had been subjected to Regina's jealous remarks. "Thank God none of *your* children will look like Major Drummond," she replied as she pulled Brand through the door and walked briskly away from the restaurant. Bewildered, Brand had to run to keep up. His complaints finally penetrated Aimee's rage and she slowed her steps to meet his shorter gait.

That night Nick arrived back at the hotel early, announcing somewhat grandly that he was taking them all to a restaurant instead of eating in the hotel as was their usual habit. Recalling her earlier experience with Regina, Aimee promptly demurred.

"Why are you being difficult, sweetheart?" Nick asked, puzzled by Aimee's curt refusal.

"I don't feel like going out tonight," Aimee said. She had already decided not to tell Nick about her meeting today with Regina. It was difficult to speak of the humiliation she felt when Regina had deliberately insulted her before an audience.

"Are you sick?" he asked, concerned.

"No, I'm fine."

Brand was sitting nearby listening to the conversation when he suddenly blurted out, "What's a mistress?"

Aimee gasped in dismay.

Nick's head swiveled around to stare at Brand. His face wore a scowl. "Where did you hear that word?"

"From a lady I met at Tall Oaks. We saw her at the restaurant today. She said Mama was your mistress. I didn't know what it meant, but the way she said it wasn't very nice."

A vile oath slipped past Nick's lips. "That's it!" he said, rounding on Aimee. "You've had your way long enough. Now we'll do things my way. Like a fool I thought you'd come to want our marriage. But now that rumor has touched Brand, I must insist that we stop the gossipmongers." Suddenly he noted that Brand was staring at them and said, "Go find Savannah, Brand. Tell her to clean you up and keep you in your room until I tell her otherwise."

Reluctantly Brand did as Nick bid. He was acquainted with most of Nick's moods, and this mood was one that demanded instant obedience. But before the door closed behind him, he turned and asked, "Do I really look like you, Nick?"

Nick's face turned ashen. "We'll talk about it later, son." When he turned to face Aimee, he was hard put to control his anger.

Aimee was well aware of Nick's temper. She hadn't seen Nick this angry since he had caught her spying. The moment the door closed behind Brand, she took an instinctive step backward.

"Who was the lady and exactly what did she say?" His face was dark, his eyes narrowed, his mouth taut.

Aimee stumbled over the words. "It was Regina. She—she said she'd heard you had a mistress living with you."

"Is that all?"

"I—"

"The truth, dammit!"

She screeched the words at him. "She said Brand looked enough like you to be your son!"

"He is my son. I want the whole world to know it."

"By now they do," Aimee spat with disgust. "Regina spoke loudly enough for everyone in Washington to hear."

"I've humored you long enough. Your wishes are no longer important. I've told you repeatedly that I loved you; why do you continue to resist our marriage? What do you want from me? You're a selfish little bitch, Aimee Trevor. Are you going to let the color of my uniform ruin all of our lives?"

Never had Aimee heard Nick speak so harshly. Was she being selfish by keeping Nick from being a true father to Brand? She had spent over five years of her life hating the man who had fathered her son. Old habits don't disappear overnight. She had hated Yankees for as long as she could remember. They had destroyed everything she held dear in life, leaving her only Brand and Savannah. Then Nick had appeared: a man from her past wearing in a blue uniform, providing her with another reason to hate him. Yet against all odds, she had fallen in love with him. Refusing to marry him made no sense, except as a means of salving her damnable pride. Was it worth it?

"I'm no longer giving you a choice, Aimee," Nick continued when Aimee appeared deep in thought. "I'm going ahead with our wedding plans. Brand deserves a father, and you need me whether you realize it or not. I won't have Brand needlessly upset by cruel gossip."

"I know."

"I don't care how much you argue ... What did you say?"

"I said I know. Everything you said is true."

"Then you'll stop fighting this marriage?"

330

"Yes."

"Thank God." He took her in his arms, pulling her close.

He would have kissed her if she hadn't added, "For Brand's sake."

He shoved her away, erupting in sudden anger. He had had enough of her nonsense. "Damn you! Then let our marriage be for Brand's sake. Let me know when you change your mind. Until then, I'll not trouble you again with my vile attentions. I'll leave it up to you to tell Brand of our marriage. And when the time is right, I want him to know I'm his father."

"Nick, no! I can't tell him that, not yet. He thinks Beau is his father. Think what that will do to him."

"I didn't say you had to tell him immediately. But in time, yes, when he's able to understand. I damn well want him to know who his father is. If you don't tell him, I will. As for you, you can make what you want of this marriage. If remaining a Reb means so much to you, then so be it. I had hopes of providing Brand with a brother or sister, but I can make do with just one son if I have to."

In a rage, he stormed out the door, leaving Aimee standing open mouthed.

Aimee didn't see Nick for two whole days after that. Briefly she thought he might have washed his hands of her, until she realized that he would never leave Brand. Recalling his words, she told Brand that she and Nick were going to be married. Far from being upset, the boy was ecstatic. He had already had this conversation with Nick before they left Atlanta, and he began to wonder when it would happen. Savannah also seemed pleased.

"De major loves you, honey," she said when she noted Aimee's distress. "And I think you love him. Once you accept de fact dat de Yanks ain't so bad, you'll see dat everythin' is workin' out for de best. Brand has his papa, and you have a man who loves you."

Nick realized Aimee had told Brand they were going to be married the moment he returned to the hotel and noted the boy's pleased expression. With a pang of regret he wished that Aimee had shown her son's enthusiasm for their union.

"Mama says you're going to be my papa," Brand gushed happily. "We're going to be a real family."

"That's right, son," Nick agreed, tousling the boy's dark hair. "I've just come from making the arrangements. Why don't you and Savannah go for a walk while your mama and I discuss our plans for the ceremony."

Brand hung back shyly. "Can I call you Papa?"

Nick's smile lit up the room. "I'd like that. Now, run along, son; we'll talk later."

"At least someone is happy about our marriage," Nick said sourly once the lad had skipped from the room.

"Savannah is pleased."

"And you? What about you, Aimee? Have you come to grips with your feelings yet? Will this be a marriage made in heaven or hell?"

"A marriage of convenience," Aimee countered softly.

"I see you haven't changed your mind," Nick said harshly. "Neither have I. I won't force myself on you. I dropped by to tell you that our marriage will take place the day after tomorrow. We'll be married at city hall at two o'clock in the afternoon. I'll come by for you in a buggy." He handed her a sheaf of greenbacks. "Buy whatever you need for the ceremony. Now if you will excuse me, I've neglected my work long enough."

His voice was so remote, so damn cold, Aimee couldn't repress the shiver that raced down her spine. Why couldn't she just admit she loved a Yankee, that she wanted Nick in her bed forever? The answer was simple yet complicated. Because her damn southern pride wouldn't allow it. She had hated Nick longer than she had hated Yanks.

"Nick, wait!"

He turned expectantly. "Have I left out anything?"

"Are we to live in the hotel?"

"For the time being. I've made arrangements to rent a house as soon as the current tenants move out. It's fully furnished, and I think you'll be pleased."

"I don't like Washington."

"I'm aware of that. But right now we'll have to make do. The end of the war is in sight, and we'll soon be free to live where we please."

"The South isn't defeated yet," Aimee declared stubbornly.

"Wilmington fell two days ago, and most of the North Carolina coast is in Federal hands," Nick declared. "Desertions from Lee's army, especially of North Carolina troops, rose to disastrous levels. Most of those men are going home to protect and sustain their families, but some went over to our side, where they knew they could find food and shelter. It's no secret that soldiers can't fight while their families are destitute and starving."

"Lincoln should be proud of himself," Aimee said with biting sarcasm.

"Aimee, this war wasn't our idea. Can't we forget war for once and just be ourselves? I never wanted to be your enemy."

"I'm going to be your wife; what more do you want?"

He searched her face. The intense green of his gaze had the ability to search deeply into her soul. "I want the opportunity to make you happy, sweetheart. I want to love you, to be a part of you, to be a husband in every sense of the word. But unless you tell me you want the same thing, we'll end up living like strangers in the same house. Do you want that?"

Silence.

His face hardened. "Aimee?"

More silence.

Without a backward glance, Nick turned abruptly and slammed out the door.

When the day arrived for their wedding, Aimee realized just how angry Nick had been. Instead of showing up in person, he sent a buggy for them with a message that he'd meet them at city hall.

"You brung it on yourself, honey," Savannah observed as they rode to city hall.

Aimee looked ravishing in a lovely winter white wool suit trimmed in rabbit fur. When Nick saw her he nearly lost his resolve to remain aloof until she admitted that she loved him. No matter how badly he wanted her, he was determined that she come to him before he made love to her again. He didn't know how in the hell he was going to survive until then, but somehow he must. If their marriage was going to prosper, Aimee must be made to acknowledge her feelings and let go of the hatred she'd harbored for him all these years. They had been making good progress until Regina Blakewell had arrived at Tall Oaks.

Marriage wasn't the only plan Nick had for their future. He had put other plans into motion that Aimee knew nothing about—ones that would prove to her how desperately he loved her. Of necessity his plans must wait, but with the way the war was going, he doubted the delay would be a long one.

The ceremony was blessedly brief. Aimee repeated her vows clearly, with only minimal prodding from Nick, while Brand and Savannah watched from the sidelines. Brand wore a grin from ear to ear while Savannah wiped an errant tear from the corner of her eye. At the end of the ceremony Nick briefly touched cool lips to Aimee's in a kiss so chaste and perfunctory, she thought she had imagined the fleeting pressure of his lips on hers. Then he promptly sent her back to the hotel, claiming he had pressing business.

"Don't wait up for me, Aimee," he said as he handed her into the buggy. "I might not make it back to the hotel tonight."

Aimee was stunned. She couldn't believe Nick had actually been serious about not sharing her bed. As lusty as Nick was, she thought it highly unlikely that he'd forgo his marital rights—no matter what he had said to the contrary.

"Where will you sleep?"

"Do you care? Are you prepared to surrender to

me in every respect? Can you forget Beauregard Trevor and the fact that I'm a Yankee?"

Immediately she drew back. "You ask too much of me."

"No, sweetheart, I ask only that you be honest with yourself for once and admit that you love me despite the fact that you're a Reb and I'm a Yank."

"I—can't."

He nodded curtly. "I'll drop by to see Brand tomorrow. I wouldn't want him to think his papa is neglecting him." He motioned to the driver, and the buggy jerked into motion.

Aimee stared straight ahead, wanting desperately to turn and look at him, but she feared that he'd assume she was issuing him an invitation. With her eyes trained straight ahead, she wondered if Nick would be celebrating their marriage tonight, and with whom.

The following day Aimee decided to leave when Nick came by the hotel to see Brand. When Savannah was occupied elsewhere with Brand, she slipped out of the hotel, telling no one she was leaving. She knew Savannah would scold her for avoiding Nick, but she was too much of a coward to face the hurt and accusation in his green eyes.

Wandering aimlessly through town, Aimee stopped briefly before a store window, admiring a dress on display. The day was cold and windy, and she pulled her cloak tightly about her as she gazed into the store window. Suddenly an image appeared in the glass beside her and she whirled, looking for the face she had seen reflected in the window. It was a face she had seen before. To her consternation, Aimee saw no one she recognized.

When she glanced back toward the window, the image was gone.

Shaken by the experience, Aimee continued on her way. She had just turned back toward the hotel when a man appeared at her elbow. "Keep walking and don't let on that anything is wrong."

Aimee blanched as she glanced up at the man who had grasped her elbow. Gar Pinder! What was he doing in Washington? "I thought you were in prison."

"There's isn't a prison in the world that can hold me," Pinder sneered. "After being jailed for a time in Atlanta, I was transported to Washington for trial. I managed to escape from my guards, but I need help. You can't imagine how surprised and delighted I was to see you in Washington."

"I can't help you, Gar," Aimee said shakily. "I'm married now, to Nick Drummond, and I refuse to spy."

"You married a damn Yankee?" Pinder said, aghast. "You deceitful little bitch!" His grip on her arm tightened.

"Stop it, you're hurting me!"

His grip slackened. "I need money and a pass to get me through Union lines."

"I have no money. Besides, the war is all but over."

"Not for me," Gar said. "I'm still wanted by the Yankees. You owe me, Aimee. It's your fault the Yankees caught me. You should have known your lover was following you, and taken precautions."

"I told you, Gar, I won't help you."

Suddenly Pinder grinned evilly. "Perhaps your husband will give me safe passage out of town in return for your life."

"Don't count on it," Aimee mumbled, fully aware of Nick's anger toward her.

"What did you say?"

"Nothing. I'm not going to stand here arguing with you. Let go of my arm."

"You're coming with me."

"I'm going nowhere with you."

"If you want to see your son again, I suggest you come along quietly. I have a gun, and I've nothing to lose by killing you. On the other hand, I have everything to gain by taking you with me and demanding safe passage through Union lines from your husband."

"I don't believe you," Aimee said, eyeing him warily.

His right hand slid into his pocket and produced a gun, which he shoved into Aimee's ribs. Aimee gasped, looking around to see if anyone had noticed her plight. To her chagrin, passersby appeared too preoccupied with their own problems to pay heed to hers. She could always scream, but Gar was a desperate man, and she knew he was capable of shooting her in cold blood.

"Now do you believe me?" Aimee gulped and nodded. "Walk," he rasped, nudging her in the ribs. He led her toward the railway station.

When they reached the depot, Pinder prodded her away from the crowd, toward the rows of empty boxcars sitting on unused tracks at the rear of the station house. He seemed to know exactly where he was going. He shoved her toward a deserted area where several boxcars sat abandoned on the tracks. Stopping before one of the cars, he pushed open the door and quickly lifted her inside. He scrambled in behind her and slid the door shut.

In the light filtering from between the slats of the boxcar, Aimee could see various items of stolen apparel, half-eaten food, and sundry items littering the floor, indicating that Pinder had been using the boxcar as a hiding place for some time. From somewhere amidst the debris Pinder found a rope and advanced on Aimee.

"What are you going to do?"

"I'm going to make sure you stay put while I contact your husband," Pinder said as he grasped Aimee and wrestled her hands behind her back. Despite her struggles, he quickly tied her hands, lowered her to the floor, and bound her ankles. When Aimee screeched in protest, he tore a strip of cloth from her petticoat and stuffed it into her mouth. After making certain her bonds were secure, he let himself out of the boxcar, closing the door behind him. Never had Aimee felt so alone in all her life.

Nick let himself into the hotel suite, wondering if Aimee had slept as badly as he had last night. He would have preferred to spend the night with her, making love to her like a bridegroom instead of sleeping on the narrow cot in his office. But he'd be damned if he'd beg her.

Savannah bustled into the room, Brand trotting closely behind her. When she saw Nick, her face fell. "I thought you were Aimee." Disappointment was keen on her wrinkled, dark face.

A thrill of apprehension shivered down Nick's spine. "Isn't Aimee here?"

"Mama left early today and didn't tell us she

was leaving," Brand explained. His little face was screwed up into a worried frown.

Nick looked to Savannah for confirmation and found it in the woman's concerned expression. "Where could she have gone? Did she mention nothing to you? No errands that needed tending?"

"She didn't say a word, Major."

Suddenly a knock sounded on the door, and Nick hurried to answer it. "That must be her now. She probably forgot her key." Nick's face fell when he opened the door and found the desk clerk standing in the portal.

"This message was left for you at the front desk, sir." He handed Nick a folded square of paper and took his leave. Nick stared at the paper as if he expected it to reach out and bite him.

"What's de note say, Major?" Savannah asked anxiously.

Carefully Nick unfolded the note. His face contorted in rage as he read the message inside. "Damn him to hell!"

"Is it from Mama?" Brand asked innocently.

Dropping to his knees, Nick grasped Brand's narrow shoulders and said, "No, son, it's not from your mama. It's something I have to handle alone. Go to your room and play while I talk to Savannah." Frightening Brand was the least thing Nick wanted to do.

Brand left somewhat reluctantly, but Savannah was not so easily appeased. "Somethin's happened to my chile, I just know it!"

"I won't lie to you, Savannah; this note is from Garson Pinder. He has Aimee. He wants a pass through Union lines in return for Aimee's life."

"Oh, Lordy," Savannah groaned, rolling her eyes in genuine distress. "What you gonna do, Major?"

"I'll find Aimee, Savannah; don't you worry. Go to Brand. Try to keep him from suspecting that his mother is in danger."

"Do you think Mr. Pinder will hurt my chile?"

"Gar Pinder is a desperate man, and desperate men are capable of many things. I'd heard he'd escaped from his guards on his way to trial, but I never suspected he'd stay in Washington this long. Never fear, I'll find Aimee. I love her too much to allow anything bad to happen to her."

"Bless you, Major," Savannah said, wiping her eyes with the corner of her apron.

Before Nick left the hotel, he questioned the desk clerk and learned little except that the description of the man who left the message clearly resembled that of Gar Pinder. According to instructions in the note, he was to bring a legal paper guaranteeing safe passage through union lines to the railway station at midnight tonight. He was to come alone and meet Pinder behind the depot. He promised to release Aimee after he had the document in his hands, but Nick didn't trust him to keep his word. Nor did Nick intend to comply himself. He planned on having Aimee back safely long before midnight.

Nick returned to his office immediately, changed his uniform for civilian clothes, and spoke in strict confidence to the officer in charge of the garrison. Then he went to the train station, mingling with the crowd as he kept surveillance on the area. Since Pinder asked Nick to meet him behind the depot, Nick astutely surmised that the Reb had been hiding nearby and probably had Aimee with him. The area behind the station seemed a logical place to focus his attention, and the dozens of deserted boxcars looked like a good place to start his search. His main concern was searching the area without attracting Pinder's notice. If the Reb thought he had been discovered, Nick feared he would harm Aimee.

Aimee's arms felt numb, and her legs had lost their feeling long ago. Pinder had returned to the boxcar a short time ago but made no effort to untie her or remove her gag.

"By now your Yankee husband has my note," Pinder said as he stood glaring down at Aimee. "Once he hands over the pass, he'll never leave the railyard alive." Aimee's eyes grew wild. "If you're wondering what I intend to do with you, you'd best start saying your prayers. Beau Trevor would turn over in his grave if he knew you'd betrayed him with a damn Yank. When I kill you, I'll merely be ridding the world of another traitor. I'm only keeping you alive in case I have to show you off to Drummond to get my pass. After that you'll both die."

Aimee's heart thudded frantically in her breast. She should have known a man like Pinder wouldn't let her leave alive. Oh please, God, don't let Nick come, she silently pleaded. She didn't care what happened to her as long as he was safe to care for Brand and Savannah.

Nick slipped silent as a wraith from boxcar to boxcar, keeping to the shadows as he paused beside each car, listening for signs of life inside. He was almost to the last of the cars now, having examined each in turn until he had nearly given up hope of finding Aimee and Pinder in one of him. Evidently his thinking had been flawed, for he had found no indication that Pinder and Aimee were anywhere in the vicinity. Then suddenly the sound of a human voice from inside one of the cars brought him instantly alert. The voice was coming from a boxcar directly ahead of him. Then the voice abruptly ceased. Nick had a decision to make.

He was almost certain Aimee was inside the boxcar with Pinder, and if he was speaking to her, she was still alive. But if he stormed the boxcar or let on that he was outside, Aimee was likely to be hurt—or killed. After several minutes of careful consideration, he hunkered down behind the boxcar to wait. Just knowing that Aimee was inside with a dangerous man nearly drove him mad, but Nick was a seasoned soldier and knew his best chance of rescuing Aimee alive would come when Pinder left the boxcar at midnight.

"It's time," Pinder said, rising to his feet. Outside, darkness was a curtain that covered the land in a black shroud. Thin clouds obscured the moon, making the darkness even more impenetrable. "Enjoy your last minutes on the earth." His nasty laugh lingered in the air long after he had slipped out into the night.

Stiff with cold, Nick heard the whisper of the door as it slid across the boxcar opening. He rose to his feet, his body tense, his mind alert. A few moments later he saw a lone figure emerge through the opening and move stealthily through the darkness. Nick waited until Pinder was lost amidst the boxcars before leaving his hiding place.

Aimee heard the door slide open, and her first

thought was that Pinder had decided to kill her before he met Nick. The darkness was so complete, she saw nothing, not even a shadow. She nearly fainted when Nick's voice came to her from out of nowhere.

"Aimee, where are you?"

Gagged as she was, all Aimee could do was make desperate sounds deep in her throat. But they were enough for Nick to locate her. "What has he done to you, sweetheart?" he said when he felt the ropes binding her limbs. Moving his hands upward, he felt the gag and gently drew it out of her mouth.

Aimee drew in a ragged breath as the dryness left her mouth. "Oh, Nick, thank God. He was going to kill us both."

"We have to hurry, love." From somewhere inside his clothing he produced a knife and carefully cut her bonds. Aimee nearly screamed when blood spurted through her abused limbs, causing untold pain. "Can you walk?" he asked as he helped her to her feet. "Pinder will be back the moment he realizes I'm not behind the depot to meet him."

At first Aimee's legs felt wooden, but because their lives depended on her ability to move swiftly, she forced herself to place one foot before the other. Taking her hand, Nick helped her from the boxcar. Then, realizing that she was unable to move as effortlessly as he would have liked, he lifted her in his arms and carried her from the railyard.

"What about Gar?" she asked breathlessly.

Just then a Union soldier materialized from the darkness. "Is your wife safe, Major?" the young lieutenant asked.

"She's fine, Lieutenant. You have your orders. You can take Pinder now without endangering my wife's life. And, Lieutenant, send a man over to the hotel to tell my son and my wife's companion that we are both safe."

Saluting, the soldier melted back into the shadows.

"What was that all about?" Aimee asked as Nick set her carefully on her feet.

"Before I left headquarters, I arranged for Pinder's capture. The men have been here for hours, waiting for a signal from me. They weren't to show themselves or move until I had you safely away from the Reb."

"I was so frightened," Aimee sighed shakily as she leaned against Nick for support. "I should have known you'd find a way to outsmart Pinder. Take me home, Nick."

"That's exactly where I'm taking you, sweetheart. To the house I rented for us. The previous tenants moved just this morning, and it's ready to move into. I'll send for Brand and Savannah tomorrow."

The brownstone Nick had rented was only a short distance from the railway station. When he ushered her inside, she grew warm at the thought of Nick spending the night in her bed. She couldn't deny the fact that she missed Nick's arms around her at night. She had grown accustomed to the heat and strength of his big body, and sorely missed the comfort and protection of his nearness. But did he feel the same? she wondered as Nick lit a lamp and walked her up the stairs.

Nick threw open a door at the top of the stairs and stood aside so Aimee could enter. He watched her carefully, his body tense, waiting. "I thought you'd like this room. It's large and overlooks the garden."

"It's lovely," Aimee said, hardly aware of the huge bed and comfortable furnishings. She had eyes only for Nick, waiting, fearing he no longer wanted her. "But . . ."

"But what?" Nick asked hopefully.

"I—don't think I can sleep after everything that's happened tonight."

"Would you like me to rub your back?"

Aimee bit her lip in consternation. She'd like him to do more than rub her back, but feared such a declaration would be tantamount to admitting she loved a Yank and was ready to accept their marriage on his terms. Hadn't Nick said he wouldn't touch her unless she asked him?

"I don't think . . ."

"Lie down, sweetheart," Nick said. His voice was low, sensuous, softly cajoling. When she merely stared at him, he grasped her arm and led her toward the bed. He set the lamp down and lowered her to the soft surface. Then he turned her on her stomach and began massaging her back.

"This really isn't necessary, Nick," Aimee protested.

"Relax, sweetheart, it will help you sleep." He continued his gentle pummeling, his teasing strokes moving from her shoulder to her buttocks.

It really did feel wonderful, and Aimee sighed in response to his soothing touch. She began to wish there weren't a layer of clothing between them. Just when she began to doze, she felt his hands slide beneath her dress and move up the inside of her leg. It felt wonderful, and she sighed contentedly. His hand traveled higher, higher still, stopping just short of that place between her legs that ached for his touch.

"Let me help you with your clothes," he offered as he began undoing the fastenings on the back of her dress. Within minutes he had stripped her bare. When he lowered his head and pressed his mouth to the soft mound of her buttocks, Aimee groaned. He slid his tongue upward along her spine, and she nearly flew from the bed.

"Nick! What are you doing?"

"You're not sufficiently relaxed yet."

Abruptly he flipped her to her back. Then his hands were kneading her breasts, moving lower to massage the satiny flesh of her belly and thighs, then returning to her breasts. Her nipples hardened into tight little buds as he paid special homage to them with the gentle friction of his thumb and forefinger.

"Does that feel good?"

Aimee could barely reply.

"Do you want me to continue?"

She shook her head no.

"Are you sure?"

She nodded her head vigorously.

Suddenly Nick's hand searched the cleft between her legs, encountering the flooding moisture his teasing massage had created, and a knowing smile lifted the corners of his wide mouth. Unrelenting in his subtle seduction, he thrust a finger inside her. Aimee jerked and cried out.

"Are you absolutely certain you want me to stop?"

Aimee gulped convulsively.

Slowly, teasingly, he withdrew his finger, waiting for her to tell him what she desired. He had vowed not to make love to her unless she truly wanted it.

Aimee gasped. "No, don't stop! Please don't stop."

"What do you want, sweetheart?"

His finger returned to her hot sheath, thrusting deeply, withdrawing, thrusting again—deeper.

"Oh, God, I want . . ."

"Tell me, Aimee. Unless you tell me what you want, I'll leave and sleep in another room. Perhaps then you'll have some idea what it feels like to ache for someone you can't have."

"Make love to me, Nick. Please."

"Gladly, sweetheart. You deserve a proper wedding night. But before I do, I want to hear you say you love me."

Sobbing in frustration, Aimee cried, "I love you, Nick Drummond. God help me, but I love you."

Chapter 19

"It seems I've waited half my life to hear you say that," Nick groaned as the weight of his body shifted over hers. He was fully aroused, taut and heavy with his need. He had denied himself so long, he wanted to thrust into her again and again and stroke himself to climax.

But he didn't. He had learned perseverance long ago. Instead, he stretched full length atop her, rubbing his body against hers, making her aware of his arousal and how desperately he needed her.

"Oh God, Nick, hurry."

"We've got all night, sweetheart. And all the nights to come." The inflection of his voice registered a surprising vulnerability when he added, "This time surrender is forever."

Aimee did not argue with him, too consumed with touching him, with holding him against her. She felt the warmth of his breath, sensed the heat and tension in him, felt his muscles flex beneath her fingertips, and realized how desperately she had missed him. Needed him. Wanted him.

When she pulled his head down to hers to kiss him, opening her legs in blatant invitation, Nick's restraint shattered. Reaching down between his legs, she guided him inside her, then clamped tightly around him. Her hips rocked in invitation, intensifying the delicious burning in her tender depths. Nick groaned as raging passion seized him and he could no longer control the fury that drove him.

He rode her hard, but not hard enough to satisfy Aimee, who urged him to even greater effort with her little cries and gasps. Her hands were never still as they committed to her memory every inch of his flesh. She knew the location of each scar that scored his skin, memorized every curve and indentation, instinctively knew where to touch him to give him the most pleasure. She closed her eyes when his stroking drove her close to the edge.

"Open your eyes, sweetheart," Nick gasped raggedly. "I want to watch your expression when I take you to paradise." Her eyes, honey-warm and glowing, slowly opened, meeting the emerald green of Nick's intent gaze. "Now, Aimee, oh God, now."

He thrust hard.

"Nick!"

She grasped his shoulders and held on for dear life as his frenzied thrusts lifted her nearly off the bed. Wrapping her legs around his hips, she squeezed tightly, making the pleasure almost unbearable for both of them. The end came to her explosively, at the same time Nick arched hard and held. She felt the hot spurt of his seed and heard his cry moments before shattering into a million pieces.

Sweat blinded his eyes as Nick strained over her, holding his own climax under strict control until he was certain of Aimee's rapture. Not until he felt the tiny tremors squeezing him and felt her body convulse around him did he surrender to the clamor of his own pounding blood.

Aimee fell asleep almost immediately, content for the first time in many days. Nick stayed awake awhile longer, watching her sleep, pledging that he'd never allow her to refuse him her bed again. Whether she knew it or not, Aimee needed and loved him as much as he needed and loved her. One day, he vowed, she'd forget that he was a Yankee and remember that the location of one's birth had nothing to do with love. It was what was in one's heart that counted. True, they had had a rocky beginning, but all that was in the past. They were married, had a son together and a bright future. He fell asleep dreaming of the day he could show Aimee what he would do for her in the name of love.

Aimee accepted the news that Sherman's sixty thousand blue avengers left Savannah for their second march through the heart of the South with almost fatalistic calm. Nick had told her that Jefferson Davis had rejected unconditional surrender as degrading and humiliating. He explained that Sherman's march into the heart of South Carolina and Alabama had two strategic purposes: to destroy all war resources in Sherman's path; and to approach Lee's rear guard, thereby crushing the Army of Northern Virginia in a vise between two larger Union armies and so wipe out Lee.

Aimee had little to keep her busy in the waning days of winter 1865. She knew for sure now that she was pregnant, but still hadn't told Nick. She feared that once she told him, her surrender to

351

him would be complete, leaving nothing of her
former self. It would all belong to Nick. Brand, the
new baby, herself. That was what he had wanted
from the beginning, wasn't it—to own her body
and soul?

One day in March Nick came home bursting
with excitement. "My mother is coming to Washington to meet my new wife," he said. Aimee had
known that Nick had a close relationship with his
family in Chicago but hadn't concerned herself
with the possibility of meeting them yet. She knew
one day she must, but imagined it would be after
the war.

"Mother is coming alone. My sister is expecting
her first child in two months and doesn't care to
travel at this time."

"How—wonderful," Aimee said somewhat hesitantly.

"Don't worry, sweetheart, she'll love you just
like I do. I've written her so much about you, she
decided to travel to Washington to meet you.
We've plenty of room here for her."

"How long will she stay?"

"No longer than two weeks. She wants to be
back in time for my sister's lying-in."

"When will she arrive?"

"Day after tomorrow. The telegram just arrived
telling me of her visit."

"I know so little of your family," Aimee said
thoughtfully.

"That's because you never cared enough to ask."
His mild rebuke made her aware that her callous
disinterest in his family had hurt him.

"Tell me about them."

Nick looked pleased as he settled down beside

her. "My mother's name is Elizabeth. Father died ten years ago, leaving his munitions plant to me and my sister."

"Munitions plant!"

"Does that bother you?"

"A little," she said truthfully. "One of the bullets from your factory could have killed Beau. Continue, please."

"There's little else to tell." Nick shrugged. "My sister's husband is in charge now, and doing a damn good job of it. I've decided to sell out my share and invest in something else. Sitting behind a desk never did appeal to me."

"You weren't sitting behind a desk when we met aboard the *Dixie Bell*," Aimee said with a hint of accusation. "I thought you were a professional gambler."

Nick flashed a wicked smile. "I was on a business trip, and on the spur of the moment I decided to combine it with a little relaxation. Truth to tell, I boarded the *Dixie Belle* because I was intrigued by the notion of a woman gambler. I heard about you long before I ever set eyes on you. I had to see for myself if you were as lovely as they said. I never thought I'd fall in love with you."

"Did you, Nick? Did you really fall in love with me?"

"How can you doubt me? I told you I searched for you for months afterward."

"I know that's what you said . . ."

"But you don't believe me."

"It's possible," she temporized. "But go on; you were telling me about your mother."

"There's little else to tell. You'll like her. She's most anxious to met you and Brand."

* * *

Elizabeth Drummond was just as Nick had described her—a small, energetic woman who seemed to be in constant motion. She wore her graying dark hair in a loosely draped bun set askew atop her head. She still showed hint of the great beauty she must have been during her youth. Aimee liked her immediately. When Elizabeth Drummond met Brand for the first time, she appeared surprised, but quickly recovered herself, asking him to call her Grandma, though she hadn't yet been told of his true parentage. Brand happily obliged.

Even Savannah was impressed by the woman's charm and graciousness. Her presence seemed to take some of the strain away from the volatile relationship between Nick and Aimee. Nick had already told Elizabeth that Aimee was a southerner, so she was careful not to mention the war and the terrible things that were happening now to the oppressed and starving people of the South.

When Elizabeth suggested an outing on a sun-drenched March day, Aimee readily agreed. They decided to stroll a bit since the weather was so mild. Elizabeth looked as if she had something on her mind, and Aimee waited patiently for Nick's mother to say exactly what was bothering her. She didn't have long to wait.

"You can't believe how happy I am to see Nick settled down and so obviously in love with his wife."

Aimee flushed, feeling a little guilty over the amount of anguish she had caused Nick.

"You're just what Nick needed, Aimee dear. And that precious son of yours. The first time I saw him I could have sworn—well, never mind, but he does look much like Nick did when he was a child. How old is Brand?"

"Nearly six."

"Six. My, my, he certainly is a big boy for his age. Was his father a large man?"

"His father?" Aimee asked dumbly. She realized that Nick hadn't told his mother that he was Brand's father, and that she must be referring to Beauregard Trevor.

Aimee was quiet so long that Elizabeth hastened to add, "You need not speak of your dead husband if it's too painful, my dear. I don't mean to pry. I merely wanted you to know how pleased I am with you and Brand. I always knew that Nick would one day find someone he could love as much as he loved that— Oh, my, there I go again, talking too much."

"It's all right, Elizabeth, really. What were you going to say? I'm sure there must have been many women before me in Nick's life."

"Are you sure you don't mind?"

"Positive."

"Well, then, I was merely referring to a time in Nick's life when he fancied himself in love with a woman he barely knew. Actually, he had only met her one time, but she must have made quite an impression upon him. He couldn't seem to forget her."

Aimee was fascinated. "What happened?"

"She was a southerner, just like you. I forget her name, it's been so long. That's really all I know about her, except that she was from New Orleans. I don't know how they met, but when Nick returned from a business trip, he was obsessed with the woman. He returned to the South time and again to search for her, but it was as if she had disappeared into thin air.

"I finally convinced Nick that she didn't want to be found. For a while he was inconsolable, but then the war started and he turned his energies to fighting for his ideals and beliefs. Now that he's found you, I'm certain there's no room in his heart for some dim memory from his past."

Elizabeth's words affected Aimee deeply. Her thoughts were confused, her brain muddled. Elizabeth couldn't help but know that Aimee was moved by her words.

"Oh, dear, I knew I should have kept my mouth shut," Elizabeth said, clearly distraught. "I didn't mean to offend you, Aimee. What happened between Nick and that other nameless woman occurred so long ago, I thought it would no longer matter."

"You're wrong, Elizabeth, it matters a great deal." Aimee's voice held a strange note, one that Elizabeth could not easily decipher. She wouldn't have hurt Aimee for the world.

"Oh, dear," Elizabeth repeated, wringing her hands. "Perhaps I shouldn't have come to Washington, but I did so want to meet you and your son."

"You couldn't have picked a better time, Elizabeth, dear," Aimee said, smiling. "What you just told me makes me extremely happy."

"You're—happy? I—don't understand."

"I don't suppose you do. I owe you an explanation, and you shall have it."

"You don't owe me anything," Elizabeth insisted, though actually she was curious to know what she had said to make Aimee happy.

"Nick and I met more than six years ago."

Elizabeth stopped abruptly in the middle of the sidewalk, turning to face Aimee. "Over six years ago? But I thought . . ."

"We met aboard the *Dixie Belle,* a riverboat plying the Mississippi River." An awkward silence ensued. Briefly Aimee considered telling Elizabeth that she was engaged in a poker game with her son at the time, but decided there were some things her mother-in-law didn't need to know.

Elizabeth was a bright woman. Understanding dawned in her wide green eyes. "Then Brand—"

"Is Nick's son."

"A son Nick never knew existed," Elizabeth said with mild reproof.

Aimee flushed. "It's a long story, Elizabeth."

"One I don't need to know," Elizabeth replied. "Suffice it to say you've found one another again and all is well. Nick has his adorable son now, and he couldn't be happier."

"And Brand will soon have a brother or sister," Aimee added, unable to keep the news to herself a moment longer.

Elizabeth's eyes sparkled. "How wonderful!"

"Only you mustn't tell Nick until I've told him myself."

"I wouldn't think of it, my dear."

The final week of Elizabeth's visit was spent becoming acquainted with her grandson. The two had taken to each other immediately, and by the time they put Elizabeth aboard the train for Chicago, everyone was sorry to see her visit end. When she gave Aimee a final hug, she whispered into her ear, "Hurry and tell my son about the baby."

* * *

Several days after Elizabeth left, Nick returned home in a serious mood. He explained the reason when they were alone, after Brand had been put to bed.

"Jefferson Davis abandoned Richmond. He took the Treasury's remaining gold and as much of the archives as could be carried," he said. "They boarded ramshackle trains and any other conveyance they could beg for, borrow, or steal. Everything else was put to the torch. They burned more of their own capital than we did of Atlanta or Columbia."

"My God," Aimee said shakily. "It really is the end."

"President Lincoln followed Union soldiers into the city. Do you realize that the president of the United States sat in the study of the president of the Confederacy mere hours after Davis left it?

"Word has it that Lincoln walked the streets with only an escort of ten sailors. Then he was surrounded by an impenetrable cordon of freed slaves shouting, 'Glory to God! Glory! Glory! Glory! Bless the Lord!' God, Aimee, they're free! I feel a part of history."

Aimee gulped, unable to speak for the lump in her throat. The Yankees had finally succeeded in beating the South into the ground. What was in store now for the valiant citizens of the South? Starvation? Deprivation? Subjugation? Would she ever see Tall Oaks again? Unlikely, she thought bitterly. She was married to a Yank now and must follow where he went. The new baby she carried in her belly made any other alternative unthinkable.

"I know this comes as a blow to you, sweetheart," Nick said when he noted Aimee's pallor. "But the outcome was inevitable from the beginning. Now the South can get back to the business of normal living. When the end comes, which we believe will be in a few days, for Lee has nowhere else to turn, men can return to their families. Our lives will change, too, sweetheart. I can spend more time with you and Brand. And maybe," he hinted with a twinkle, "there's a new baby in our future."

Aimee looked at him sharply. Had Elizabeth told him about the baby? She doubted Nick's mother had broken her promise, and assumed that Nick was merely guessing. She chose to ignore his subtle hint. "You've won," she said bitterly. "I know how happy that makes you."

"It's something you're going to have to live with, Aimee. Neither side has won. Not when you consider the staggering numbers of dead and wounded. People without homes, or food, or clothing. Come on, sweetheart, let's go to bed. I have this terrible urge to hold you in my arms. The only thing about this war I'm grateful for is that I found you again."

Once in bed, Nick made no move to do more than hold Aimee. Sensing her sadness and her need to come to grips with the imminent fall of the South, he offered comfort with no strings attached. Aimee felt his warmth envelop and enfold her, felt his compassion, and something inside her broke loose. Instinctively she knew this man would always be there when she needed him. He offered comfort in times of stress, gave her love when she had scorned it, brought passion and fire into her life when she had been empty. He had filled her with his child when she wasn't sure she wanted to bring another Yankee into the world, made her love him despite the hatred she bore him throughout the years.

"Nick . . ." Her voice faltered and she tried again. "Nick—I do love you."

Nick's arms tightened, but he said nothing. He was too choked up to speak. Before, he'd always had to pry those words from Aimee's lips. And once she'd spoken them, he never knew whether they came from the heart. This was the first time she had given them freely.

"Did you hear me? I said I loved you."

"I heard you, sweetheart. I'm just too shaken to speak. I never thought you'd give up that damn southern pride long enough to admit you could love a Yankee."

"I believe you now about looking for me after that night aboard the *Dixie Belle*. Hate is such a destructive emotion that I've had a difficult time accepting that you truly love me."

"Why in the hell do you think I married you?"

"So you could have Brand."

"If I had wanted Brand and not you, I'd have found a way to get him. There would have been no one to stop me."

Aimee chewed on that thought for a while. Then she decided that the time had come to tell Nick about the new baby, but to her shock, Nick forestalled her.

"Is there something else you wanted to tell me, sweetheart?"

Aimee's breath quickened. "You know?"

"If you're referring to the child you're carrying,

yes, I know. I've been wondering when you were going to tell me."

"How did you know? Did your mother tell you? I haven't been sick in the mornings like I was with Brand, so you had no clues."

Nick laughed. "No clues, you say. Ah, sweetheart, you're wrong. I know your body as well as I know my own. There were too many subtle changes for me not to know. What about this?"

He touched her breasts, and she inhaled sharply. The sensitive flesh responded to his touch almost violently. "And this?" He slid his hand over the ever so slight protrusion of her belly. "Not only are your breasts and nipples more sensitive to my touch, but they are fuller. And your stomach is softly rounded against my palm. I'd have to be blind not to notice the changes in your body. So when am I to be a father again?"

"In late summer."

"Are you happy about it?"

"Yes, yes, I am," she said, surprising herself. Suddenly this new baby was very important to her.

"I'm surprised you and Beau had no children."

"We were together a very short time before he left for war."

"Long enough," Nick said dryly. "You conceived Brand on our very first night together. Aimee, I've deliberately refrained from asking you this before because I've been afraid of the answer, but it's something I have to know. I can't live with a dead man's memory. It's hell not knowing whether you think of your dead husband when we make love. Or if he's in your mind and heart more often than

I am. Do you love me as much as you loved Beauregard Trevor?"

Aimee was silent a long time, choosing her words carefully. So long, in fact, that Nick finally blurted out, "No, don't tell me! I think I already know the answer."

"You don't know a damn thing, Nick Drummond. Beau was a wonderful, kind man who came into my life when I needed him most. He never thought less of me for having an illegitimate child, nor did he ever consider Brand anything but his child. We might have been happy together had he lived."

"Might have been?" Nick asked, quickly picking up on her words. "Did you enjoy making love with him?"

"We were together such a short time . . ."

"Tell me, Aimee."

"Beau never made me feel the way you do," she admitted slowly. "And I refuse to continue with this conversation. Beau is dead—he'd want me to be happy with someone else. When you and I make love, there is room for no one in my heart but you. You consume my thoughts and fulfill my body in ways I never thought possible. That's all I'm going to say on the subject of Beauregard Trevor."

"That's all I wanted to know. I'm the jealous sort. Though I begrudge Beauregard Trevor his possession of you, I'm grateful he was there when you and Brand needed him. But as long as I'm alive, you'll never need to turn to another man for comfort or love. I love you, Aimee Drummond. I've loved you for more than six years. Until I found you again, I never knew why my life felt incomplete."

"Oh, Nick, just think of all those years we've wasted," Aimee sighed.

"About the baby, sweetheart; shall we stay in Washington for the birth or would you prefer to go to Chicago, where my mother can look after you and Brand?"

"I want to go home, Nick. I want our baby to be born in the South. Is that impossible?"

"Still the little Rebel, aren't you? If it's at all possible, I'll grant your wish. But don't count on it."

They lay in silence for a while, both consumed with their separate thoughts. Suddenly Nick turned to her, drawing her close and kissing her. "Is it all right if I love you now? I thought I could lie here without making love to you, but I hadn't counted on the aching hunger that gnaws at me each time I touch you."

"I'd prefer you didn't make love to me."

"What!" Keen disappointment sent the word hissing through his teeth, but he'd not force the issue if Aimee truly felt unable or unwilling to make love with him.

"Let me make love to you instead."

"Oh God!"

She began by kissing him everywhere, running her tongue the length and breadth of his hair-roughened skin, tasting and biting his flesh with teasing little nips. When she lay full length atop him, Nick tried to raise her so he could push himself inside her, but she wouldn't allow it. Instead, lying groin to groin, she rubbed her sensitive breasts against his chest until her nipples became engorged and aching, until she burned between her legs with the fires of hell. But still she resisted his attempts to press her to her back and thrust into her.

"Not yet," she told him. Nick groaned and persevered, vowing to pay her back in kind for the torture she was inflicting. Finally, when her mouth grew bolder still, tormenting him with wet kisses in places that drove him mad with wanting, he flipped her over on her back and shoved himself inside her.

"You little tease," he grunted as he buried himself deep into her throbbing heat.

She was laughing until he began thrusting furiously. And then her laughter turned to gasps, sighs, and incoherent cries as he drove her to the brink of ecstasy, then tumbled her over the edge.

Aimee accepted the news of General Lee's surrender to General Grant at Appomattox Courthouse in April with a heavy heart. It was no more than she had expected, but painful nevertheless. Nick tried to comfort her by telling her about the generous settlement offered the vanquished army.

"Terms of the agreement left Confederate officers and men free to go home without being disturbed by U.S. authority so long as they observe their paroles and the laws in force where they reside." He had explained all this to Aimee and Savannah as he paced back and forth in the parlor. Brand sat quietly beside Aimee, listening carefully.

"Does that mean none of the Southern army can be tried for treason?" Aimee asked.

"That's right," Nick replied. "And they were granted another boon. At Lee's request, Grant allowed each man who claimed a horse to keep it, privates as well as officers. They'll be needed to put in crops to carry them and their families through the next winter."

"That was generous," Aimee allowed somewhat grudgingly.

"We're all Americans, sweetheart," he reminded her.

"Can we go home to Tall Oaks now?" Brand said anxiously. He had remained so quiet, they had forgotten he was there.

"Don't you like it in Washington, son?" Nick asked, unaware that he had been following the conversation so closely.

"It's all right, but I like Tall Oaks better." Suddenly he grew thoughtful.

"What is it, Brand?" Aimee asked.

"If the North won the war, is my papa still a hero?"

Nick winced.

Aimee groaned.

Savannah said, "Oh, Lordy."

"I think it's time we told him," Nick said, sending Aimee a meaningful look.

"I'll go start supper," Savannah said, hauling herself from the chair and moving with alacrity toward the kitchen.

"Tell me what?" Brand asked curiously.

Aimee sent Nick a helpless look.

"Beauregard Trevor was indeed a brave man, Brand, but he wasn't your father. Your mother and I were waiting for the right time to tell you."

Brand looked confused. "If he wasn't my papa, who is?"

"I'm your papa, son."

"I know. You've been my papa since you married Mama, but who is my real father?"

"That's what I'm trying to tell you, son. Your mother and I knew one another a long time ago, before you were born."

"But you weren't married," he said with guileless innocence.

"Sometimes mamas and daddies aren't married when their children are born. But I always loved you and your mother. It just took me a long time to find you."

Brand was so quiet, Nick began to fear he had done the wrong thing by telling the child. He looked at Aimee as if to say, I'm sorry.

"Can I still think of Beauregard Trevor as my second papa?" Brand asked after a long pause.

"I think he'd like that, son."

"There are still things I don't understand."

"I know, Brand, but please trust me. I promise one day, when you're old enough to understand, I'll explain everything. All you need to know right now is that both your mama and I love you dearly. And one day soon you'll have a new brother or sister. Does that please you?"

"I love you, too, Papa," Brand said solemnly. "Do you think I can have a brother? A little sister might not want to play the same games I do."

Aimee laughed delightedly. "If the baby turns out to be a girl, perhaps the next will be a boy."

Nick grinned, the dimple in his cheek deepening. "I'll certainly do my part, son.

Chapter 20

❦❦❦

"**A**re you all right, sweetheart?" Nick asked for the hundredth time since they boarded the train in Washington on a hot summer day in late July 1865. "We'll be arriving in Atlanta within the hour."

"I may look like an elephant and waddle like a duck but I feel fine," Aimee assured her anxious husband.

"You look beautiful. I'm sorry I missed Brand's birth. You must have been beautiful then, too."

The train was crowded. During this Reconstruction period following the end of the war, Atlanta had become the center of federal government activities. Aware of how much Aimee hated Washington, Nick had promptly applied for a transfer to Atlanta. His new assignment placed him in a high position in the Freedman's Bureau, created in March and placed under the jurisdiction of the War Department. The function of the bureau was to dispense rations and relief to hundreds of thousands of whites, as well as black refugees, uprooted by the war and to assist freedmen during the difficult transition from slavery to freedom.

Aimee watched out the window at the passing

scenery, wondering what had become of Tall Oaks. Since she had paid no taxes for several years, she assumed the land had been sold to northern speculators. The South was already swarming with carpetbaggers, the term applied to northern Republican politicians arriving with few possessions in the ravished South. Their aim was to exploit Negroes as a means of obtaining office or financial gain for themselves in the southern states.

Aimee thought back to that day in April when Lee surrendered at Appomattox Courthouse. People rushed into the streets following a 900-gun salute. From one end of Pennsylvania Avenue to the other, the air seemed to burn with bright hues of the flag. Hundreds of people were embracing, talking, laughing, cheering. For Aimee it was a time of sadness, not rejoicing. Oh, she was happy the bloodshed was finally over, but she realized that southern society would never be the same, and that a great gulf would always exist between the conquerors and the vanquished.

"What are you thinking, sweetheart?" Nick asked when he noticed Aimee's preoccupation.

"Will life ever be the same again?" Aimee asked wistfully.

"It will be better," Nick predicted. "I intend to resign my commission one day soon and we can get on with our lives."

"Then what? I don't think I'll like living in the North if all the cities are like Washington."

"Perhaps you won't have to," Nick said cryptically.

Aimee fell silent, her mind transgressing to that terrible day in April when Lincoln was assassinated by John Wilkes Booth, an actor who interpreted Lincoln's last speech on April 11, 1865, as the words of a radical Republican. To Booth, the last straw was Lincoln's promise of Negro citizenship.

"Are we going to Tall Oaks, Mama?" Brand asked excitedly.

Aimee's thoughts returned abruptly to the present. "I'm afraid that's impossible, darling. The taxes haven't been paid in years. It no longer belongs to us."

Brand looked to Nick for confirmation, and when he said nothing to dispute Aimee's words, the boy's enthusiasm dimmed.

"Don't worry, son, I'll find us a place to live," Nick promised. "I already have something in mind for us. We have to get your mother settled before the new baby arrives."

Savannah cast a wary glance at Aimee's bulging girth and remarked, "Den you better do it fast, Major. Dat child ain't gonna wait too long. Aimee wasn't near this big with Brand."

"Don't worry about me," Aimee returned somewhat testily. Her mood swings these days weren't always predictable.

Nick laughed and patted her hand indulgently. "I'll worry about you until that child is in my arms."

Atlanta was a beehive of activity, teeming with men in blue uniforms interspersed with civilians returning to their homes and freed Negroes wandering the streets. The train arrived two hours late and Nick hurried them off to the hotel where he had wired ahead to reserve two rooms. Due to the crowded condition of the city and the number of speculators arriving daily in increasing numbers, he considered himself lucky to have obtained ample space for his family.

Aimee was more exhausted than she cared to admit. She was so big and awkward that just standing up was an ordeal. She had been unable to rest comfortably on the train and her deprived body cried out for rest. Nick left her almost immediately to report to his duty station and to check into some unfinished business. Dimly, Aimee wondered what unfinished business he could have in Atlanta but was too tired to question him. She naturally assumed he was going to try to find them a place to live.

One day about a week later Nick showed up at their hotel room at mid-morning, having left at his usual time of seven that same morning. Aimee thought it odd to find him home so early since his work consumed nearly all his waking hours.

"Are you up to a ride in the country, sweetheart?" Nick asked as he burst into the room. He was grinning from ear to ear, his mood so exuberant her curiosity was piqued.

"A ride?" she asked incredulously. Actually, riding was the last thing she felt like doing. But Nick seemed so adamant about her going she didn't have the heart to refuse.

"I have a horse and buggy waiting outside and I promise to take it easy. A ride will do you good. You've been cooped up far too long in the hotel, and before that in Washington."

"Shall we take Brand and Savannah? I'm sure they'll appreciate an outing as much as I will."

"Not this time, Aimee. I want you all to myself."

Aimee was more than a little puzzled by Nick's curious mood. She hadn't seen him like this in a

long time. Usually he jumped at the chance to be
with Brand and she couldn't understand why he
didn't want their son with him during this particular outing.

"I had the hotel prepare us a basket of food to
eat along the way."

"Where are we going?"

"Does it matter?" Aimee was dazzled by the
brilliant green of his eyes. What was he up to?

"Not really. But I should tell Brand and Savannah that I'm leaving. Brand will be disappointed."
She glanced at him from beneath long feathery
lashes, waiting to see if he'd change his mind
about bringing Brand and Savannah along. He
didn't.

"I stopped by their room before I came here,"
Nick said blandly. "Everything is taken care of."
The way he said it gave Aimee the distinct impression that there was something Nick wasn't telling
her about this proposed outing. Had he found
them a place to live and wanted to surprise her?
Yes, that was it, she decided.

The day was as hot and humid as only a day in
July could be in the South. Since arriving in Atlanta, Aimee had shed all her petticoats except one
and wore only loose, sleeveless garments that
hung from her shoulders and skimmed her bur-
geoning figure. She added a parasol to shade her
from the sun and pronounced herself ready.

True to his word, Nick took his time as he drove
the buggy along Atlanta's crowded streets into the
countryside. Relaxing against the leather backrest,
Aimee breathed deeply of the fresh scent of wild-
flowers after an afternoon rainstorm and was glad
Nick had persuaded her to go on this outing. He

seemed to have no particular destination in mind, or so it appeared to Aimee, and early in the afternoon they stopped to partake of the lunch prepared by the hotel. After a pleasant hour spent beneath a lofty oak tree, Nick suggested they leave.

"This looks like the road to Tall Oaks," Aimee said as Nick turned the buggy onto a road she recognized immediately. She had traveled it many times in the past.

"It is. Colonel Mullins asked me to look at some land he's interested in buying."

Aimee's bottom lip trembled. "Is it Tall Oaks he's interested in buying?"

Nick smiled a secret smile. "No, sweetheart, Colonel Mullins doesn't want Tall Oaks."

Aimee hadn't the courage to ask if someone had already bought Tall Oaks. Nor did she wish to see the burnt wreckage of the house she had come to love. Instead, she concentrated on the shimmering summer day and the baby she carried inside her. With a sense of wonder she touched her belly, speculating on whether her child would be a girl or boy and if it would resemble Brand.

How different things were with this pregnancy, she mused thoughtfully. When she carried Brand the only thing that got her through the ordeal was her consuming hatred for Nick Drummond. Without that hatred to sustain her Aimee wasn't certain she could have survived. Now she had Nick's love to nurture and support her and her future had never looked brighter.

As the horse plodded forward beneath the blazing sun, Aimee's eyes grew heavy and her head nodded sleepily.

"Rest your head on my shoulder, sweetheart," Nick said, placing an arm around her so she could lean against him. "Take a nap, if you'd like. It will do you good. Do you feel all right?"

"I'm fine. The heat and sun make me sleepy."

Soon she was nodding off. She was deep in slumber when Nick turned off onto a narrow road beneath an avenue of stately oaks.

"Wake up, sweetheart, we're home."

He shook her gently, trying not to startle her. Aimee came awake slowly, still groggy from the heat and rhythmic motion of the buggy. She looked at him dumbly, her eyes wide as she tried to dispel the mantle of sleep.

"We're home," Nick repeated. His face wore an expression of tempered exuberance and expectancy. He looked like Brand when he had done something admirable and wanted approval for his good deed.

Slowly Aimee became aware of her surroundings, so familiar her heart jerked in instant reaction. Of the dappled shade of the tall oak trees standing like ancient sentinels above them. Of the wide expanse of lawn leading up to the house she had sought to protect and failed. She saw the columns first, all twenty of them surrounding three sides of the house, rising majestically in all their former glory. The verandas and railings were no longer peeling or blistered. Every inch of the newly restored house was painted a pristine white. Frilly curtains hanging in the windows in front of the house billowed gently in the breeze.

The last time Aimee had seen Tall Oaks, little remained but the outside walls and virtually unscathed front pillars. Even the outbuildings had been restored, except for the slave huts which had been torn down. Was she dreaming? She blinked repeatedly, dashing aside the tears gathering in her eyes.

"You're not dreaming, sweetheart," Nick said, as if reading her mind. "It's real."

Suddenly her composure crumbled. "Why did you bring me here? Why? Didn't you know how it would affect me?"

"I knew, Aimee, and I—"

"The new owner did a wonderful job," Aimee continued before Nick could explain. "It looks far more grand than I remembered. It hurts to think of Tall Oaks belonging to anyone but Brand. Beau wanted Brand to have it even if we had children of our own one day." Turning away, she sighed deeply. "I'm ready to leave now."

"Wouldn't you like to see the inside?" Nick's eyes gleamed with deviltry. Aimee couldn't understand why he was being deliberately obtuse about her feelings. "I'm sure the new owners won't mind."

"I—no, I don't think so. Please, Nick, I couldn't bear it. Let's leave now before we're noticed."

"Too late, we've already been seen."

Sure enough, a black woman and small child appeared in the doorway. Aimee blinked, then cried out. They looked almost like—dear God, it was them! Savannah and Brand stepped onto the wide veranda. Savannah wore a grin that spread from ear to ear. Brand broke away and ran down the stairs, waving his arms in exuberant welcome.

"What kept you?" he cried happily. "We've been waiting here for you ever so long."

Aimee paled, so confused all she could do was

sit there in the buggy with tears rolling down her cheeks.

"I arranged for them to leave the hotel shortly after we did," Nick confessed somewhat guiltily. He wanted to surprise Aimee, not upset her. He should have realized her emotional state was far too fragile for this kind of shock so late in her pregnancy. "I had Savannah pack our belongings and meet us here. While we were taking the long way and stopping for lunch, they came directly to Tall Oaks."

She looked at him, her eyes luminous with tears. "I—don't understand. What are Savannah and Brand doing here? Have the new owners rented Tall Oaks to us?"

"Aimee, sweetheart, Tall Oaks is ours. Yours, mine, and Brand's. It's your wedding present. I couldn't tell you about it before because I wasn't sure if I could hire the manpower necessary to renovate the place."

"Renovate! There was little left after the fire but four walls. It must have cost a fortune to rebuild."

Nick shrugged. "I told you I was thinking about selling my share of the munitions plant, didn't I? We'll, my brother-in-law was eager to buy me out. I used the money to rebuild the house. Now, seeing your face, I feel it was well worth the expense. Don't worry, sweetheart, there's still enough money left to keep us in style until our land produces, and even beyond that, if need be."

"Why? Why would you do such a thing? You're a businessman, not a farmer. I know you brought me to Atlanta merely to humor me, but surely you aren't planning on setting down roots here, are you?" Her voice held a ring of hope that tugged at Nick's heart.

"Tall Oaks is our home now. It's our children's heritage. I paid the taxes and rebuilt it to its former elegance because I love you and intend to use the land as God meant it."

He leaped from the buggy then turned to lift Aimee to the ground. He set her on her feet, kissing her lightly before placing an arm around her waist and drawing her toward the house. "Come and inspect your domain, Mrs. Drummond."

Nick's memory of the house was phenomenal, Aimee thought as she lay in bed later that night waiting for Nick to undress and join her. Every room was nearly identical in size and proportion to those that had been destroyed in the fire. Every detail had been meticulously duplicated.

"How did you manage everything?" Aimee asked once Nick was settled beside her in the new bed. "When did you have the time?"

"It wasn't easy," Nick allowed. "I knew how much Tall Oaks meant to you and Brand and I paid the taxes before we left Atlanta in the winter of 1864. Sensing the end of the war, I made arrangements for rebuilding to begin immediately. I drew a diagram and communicated through letters and telegrams. I had no problem finding an overseer and workers willing to put in a full day's work for a full day's pay."

"I can't believe you did this for me."

"I love you, Aimee Drummond. I've been telling you that since I found you again nearly a year ago. You were so brave challenging me in the foyer of Tall Oaks with that small, ridiculous handgun. It reminded me of one other time when you threatened me with a gun. It was aboard the *Dixie Belle*, remember? I don't ever want you to doubt my love again. Restoring Tall Oaks to you is my way of proving how deeply I love you."

"I don't need proof, Nick," Aimee sighed contentedly. "As much as I appreciate what you've done in my behalf, it wasn't necessary. I've finally come to grips with loving a Yankee. Wherever you chose to live would have been fine with me."

"I chose Tall Oaks." A comfortable silence settled between them. Suddenly Nick stirred and said, "Did I ever thank you for Brand? He's a wonderful boy. You did a fine job raising him. Having another child with you makes my life complete."

"I might want more than two children," Aimee teased as she snuggled against him.

"I'll do all in my power to oblige, sweetheart," Nick said with a roguish grin. "I love you. I'll do whatever makes you happy."

"I'm happiest when you're making love to me."

"Then I promise to keep you deliriously happy forever and ever."

Epilogue

April 1866

Aimee tucked another seed into the small furrow she had just dug in the ground and packed the fertile earth around it with the back of her small spade. She loved springtime. This year the war-ravaged land was showing signs of renewal, and the citizens of the South had begun their long trek toward Reconstruction.

Kneeling in the dirt, she sniffed appreciatively of the rich soil made fertile by frequent rainstorms, and recalled all the things she had to be grateful for. Leaning back on her heels, she dashed away beads of sweat clinging to her brow with the back of her hand, leaving a smudge of dirt across her smooth forehead. The kitchen garden should produce well this year, she thought idly as she pushed another seed into the ground.

Glancing out across the wide expanse of green lawn, she saw Nick riding toward the house. As usual, Brand rode beside him on the pony Nick had purchased for him on his sixth birthday. She smiled in response to Nick's wave when he saw her kneeling in the dirt. He turned his mount in her direction. Brand followed close behind. Father and son were so alike, it was uncanny.

Nick dismounted, pulled her to her feet, and planted an exuberant kiss on her lips. "We'll start plowing tomorrow," he said. "The fields have dried out enough to start putting in crops."

Aimee smiled, surprised at how good a farmer Nick had become in the short months since he had resigned his commission in the army. Some of the former slaves had drifted back to Tall Oaks seeking work, and Nick had offered them jobs. He paid them a fair wage, and they seemed content with the arrangement. Nick had field hands to farm the land, and the workers had a place to work and live.

Conditions in Atlanta were appalling. Most of the former slaves had no place to go, so they roamed the streets looking for handouts and getting into brawls. The federal government was trying to help, but embittered Reb soldiers returning from war and finding nothing left of their former lives added considerably to the chaos and woes facing Reconstruction.

"It will be good to see crops growing on the land again," Aimee said wistfully. "I feel badly for all our neighbors who weren't as lucky as we were. Their land is lost to them forever."

"No one said war was fair."

Suddenly a loud wail pierced the air, and Aimee glanced toward the house. "That must be Jamie. He's as impatient as his father. Run into the house, Brand, and tell Savannah I'll be right in to feed the little scamp."

She and Nick watched fondly as Brand's little legs churned into motion. "I can't recall ever being this happy," Nick said with a sigh of contentment. "Though you did give me quite a scare when you gave birth. I don't think I ever want to go through that again."

Aimee started to reply when another loud wail joined the first, creating an earsplitting din that made Nick roll his eyes heavenward in mock surrender. "I'd better hurry before the house falls down around us," Aimee said.

Before she reached the house, Savannah appeared in the doorway holding a bundle in either arm. "Dey ain't gonna wait much longer for dere dinner," she said, juggling a child on each ample hip.

"Feed Jamie first, Mama," Brand yelled, trying to be heard over the babies' screeching. "He's crying the loudest."

By now it was difficult to tell which child was creating the most noise. Nick strode purposefully toward Savannah, took one baby from her, and rocked it awkwardly in his strong arms. Immediately the child fell silent.

"At least my daughter appreciates me," he said. His face was aglow at the wonder of his twins. "See how Janie stopped crying when I picked her up."

"I appre—appreciate you, Papa," Brand said, stumbling over the long word.

"And I appreciate you, son. And also your mama for giving me these wonderful children. Twins; I still can't get over having two babies at once."

"I was so big, I should have suspected something," Aimee said as she plucked Jamie from Savannah's arms and carried him inside. Brand followed Savannah into the kitchen while Aimee and Nick continued upstairs to the bedroom, each carrying a squalling child.

Settling herself in a rocker, Aimee opened her dress and offered a breast to her irate son. Immediately he latched on to an engorged nipple, sucking lustfully as milk gushed into his mouth.

"Greedy little devil, isn't he?" Nick remarked as he watched his son suckle.

"He comes by it naturally," Aimee said, flashing Nick a cheeky grin. Aimee recalled the many times in the past when she had called Nick a devil and truly meant it.

"They're going to have to learn to share with me," Nick said. His green eyes sparkled mischievously. "Besides, there's only one devil in this family, and I have no intention of sharing the title."

"As long as you are *my* devil, Nick, you can keep the title."

"Thank you, sweetheart, for all the happiness you've brought into my life. Now, hurry up and feed those two; they have a father who is anxious to take their place. And if I haven't told you lately, I love you, Aimee Drummond."